The Devil in Music

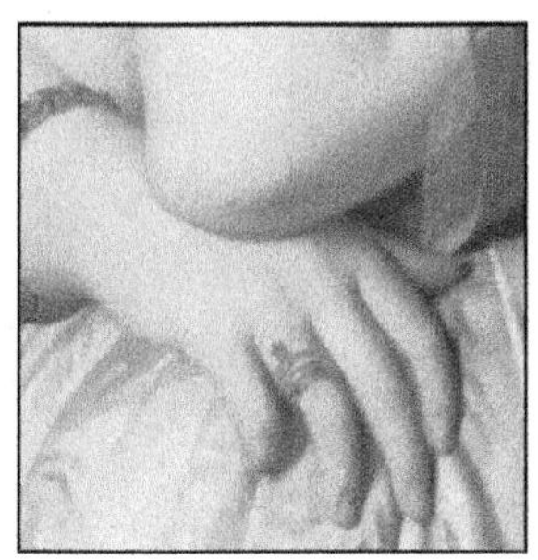

THE DEVIL IN MUSIC

Kate Ross

Felony & Mayhem Press • New York

All the characters and events portrayed in this work are fictitious.

THE DEVIL IN MUSIC

A Felony & Mayhem mystery

PRINTING HISTORY
First UK edition (Viking): 1997
Felony & Mayhem edition: 2013

ISBN: 978-1-937384-71-5

Manufactured in the United States of America

Library of Congress Cataloging-in-Publication Data

Ross, Kate.
The Devil in music / Kate Ross. -- Felony & Mayhem Edition.
pages cm
ISBN 978-1-937384-71-5
1. Kestrel, Julian (Fictitious character)--Fiction. 2. London (England)--Fiction.
3. Singers--Fiction. 4. Opera--Fiction. 5. Italy--Fiction. I. Title.
PS3568.O843494D48 2013
813'.54--dc23

2013010232

A NOTE ON THE MILANESE DIALECT

For much of this book, readers are asked to pretend that the characters are speaking Italian—or, more precisely, Milanese, the old dialect of Lombardy. A few Milanese words are used, such as *signor* for *signore*, *popola* for *signorina*, and *palazz* for *palazzo*. But by and large I've chosen not to throw foreign words into the dialogue, except when they are mixed into an otherwise English conversation. My reasoning was that those of the characters who speak Milanese would not sound "foreign" to one another.

CHARACTERS

The Malvezzi Family

LODOVICO MALVEZZI, *a Milanese marquis (*marchese*)*
BEATRICE MALVEZZI, *his wife*
RINALDO MALVEZZI, *Lodovico's son by a previous marriage*
FRANCESCA ARGENTI MALVEZZI, *his wife*
NICCOLÒ MALVEZZI, *their son*
BIANCA MALVEZZI, *their daughter*
CARLO MALVEZZI, *Lodovico's younger brother, a count (*conte*)*

Malvezzi Servants

ERNESTO TORELLI, *Lodovico's manservant*
GUIDO GENNARO, *Carlo's manservant*
NINA CASSERA, *Beatrice's maid*
BRUNO MONTI, *footman*
TOMMASO AGOSTI, *footman*
MATTEO LANDI, *gardener of Villa Lealtà*
LUCIA LANDI, *his daughter*
ABBÉ MOROSI, *tutor to Niccolò and Bianca*

The Musical World

"ORFEO", *an English tenor*
PIETRO BRANDOLIN ("VALERIANO"), *a male soprano*
MAESTRO FILIPPO DONATI, *a singing teacher and composer*
ANTONIO FARESE ("TONIO"), *Maestro Donati's "Eyes" (1821)*
SEBASTIANO BORDA, *Maestro Donati's "Eyes" (1825)*
GASTON DE LA MARQUE, *a dilettante music scholar*

British Visitors to Lombardy

JULIAN KESTREL, *a gentleman*
THOMAS STOKES ("DIPPER"), *his manservant*
DUNCAN MACGREGOR, *Mr. Kestrel's friend; a surgeon*
THE HON. BEVERLEY ST. CARR, *a young man on the Grand Tour*
HUGO FLETCHER, *his tutor*

Inhabitants of Solaggio

FRIEDRICH VON KRAUSS, *garrison commander*
BENEDETTO RUGA, *mayor (*podestà*)*
DON CRISTOFORO, *parish priest*
LUIGI CURIONI, *physician*
MARIANNA FRASCANI, *landlady of the Nightingale*
ROSA FRASCANI, *her daughter*

Miscellaneous

GIAN GALEAZZO RAVERSI, *a Milanese count (*conte*) friend of Lodovico Malvezzi*
CAMILLO PALMIERI, *the Malvezzi family lawyer*
ALFONSO GRIMANI, *a police official (*commissario*)*
PAOLO ZANETTI, *his clerk and interpreter*

The icon above says you're holding a copy of a book in the Felony & Mayhem "Historical" category, which ranges from the ancient world up through the 1940s. If you enjoy this book, you may well like other "Historical" titles from Felony & Mayhem Press.

For more about these books, and other Felony & Mayhem titles, or to place an order, please visit our website at:

www.FelonyAndMayhem.com

Other "Historical" titles from

FELONY & MAYHEM

ANNAMARIA ALFIERI

City of Silver

Strange Gods

DAVID STUART DAVIES

Forests of the Night

FIDELIS MORGAN

Unnatural Fire

The Rival Queens

KATE ROSS

Cut to the Quick

A Broken Vessel

Whom the Gods Love

The Devil in Music

CATHERINE SHAW

The Library Paradox

The Riddle of the River

TYLER, LC

A Cruel Necessity

LAURA WILSON

The Lover

The Innocent Spy

An Empty Death

The Wrong Man

A Willing Victim

The Riot

The Devil in Music

Part One

MARCH 1821

He loves to sit and hear me sing,
Then, laughing, sports and plays with me;
Then stretches out my golden wing
And mocks my loss of liberty.

William Blake
Song

Lodovico Malvezzi signed his name with a flourish and sat back to read what he had written:

Castello Malvezzi
13 March 1821

Signora,—

My son has very properly passed your letter on to me. Neither he nor I can be moved by such appeals. I swear by God and the Madonna that you will not see Niccolò and Bianca or hold any communication with them, as long as you remain with Signor Valeriano. I think you know that I am a man of my word.

You say that they are your children—that in charity to them, if not to you, I should not keep them from their mother. I say that they now have only one parent: my son, who has not disgraced them. My God, do you think I would allow those precious children—the blood of my blood, the sole hopes of my line—to fall into the hands of a woman who has brought infamy on their name? My one consolation is that, situated as you are, you cannot bring into the world bastards whom they must own as brothers or sisters.

I might have known that, as soon as Rinaldo returned from his travels, you would turn up and try to come round him with your prayers and persuasions. I understand that you and your friend have even had the audacity to take up residence just across the lake from my castle. (I use the word "friend," not out of any consideration for your feelings, but because to call him your lover would be an outrage against nature.) Your hopes are vain, and your journey from Venice useless. Rinaldo will not see you, and my servants know that anyone who admits you to my house or breathes a word to you of the children will feel the full weight of my displeasure.

If your punishment seems harsh, ask yourself— or better still, ask a priest—if it is any more than you have deserved. It is never too late to repent, this side of Heaven. Renounce Signor Valeriano and return to my son. Otherwise, your children are as dead to you as if you had buried them with your own hands.

I remain, to my lasting shame and regret, your father-in-law,
Lodovico Malvezzi

Lodovico smiled with satisfaction. It would do. He folded the letter, addressed it, and went to the window, where he had left a stick of wax to warm in the sun. A candle-flame would have melted the wax far more quickly, but Lodovico would have thought it a shocking extravagance to keep a candle burning in broad daylight, just to seal a letter. He placed a dollop of wax on the letter and ground his seal into it. The seal left a bold, clear imprint of his family device: a sword pointing upward, with a serpent coiled around the blade.

He was about to ring for a servant to take the letter. Then a frown gathered on his brow, and he took a turn about the room. His study was on the topmost floor of the castle's largest tower. One window faced west, over the castle courtyard with its high, spiked curtain wall, toward an expanse of tree-covered hills dotted with hardy stone cottages. In the distance rose a range of purple Alps, mantled in mist and crowned with snow. The window opposite looked out on the silver-blue ribbon of the Lake of Como, and the jagged promontories, plunging ravines, and wooded slopes that lined its shores. Lodovico was master of all he surveyed: what he did not own outright, he dominated by virtue of his rank, wealth, and high standing with Milan's Austrian overlords.

And yet his daughter-in-law—a mere woman, hardly more than a girl!—had defied him for nearly two years, cleaving steadfastly to her monstrous lover and resisting all his threats. Her infidelity was the least of her crimes: in Milan, many a married lady of rank had her cavalier, and society viewed them both with an indulgent eye, if the lover was well born, and the affair was conducted discreetly. But Francesca had attached herself to a singer—one who could not even be dignified with the title of a man. What was worse, she had left her husband to live openly with him. It was not to be borne.

Lodovico strode back to his desk, took a new sheet of paper, and dashed off:

Castello Malvezzi
Tuesday morning

My dear Rinaldo,—

I have answered your wife's letter in the manner it deserved. If I could rely on you to act with firmness and resolution, my intervention would not be needed. But I know too well that you are the plaything of any strong will brought to bear on you. That being so, you did right to pass her letter on to me.

What I wish to know now is, are you a man? Do you mean to behave, for once in your life, like the future head of this house? Francesca may well approach you again, thinking—no doubt rightly—that you are weak enough to yield to her entreaties and allow her a glimpse of Niccolò and Bianca. If you do, you will find yourself without an income, or even a roof over your head. I swear to you that I will throw you into the street, sooner than let you cross me in this.

I might have hoped, since Heaven saw fit to give me only one child, that he would be a man of character and courage. But God's will be done. You have already failed once to defend your honour. Fail now, and I wash my hands of you for good and all.

Believe me, yours most sincerely,

Lodovico Malvezzi

Lodovico folded and sealed the letter, then tugged on the bell-pull. Footsteps, increasingly laboured, approached up the spiral stairway. At last Lodovico's servant Ernesto appeared, panting from the climb up the tower. Lodovico prided himself on being able to take those stairs at a gallop, although he and Ernesto were of an age. But Ernesto was grey and grave and looked his full fifty-six years, while Lodovico was still a fine figure of a man, his hair more black than white, his hazel eyes brilliant, his tall form straight and commanding. What was more, his strength and energy were unimpaired—he flattered himself that plenty of women could attest to that.

"Here." Lodovico handed Ernesto the letters. "Send these by courier. They're too urgent to entrust to the post."

"Yes, Your Excellency." Ernesto bowed. "Will you be going to the villa this morning? I wasn't sure if I was to send for your horse as usual."

"The villa!" Lodovico slapped his forehead. "Body of Bacchus! How could I forget?" He pulled out his watch. "Half-past nine already! Have my horse brought round at once! And let me know the moment it's here!"

"Excellency." Ernesto bowed himself out.

Lodovico's heart beat fast with anticipation, and he felt the guilt that assails a lover who has let his thoughts stray too far from the object of his passion. This was the first day in weeks that he had not looked at his watch every moment as the time approached to depart for the villa. Curse Francesca: her letter had spoiled the hour of sweet expectancy that was one of the most delectable pleasures of love.

He went to the window on the east side of the tower, and his eyes travelled down the high, rocky crag where Castello Malvezzi was perched, to the villa set in its green garden on the lake. Once the sight of it—white and perfect, like a pretty, pristine doll's house—had made him gnash his teeth. That was in the days when Napoleon Bonaparte, that devil incarnate, had ruled over Lombardy, bringing war, anarchy, godlessness, and every sort of depredation from taxation to outright looting. Right-thinking men like Lodovico had remained loyal to the Austrian Emperor, Lombardy's legitimate ruler, guardian of tradition and the Catholic faith. But Lodovico's younger brother, Carlo, had embraced liberalism and made common cause with the French. With the wealth that came to him, he had purchased this very villa and, under Lodovico's outraged eyes, held lavish entertainments there for upstart French officials.

Seven years ago—thank God and the Madonna!—the French were driven out, and the Austrians returned to Lombardy to reestablish order and bring peace. Carlo took refuge at the court of Parma, south of Milan. Deep in debt, he had no choice but to sell the villa to Lodovico. By all accounts, he was still in financial straits, with a courtier's lifestyle to maintain and six children to launch in the world. It would not surprise Lodovico if he came seeking a loan. Lodovico might even give it to him—depending on how he asked.

Lodovico consulted his watch again. Twenty minutes to ten! Where the devil was his horse? He started down the stairs, and met Ernesto coming up. His horse was saddled and waiting in the courtyard. He sped down the remaining stairs, mounted, and set off.

The road from Castello Malvezzi descended the crag by twists and turns, hugging cliff walls leprous with moss and lichen. Dark, solemn cypresses blocked out all but an occasional ray of sunlight or sliver of gleaming lake. At the base of the crag, the road ran behind the villa gardens. It was an indirect route, since the villa lay just beneath the castle, but that side of the crag was too rocky and steep for horse or man to descend. So Lodovico had to ride halfway around the villa grounds to the gate in the south garden wall.

This was the balmiest day so far this year. All the trees were in bud. Birds wheeled and sang, and lizards skittered along the garden wall. In the mountains to the north and west, the thaw had set in with a vengeance: Lodovico could hear the rush of streams swollen to torrents by melting snow. A group of peasant women trudged along the road, lugging baskets of earth to build up their terrace farms. They curtsied to Lodovico and moved aside to let his horse go by.

All at once he saw another rider coming toward him at a trot. He cursed under his breath. Ordinarily he would not have minded passing the time of day with Conte Raversi, who had a villa further up the western shore of the lake. Raversi and he were near in age and like-minded about politics. But just now his only thought was to reach the villa.

"Lodovico!" Raversi hailed him. "I was on my way to see you."

"Good morning," said Lodovico, with all the courtesy he could muster. "I'm afraid I can't stop—I'm on urgent business."

"But I have to tell you the news!" Raversi pushed back the disorderly locks of black hair from his brow. His dark eyes burned in his long, pale face.

"What news?"

"The revolt in Alessandria has spread to Turin. The rebels are demanding a constitution, and the King may have to abdicate."

He was speaking of the revolt that had broken out a few days earlier in Piedmont, the state on Lombardy's western border. "It won't come to that," said Lodovico. "There's a loyalist garrison at Novara. They'll soon make short work of the rabble."

"But don't you see? They'll have to concentrate on retaking Turin—they can't leave the capital in the rebels' hands. And that means there won't be anyone to guard our border. The revolt will spill over into Lombardy. The secret societies here are champing at the bit to rise up against us. All that's needed is a spark to set the revolution alight—"

"Gian Galeazzo, Gian Galeazzo." Lodovico shook his head in amused exasperation. "Do you think a handful of badly armed Carbonari would be any match for Austrian troops?"

"Austrian troops can't fight an enemy they can't find," argued Raversi. "The Carbonari are a deadly danger because no one knows who or where they are. They belong to secret lodges, communicate in cipher, swear not to reveal each other's names on pain of death—"

"They'll have to come out into the open in order to attack us," Lodovico said reasonably. "And they'll be shot down like dogs, and that will be an end of it. I'm late, Gian Galeazzo, so if you'd be good enough to let me pass—"

"But I thought you'd be especially worried about the revolt in Turin. I know Beatrice is there."

"Yes, she is," said Lodovico, rather sharply. "And if I thought she was in any danger I would go to her. I'm well able to look after my wife."

"Of course. But—"

"There are no buts. You know Beatrice: she's clever and clear-sighted—the one woman in a thousand who can be trusted not to panic in a crisis. She'll know whether to leave Turin before the rebels arrive or lie low and not draw attention to herself until the revolt's been quelled. I wish she hadn't chosen this particular time to visit Turin, but there's no help for it now."

"Why is she there?"

Lodovico shrugged. He was proud of his ignorance of his wife's activities. Not many men could marry a woman so much younger, and so beautiful, and yet resist the temptation to keep a jealous eye on her. So many husbands turned their houses into prisons, their servants into spies. Beatrice and he were above that sort of thing. She was not wanton, and he was not weak. He had the luxury of trusting her.

"Now I really must go," he said, digging his heels resolutely into his horse's sides.

"One more thing," Raversi said quickly. "I'm having a meeting at my villa today at one o'clock. Von Krauss will be there." Von Krauss was the commander of the Austrian garrison headquartered in the nearby village of Solaggio. "I want to talk about how we might defend the neighbourhood in the event of an insurrection. Will you come?"

"Yes, yes. Now, good day to you, Gian Galeazzo."

Lodovico spurred his horse to a canter, determined to get away at last. Raversi's heart was in the right place, but he was an alarmist. He thought Carbonari were lurking around every bush and under every bed. Lodovico had no doubt that the trouble in Piedmont, like the recent revolution in Naples, would be put down. Demanding a constitution! Any idiot ought to be able to see that a ruler could not apply the same laws to everyone—nobles and peasants, enemies and friends. Yet every political idealist and disgruntled bourgeois thought a constitution the answer to all their problems!

Lodovico rounded the southwest corner of the garden wall. On his right, the whitewashed, red-roofed houses of Solaggio began to appear, linked together by daisy-chains of washing hung out to dry. The lake lay ahead, slender fishing boats skimming its polished surface. The road ended just short of the lake, the garden wall giving way to an elegant wrought-iron gate. Lodovico jumped down from his horse and flung its reins over a gatepost. He was not afraid to leave it unattended: the whole neighbourhood knew it was his, and no one would dare to steal it. For longer visits, he stabled it at the Nightingale, Solaggio's only inn.

He went through the gate and strode along the lakeside path, which was the quickest way to the villa. It was paved with flagstones and raised some fifteen feet above the lake by an embankment. Halfway to the villa, a dainty little Moorish pavilion jutted out over the water to serve as a belvedere.

Lodovico looked at his watch, swore, and quickened his pace. In the distance, he glimpsed the elegant arc of the villa terrace, with its marble balustrade over the lake. Then the villa itself appeared: a white rectangle, simple and almost severe, with grey-shuttered windows and marble balconies. He was almost running by the time he crossed the terrace and ascended the majestic double stairway to the entrance. As he reached the top, a girl came out through the door.

She was about sixteen, dressed in a white blouse with the sleeves rolled up to her elbows, a blue bodice and skirt, and a red shawl. Her dark brown hair was sleekly drawn up into a knot and secured by a coronet of gleaming hairpins. She curtsied, keeping her lustrous dark eyes lowered. "Good morning, Excellency."

"Good morning, Lucia! Do you know how it gladdens a man's heart to see your blooming face on a spring morning?"

"No, Excellency," she said, without looking up.

"Where are you off to in such a hurry?"

"To speak to my father, Excellency." Her father was the gardener. "About provisions we need from the castle."

"Take care you speak to no one else," he teased. "Those eyes of yours could drive poor farmers and fishermen mad with love. And better men than they," he added meaningfully.

"I wouldn't know about that, Excellency."

"Wouldn't you, Lucia? You will soon enough."

"May I go now, Excellency?"

Lodovico's eyes ran over her. She was more of a woman every day: her breasts deliciously full, her arms strong but shapely, her ankles trim. Her skin was the colour of honey, and no doubt as sweet to the taste. Ah, he would like to have her, especially if he could be the first. To conquer her maiden shyness, feel her soft skin hot with blushes under his exploring hands—

Enough of these thoughts, he told himself. He had a better use for Lucia. Besides, it was almost blasphemy to lust for a peasant girl, when he was so near the object of his adoration. He waved Lucia on her way and went into the villa.

They had started without him. The sound met his ears as he entered the Hall of Marbles, the large square entrance salon. They were working on *"See, the lovely dawn is breaking,"* the air sung by the enamoured young Count Almaviva beneath his sweetheart's balcony in *The Barber of Seville.* Lodovico's heart leaped in his breast as he heard the clear, brilliant strain. He did not go into the music room yet, but stood just outside the door, where he could be alone with his beloved. Lightheaded with exultation, he closed his eyes and let the skeins of melody enfold him. What did flesh and blood matter? Lodovico was in love with a voice.

CHAPTER 2

Lodovico had been in love with voices before. When he was younger, he had had a new musical passion every few months. Nowadays, he was a little more jaded. That was inevitable in Milan, where people of his class went to La Scala six nights a week, three seasons a year, and every fruit vendor or café waiter was a discerning opera critic. Yet now and then there would come a voice that penetrated Lodovico to the heart—consumed him with a desire all the sharper and more rapturous because it could never be satisfied.

The bodies his voices inhabited were unimportant. They might be male or female, young or old, comely or hideous. This one happened to live in the chest and throat of a twenty-one-year-old Englishman. He was a tenor, with a warm, alluring chest voice and an upper register that rivalled any soprano's for limpid beauty and sweetness. Lodovico called him Orfeo, after Orpheus, the Greek singer whose music charmed wild beasts and moved rocks to tears.

Orfeo had reached the bravura climax of his song. His voice darted agilely from note to note, with a fire and intelligence that turned pure acrobatics into art. He finished; the piano played the concluding notes, then a pair of hands was heard applauding.

A man's voice spoke: "Bravo, my son! That's coming along very well!—the high notes firm and assured, the cadenzas accurate to a semitone. Of course you know where you breathed in the wrong place?"

"Yes, Maestro," the young man said ruefully. "And when I tried to put it right, I fell out of time."

"Let's try that passage again."

They went over and over it, till it was as close to perfect as Lodovico could imagine possible. He still concealed his presence, finding it sweet to listen unseen. While Orfeo rested his voice, Donati discussed the technique of famous tenors he had heard or trained: Crivelli, Garcia, the elder and younger Davide. At length he said, "All right, now let's hear you in the cantabile style. Sing *'My dear love,'* and ornament the reprise. But keep your improvisations few and simple—nothing ruins a sentimental air like loading it down with trills."

The piano played the introduction. Orfeo began:

"My dear love, at least believe me,
Without you, my heart languishes."

Lodovico listened transported, his eyes filling with tears. Of all Orfeo's styles, the tender cantabile was his best.

Lodovico stole a glance into the room. Donati was at the piano, listening to his pupil with the complete concentration he could bring to bear on sound, now that he could no longer see. He was a thin, elderly man, with skin like fine parchment and a bald crown ringed by wispy white hair. Orfeo stood with his back to Lodovico, observing his posture and facial expression in a full-length mirror as he sang. This was one of Donati's exercises, and no doubt it helped the vulgar run of singers learn to look distinguished on the stage, but in Orfeo's case it was hardly necessary. He stood and moved like the gentleman he was. Breeding would always tell.

When the song was over, Donati applauded enthusiastically. "My son, that was lovely! Your diminuendo is exquisite. Use it sparingly—it will astonish all the more."

Lodovico agreed. Orfeo had thoroughly mastered the art of holding a note and making it ever softer, till it faded away like a dream. Moreover, he could do it without revealing, by either a gasp or a grimace, the iron control it required.

Donati went on, "Once or twice I caught you forcing your chest voice up into your head. That won't do at all. The greatest vulgarity a singer can fall into is to sing a high note—indeed, any note—at the top of his voice. A tenor is not an Alpine goatherd, or a drunken gondolier. Anyone with a healthy pair of lungs can be merely *loud*. But to sing with refinement, accuracy, delicacy of feeling—that is the mark of an artist."

"I'll try to remember, Maestro."

Lodovico could restrain himself no longer. "Bravo!" he cried, coming into the room and applauding vigorously. "You're in rare voice, my songbird!"

Orfeo's head came up. The mirror caught the look in his eyes: startled, constrained, as if he had suddenly been jerked by a rope. But when he turned toward Lodovico, he had regained command of his face. "Signor Marchese. I didn't see you."

"You weren't meant to." Lodovico spoke easily, but there was an imperious gleam in his eye. This was his house. He was under no obligation to have himself announced.

"Signor Marchese." Donati rose and bowed in the direction of Lodovico's voice. "We feared you wouldn't be with us this morning."

Lodovico felt the chill of formality in the air, and resented it. Must they make it so obvious that his presence disrupted their rapport? Of course they owed him respect, but they ought to make him feel welcome, too. They would never have met if it had not been for him. Orfeo would not have had a singing teacher at all, let alone one of the finest in Italy.

"You might have known I would come," he said testily. "I never miss Orfeo's lessons."

"I hope there was nothing amiss at the castle to detain you," Orfeo interposed in his usual quiet, courteous tone.

"No—just some family business I had to attend to."

Lodovico softened toward him, remembering how sublimely he had just sung. "You're making splendid progress! How long do you think it will be, Maestro, before our songbird is ready to try his wings?"

"Perform in public, you mean, Signor Marchese? I need at least a few more months with him. You know how raw he was when he came to me."

"No hurry." Lodovico nodded approvingly. He was looking forward to launching his protégé on the operatic stage, but not just yet—not till he had drunk his fill of the pleasure of having him all to himself. "By the time he's ready to make his debut, all Milan will be consumed with curiosity about him. And then—and then, my songbird, you will have such a triumph as Milan has never seen! Poets will write sonnets about you, impresarios will contend for you, women will throw themselves into your arms! What's this? You look dubious."

"I don't doubt your judgement, Signor Marchese—only my ability to live up to it."

"Tut!—no false modesty. Save that for your public appearances. You are a marvel, and soon all Italy will know it. In the meantime, be patient, and continue to be guided by me."

Donati looked troubled. "Do you mean he isn't to show his face outside the villa for several more months?"

"You needn't make it sound as if I've forbidden him even a breath of air," Lodovico said impatiently. "He can go into the garden, as long as he stays inside the walls and away from the lake. I don't want to make him a prisoner—only to prevent his being seen. You *have* been keeping out of sight, my Orfeo?"

"I've complied with your wishes in everything, Signor Marchese."

Lodovico ordinarily took it for granted that his dependents would obey his orders. But with Orfeo, he never knew quite what to expect. The young man had been bred a gentleman and had a mind of his own. He was not awed by Lodovico's rank, as most singers would be. He was respectful toward Lodovico and showed himself grateful for all Lodovico had done for him. But there was much he kept hidden from Lodovico. He had not always been so reticent. When they first met in Milan, he had talked of his family, his home in England, his feelings about pursuing a career in music. Now he seemed to have withdrawn behind a veil. His reserve puzzled Lodovico—sometimes angered him. Bodies might be immaterial, but the soul of a singer was inextricably bound up in his art. While the *man* remained so elusive, how could Lodovico wholly possess *the voice*?

"The course I've set for you may seem hard," Lodovico told him. "You're young—naturally you chafe against confinement. But believe me, nothing will serve you better in the future than to make a mystery of you now. The public is mad for novelty. Why do you think singers constantly travel, performing now in one Italian state, now in another? So that people everywhere will hear something new. Now, you, my songbird, have never sung in public anywhere! You are a complete unknown, and we must keep you that way."

"But, Signor Marchese," protested Donati timidly, "why should he have to hide his face and name as well as his voice? Isn't it enough if he appears in public but doesn't sing?"

"Body of Bacchus, Maestro!—you quite fail to understand my strategy. By now all Milan knows I've taken an English tenor under my wing and brought him here to be trained by you. They'll be wondering about him: what he looks like, where he comes from, if it's true he's of good birth. So we tell them—nothing! Soon they'll start weaving stories about him. They'll say he was captured from a British ship by pirates, that he's the King of England's bastard son, that he had to leave his country for killing a man. By the time he makes his debut, people will come just to *see* him—never mind how he sings! There now, Maestro: are you content?"

"If Orfeo is," said Donati.

"He'd be a fool if he weren't," Lodovico declared.

Orfeo looked at him opaquely. Lodovico supposed he had been a little rude. He set out to smooth the young man's ruffled feathers, in order to put him in the right frame of mind to sing again. "All I meant, my Orfeo, was that, being the sensible young man you are, you would understand how my plan will further your career. Now then: sing me something else. Sing something by Cimarosa."

Orfeo complied. But all too soon Donati put an end to his lesson, saying he had sung long enough and must not strain his voice. Lodovico acceded with a sigh. In matters of technique and training, Donati's word was law.

Orfeo went to the window and looked out, screening himself with the curtain so that he could not be seen from outside. Donati felt for the little bell he always kept by him, and rang it. His servant, Tonio Farese, a thickset young man with a ruddy face and big, ungainly hands, came in to pour them all some wine. Lodovico observed distastefully that he spilled a little on the carpet. "Fetch a cloth," he ordered. Tonio sidled out like a whipped dog.

"That servant of yours isn't good for much," Lodovico told Donati.

"No," said the maestro regretfully. "I only engaged him because his parents were favourite pupils of mine, and after they died, I felt I should do something for him. I happened to be in want of Eyes, and he could read music, so I offered him the post." *Eyes* was Donati's term for a young man who served him as both valet and secretary.

Lodovico regretted that Donati should have to keep a servant at all. The fewer people who saw Orfeo, the better. But a blind man, and a distinguished teacher at that, could not be expected to look after himself. At least the list of people who knew Orfeo was not long: just Lodovico, Donati, Tonio, Lucia, and her father, Matteo. Lucia cooked Donati's and Orfeo's meals and took care of the few rooms in the villa that Lodovico had opened for their use. Matteo kept the grounds in order as well as one man reasonably could, and fetched food and candles from the castle or the village. Orfeo, Donati, Tonio, and Matteo lived at the villa, but Lucia spent her nights at the castle. No doubt Matteo did not want her sleeping under the same roof as Orfeo and Tonio.

Lodovico himself lived at the castle and only came to the villa for Orfeo's lessons at ten in the morning and six in the evening. He could not do without a retinue of servants at his beck and call. He had little practical need for them, since his domestic wants were simple, but they were part of the indispensable panoply of his rank. Then, too, although he was proud to have secured the villa, he did not like it much. His brother Carlo had polluted it with statues and friezes glorifying Athenian democracy and Roman republicanism.

Thinking of politics reminded him of his conversation with Raversi. "The devil! I must go. I promised Conte Raversi I would go to a meeting at his villa to talk about defending the neighbourhood in case of a revolt."

Orfeo looked around. "Is that likely?"

"I shouldn't think so. But of course Conte Raversi is wise to take precautions." Lodovico might think Raversi an alarmist, but he would not criticize a fellow nobleman to outsiders.

"Is there any news from Piedmont?" Orfeo asked.

"The rebellion has spread to the capital. But that's no matter—it will be put down. And our own Carbonari are too disorganized and cowardly to revolt. Most radicals are nothing but talk. They play childish games, but they'd never risk their lives in a real rebellion."

Orfeo seemed interested. "What sort of childish games do you mean, Signor Marchese?"

"Never mind, my songbird." Lodovico smiled enigmatically. "One of these days perhaps I'll tell you all about it, but the time isn't ripe."

Tonio came in with a cloth to mop up the wine. Lodovico retrieved his hat and riding whip. Donati began dreamily playing an air he himself had composed long ago. Orfeo looked out of the window and, as always, kept his thoughts to himself.

Raversi's meeting made Lodovico take the threat of rebellion a little more seriously. Von Krauss, the level-headed garrison commander, was worried, and so were other men of standing in the neighbourhood. They all resolved to keep close track of events and report any ominous incidents to Von Krauss immediately. At Raversi's urging, Von Krauss agreed to dispatch a contingent of soldiers to guard the approaches from Piedmont, and from Lugano just over the Swiss border, where many exiled Italian radicals gathered to plot against the Austrians.

On his way back to Castello Malvezzi for dinner, Lodovico pondered whether he ought to go to Turin and bring Beatrice home. He did not want to leave the Lake of Como—he was too enthralled by Orfeo's lessons, and besides, he had a project he wanted to accomplish first. He wished he could send Rinaldo to fetch his stepmother, but he did not trust him not to make a muddle of the task, or worse. For the thousandth time, he asked Heaven why he was cursed with such a son.

By the time he reached home, he had decided on a compromise. He wrote to Beatrice adjuring her to send him frequent word of her safety, and to leave Turin at the first outbreak of violence. He knew she was well supplied with male servants to guard her on the roads. He still thought this much-vaunted rebellion would prove to be a damp squib, but at least Beatrice would know he was thinking of her, and the letter bearing his seal would warn all who saw it that, even from afar, Marchese Malvezzi was watching over his wife.

After dinner, he went to the villa for Orfeo's evening lesson. Night was falling when he returned to the castle. The wooded mountains were mere slate-blue shapes against the sky. On the lake, lanterns glimmered in the prows of boats, casting gold reflections on the water. A chill breeze carried snatches of boatmen's songs to Lodovico as he rode up into the hills. Church bells chimed mournfully from distant belfries; Lodovico dutifully bent his head to offer up a prayer.

He gave his horse to a groom at the castle gate, crossed the courtyard, and entered the vast, cold entrance hall. There he encountered Bruno Monti, one of the footmen. Bruno was booted and spurred, his dark curls lacquered to his forehead with sweat. He reported that he had just returned from delivering Lodovico's letters: one to Marchesina Francesca at her villa across the lake, and the other to Marchesino Rinaldo in Milan.

Lodovico commended him for his speed and sent him off to find some supper. He himself took a single candle and ascended his tower. The faint light flickered over the uneven stone stairs and damp brick walls with their slots for shooting arrows. At the top, Lodovico entered his study, which was square and took up an entire floor. It was dark and cold; Lodovico did not permit fires in March. The furnishings consisted of a large, heavy writing-table, a narrow wooden chest standing on claw feet, and two high-backed chairs upholstered in frayed and fading tapestry. The walls were covered with discoloured, peeling white plaster and hung with dark, solemn portraits of dead Malvezzis.

Lodovico placed the candle in a tall iron stand, which he drew up to the writing-table. At last he had leisure to work on his secret project—one he felt sure would bring new glory to his name, if only he could complete it. Taking a key from his watch-chain, he unlocked the chest and drew out a notebook bound in russet leather. He brought the notebook to his desk, took out some loose sheets from under the front cover, and set them before him. Then he opened the notebook. Its pages were ruled with bass and treble staffs, filled in with musical notes in a quick, elegant hand. Dipping pen in ink, he began writing furiously on the loose papers, pausing only to turn pages of the notebook and stare hard at their contents.

The work absorbed him for two or three hours. When his concentration failed him, and the musical notes became meaningless black specks before his eyes, he went to the window that looked out on the lake, and opened the lattice to let the chill breeze cool his face. It was frustrating, how long this task was taking. He had thought it would be so easy when he began.

There were no more boats on the lake, and few lights glimmering on the shores. The mountains were all but invisible against the sky. Stars twinkled here and there through rents in the veil of mist. A mere mile away across the lake, his daughter-in-law was sleeping—or, more likely, lying awake beside her preposterous lover, eating her heart out over Lodovico's letter. He hoped they would quarrel and come to hate each other. They deserved no less, because each of them had betrayed him. Francesca had made his family name a byword for the most grotesque cuckoldry imaginable. And Valeriano had inflicted a pang that was, if anything, worse.

Lodovico remembered the first time he had heard Valeriano sing. That haunting, brilliant soprano had thrilled him—he had set about wooing the singer at once. Valeriano had had little need for his patronage: he was already famous and successful, despite increasing public distaste for the castrato voice. But he was not well known in Milan, so Lodovico had introduced him everywhere, helped him to secure the best engagements, even made him welcome under his own roof. That was how Valeriano had come to know Francesca—and he had repaid all Lodovico's kindness by running away with her!

Lodovico shut the lattice with a crack that resounded like a gunshot in the silence. Returning to his desk, he gathered up the notebook and papers and locked them away in the chest. Then he snuffed the candle, shrouding the room in darkness. He did not need a light to get to his bedchamber, which was just beneath this room. But as he was passing the window that faced away from the lake, to his surprise he glimpsed a light in the courtyard below. None of his servants ought to be up at this hour, wasting lamp oil and making themselves too tired to work the next day. He went to the window to investigate, but when he got there, the light was gone.

He opened the lattice and put out his head, letting his eyes adjust to the darkness. Soon he could trace the outlines of the mountains against the misty sky and, more vaguely, the curtain wall edged with sharp stone teeth, the massive gate, the square watchtowers, and the litter of sheds and carts in the courtyard. But there was no light. Either he had imagined it, or it had been put out

No, there it was again! It was only a hand-held lantern, but in this gloom it shone as conspicuously as a beacon. Lodovico peered hard at the figure holding it: a man in a long dark cloak and a tall hat, moving cautiously along the curtain wall toward this very tower.

The light disappeared again. It must be a dark lantern, with a shutter to conceal the flame. Without taking time to relight his own candle, Lodovico felt his way swiftly to the door and down the stairs. At the bottom, where the tower met the curtain wall, there was a door leading into the courtyard. Lodovico lifted the latch very slowly so as not to make a sound, and opened the door.

The man in the cloak had nearly reached him. His lantern was shuttered again; he was using the wall to guide his steps. Lodovico could just make out his dark figure silhouetted against the paler stone. When he reached the tower door, he unshuttered his lantern. The light shone on Lodovico's face.

Lodovico heard his sharp intake of breath. He took the lantern and turned it around to illumine the intruder's face.

"Good evening, my songbird. You've flown very far from your nest."

"I'm sorry, Signor Marchese." Orfeo's eyes were wide, his face a little drawn, but he spoke quite steadily.

"How did you get through the gate?"

"I found a key at the villa."

"You found the lantern there, too, I suppose?"

"Yes."

"You've breached my terms, straying so far from the villa."

"I hoped at this hour it might not matter."

"It matters at any hour. We had an understanding, and you've broken it. Why?"

"I was restless."

"You could have walked in the garden."

"Forgive me, Signor Marchese, but I was tired of the garden."

"What brings you here?"

"Curiosity. I've often looked up at the castle and wondered what it was like."

That was too much for Lodovico. He threw back his head and laughed.

Orfeo opened his eyes at him, then waited politely till his mirth subsided. "May I ask how I've amused you, Signor Marchese?"

"My dear Orfeo, do you really think I don't know why you're here?"

"What do you mean?"

Lodovico shook his head tolerantly. "Ah, well, you can't help being English. An Italian would have owned up at once. Is she expecting you?"

"I don't understand."

"Because if she is, she'll be disappointed. I'm sending you back to the villa at once. Holy Virgin, you have all day to make love to her! There must be hollows enough in the bushes for what you have in mind. Or better still, take her to the caves. But don't come seeking her here."

Orfeo's face became very still. He said nothing for a few moments. Then: "I have no assignation with Lucia. She's never given me any encouragement."

"But you've come to see her all the same—you can't deny that."

Orfeo was silent.

"My boy, do you think I'll disapprove? Why do you think I chose such a comely, lusty girl to look after the villa while you're there? I know some people think it's bad for a singer to expend too much of his vital energy on women, but I think that's rubbish. A man your age shouldn't be deprived of female companionship. It upsets his physical balance—makes him depressed and discontented. And then how can he sing? So take Lucia by all means. Consider her yours to do what you like with. That's why she's here."

"And when I finish with her?" Orfeo asked quietly.

"I'll give her a dowry. That and my gratitude will bring potential husbands flocking round her. If there's a child, you can visit it. You see how easily these things are arranged? But now you must go back to the villa before the servants see you. And mind you don't leave it again till your training is finished."

"As you wish, Signor Marchese." Orfeo held out his hand for the lantern.

"One more thing." Lodovico's hand closed around the young man's upper arm in a grip that must have been painful, and was meant to be. "This damp night air is ruinous for your voice. If I catch you out in it again, I'll lock you up. So be wise, my Orfeo. Don't make me put my songbird in a cage."

As usual, Lodovico slept well, but not long. Soon after dawn, he rose, wrapped himself in his worn wool dressing-gown, thrust his stockinged feet into slippers, and pulled his nightcap down over his ears to keep them warm. Then he padded upstairs to his study. Unlocking the claw-footed chest, he drew out the notebook and papers again. He worked for an hour or two by the pale dawn light, pausing frequently to rub his hands and flex his cold, stiffening fingers.

At length he heard measured, methodical footsteps approaching up the stairs. He hastily scooped together the papers he was writing on and shut them in the notebook. He trusted Ernesto more than any of his other servants—more even than most of his friends—but this project was special. No one must know about it until it was finished.

Ernesto came in and bowed. "Good morning, Excellency. I've left your shaving-water in your room, when you want it."

"Thank you. I'm going to work a while longer before I'm shaved and dressed. What's that?"

Ernesto was holding a package wrapped in brown paper and tied with a cord. He handed it to Lodovico. "Bruno found it this morning, on the flagstones just outside the castle gate."

It was roughly oval in shape, about two feet long, soft and pliable. When bent, it made a rustling sound. "FOR MARCHESE LODOVICO MALVEZZI" was written on one side, in anonymous block capitals.

Lodovico frowned at it. He did not like mysteries or surprises. "You may go," he said. Ernesto bowed and went out.

Lodovico cut the cord with his penknife and opened the brown wrapping. Inside was a layer of crinkly silver tissue paper, of the kind used to wrap purchases in ladies' shops. A piece of parchment, folded in quarters, was pinned to it—a note, evidently, but Lodovico did not stop to read it. He tore apart the tissue paper to see what was inside.

It was a lady's glove, made of soft, fine, cream-coloured kid, a little discoloured with age. The part extending from wrist to elbow was embroidered with myrtle leaves in fraying green silk. Nestled among the leaves was a heart made all of rubies, pierced by a diamond shaft.

Lodovico drew the glove out of the wrappings. It was flapping wildly; he realized this was because his hands were shaking. He clenched them around the glove to keep them still—then, seeing the soft kid crushed and twisted, he dropped the glove fearfully.

With hands not yet quite steady, he unpinned and unfolded the note. The writing was wavering and erratic, as if a right-handed person had penned it with his left hand. It said:

> *I know who owned this glove and how she came by it. Unless you wish all the world to know her story, meet me on the night of 14 March, after 11.00, at the Moorish belvedere at Villa Malvezzi.*

Lodovico's cheeks flamed. Blackmail! He, Marchese Malvezzi, the prey of an extortionist! Rage brought his strength and energy flooding back. He leaped up, scraping his chair, and strode fiercely about the room. Who could the blackmailer be? Only one person knew the story behind the glove—but how could the glove have come into that person's hands? And why should that person have waited so long to use it?

Whoever the blackmailer was, he had mistaken his victim. He would soon find out what it was to make an enemy of Lodovico Malvezzi! Perhaps Lodovico would set the law on him, using the note as evidence. Then again, he might simply send half a dozen footmen with staves and cudgels to keep the belvedere rendezvous. One thing was certain—the blackguard would not extort a single soldo. Let him talk—let him do his worst! Nothing he might say could hurt Lodovico now.

Or could it? Lodovico's steps faltered. He went to his desk and picked up the glove again. A voice he had not heard in years came back to him, silvery and sweet. He shivered, as if someone had walked over his grave.

"No, no," said Donati, "chromatic thirds, transposed up one semitone at a time. Like this." He played a few bars on the piano.

Tonio's pen scratched with maddening slowness. Donati only hoped he was not making too many mistakes. Sometimes it seemed more trouble than it was worth to dictate the vocal exercises he devised to Tonio. He had no need for a record himself, since his blindness had only intensified his already formidable memory for music. But his pupils required a transcription to sight-read and study. Orfeo in particular took a great interest in exercises and other training techniques, and often talked with Donati and the marchese about them.

Donati knew Orfeo had fallen into the habit of correcting Tonio's errors. He would glance over Tonio's work, ask a few questions, and then take the exercises away where he thought Donati could not hear him rewriting them. He was always doing Donati little unobtrusive favours like this. But he should not have to take on Tonio's duties—he was a gentleman, after all, even if he was being trained for the stage.

There was no shirking the unpleasantness any longer: Tonio must go. When they returned to Milan, Donati would help him find some other position. It would not be easy, for Tonio was as sullen and unlovable a young man as Donati had ever encountered. The untalented son of talented parents, he seemed to think the world owed it to him to make up for this unfairness, and he himself owed the world nothing in return. The one person at the villa he readily obeyed was the marchese, and that was only because he was afraid of him. Donati was far too soft-hearted a master for him. Orfeo clearly thought so too, though he did not say it in so many words.

Donati heard a faint sound from the direction of the window: a short sigh, abruptly cut off. Orfeo had stifled a yawn. "Have I been working you too hard, my son?"

"No, Maestro." Orfeo's voice had the added warmth that told Donati he was smiling. Unlike many of Donati's pupils, Orfeo always seemed amused to realize how much Donati observed about him. But the next moment his tone changed—became subtly guarded. "The marchese is coming."

"He's early," said Donati. "The church bells haven't struck ten."

"He was late yesterday," Orfeo reminded him.

Donati knew what he meant. Having missed part of yesterday's morning lesson, Lodovico would take care to exact all that he was entitled to today.

The marchese's quick, sharp footsteps approached the music room. He swept in. "Good morning, Maestro. Orfeo." He did not deign to greet Tonio, who sat shuffling his feet beside Donati at the piano. "I have something to tell you before we begin. I haven't been sleeping well at the castle, so I've decided to spend the night here."

"Here?" Donati was taken aback. "Tonight?"

"Of course tonight, Maestro, what did you think?"

"I think Maestro Donati meant that we're hardly prepared for this honour," Orfeo said. "Only a few of the rooms are open, and no servants' quarters are prepared."

"I'm not bringing any servants," the marchese rejoined. "You know I don't want any more people seeing you than I can avoid. You." He must be addressing Tonio. "Tell Lucia to get one of the bedrooms ready for me—I don't care which—and to expect me for dinner tonight and breakfast tomorrow."

"Yes, Your Excellency." Tonio plunked down his little portable desk, setting the inkwell rattling in its hole, and hurried out.

"Now then, my songbird," said the marchese, "let's see what sort of voice you're in today."

Donati did not quite like his tone. He sounded as if he expected his protégé to disappoint him. But Orfeo was more than equal to the challenge. He had never sung better than he did this morning.

The marchese ought to have been pleased—and he was, when he could concentrate sufficiently on Orfeo's performance. But he was restless and distracted, often walking about while Orfeo was singing. At one point Donati even heard him scribbling with Tonio's quill. He had a habit of writing absently with any pen and paper that came to hand, but he had never done this during Orfeo's lesson before.

Was the infatuation fading? Donati did not think so. Something must be preying on the marchese's mind. Could it have anything to do with his impromptu plan to spend the night at the villa? Donati still thought this extraordinarily strange. Lodovico had always maintained a strict social distinction between himself, on the one hand, and Orfeo and Donati, on the other. They rarely dined together and never slept under the same roof. Indeed, Lodovico never passed a night anywhere without a retinue of servants.

When the lesson was over, Lodovico applauded vigorously. "Bravo! Bravo, my songbird! Your portamento is sublime—you glide from note to note with the natural grace of a bird in flight."

"Thank you, Signor Marchese."

"Your little bout with the night air doesn't seem to have affected your throat."

There was the briefest of pauses. "No, Signor Marchese."

"Thanks be to the Madonna for that!"

"What bout with the night air?" asked Donati.

"Didn't he tell you?" The marchese burst out laughing. "Our Orfeo was smitten with love last night, and scaled the wall of Castello Malvezzi in search of his lady."

"Scaled the wall?" Donati exclaimed. "My son, what were you thinking of?"

"His Excellency is pleased to be metaphorical," said Orfeo. "I got in through the castle gate, with a key I found in one of the storerooms here."

"I'd best take that key back to the castle with me," said Lodovico. "Just to put temptation out of your way."

"As you wish, Signor Marchese."

"Or better still, I'll give it to Matteo for safekeeping. You can't very well ask the girl's father for the means to get to her bed, now can you?"

"I hope I should have sufficient taste to ask the girl herself first. Which, as I told you last night, Signor Marchese, I haven't done."

"See how he protects her reputation!" mocked Lodovico. "Anyone would think she was a duchess. Why, he won't even own up to the assignation!"

Orfeo rose. "If you require nothing further of me, Signor Marchese, I should like to go for a walk in the garden."

"Now I've ruffled his feathers," said Lodovico. "Apparently Englishmen don't like to boast of their conquests of peasant girls."

"I wasn't aware that a gentleman of any nation boasted of his conquests at all. Good day to you, Signor Marchese. Maestro."

Orfeo walked out unhurriedly. Donati could eerily feel the marchese looking after him. At last Lodovico said, "He came dangerously close to insulting me."

Donati summoned his courage. What had he to be afraid of, after all? He was a famous teacher, dependent on no one for money or patronage. And he was at the end of his life—a time, surely, when a man could, and ought to, take chances. "You goaded him, Signor Marchese. And—pardon me—but I think you did it deliberately. Why?"

There was a faint rustling among the sofa cushions, as if Lodovico were settling himself more comfortably. "Because his pride needs curbing. He can't afford to be too sensitive about his honour, once he goes on the stage. You know how singers elbow each other for the best operas, the choicest arias, the topmost rank on the bill, the highest fees. If Orfeo succeeds, his rivals will plague him with spiteful tricks and gossip. If he disappoints the public, they'll turn on him, snapping at his heels, just as surely as they fawned on him before. What, will he send out challenges to every man in an audience that boos him the first time he has to sing with a cold in his head? He must learn to court the public's favour—accept humiliation when necessary. And the sooner he learns that, the better."

"Not all singers resort to underhand tactics," Donati argued. "And those who do usually lack the talent to succeed any other way. Orfeo has the talent—what's more, he has fire and charm that come in large part from his high breeding. To break his spirit might well undermine his art."

"Tut!—a thoroughbred horse is none the worse for a little schooling, and that's all I mean to give Orfeo."

"Horses are animals, Signor Marchese. They respect a strong hand—they may even come to love the one who tames them, as a child loves a fond but firm parent. A proud young man doesn't love where he's forced to submit. When you give to such a man, and he discovers you believe you've bought him, he will neither love nor respect you; even his gratitude may wither away. Orfeo will come to feel he owes you nothing. He will leave you, even turn on you, without compunction."

"I don't know what you're talking about!" Lodovico cried angrily. "I've never mollycoddled Rinaldo, and he's loyal and respectful toward me!"

He wouldn't dare be anything else, Donati thought sadly. Poor boy—the marchese had cowed him so thoroughly that he had no will of his own. There was a joke in Milan that Rinaldo and his wife's lover had not enough balls between them to make up one whole man. Lodovico's tragedy was that he admired strength and courage but could not bear to have them exerted against himself. He was always trying to bend people to his will, yet once he succeeded, he despised the puppets he had made. He was like a child forever breaking his favourite toys. Only one person seemed able to keep both his love and his respect: his second wife, Beatrice, who by all accounts was as beautiful as a goddess and as subtle as a sphinx.

Donati gave up the dispute. He had known the marchese too long to have any hope of changing his mind, once it was firmly made up. Better to keep on his good side, so that he might intervene on Orfeo's behalf if a serious quarrel blew up between them. Orfeo had too fine a voice to blight his prospects by making an enemy of a man of Lodovico's influence. Lodovico must not be allowed to destroy his career, as he had Valeriano's.

"Please forgive me, Signor Marchese," Donati said meekly. "I'm afraid I was carried away by my zeal as a teacher."

"I understand, Maestro. That's only natural. If you didn't care passionately about your pupils, you couldn't bring out the best in them. But your province is voices, not character."

Donati nodded submissively. His fingers ranged over the piano keys, picking out an old melody by Paisello. *I no longer feel youth shine in my heart.* Sometimes he wished it were true.

He left off playing to listen to the sparrows, who were filling the air with song as they built their spring homes in the villa's cornices and balconies. It was a fine day: he could feel the sun streaming through the window and smell the first blossoms opening. "Orfeo's idea of a walk appeals to me, too. With your permission, Signor Marchese, I'd like to ring for Tonio to take me round the garden."

"I'll take you, Maestro," Lodovico said genially. "This isn't a day to be indoors."

He helped Donati up and gave him his arm. They went out onto the terrace. If Donati had not known the terrace overlooked the lake, a hundred things would have told him so: the restless plashing of the waves against the embankment, the gulls' cries, the smell of fishing nets, the beating of oars, and the extraordinary natural harmonies of the boatmen, who had never studied music and could not read a note.

Lodovico led Donati away from the lake. Donati knew this path: it snaked around the back of the villa and continued north by a series of twists and turns, till it reached the cliff on which Castello Malvezzi was perched. This formed the northern boundary of the villa garden. Donati took off his hat to feel the alternating sun and shade on his bald crown, as the path passed in and out of the shelter of trees. Bees hummed, and there were sudden rustlings in the bushes that must be lizards darting to and fro.

All at once there was a new sound: a babel of raised voices, mostly male, and a sharp, confused scuffling. "What is it?" Donati asked anxiously.

"It's coming from the caves," said Lodovico.

Donati knew there were several small caves hollowed out of the cliff on which Castello Malvezzi stood. Beneath the caves were fanciful grotto rooms, now used as wine cellars.

"Do you think someone is trying to steal the wine?" Donati asked.

"I'll soon find out!" said Lodovico. "Wait here!"

Donati wanted to obey, but he was frightened—he hardly knew of what. When the marchese let go of his arm, he stretched out his hands and took a few faltering steps. There was nothing to hold onto—he did not even have the light rattan cane he usually used to find his way about. His foot caught on a tree root, and he almost fell.

"Oh, here, Maestro, come with me." Lodovico caught his arm impatiently and hurried him along.

The fracas ahead grew louder. Donati made out Tonio's coarse voice cursing, and Matteo's shouting to him to shut his mouth. But when the marchese and Donati reached them, there was dead silence.

Lodovico's arm went stiff in Donati's grasp. "What's happening here? My God, Orfeo, are you all right?"

"I'm perfectly all right, Signor Marchese." Orfeo's voice was level, but a little breathless.

"Perfectly all right! Body of Bacchus! Your face is covered with blood!"

"My lip is split. That's where all the blood is coming from."

"You've been fighting!" said Lodovico. "And with this cur of a servant! Well, sirrah! What have *you* to say for yourself?"

There was no reply—only the shuffling of feet that was Tonio's usual response to a difficult question. A smell of sweat came from his direction, mixed with the reek of wine around both young men.

"I will have an explanation of this!" Lodovico stormed. "Matteo, what's going on here?"

"They were fighting down in the grottos, Excellency—Signor Orfeo and Tonio." The gardener hesitated; he was not a man of many words. "Lucia here, she heard the noise and fetched me to break it up. I did—or I had most nearly, when Your Excellency arrived."

"What was this fight about?" Lodovico demanded.

Orfeo said quickly, "Tonio and I had a difference of opinion over a game of cards. He accused me of cheating. I tried to explain that he was mistaken, but he wouldn't be persuaded, and finally I was obliged to knock him down. He objected."

"You got yourself into this state, risked doing yourself grievous harm, demeaned yourself by fighting a common servant—all over a game of cards?"

"In retrospect, Signor Marchese, it does seem hardly worth the trouble."

"You are impudent, signor. You forget yourself—and me."

"I could never forget you, Signor Marchese." Orfeo's voice was just a little wry.

Donati wished with all his heart that Orfeo would sulk or rebel or lose his temper. Anything was better than this cool composure. For Lodovico, it was like a red flag to a bull. "So this is what your fine manners and breeding amount to!" he spat out. "Grappling with a servant in a wine cellar! Maestro, you should see your pupil: his lip split, his hat gone, his collar half torn off, and his clothes all stained with wine! How did that happen, pray?"

"We broke a bottle of wine in the fight, and rolled in it while we were struggling on the floor."

"Better and better!" Lodovico taunted. "And who is going to pay me for the bottle of wine I've lost?"

"As you know, I haven't much money," said Orfeo in a low voice. "But you may have my gold cravat-pin if you like."

"I don't want your damned cravat-pin! I can buy a hundred like it! What I want is an apology!"

"For what, exactly?" asked Orfeo consideringly.

"For conducting yourself like a common ruffian. For disgracing yourself and me."

"I can't apologize for that, Signor Marchese, because I haven't done that."

Lodovico drew in his breath. Don't, Donati pleaded silently, don't insult him again, he won't stand much more.

"How dare you?" Lodovico let fly. "How dare you defy me like this? What would you be without me? A shreds-and-patches gentleman, reduced to giving music lessons or accompanying rehearsals of third-rate opera companies! I found your voice going to seed and took you under my wing—gave you the greatest singing teacher in Italy! And you repay me like this! You make me ashamed I ever took you up!"

Orfeo said nothing. Donati knew by his laboured breaths that he was fighting for self-command.

"I want an apology for your rudeness and ingratitude," Lodovico went on. "If I don't get it, I swear by the Madonna I'll send you packing, even if it breaks my heart to lose your voice!"

There was a long pause. Donati thought he would run mad with suspense. At last Orfeo said quietly, "I beg your pardon for my rudeness and ingratitude."

"Ah." Lodovico let out a breath of satisfaction.

"May I have leave to return to the villa to wash my face and change my clothes?" Orfeo asked.

"Yes, by all means. Get rid of all trace of this brawl."

"Yes, Signor Marchese." Orfeo departed in the direction of the villa.

"As for you"—the marchese turned in Tonio's direction—"you'd no business fighting with your betters."

"H-he started it, Excellency—"

"I don't care a dried fig who started it!" bellowed the marchese. "The end of it is that you're dismissed. Pack your things, and get out."

Donati considered pointing out gently that Tonio was his servant to dismiss, not Lodovico's. But really, it was just as well. He had meant to sack Tonio anyway. "I'll give you a month's wages," he promised. "And if you let me know where you're going, I'll help you find another place."

"Thanks, Maestro," Tonio muttered.

"Be off with you!" said the marchese. Tonio took to his heels.

"Hadn't I best go after him, Excellency?" ventured Matteo. "He might run into Signor Orfeo again, and—"

"Yes, yes, I see. Go on. No, wait—I've something to tell you first. You may have heard from Lucia that I'll be staying at the villa tonight. I'm giving you a holiday. You can spend the night up at the castle with your daughter."

Donati shook his head forebodingly. That would leave no one at the villa but Lodovico, Orfeo, and himself—hardly a congenial group, after what had happened today.

Matteo and Lucia murmured their thanks and took the path back to the villa. Donati had almost forgotten Lucia was here. She had been so silent throughout this scene. He wondered what she thought about it all.

"Well, Maestro?" said Lodovico. "Shall we continue our walk or go back to the villa?"

Donati supposed he should not be surprised by the marchese's cheerful tone. He rarely held grudges, once he had got his own way. "I'd as lief go back to the villa, if you wouldn't mind, Signor Marchese. All this has tired me out."

"Of course, Maestro. This way." Lodovico gave Donati his arm. As they proceeded along the path, he said, "You see, my songbird is all the better for having his wings clipped a bit. He's a sensible young man at bottom, and knows on which side his bread is buttered. You'll see he won't be quite so saucy to me in future."

Donati did not answer. Why? he kept asking himself. Why did Orfeo give in? Not because he was afraid of Lodovico—Donati was sure of that. No: he had made a calculated decision to keep on his good side. For his patronage? His money? Or for some other reason beyond Donati's grasp? Whatever the cause, Donati guessed what that submission must have cost him. And he suddenly knew that, in this clash of wills between a powerful nobleman and a penniless singer, it was Lodovico Malvezzi he was afraid for.

A fleeting tranquillity returned to the villa. The marchese went back to the castle till dinnertime. Orfeo changed his clothes and had his split lip attended to by Lucia. He made no comment about Tonio's dismissal, but Donati had an idea he was not sorry to hear of it.

Donati was relieved to be rid of Tonio, but now he had no valet and secretary to be his Eyes. The marchese had promised to send him a servant from the castle tomorrow, but how would he manage tonight? "Orfeo will help you," the marchese had said, but Donati thought Orfeo had been humiliated enough for one day, without being made a servant to his own singing teacher. In the event, however, the problem was easily solved: Orfeo stepped into Tonio's shoes without being asked.

In the late afternoon, the marchese returned with a carpet-bag, having left his horse at the Nightingale in Solaggio. Lucia had prepared the largest and grandest of the villa's seven bedrooms for him. He, Donati, and Orfeo all occupied rooms on the upper floor at the front of the villa, overlooking the terrace and the lake. Donati's and Lodovico's rooms flanked the main staircase; Orfeo's was on the other side of Donati's.

Lodovico took his carpet-bag to his room himself, refusing to let Lucia unpack it for him. He, Orfeo, and Donati sat down to an uncomfortable dinner. At six o'clock, Orfeo had his evening lesson. He sang as well as ever, but Donati perceived it was costing him an effort. When Donati questioned him, he reluctantly admitted that his split lip had opened again and was bleeding profusely. "You ought to have told me at once," Donati said severely. "How can I teach you properly, when I don't know what obstacles you're facing?"

"I'm sorry, Maestro. But if I'd been on stage, I couldn't have complained to anyone. I should have had to go on singing as best I could."

Donati was about to point out that a lesson was not a stage performance. But he let the argument drop, because he understood what it was really about. The young man would sooner have choked on his own blood than complained of pain or difficulty in front of the marchese.

In the evening, Matteo and Lucia departed for the castle. Lodovico paced up and down the music room in an agitation Donati could not account for. Orfeo played the piano and sang softly to himself. Donati did not allow him to practise at full volume for more than two hours a day, but he could sing a little longer in half-voice, to develop interpretation and expression. He was working on one of the old songs Donati loved:

"I am all sorrow,
I have only cares,
A cruel pain is killing me.
For me, the stars, fate, the gods, Heaven are nothing but tyrants."

"Do you have to go on in that dreary vein?" snapped Lodovico. "Can't you sing something more cheerful?"

Without comment, Orfeo changed to Mozart's droll air

about the advantages of hiding under an ass's skin. Lodovico resumed his pacing. Donati was profoundly relieved when the church bells struck ten, and Lodovico sent him and Orfeo off to bed. As he ascended the stairs on Orfeo's arm, he heard the marchese restlessly playing scales on the piano, and wondered when he meant to go to bed himself.

Orfeo helped Donati to wash and undress, his touch as gentle and patient as a woman's. Donati could not imagine how he had endured Tonio's ministrations for so long. He hated to raise a sore subject, but he knew he would not sleep unless he did. "My son, there's something you ought to know. Tonio made a vow to give up cards during Lent."

Orfeo's hands paused briefly in the act of tying Donati's nightgown at the neck. When he spoke, Donati could hear the smile in his voice. "I made a misstep there."

"Don't worry, I won't tell the marchese. But, my son, what were you and Tonio really fighting about?"

"Believe me, Maestro, it was a matter of no importance."

"Then why can't you tell me about it?"

"I will, if you'll worry otherwise. But I give you my word, there's no need."

Now Donati was in a quandary. To insist would be tantamount to saying that he did not trust his pupil. Orfeo was at an age when a man was entitled to keep a quarrel private if he chose. So Donati asked him nothing more. But when Orfeo had helped him into bed and drawn up the covers, Donati said tentatively, "I was thinking—"

"Yes, Maestro?"

"I know you and the marchese haven't been getting along of late. He does care about you in his way. I heard the fear in his voice when he asked if you were all right after the fight—"

"I think, Maestro," Orfeo said quietly, "you must know as well as I do that *Are you all right?* really meant *Can you still sing?*"

Donati sighed. "Well, anyway, I thought perhaps if you wanted to continue your training and didn't want to be indebted to the marchese, you might come and live with me till I find someone to take Tonio's place. The work wouldn't be hard, and you could go on with your lessons. I know it seems demeaning for a young man of your background—"

"Maestro, it would be an honour! But—my plans are unsettled. I can't say for certain where I'll be or what I'll be doing in a week, or a month."

"I don't understand. You would go away before your training is finished?"

"Not of my own choice. But it's possible, yes."

"Is it something to do with your family in England?"

"In a way. I'm sorry to be so mysterious. I would tell you if I could. There: I've put your bell in the compartment of the headboard behind you—so." He guided Donati's hand to it. "If you need anything during the night, you've only to ring."

"I can't summon you with a bell!"

"Then I shall have to sleep at the foot of your bed like a spaniel, so that you can nudge me awake if you need me. I really think the bell is more practical. Good night, Maestro. Pleasant dreams."

Donati heard the door close softly behind him. He expected him to go to his own room, but instead heard his footsteps descending the stairs. The marchese would be annoyed if he caught him up and about—he had seemed to want him and Donati out of the way. But why?

Donati slid out from under the covers and knelt on the chill floor beside the bed. He said an Our Father and a Hail Mary. Then he pictured Santa Cecilia as he loved her best, dressed in her bridal finery, hearing musicians play at her wedding feast, while she sang to God in her heart that she would always remain a virgin. He begged her to bless both Orfeo and the marchese and to heal the rancour between them. And he asked that, if Orfeo would not suffer by it, he might remain with Donati and become the great singer he was meant to be.

The marchese's fitful piano playing had long since ceased. As Donati got back into bed, he thought he heard the front door open and close. He lay still and listened, but all he could hear was the ceaseless, sorrowing murmur of the lake. He fell asleep.

Donati woke to the song of a lark. He reached up, feeling for the silken watch-pocket that hung over his bed. His watch had no glass covering on the face, so that he could feel the hands. He ran his fingertips lightly over them. It was a little after six, the hour when he and Orfeo were accustomed to rise. He took his bell out of the headboard compartment and rang.

No one came. The villa was strangely silent. Donati supposed Lucia and her father had not yet returned from the castle, and Orfeo and the marchese were still abed. Yet the bell was very loud—it ought to have awakened Orfeo, whose room was next to Donati's, and perhaps Lodovico as well. Could they have gone out for a walk? No: Orfeo would not have left Donati to shift for himself. Perhaps he had gone to fetch water for washing and shaving.

Donati waited a while, then rang again. Still no one answered. He lay quiet, straining to hear footsteps or the opening of a door. Outside his window, the birds were singing in chorus. But in the villa, there was not a sound.

When the church bells around the lake struck seven, Donati began to be frightened. Orfeo would not have deserted him. Suppose he were lying ill in his room, hearing Donati's bell but unable to answer it? Donati scrambled out from under the covers and felt with his feet for his slippers. That was when he heard the front door open and close. He fumbled for his bell and rang it as hard as he could.

There was a light step on the stairs, then his door opened. "Good morning, Maestro," said Lucia's voice. "I'm sorry to be so late this morning, but one of the maids at the castle had a toothache, and I had to help look after her. I'll put the coffee on straightaway."

"It doesn't matter about the coffee. Lucia, I've been awake nearly an hour, and there's not a sign of His Excellency or Orfeo."

"That's funny. Wait here a minute, Maestro."

He heard her walk to Orfeo's room, then to Lodovico's, and finally back to his own. "They're not there," she said slowly. "And their beds haven't been slept in."

"But—where can they be?"

"I'll look downstairs."

Donati waited, torn between hope and anxiety. At last Lucia returned, saying, "They're not downstairs. I couldn't find any trace of them. But I've put the coffee on, so you'll soon have that to warm you. There's not much sun today."

"For the love of God, Lucia, never mind about the coffee! Where can the marchese and Orfeo be?"

"Wherever they are," she said reasonably, "they wouldn't want you going without breakfast, Maestro. Here, I've brought you water to wash with, and fresh towels, and when that's done I'll help you dress. Do you mind going without shaving for the time being? I've never shaved a man."

"I can shave myself," Donati said hastily. "You needn't do anything else for me, really, Lucia—"

"Now, Maestro, there's nothing to be embarrassed about. I looked after Papa when he had fever last year and was as helpless as a baby. I'll just go out for a few minutes while you do anything you need to do alone, and you ring your bell when you're ready for me to come back."

Donati could see it was useless to resist. Between them, they got him washed, shaved, and dressed, though Donati kept urging Lucia to go out and look for the marchese and Orfeo. "I will just as soon as I've got you settled," she promised. "Don't worry. I wouldn't be surprised if His Excellency heard some singer he admired on the lake last night, and he and Signor Orfeo went out in a boat to find out who it was. You know what His Excellency is like."

Donati detected the undercurrent of tension in her voice. She had fears, but she was willing herself not to give way to them.

When she had led Donati down to the drawing room and put a steaming cup of coffee in his hands, she went out to search for the marchese and Orfeo in the garden. If she could not find them, she said, she would seek help from her father, who was doing an errand in Solaggio.

Donati drank his coffee, then went into the music room and tried to play the piano. It was no use—for once music failed to distract him. He walked out onto the terrace. The air was close and a little chilly, the wind fresh. It would rain by and by.

The waiting seemed interminable. When the church bells rang the half-hour after eight, Donati fetched his hat from its stand and went out for a walk. He knew it would be more sensible to remain at the villa in case the marchese and Orfeo returned, but this hanging about doing nothing was unbearable, even for one as schooled in patience as himself. If he kept to the lakeside path, which was flagstoned and fairly straight, he would not need anyone to guide him. And there was always the chance he might meet the marchese and Orfeo or hear some news of them.

Using his light rattan cane, he found his way to the point where the lakeside path branched off the terrace. He strolled along, swinging the cane lightly back and forth in front of him to guard against obstacles. Fishermen's voices, snatches of song, and gulls' hoarse cries came from the lake to his left, muffled by the plane trees that he knew ran along this part of the path. He still felt no sunshine; that might have been the effect of the plane trees blotting out the eastern sky, but the air hung heavier than ever, and before long it began to rain. Donati did not want to return to the villa, but the drops fell ever faster, pattering on the grass and leaves. Just then his feet crunched on shifting, uneven ground, and he knew he had reached the gravelled yard outside the little Moorish pavilion that served as a belvedere over the lake. He had never been inside it—a view naturally meant nothing to him—but it seemed to provide an opportune shelter from the rain.

He turned left, toward the lake, and felt ahead with his cane till he found two shallow stairs leading up to an open doorway. He went in, shuffling along the smooth, tiled floor, with his left hand outstretched and his right hand swinging the cane before him.

The obstacle was so low, he missed it. He tripped and fell sprawling, but could not make out what he had fallen on.

It seemed to be furniture—at all events, it was covered with cloth—yet it lay inexplicably along the floor and was too hard and awkwardly shaped to sit on. His hand lit on a flap in the wool covering. He lifted it, felt it between his fingers. It was not a flap. It was a lapel.

He cried out, struggled off the thing he had been lying on. He wanted to grope his way to the door and escape. But he knew he must not. There seemed to be no one here but him to do whatever must be done.

He crossed himself, then reached out trembling hands. His fingers met the fine, smooth wool again. A coat—a man's dress coat, with tails. It was unfastened, and the tail nearest Donati was stretched out unnaturally along the floor. He left it there. His hands found a silken waistcoat, a watch-chain, and a linen cravat. The waistcoat was torn in one place. Donati unthinkingly poked a finger between the frayed edges, and it sank into something cold and pulpy, like a rotten spot in a piece of fruit. He had put his finger through a hole in the man's chest.

He spun away, his stomach heaving. Santa Cecilia, Santa Cecilia, take this thing away! Make this all a dream, please, Santa Cecilia! Please, dear God!

He crossed himself again and again, shaking violently, drawing long shuddering breaths. Then suddenly his chest contracted, and his sobbing ceased. He must know *who.* He steeled himself, turned back to the thing on the floor, and groped above the cravat. The head was hatless, the cheeks pricked with stubble, and cold as stone. A square chin, a nose beaked like a hawk's, thick, jagged brows above staring eyes, which Donati gently closed. He was almost sure he remembered the face from the days before he lost his sight. But there was a way to be sure. He felt along the man's watch-chain till he found an ornate seal. His sensitive fingers made out the device on the end: a serpent coiled around a sword. Donati folded his hands, bent his head, and prayed for the soul of Lodovico Malvezzi.

All at once Donati heard footsteps crunching the gravel outside the belvedere. His heart lurched. But the next moment he recognized Matteo's voice: "Did you look in here?"

"No," Lucia's voice replied.

Donati opened his mouth to warn them of the shock in store, but no sound came. He heard them coming into the belvedere. Lucia gasped, and Matteo cried, "Mother of God! His Excellency!"

Lucia ran to Donati. "Let me help you up, Maestro."

"I don't think I can stand," Donati said shakily.

The girl dropped down beside him. He could sense her staring at the body. "He's dead, isn't he?"

"Yes. I think he's been dead for hours. There's—there's a hole—" He pointed a quavering finger toward Lodovico's body.

"A bullet hole," she said sombrely. "His waistcoat and chest are all charred."

"What should we do?" asked Matteo from the doorway, his gruff voice unnaturally high.

Lucia drew in her breath sharply. "Orfeo!"

"Where?" exclaimed Donati, starting up.

"I don't know!" she said in a choking voice. "You don't think he—Oh, God!"

What was she afraid of? Donati thought. That Orfeo was murdered—or murderer? He could not bring himself to ask.

"What shall we *do*?" Matteo almost wailed. He still had not come any closer—perhaps in the grip of a peasant's superstitious horror of the dead.

His daughter was made of sterner stuff. "He must have the Last Rites. Papa, will you fetch Don Cristoforo from the village?" Don Cristoforo was the parish priest. "And—I know!—go and tell His Excellency's friend, Conte Raversi. He'll know what to do."

"That's a good thought!" Matteo's voice was fervent with relief at the prospect of laying this burden on someone else's shoulders. "I'll go at once! But—I don't know if I should leave you here—"

"I think we'll be all right." She sounded as if she were trying to persuade herself. "You don't think whoever did this will come back, do you, Maestro?"

"I don't know," Donati admitted. "So you'd better go with your father. I'll stay here with—the marchese."

"I'm not leaving you alone," she declared. "We'll both stay."

When she spoke in that tone, there was no gainsaying her. Matteo hurried off.

Lucia helped Donati up and guided him to a little stone seat close by. He asked uncertainly, "Should we do something for him? Fold his hands, button his coat—"

"I don't think so. I think we should leave him just as we found him. People might want to know how he was lying, and how his clothes were pulled about."

"One of his coat-tails is sticking out," said Donati, though it seemed silly to mention such a small thing.

"They both are." Realization dawned on her. "Someone's been through his pockets!"

"Robbery!" said Donati. "So that's what it was!" He felt a weight lifted from his heart. Orfeo might conceivably kill to right a wrong or avenge an insult, but he would never steal from his victim.

He heard Lucia move quickly toward the body again. There were rustling and clinking sounds. "His watch is still here," she sighed. "So is his pocketbook. And his trouser pocket is full of coins."

"So it wasn't robbery. Unless whoever killed him was interrupted before he could steal anything. You don't suppose Orfeo came along and took the murderer by surprise?"

"And did what?" she asked indignantly. "Ran away?"

"He might have been killed himself, and his body thrown in the lake."

"No! That's not possible. The robber would have thrown the marchese in, too."

Donati thought this was by no means certain, but he saw no point in saying so. "Conte Raversi will help to sort it all out. It was clever of you to think of sending for him." Donati knew Raversi and thought him honourable and conscientious, despite his well-known obsession with the Carbonari.

There was a short silence. "We should pray for him," Lucia said.

She began dutifully reciting the prayer for the dead known as the *de profundis*: *"Out of the depths I cry out to thee, O Lord..."* Donati joined her, taking comfort in the solemn, familiar chant that lulled his thoughts to sleep, leaving only reverence for God and pity for the dead.

To Donati's surprise, Conte Raversi came to the belvedere without priest, gendarmes, or any servant but Matteo. Raversi explained that he had sent a footman to Solaggio to fetch Don Cristoforo, as well as Luigi Curioni, the village doctor; Benedetto Ruga, the podestà, who had the duties of a mayor and chief magistrate; and

Friedrich Von Krauss, the commander of the Austrian garrison. Donati had no doubt that, although Ruga would be officially in charge of the investigation into Lodovico's murder, it was really Von Krauss who would organize and direct it. In Lombardy, Italians might propose, but the Austrian military disposed.

Raversi went over to the body. "So it's true," he said in his hollow, melancholy voice, which always sounded to Donati as if it were coming through a long tunnel. "Matteo told me, but I hoped against hope that it was all a ghastly mistake. My poor friend." He prayed softly for a few moments. "To die so far from his wife and family—at the hands of an assassin!"

Donati did not know what to say. Lucia spoke up. "So please you, Excellency, we think someone went through his pockets, but there doesn't seem to be anything missing."

"You're Matteo's daughter, I think?" said Raversi.

"Yes, Excellency. I'm Lucia Landi."

"Have you moved the body or disarranged it in any way?"

"No, Excellency."

"You're all witnesses to the fact that I'm not doing so, either. But I wish to confirm what you've told me. Yes, his pocketbook and watch are here. And in his breast pocket—a pistol! Why should he carry arms in his own garden? Ah, Madonna!—he must have known he was the target of an incendiary! And yet he was gallant to the end—scorning the Carbonari and refusing to take them seriously."

Donati was taken aback. "Signor Conte, are you so certain that the murder was political?"

"Can you doubt it, Maestro? When a man like Lodovico—a staunch friend to the Austrian government and the Church—is killed for no apparent reason, the crime must be political. Consider the times we live in: rebellion in Naples, rebellion in Piedmont, a massive conspiracy just beginning to be uncovered here in Lombardy!"

Donati had heard all about the arrests in Lombardy this past autumn. A group of distinguished men, including some of northern Italy's foremost writers and journalists, stood accused of plotting to overthrow Austrian rule in Milan and Venice. A special commission had been established in Venice to deal with the conspiracy, and if Donati did not miss his guess, it would soon aggrandize its importance by finding more traitors. Those already arrested were pent up in wretched cells, subjected to secret interrogations, denied the assistance of lawyers and the consolation of friends.

Lucia broke the silence. "Maybe the marchese shot himself, Excellency. He did have a gun."

"But it hasn't been fired," said Raversi. "It's loaded, but he never had a chance to use it. Though it's true that the extent of the wound and the blackening around it show he was shot at very close range. This young man you call Orfeo must have come into the belvedere with him—he didn't, for example, shoot him through a window from outside. Of course, he might have killed him outside and dragged his body in here to conceal it."

Donati said as politely as he could, "You seem to have made up your mind that Orfeo killed him, Signor Conte."

"Of course he did!" said Raversi eagerly. "He was the perfect Carbonaro agent: a foreigner without connexions in Milan, of whom nothing was known for good or ill. He kept his name and background a secret, and now he's disappeared. That's how the Carbonari work—in silence and deceit."

"But Signor Conte," Donati protested, "it was the marchese's idea to make a mystery of Orfeo's name and background. He thought it would stir up public interest in him."

"The Carbonari are very clever," said Raversi. "No doubt Orfeo made Lodovico think it was all his own idea."

"With respect, Signor Conte, I don't think anyone ever put a thought in Marchese Malvezzi's head against his will."

Raversi thought briefly. "Do you know Orfeo's real name, Maestro?"

"No, Signor Conte. I know almost nothing about him, except that he has a beautiful voice. Surely that can't be said of many Carbonari."

"There are Carbonari in all walks of life, Maestro. What more natural than that they should choose a singer to attach himself to Lodovico? My poor friend's mania for music was well known."

Donati was shaken. It might be true. What did he know about Carbonari? He was fond of Orfeo, but the young man had been something of an enigma to him. *I can't say for certain where I'll be or what I'll be doing in a week, or a month… I'm sorry to be so mysterious. I would tell you if I could.* Mightn't these be the words of a radical incendiary?

"Excellency," broke in Lucia, "how do we know Orfeo hasn't been killed, too? Or that he isn't lying wounded somewhere, needing us, while we stand about here making up stories?"

"Comandante Von Krauss and the others will be here soon, and a search can be made," said Raversi. "Until then, I must require you all to stay here. Tell me, Maestro, how did you meet Orfeo?"

"I'd known Marchese Malvezzi for some years. He'd sponsored promising pupils of mine, and I'd trained protégés of his. He told me how he'd met this young Englishman and taken it into his head to have him trained at his villa on the Lake of Como. He wanted me to be his teacher. I could gauge the extent of his infatuation by his willingness to leave Milan in January—the best opera season of the year—to live on the lake in winter weather, with hardly any company of his own rank. I told him I was old and blind—my days of intrigue and adventure were long past. I wanted to work in comfort, without having to hide from anyone."

"And yet you agreed to teach Orfeo. Why?"

"Signor Conte," Donati said simply, "I heard him sing."

There was a pause. Donati heard Raversi walking deliberatively back and forth. "How long have you and Orfeo been living here?"

"About six weeks, I think."

"What language did you and he speak?"

"Milanese, Signor Conte. I don't speak English."

"Did he speak Milanese well?"

"Extremely well."

"So you could converse quite fluently. Didn't he ever tell you anything about himself?"

"No, Signor Conte. But I never asked. I wasn't curious. We lived for music—we talked and thought of nothing else. The rest of the world seemed very far away."

"What about you, Matteo?" asked Raversi. "Can you shed any light on who Orfeo was or where he came from?"

"Excellency, I hardly ever saw him. I was always out working in the gardens or going on errands to the village and the castle."

"And you, Lucia? Do you know Orfeo's name?"

"No, Excellency."

"You were close to him in age," Raversi said persuasively. "The two of you must have been thrown together—become friends."

"A girl like me doesn't make friends with a gentleman like him, Excellency—not unless she wants to be ruined out of hand. I wouldn't take that chance. I want to be properly married some day."

"Hm. Well, at least you can give me a description of him."

"A description, Excellency?"

"Yes, a description. What did he look like?"

"That's hard to say, Excellency."

"How can it be hard to say? Haven't you been living here with him all this time?"

"I didn't *live* here, Excellency," she said primly. "My father wouldn't allow it. I only came to cook and clean during the day."

"All the same, you must have seen Orfeo frequently. Was he tall?"

"Taller than I am, Excellency."

"That's as might be expected. How much taller?"

"I don't know, Excellency. I never stood close by him."

"Was he heavily built?"

"I wouldn't say so, no."

"What colour was his hair?"

"Brown, I think."

"What shade of brown?"

"I didn't especially notice."

"What about his eyes?"

"I'm not one to be looking into gentlemen's eyes, Excellency!"

"For the love of God, girl, you must remember more about him than this! Was he good-looking? Had he any scars or moles or disfiguring marks?"

"I really didn't take any notice of his looks, Excellency. He was above my touch."

Donati shook his head dazedly. Lucia, who had not flinched from helping him dress this morning, turning priggish! Shrewd, sharp-eyed Lucia, unable to describe a young man she had seen every day for the past six weeks! Oh, Orfeo, Orfeo, you have a great deal to answer for!

"Mother of God!" cried Raversi in exasperation. "Matteo, *you* describe him."

Matteo cleared his throat and shuffled his feet. "I didn't see half so much of him as my girl here did. If she can't describe him, then nor can I, Excellency."

"This is preposterous! Maestro Donati, surely Lodovico told you something about what this young man looked like?"

"He told me he was twenty-one years old. But he never said whether he was fair or dark, tall or short. He did say he would cut a fine figure on the stage and be pleasing to the ladies, but I had the impression he meant that he was graceful and gentlemanly, not necessarily that he was handsome."

"Didn't you have to feel Orfeo's face or throat in order to teach him?"

"No, Signor Conte. I knew just by listening to him what he was doing right or wrong.—But wait!" Donati held up his hand. "We're forgetting Tonio!"

"Who is Tonio?" asked Raversi quickly.

"My servant. Or rather, he used to be. The marchese made me dismiss him yesterday."

"Why?"

Donati recounted how Orfeo and Tonio fought in the wine cellars under the caves, and how the marchese came upon them after the fight, lost his temper, and quarrelled with Orfeo. Of course Raversi wanted to know what Orfeo and Tonio were fighting about. Donati answered that he did not know.

"Where is Tonio now?" Raversi asked.

"I don't know, Signor Conte. But he can't have gone far. I promised I'd give him a month's wages and help him find another post. So he's probably in Solaggio waiting for a chance to come back and see me after the marchese leaves—" Donati stopped short, remembering that Lodovico would never go anywhere of his own accord again. "He wouldn't have wanted to come back while the marchese was here," he finished. "He was afraid of him."

"Angry with him, too, probably," said Lucia shortly.

"What are you trying to suggest?" Raversi asked her sternly.

"It's not my place to make suggestions, Excellency. I was just wondering, that's all."

"You're thinking Tonio might have killed the marchese?" said Matteo. "How could he have got into the garden? I left the gate locked last night, and he didn't have a key."

"It wasn't locked this morning, Papa. I forgot to tell you."

"Are you sure?" asked Raversi.

"Yes, Your Excellency. When Papa and I came down from the castle this morning, he gave me the key to unlock the gate, because he had to go to the village. But I didn't need to use it, because the gate was already unlocked."

"How many keys are there?" asked Raversi.

"Two, Excellency," said Matteo. "One I took with me to the castle last night, and the other's kept in a shed in the garden."

"Well, there you are," said Raversi. "Orfeo took the key from the shed and let himself out of the garden after he killed Lodovico."

Donati was only half listening. Something of the greatest importance had dawned on him. There might be dozens of brown-haired young men wandering about the mountainous countryside or trying to cross the borders into Piedmont or Switzerland. But not many of them would have a split lip.

Raversi seemed uncannily to read his mind. "Was Orfeo hurt in this fight with Tonio?"

Somebody has to tell him, Donati thought. Lucia won't, and Matteo is taking his cue from her. So it's up to me. Orfeo may be a murderer. He mustn't escape.

"I don't know," he heard himself mumble. "As you know, I can't see."

He heard Lucia's quick release of breath. Now we're all guilty, he thought. Heaven help us if this young man isn't worth lying for!

His keen ears caught voices in the distance. "Someone is coming."

Matteo's heavy tread moved toward the door. "It's Comandante Von Krauss and some soldiers," he reported. "And I can see Don Cristoforo and Signor Ruga—oh, and Dr. Curioni. They're all coming from the direction of the village."

"The devil!" muttered Raversi. "I didn't want such a great group all at once. Tell me: does anyone know of this crime except ourselves?"

"We told no one else," said Donati. "But I expect that, now you've sent for the most important people in the neighbourhood, the news will be all over Solaggio, and boatmen will be carrying it to all the villages round the lake."

"No," said Raversi. "I had notes delivered to Von Krauss and the others, telling them about the murder but urging them not to reveal it to anyone yet. Even the servant who delivered the notes wasn't privy to what they said."

"But Signor Conte," said Donati, "people will have to know about the murder soon enough."

"I'm afraid I've kept you talking too long, Maestro," Raversi said solicitously. "You must be exhausted after such a terrible shock. Matteo, Lucia, will you take Maestro Donati back to the villa? Remain there, all of you, until I come to join you. And speak to no one—no one, do you understand?—about what you've seen and heard here today."

Of course the first thing Lucia did on their return to the villa was to look for Orfeo. He was not there. "Some of his things are missing," she reported to Donati. "A change of linen, his riding coat, and his top-boots. And the dress coat he was wearing last night is hanging in the wardrobe."

"So he left deliberately," said Donati. "And very quietly—he didn't wake me when he came to get his things, and I sleep lightly."

"That's not the worst of it," she said. "His pistol is gone, too—the one he kept in the night-table drawer."

Donati crossed himself. "God help the boy. I hope he wasn't a Carbonaro. I'd rather think he killed the marchese out of anger at his treatment of him. It's more human, somehow."

"Maestro," she said reproachfully, "didn't you know him any better than that?"

Donati set his face resolutely. "We have to tell Conte Raversi and the others what you've discovered."

"I was going to tell them, Maestro," she said calmly. "They might find Orfeo with his pistol and the other things he took away, and then they would know I was lying. And what good could I do Orfeo after that?"

They waited an hour or more for Raversi to come and tell them what was to happen next. Donati sat at the piano but was too shattered to play a note. Matteo, unused to being indoors, went tramping about, knocking into tables and candle-stands. Lucia kept the coffee-pot replenished and went about her usual household tasks.

At about noon, Raversi, Ruga, and Don Cristoforo brought back Lodovico's body, along with one of the villa lanterns that had likewise been found in the belvedere. Von Krauss had returned to his barracks to send out parties of soldiers to hunt for Orfeo. Don Cristoforo had given Lodovico the Last Rites, and Curioni had examined his body. Now Curioni was on his way to the village to engage a trustworthy woman to help prepare Lodovico's body for display in the parish church. There it would remain until the Malvezzi family determined where, and with what pomp and ceremony, it would be buried.

Raversi said Curioni was reasonably certain the body had not been moved after the murder. This scotched any theory that Lodovico had been killed outside the belvedere, and his body hidden there afterward. Curioni had also confirmed that the shot that killed Lodovico was fired at close range—probably within six feet. Not only was Lodovico's chest badly blackened and torn, but the wad that had been used to ram the bullet up the gun's muzzle was lodged in the wound. It proved to be a piece of paper ruled with staffs for composing music. As best as Raversi could tell through the blood and powder burns, there was no writing on it. "Could Orfeo have got hold of paper like this?" he asked Donati.

"Yes, Signor Conte, very easily. Both he and Tonio used that sort of paper to copy out exercises I composed. The marchese himself used to scribble on it—a restless habit he had. But there was nothing unique about it. You could buy it at any stationer's in Milan."

"When was the last time you saw—I mean, encountered—Marchese Lodovico alive?"

"He sent Orfeo and me to bed when the church bells chimed ten. I heard him playing scales on the piano downstairs, but not for very long. Just before I fell asleep, I thought I heard someone go out through the front door. But that might have been Orfeo. He went downstairs after he helped me prepare for bed."

"Lodovico sent him to bed, but he went downstairs again?"

"Yes," said Donati unhappily.

"Curioni thinks Lodovico was dead by three or four in the morning, but might have died much earlier. So we know he was killed some time between ten and four. If it was earlier rather than later, Orfeo's had a very great start of us. God knows if it will be possible to find him, especially with such a vague description. Still, he hadn't a passport to leave Lombardy. If he tried to cross any border, he would have been stopped."

Unless he had enough money to bribe the customs officers, Donati thought. Or someone provided him with a false passport. Or he tramped over the mountains into Switzerland, as the smugglers do. Oh yes, for an unscrupulous or desperate man, there are many ways out of Austrian Italy.

Lucia told Raversi about Orfeo's missing clothes and pistol. Raversi was more confident than ever that Orfeo was a Carbonaro. "This confirms me in what I've proposed to Comandante Von Krauss. You know that Piedmont, right on our border, is in the throes of a revolt, but you may not have heard yet that the King has abdicated, and the Regent, Carlo Alberto, has been forced to proclaim a constitution. The Piedmontese rebels' success has emboldened our own Carbonari. If it's known that Marchese Malvezzi has been assassinated, and his killer has escaped, the murder will be hailed as a signal for radicals all around the lake—perhaps all over Lombardy—to rise in revolt. Lodovico was so closely identified with our Austrian rulers that his murder will be seen as a blow directly against the government."

"What are you saying, Signor Conte?" Donati stammered. "You want us to keep the murder a secret?"

"Not for long, Maestro," Raversi assured him. "Just until the political situation calms down—or until Orfeo is found and can be made an example of. It's an extreme measure, and Comandante Von Krauss was sceptical about it at first. But in the end he couldn't take the responsibility for inciting an insurrection."

"But how can you hide the marchese's death from his family, his servants, his friends?"

"My dear Maestro, no one said anything about hiding his death. Dr. Curioni has agreed to certify that he died of heart failure. I regret carrying the deception so far, but I have no choice. Curioni was persuaded of the urgency of the need."

Donati had no doubt that an Austrian commander and a contingent of soldiers could persuade Curioni of almost anything. "But Signor Conte, how can you search for Orfeo without revealing that he's suspected of killing the marchese?"

"A man can be sought without anyone's knowing what he's wanted for. Von Krauss has agreed he won't even tell the soldiers hunting for him why they're to find him. They may have ideas—so may the people they question. But they won't know for certain, and in the inevitable flood of rumours, murder will be only one possibility."

Donati shook his head. Raversi might prevent an insurrection, but he would never find Orfeo at that rate. He himself had been a city dweller all his life, but even he knew that the peasants living around the lake profoundly distrusted Austrian soldiers and cooperated with them as little as possible. They had long protected smugglers against them, and they would do as much for Orfeo, if they did not know he was suspected of a crime as serious as murder. In his zeal against the Carbonari, Raversi seemed to have forgotten what he owed to his friend, whose murderer might well go unpunished.

"Now then," Raversi proceeded, "here's what we've decided to do. Our good Don Cristoforo will break the news of Lodovico's death in the village. Signor Ruga will send out gendarmes to assist in the search for Orfeo and to look for Tonio. I've suggested they make enquiries for Tonio at the Nightingale. It's the only inn in Solaggio—he's quite likely to have stayed there last night."

"Signor Conte," remonstrated Don Cristoforo, the priest, "surely you can't mean to conceal the true manner of Marchese Malvezzi's death from his family."

"I'm afraid I must, Your Reverence. Lodovico's family pose the greatest danger of all. If they find out he's been murdered, they'll make a public outcry and demand drastic action by the government. Secrecy will become impossible."

The others had no choice but to fall in with Raversi's scheme, and promise to keep dark that Lodovico had met his death by foul play. Raversi said he would write to Marchese Rinaldo in Milan, telling him only that his father had died unexpectedly, and that he, Raversi, awaited Rinaldo's instructions about property matters and funeral arrangements. He would also write to Marchesa Beatrice in Turin, though it might take some time for the news to reach her, given the political chaos there.

Ruga and Don Cristoforo returned to Solaggio. Soon after, Donati heard the passing-bell toll solemnly for Lodovico's soul. An old woman came from the village to wash and dress Lodovico's body. Since she would see the bullet hole in his chest, she too had to be sworn to secrecy.

Raversi made a thorough search of the villa, keeping Matteo with him to bear witness that he neither removed nor disarranged any of Lodovico's or Orfeo's possessions. If anything interesting came of the search, Donati was not told about it. He was present, however, when Raversi asked Matteo and Lucia where they had been between the hours of ten and four last night. They both said they had spent the night at the castle. Matteo had lodged with the gardener, while Lucia had shared a bed with two maidservants, Maria and Bona. Maria had had a toothache, and the other two had sat up with her all night. Donati supposed this story would be easy enough to verify.

"You have an alibi," he told Lucia.

"What's that, Maestro?"

"Someone who can swear you were somewhere else when the crime was committed."

"Oh," she said shrewdly.

"What are you thinking?"

"I was just wondering if Tonio has one of those."

Tonio did have an alibi—but Tonio was missing. Marianna Frascani, the landlady of the Nightingale, reported that he had come to her inn yesterday evening in a sullen, angry mood, and had drunk himself into a stupor in the public room. He had bespoken a bed, but no one wanted to carry him upstairs to it. He was a big young man, and neither plump enough in the pocket to make it worthwhile to do him favours, nor agreeable enough to make people want to help him for his own sake. Marianna had left him lying on the brick floor in the public room. As she was not a trusting woman, she had tied a bell to his ankle and made a waiter sleep close by him, in case he awoke and took this opportunity to steal something. She and the waiter were absolutely certain that he had remained there all night.

In the morning, said Marianna, Tonio woke up with an aching head, sluiced his face at the pump, and wandered away from the inn. After a short while, he came back, packed up his belongings in a bundle, paid his reckoning, and ran off as if the devil were at his heels.

"When was that?" Raversi asked Ruga, who had brought this information to the villa.

"Marianna said, between eight and half-past." Ruga's voice took on the questioning lilt it always had when he spoke to men of rank, as if he hesitated to make any definite statement without their approval. As usual, he sounded a little breathless. Donati surmised that he was a portly man, with muscles too slack to support his weight.

"Did he say where he was going?" Raversi asked.

"No, Your Excellency."

"Did he mention anything about Orfeo?"

"Not so as Marianna could recall."

"Are you sure about all this?"

"Yes, Excellency. I spoke to her myself."

"He can't have committed the murder," Raversi said slowly. "So why did he run away?"

"I can't imagine," said Donati. "He knew I was going to do something to help him. Perhaps he'll come back, or write to me."

"Let me know at once if he does. He may well be the person best able to give a description of Orfeo. He fought with him—he must have had to take a good look at him. I wonder—Ah, Madonna! Of course!" Raversi began walking excitedly back and forth. "Orfeo deliberately picked that quarrel with him! He wanted to drive him away from the villa, so that there would be no one young and able-bodied to protect Lodovico! Maestro, have you any idea where Tonio might have gone?"

"No, Signor Conte. He had no family, and few friends."

"Hm. I'll ask Comandante Von Krauss to have his men look for him as well as Orfeo. But now I must go to Castello Malvezzi and break the news of Lodovico's death to his servants. Signor Ruga, will you be good enough to come with me? I wish to make a search for evidence, and your assistance would be useful."

"Yes, of course, Excellency! I'm at your service."

Left alone, Donati played the piano and considered where to find new Eyes. Perhaps some young singer at the Conservatory in Milan would barter his services for lessons. Donati would make enquiries directly he returned to Milan. He hoped that would be soon. He longed for the familiarity of the city streets, the spring season at La Scala, Ricordi's music shop. This lake was an ill-omened, treacherous place. He wished with all his heart he had never come—never known that sweet-voiced Englishman who might be criminal or victim, fugitive or martyr.

Two days passed. Nothing was heard of Orfeo or Tonio. Peasants poured into Solaggio to see the marchese's body laid out in all its finery in the church, but no one seemed to suspect he had met his death by foul play. There was a good deal of speculation about why the soldiers were seeking Orfeo. It was rumoured he had run away when his patron died because he did not want to be forced to account for the favours he had received. But the more popular theory was that he had taken advantage of the marchese's death to pinch something.

On the third day after the murder, Rinaldo and his stepmother Beatrice arrived at the lake. Donati had expected Rinaldo much earlier, since Milan was only a few hours' journey away. But it seemed Rinaldo had not been in Milan when Raversi's messenger arrived. Donati did not hear the details about this. He was given permission to leave the lake and lost no time in returning to Milan.

Soon after he arrived at his flat near the Conservatory, Conte Carlo Malvezzi, Lodovico's brother, called and talked with him a while about Lodovico's last days. Carlo lived in the neighbouring state of Parma but happened to be paying a visit to Milan when Lodovico died. Now he was staying on to meet with the Malvezzi family lawyer, because Lodovico's will had appointed him executor.

At intervals over the next few weeks, high-ranking police officials came to question Donati about the murder. But either their efforts to solve it slackened, or they ran out of things to ask; at all events their visits tapered off, and there was silence.

In token of her husband's high regard for Donati, Marchesa Beatrice settled a pension on him, which he accepted gratefully. Freed from financial worries, he retired to the university town of Pavia, some twenty miles south of Milan. There he heard with increasing concern about the political repression that was sweeping the Italian states. The revolts in Naples and Piedmont were brutally put down. In Milan and Venice, the special commission appointed to deal with the Carbonari flourished. Respected aristocrats, artists, and professional men were arrested, subjected to secret trials and humiliating public sentences, and trundled off to prison fortresses in the far corners of the Austrian empire.

Donati wondered whether, in this atmosphere of suspicion and secrecy, it would ever be deemed safe to reveal that Lodovico had been murdered. How could the government do so, when it must admit it had neither solved the murder nor found any trace of Orfeo? Donati tried not to think about it. He had plenty to keep him occupied: he was writing a treatise about singing techniques, and he still took pupils occasionally. Yet he could never hear the *de profundis* without thinking of Lodovico's soul unquiet, his murder unavenged. *Out of the depths I cry out to thee, O Lord.* But no one seemed to be listening anymore.

Part Two

SEPTEMBER 1825

In Italy? Unhappy land! she has ever been the reward of victory... What can be attempted between two powerful nations, which, sworn ferocious and eternal enemies to each other, make alliance together, merely to enfetter us? Where their strength is insufficient, the one deceives us with the enthusiasm of liberty; the other, with the fanaticism of religion. And do we, wholly undone by our ancient servitude, and our modern licentiousness, groan like vile slaves, betrayed, famished, and instigated to action, neither by treachery nor by want?

Ugo Foscolo
The Last Letters of Jacopo Ortis
(from an 1818 translation)

For the third day in a row, the newspapers were full of the murder of Lodovico Malvezzi. Julian Kestrel collected all the latest accounts and took them into the window-seat of the little inn parlour he shared with Dr. MacGregor. The rain was falling in sheets, as it had ever since they arrived. Geneva was a grey city on a greyer lake, against a pale grey sky.

MacGregor came in, plunking down a china cup disgustedly on a table. "They've made the tea too strong again. I might as well chew the tea-leaves and be done with it! No use asking them to do it over—it comes back as hot water with a leaf or two floating on the top."

"The natives prefer coffee," said Julian, almost as patiently as if they had not had this conversation a hundred times.

"Hmph! That bitter black stuff *you* drink!"

Julian went to the coffee-pot and poured himself another cup. It was the closest he cared to come to a gesture of defiance. Why quarrel with MacGregor now, when they had travelled so far without an open row, and would soon be parting company?

He had meant well, inviting MacGregor on this journey. The two of them had known each other a little over a year, having met when Julian solved what was now known as the Bellegarde Murder. Since then, they had formed as close a friendship as was possible between a sixty-year-old country surgeon and a London *beau* less than half his age. A month ago, Julian stopped to visit MacGregor on his way home from a shooting trip, and learned that MacGregor's old friend and mentor, Dr. Greeley, had died after a long illness. Ordinarily MacGregor soon rallied from any disappointment or sorrow: hard work was his tonic, and religion his consolation. But neither seemed able to lift his spirits now. One day he happened to mention that he had spent his whole adult life in Alderton, his Cambridgeshire village, and had never been out of Great Britain. Julian thought it would do him good to get away from his patients and obligations—to see that there was more to life than his work, and much more to the world than Alderton. He himself was about to depart on one of his periodic trips to Italy, and on an impulse he asked MacGregor to go with him. At first MacGregor made all sorts of objections: this or that patient needed him, the autumn always brought on sickness, the local squire's first grandchild was due in December. In the end he consented to go, but only for a limited time, and not as far as Italy.

From the moment they docked in Calais, MacGregor did nothing but complain. The food was unwholesome, the Catholic Church was corrupt, the French were rude and sly, everything cost too much. When Julian pointed out that British tourists were largely responsible for driving up the prices, MacGregor grumbled that they would do much better to stay at home.

Of course the two of them were wholly incompatible in their tastes. Julian wanted to go to the theatre, the opera, art collections; he also liked inspecting police offices and gaols. MacGregor preferred to visit hospitals, asylums, and scientific institutions. Julian was willing to go to such places—he even found them interesting. But he resented the fact that it was invariably he who yielded graciously to MacGregor's wishes. MacGregor had none of the gentleman's skills of adapting or dissembling. His rugged honesty was one of the things Julian most respected about him—but he had never had to live with it for an extended period before. Unwilling to abandon MacGregor to struggle with foreign languages and customs, he had no choice but to forgo many of his own pursuits. In Paris, he saw little of his friends, eschewed the gaming-houses of the Palais Royale, and—hardest to bear!—got no closer to the female dancers of the Paris Opera than a third-tier box. It was his most chaste sojourn in Paris in years, which did not improve his temper.

All the while, MacGregor fretted about his patients. When they reached Geneva he announced he would go no farther, and Julian could not help feeling relieved to be rid of him. Yet he told MacGregor he ought not to leave Switzerland without getting a better look at the Alps. MacGregor rejoined that he had seen the Scottish highlands, and they were mountains enough for anybody. After all, how different was one mountain from another? Julian gave it up. As far as he could tell, MacGregor had gotten nothing whatsoever out of this journey. Perhaps his stubborn dedication to work was admirable, but Julian could only pity him for all that he missed. He himself might be too susceptible to beauty, but better that than to hear Madame Pasta sing or see Notre-Dame, and feel nothing.

MacGregor's voice recalled him to the here and now. Pointing to the pile of newspapers in the window-seat, he said, "That murder again?"

Julian nodded. "There's some fresh news today, but not as much as I'd hoped for. The Italian papers are too heavily censored, and the Swiss aren't well enough informed. Still, they can't keep away from the story. How could they? It's an opera plot, a Gothic novel—if it had happened anywhere but in Italy, it would be impossible to credit."

"It all sounds like moonshine to me. How could a nobleman like this Lodovico Malvezzi be shot to death without anyone's knowing a blessed thing about it for four and a half years?"

"The authorities put it about that he died of heart failure."

"And they got a doctor to swear to that?" MacGregor was scandalized.

"In Austrian Italy, my dear fellow, people swear to much more remarkable things."

"But why keep the murder a secret?" MacGregor jumped up and paced back and forth, as he always did when they were wrestling with a murder case. Julian felt it was quite like old times. "The authorities must have known they'd be tying their own hands when it came to solving it."

"I don't know if I can make you understand what Italy was like in those days. I was travelling there, and I remember the climate of suspicion and fear: the long stops and searches on borders, the constant surveillance by police, the arrests of men like Silvio Pellico, the greatest living playwright in Italy, and the philosopher Melchior Gioia. There'd been a series of radical conspiracies and rebellions, and the Austrian government was determined to suppress them. As best I can tell from the newspaper accounts, Lodovico Malvezzi's murder was viewed as a political assassination, and I daresay the authorities feared that, if it became known, it might spark a political conflagration."

"It sounds as if they'd lost their heads completely."

"Governments do," said Julian with a shrug. "My father told me about the anti-Jacobin panics in England after the French Revolution: political meetings suppressed, people tried for treason just for holding opinions offensive to the government. But at least we have a parliament and some semblance of liberty. Italian rulers can do more or less as they like."

MacGregor absently took up his cup and saucer and began drinking the unpalatable tea. "How did the truth about the murder finally come out?"

"The newspapers say that about a fortnight ago, an old woman who'd prepared the body for burial turned contrite on her deathbed and told how she'd been sworn to secrecy about the bullet hole in the chest. I imagine the Milanese authorities were acutely embarrassed. They probably hadn't intended to conceal the murder so long, but when they failed to solve it, they found it increasingly awkward to admit they'd kept it dark. Now I expect it will be a point of honour with them to catch the murderer—or someone they can pass off as the murderer. The marchese was a staunch friend to the Austrians, and they aren't so popular in Milan that they can afford to neglect their duty toward their friends. Besides, the marchese's family has been kicking up hell's delight. The authorities didn't tell even them that he'd been murdered, and now his brother is demanding to know why Orfeo—the English singer I told you of—hasn't been found, and what the authorities mean to do about it."

"And what *do* they mean to do about it?"

"I assume they'll move heaven and earth to find Orfeo, but the devil only knows how they're to succeed, when they don't know his name or what he looks like. And of course, after four and a half years, he could be very nearly anywhere."

"Isn't there anyone who can give a description of him?"

"Two servants lived with him, a gardener and his daughter, but the gardener is dead—of a genuine heart attack, apparently—and the authorities have lost sight of the girl. The singing teacher, Maestro Donati, is blind, and his servant, Tonio Farese, disappeared the day after the murder."

"Upon my soul!" MacGregor shook his head. "Then they'll never find Orfeo. They might as well look for an elephant in the moon!"

"Well, actually—" Julian began.

"Oh, Lord!" MacGregor groaned. "I know that look! It means you're about to tie an already tangled web into Gordian knots!"

"I just wanted to suggest," said Julian mildly, "that the authorities, the newspapers, and the Malvezzi family all seem to be ignoring the most intriguing possibility."

"What's that?"

"That Orfeo didn't kill the marchese."

"But he ran away after the murder and hasn't been heard of since. That doesn't exactly suggest he had nothing to hide."

"A man may have something to hide without being a murderer. But it isn't anything I've read about Orfeo that makes me wonder—it's what I know of the marchese's relatives. The Malvezzi are a very turbulent family. Lodovico never got on with his son. He'd quarrelled bitterly with his son's wife, because she ran away with the singer Valeriano. He and his brother were estranged by political differences. And he'd taken as his second wife a much younger woman, by all accounts a great beauty, who may have had reasons for wanting to be a widow."

"How do you know so much about it?"

"It's common knowledge in Italy. The Italians aren't like us: they have no shame or reticence about their passions. We draw a veil of decorum over our love affairs and family conflicts. The Italians unabashedly love and hate in the glare of public notice. I don't suspect any of the marchese's relatives more than another—I've never met them. But I did meet the marchese."

"You did? When?"

"Some years ago, when I lived on the Continent."

"What was he like?"

Julian's gaze turned inward. "He was a colossus of a man—over six feet tall, broad-shouldered, with a mane of dark hair streaked white at the temples, a beaked nose, and eyes very nearly gold. He had a long stride, and a vitality so powerful that it seems extraordinary a mere bit of lead could quench it. And he was as proud as Lucifer. But he forgot his aristocratic prejudices the moment he met anyone who genuinely loved music. Any fruit vendor or café waiter who had something eloquent to say about Catalani's scales or Velluti's trill could become his friend. I was very young and knew almost no one in Milan, but I did know something about music, and that gave me an opportunity to talk with him at some length."

"He certainly made an impression on you."

"I think he did on everyone who knew him. I also think he was the kind of man who made enemies, because he gave no quarter to anyone who crossed him."

"Perhaps he made an enemy of this Orfeo," said MacGregor.

"Perhaps. The newspapers don't say much about their relationship, or any reason Orfeo might have had to kill him."

"Well, I must own, you've got me interested in this business. It's just as well you're going to Italy—you'll hear how it all ends and can write to me about it."

"Yes," said Julian musingly. "I'll let you know what happens."

MacGregor looked him hard in the eyes. "Kestrel, what are you thinking? What are you going to do?"

"Well, as you know, I've had a little experience with murder investigations—"

"If you mean you've solved murders that baffled even the Bow Street Runners, I know that, yes."

"—so it occurred to me I might go to Milan and find out if I could be of any use to the police or the Malvezzi family."

"This being of use to the family—does it include finding out if one of them killed the marchese?"

"If it does, I shan't make any secret of it. They would guess in any case, by the questions I asked them."

"Well, why should they let you—a foreigner, someone they don't know from Adam—come asking them questions and trying to prove one of them a murderer?"

"My dear fellow, I don't know. Perhaps because, being English myself, I may be able to help them find Orfeo. Set a thief to catch a thief, as my friend Vance says. If they tell me to go to the devil, what have I lost? I was going to Italy in any case."

"You've quite made up your mind to this, haven't you?"

"I hadn't before," Julian reflected, "but I seem to have persuaded myself."

He pulled the bell-rope by the fireplace. A waiter appeared. "Please send my manservant up," said Julian in French. The waiter bowed himself out.

"Well, I suppose you must know what you're doing," said MacGregor, in a tone that implied the opposite.

Julian smiled. "I wouldn't make any such rash pronouncement as that. But this may be the investigation of a lifetime, and I can't miss it."

Julian's valet came in. He was small and lithe, about twenty-one years old, with a round face and iridescent brown eyes. "Sir?"

"Dipper, I'm going to Milan."

Dipper's face closed up. "I thought you would, sir."

"Dipper doesn't approve of my Italian project," Julian told MacGregor.

"It ain't my place to approve or not approve of what you do, sir."

"Good God," said Julian. "This is quite serious. It's only when I'm in your blackest books that you begin talking like a servant."

Dipper refused to be drawn. "When shall I have our traps packed, sir?"

"I should like to leave tomorrow, when Dr. MacGregor starts for England. We shall have the deuce and all to do before then. We'll need passports for Austrian Italy, and that means obtaining signatures from our own consul and visas from a representative of Lombardy-Venetia. It's an infernal nuisance getting into the Italian states—at all events, if you do it legally. Still, I daresay we can be ready to leave by noon tomorrow. Will you order a post-chaise for that time?"

I'll do it, but I won't like it, said Dipper's eyes. "Will that be all, sir?"

"Yes. I don't want to detain you—I'm sure you have a great many chambermaids and milliners' apprentices to take leave of."

Dipper went out. Julian looked after him wryly. "My valet has disowned me. I shall blow out my brains between here and Domodossola."

"What's all this about?" MacGregor demanded. "Why doesn't Dipper like this Italian business of yours?"

Julian shrugged. "Perhaps he thinks I should confine myself to domestic murders."

"He's never opposed any project of yours before. In fact, I've never seen the two of you at odds about anything."

"That's because you're not there when I dress in the morning. We have quite violent disagreements about starch."

"Seriously—"

"Seriously, as you know, Dipper was once in the habit of finding things before they were lost, and he still isn't overfond of the police. He's resigned himself to hobnobbing with Bow Street Runners at home, but the prospect of mixing with Milanese gendarmes may be too much for him."

"Rubbish! What he likes or dislikes is nothing to the purpose. He'd lie down in the road and let a coach-and-four run over him if you asked him to. So why doesn't he want to do this?"

"I can't speak for him," said Julian more soberly. "You had better ask him."

He went over to the window, which was still blurred and battered with rain. MacGregor followed, about to start remonstrating again. Then his brows drew together. "Look here: should you be travelling in this downpour? All the guidebooks warn about the autumn rains in Italy. They say the rivers overflow and flood the roads and wash whole bridges away."

MacGregor's guidebooks had been a source of dire predictions throughout their journey. Julian had often been tempted to pitch them out of the carriage window. "The worst rains are still a few weeks away. And the Simplon is an excellent road."

"A good road won't stop you catching your death of cold."

Julian laid a hand on his shoulder. "If I'm going to die in Italy, my dear fellow, I shall do it more artistically."

MacGregor was unable to catch Dipper alone for the rest of that day. While Kestrel rushed about collecting visas—if anyone as cool and unruffled as Kestrel could be said to rush—Dipper was out replenishing their stores of everything from soap and toothpowder to brandy and ammunition. MacGregor had been a little taken aback to see that Kestrel travelled with a case of pistols; it reminded him of tales he had heard of bandits on Continental roads. Certainly they had passed through some rough terrain that seemed ideal for an ambush. But the only danger that ever seemed to worry Kestrel was that he might not find a suitable place to have his linen cleaned.

The hours hung heavy on MacGregor's hands. He hated this idleness. Only old people and invalids sat about toasting their feet in the middle of a Monday afternoon. People like his friend Dr. Greeley, bored and broken, ending his days in a dreary watering place, surrounded by strangers. MacGregor had visited him there and could not forget his restless hands, his vain attempts to walk or write, the tears in his eyes when he could not even feed or clean himself. MacGregor had stayed with him as long as he could, and when he left, he had prayed, sinfully, to die before he became inactive and useless.

He sprang up, bundled himself into his greatcoat, and went out for a tramp in the rain. Geneva was as bustling and business-like as ever. MacGregor admired its cleanliness and order and its hard-working, educated people. Yet he was secretly disappointed in it for not being Continental enough. And this made no sense, because the Continent had been nothing but an ordeal to him. He found it a constant struggle to get through the simplest rituals of life: ordering meals, looking after his clothes, obtaining candles or writing-paper. He had thought he knew French, because he could read French medical treatises. But when he tried to speak it, he got all muddled, and waiters and postillions looked at him with weary patience or outright contempt. Kestrel, of course, spoke French and Italian like a native and knew all the local customs, so MacGregor rarely had to fend for himself. But it was embarrassing to be led about like a child, to be always confused and helpless.

He knew he had been testy and ungracious—had not really given Europe a chance. But how could he, when home tugged insistently at his heartstrings, and a cruel voice kept whispering in his ear: *Don't stay away too long! They may find they can do without you!* He was ashamed to confess all this to Kestrel—did not see how Kestrel could understand in any case. At his age, a man could not grasp what it was to grow old.

MacGregor walked as far as the quai on the northern bank of Lake Geneva. From here there was a famous view of Mont Blanc, but the sky had never been clear enough for MacGregor to see it. He never would see it now. Tomorrow he was departing for England, with a courier Kestrel had engaged to escort him. The prospect did not give him the satisfaction he had expected. To be sure, he was relieved to be going home, but it was the relief of a defeated army after its surrender. As he walked back to his inn in the gathering dusk, passing the little church where John Knox had preached Protestantism three centuries ago, he told himself that Knox would not have let homesickness, stubborn pride, and embarrassment drive him away from the Continent. But Knox had had the Reformation to inspire him, and his congregation to guide and protect. That was what MacGregor missed: a worthy focus for his energies. Continental travel was nothing but idleness and art, and MacGregor condemned the one and was uncomfortable with the other.

When he came into the parlour he and Kestrel shared, he saw that the door to Kestrel's bedroom was open. Dipper was inside, reverently laying Kestrel's three dozen newly laundered neckcloths one by one in their rectangular box. MacGregor came forward and stood in the doorway. "Where's your master?"

"He went out to buy a dictionary, sir."

"A dictionary? What sort of dictionary?"

"A Milanese dictionary, sir."

"Why in blue blazes does he need a Milanese dictionary? He speaks Italian."

"There ain't no such thing as h'Italian, really, sir," Dipper explained helpfully. "There's Tuscan and Neapolitan and Venetian, and I dunno what else. In Milan, they patter Milanese. So Mr. Kestrel wanted to brush it up."

MacGregor smiled in spite of himself, to hear a youthful Cockney speak so knowingly about Italian dialects. "Before you knew Kestrel, did you ever think you'd be a seasoned traveller in Italy?"

"Before I knew Mr. Kestrel, sir, the only place I ever expected to travel was Australia."

MacGregor realized he must mean the penal colony at Botany Bay. And very likely he was right. Even expert pickpockets could not evade the law forever. Something dawned on MacGregor that he ought to have perceived long since. "It's for Kestrel's sake that you don't want to go to Milan, isn't it?"

Dipper did not answer.

"Kestrel doesn't want me to know about this, does he? That's why he tried to fob me off, when I asked him this morning what you had against this Italian business of his. Finally he told me to ask you what it was about—probably because he knew I would anyway. Well, what is it? Out with it, man."

"I think he ought to keep clear of this h'Italian murder, sir. But he's got a bee in his bonnet about it."

"Well, why shouldn't he try his hand at solving it? He's solved murders before."

"Not in h'Italy, sir. Things is different there. The *sbirri*—that's the police, sir, but you don't call 'em that to their faces, 'coz it ain't a polite word—they can bone any cove and clap him in quod."

"You know I can't understand you when you talk that gibberish."

"I mean, sir, they can take any man up on suspicion and put him in prison. And if they think he's a Carbonaro—that's a radical, sir, as plots against the h'Austrians—then he won't never get out, 'coz even if the *sbirri* can't prove he's a Carbonaro, he most likely can't prove that he ain't. So they packs him off to some prison in h'Austria, loaded up with body-slangs—fetters, that is." Dipper came closer, his eyes getting very round. "In Rome, they cuts off coves' heads! I seen it, last time we was there. It ain't civilised!"

"Well, you know, the guillotine is really more humane than our hangings. It kills almost instantly, whereas a poor devil struggling on a rope can take ten minutes or more to die."

"Oh, yes, I know that, sir. Me pa was a quarter-hour about it, when they done *him*. But I still say it ain't civilised."

MacGregor was taken aback, and could not at first pick up the thread of their conversation. "But Kestrel isn't going to be mistaken for one of these Carbonaros. He's British, for God's sake! Besides, he lived in Italy for years. He must know how to keep out of trouble with the police."

"He never had reason to go near 'em before, sir. Most foreigners don't. They goes to h'Italy to look at paintings and statues. They don't keep company with the *sbirri*—nor with murderers."

MacGregor felt a chill down his back. He said, with as much conviction as he could muster. "Kestrel's handled murder investigations before. He knows what he's about."

"He knows too much, sir. Sees through a millstone, Mr. Kestrel does. And in h'Italy, them as lives longest is them as sees nothing at all."

The door from the hallway into the adjacent parlour opened and closed. Dipper at once discovered an infinitesimal crease in one of the neckcloths and bent over it with a small, slender iron he had left warming on the hob. MacGregor clasped his hands behind him and rocked back and forth self-consciously on his heels.

Kestrel came in. "I can see my ears ought to have been burning." He added, looking critically from one to the other, "In fact, it's a wonder my hat wasn't set on fire."

Dipper removed Kestrel's wet coat and helped him into his dressing-gown. Then Kestrel and MacGregor went into the parlour. Kestrel smiled wryly and lifted his brows, obviously expecting to be read a lecture. MacGregor knew he would listen pleasantly, parry MacGregor's arguments with charm and wit, and then do exactly as he pleased. For all his courtesy and tact, Kestrel could be as stubborn as—well, as MacGregor himself.

"I suppose you've considered," MacGregor said at last, "that any trouble you get into in Milan is bound to involve him, too?" He jerked his head toward the room where Dipper was still packing.

"Yes." Kestrel looked grave at that. "But what can I do? I can't tell him he needn't come with me if he'd rather not. The least one can do in return for loyalty like his is not insult it."

MacGregor sighed, acknowledging the truth of this. "Will you do one thing for me?"

"If I can," said Kestrel, a touch guardedly.

"Lay hand on heart, and ask yourself if this Italian venture of yours is worth the risk. Maybe these fears of Dipper's are all fustian—I don't know. But I do know that, if my son had lived, he'd have been about your age. And I'd like to think, when we go our separate ways tomorrow, that I'll see you again."

For once Kestrel seemed at a loss for words. MacGregor wanted to press his advantage: *Come home with me—or at least go somewhere, anywhere, other than Milan.* But if Kestrel acceded, he would always regret it. He had called this the investigation of a lifetime—wouldn't he always wonder what it would have been like? What right had MacGregor to deprive him of his adventure? One of them ought not to turn back. So MacGregor said nothing. And the next day Kestrel and Dipper set out for Milan.

The Simplon Highway, running from Paris to Milan by way of Geneva and the Alps, was perhaps the greatest gift Napoleon had bequeathed to Italy. For some fifteen years, the northern Italian states had been united under his rule, and Milan had been the Italian Paris—the dashing and elegant capital of Napoleon's Kingdom of Italy. That kingdom had fallen a dozen years ago, and the Austrians, who had held Milan before the French came, made haste to reclaim it. Nowadays, to speak well of the Kingdom of Italy was treasonous in Milan; to fly its red, white, and green tricolour was to invite arrest. Napoleon, though dead, was still a threat to Italy's overlords. To be sure, he had been a conqueror, who had kindled dreams of liberty in the Italians only to beguile them into servitude to another master. But the fact remained that, for the first time since ancient Rome, much of Italy had been united. The King of Italy might have been a French despot, but the Kingdom of Italy was now a living ideal for many Italians.

And the Simplon Highway remained. Skirting Lake

Geneva, a great flat sheet of water dotted with dipping gulls, it passed through a plain rich in orchards, vineyards, and flocks of black-headed sheep. The faraway mountains on either side of the road were featureless—just mammoth shapes of a colour neither grey nor purple nor blue. But on the third day of Julian's journey, the sky cleared, and the mountains began to close in. The road twisted and ascended; the horses laboured harder and rested more frequently. Julian laid aside his Milanese dictionary to watch the Alps rise up around him: their lower slopes covered with feathery trees tinged orange by the autumn chills, their higher reaches bare and bleak and flecked with snow. Then the sky narrowed to a ribbon of blue, as the road was caught between sheer rock faces scored with tracks of ancient streams. Sometimes the sky vanished altogether, as the road was swallowed up in a mountain cavern, while overhead there came a deafening roar of snow crashing down the cliffside. At last they reached the summit of the Simplon Pass, where Julian looked along a vast valley threaded by a foaming stream, to a row of lofty peaks as white and pure as a glimpse of Heaven.

Then came the descent, zigzagging among stark cliffs and dizzying waterfalls. The postillion had to dismount frequently to slip a skid pan under the rear wheels, in order to keep the carriage from overtaking the horses. At Iselle they crossed the frontier into Piedmont, the northwesternmost Italian state. There they spent the night at an inn that clung to the side of a precipice and was perpetually shrouded in fogs from the chasm below. Next day, the ground grew flatter, the landscape greener, and Julian felt a thrill of anticipation, as the balmier air caressed his face with the promise of Italy.

Dipper, who never brooded long over ills he could not remedy, soon regained his usual cheerfulness and made friends with postillions, ostlers, and waiters all along the way. There were gaps in his Italian, but what he could not put into words, he conveyed with gestures as fluid and expressive as the Italians' own.

The road hugged the western shore of Lake Maggiore,

winding between wooded hills and dazzling deep-blue water. At the southern tip of the lake, the Lombard frontier loomed up before them, marked by flags bearing black imperial eagles, and by the shimmer of sunlight on Austrian bayonets. Customs officials demanded Julian's and Dipper's passports, and were duly bribed to return them after a brief examination. Thereafter, all along the road to Milan, shabby police clerks kept popping out of wooden boxes, inspecting passports and extorting tips. Of course, the customs officials were mainly an annoyance to legitimate travellers: smugglers and Carbonari knew how to deceive or avoid them.

The land was flat and fertile now, criss-crossed by rows of mulberry trees, their branches gaily festooned with vines. Julian made out a speck of brilliant gold in the mists on the horizon: the statue of the Madonnina, protectress of Milan, atop the highest spire of the cathedral. Then the cathedral roof came into view: a triangular hulk that slowly, wondrously crystallized into a myriad of slender white spires. The carriage entered Milan by the Simplon Gate, where a half-finished arch of triumph stood amid rough sheds and moss-grown blocks of marble. The arch had been begun by Napoleon, and the Austrians could not bring themselves either to complete it or to tear it down.

It gave Julian a peculiar sensation, seeing Milan again. He had not been here in so long—not since his first journey to Italy. Yet it all seemed startlingly familiar: the spacious thoroughfares flanked by rabbit warrens of back alleys, the proud palaces cheek by jowl with wretched shacks, the balconies with their delicate iron railings and blowing linen, the gaudy array of blue, green, and yellow awnings on shops and cafés. But it was chiefly the people who gave the streets their charm and animation. Well-to-do young men showed off their prowess on English horses; brightly clad peasants hawked everything from chestnuts to cane chairs; Jesuits strutted like ravens in their elegant, austere black cassocks; Austrian soldiers stood about smoking cigars and conversing in German or Hungarian. But the women drew Julian's notice most. They were remarkably handsome, their eyes large, dark, and expressive, their movements impetuous yet graceful.

Julian put up at an inn called the Bella Venezia in Piazza San Fedele, convenient to the cathedral, the Scala opera house, and the Santa Margherita, Milan's principal police office and prison. Not that he intended to approach the police directly about the Malvezzi murder. They were not likely to welcome the assistance of a young English dandy, however experienced he might be in solving crimes. The only Englishman they would be eager to see was Orfeo, who had every reason to put a continent between himself and them.

No: he would rather offer his services to the Malvezzi family. But there were several things he wanted to find out first. What efforts were being made to find Lucia Landi? And Tonio Farese, Maestro Donati's servant—what had become of him? Finally, what role were Lodovico's relatives playing in the investigation? The newspapers said little about them, which suggested they had retired from public view during this crisis. But if they were showing themselves anywhere, it was bound to be at the opera.

La Scala was the nightly rendezvous of much of the city of Milan. The aristocracy in particular rarely entertained at home, partly because their *palazzi* were seldom as sumptuous inside as out, and partly because the police assumed that any group of educated Italians who gathered in private, especially at night, must be hatching a conspiracy. Instead, each of the two hundred private boxes at La Scala served as a tiny drawing room, where for four or five hours a night, six nights a week, the box-holder and his guests played cards, exchanged gossip, sometimes even took meals. In the dark depths of the boxes, lovers made assignations, and Carbonari were said to plot. No one paid much attention to the music—after all, the audience sat through the same opera twenty or thirty nights in a row. The loud talk and clinking of knives and forks subsided only during favourite arias and ensembles, which were listened to with rapt attention and a highly critical ear.

Julian arrived in Milan with just time enough to change

into evening clothes, dine, and reach La Scala before the curtain rose. He sat in the pit, which was mainly a haunt of the *cittadini,* Milan's merchant class. In Florence or Naples he would have had introductions to aristocratic boxes, but here he was practically a stranger. He knew he must set about improving his acquaintance with the Milanese nobility, whose boxes would be the best places to pick up gossip about the Malvezzis. But tonight he could not resist sitting far enough from the noise in the boxes to hear the opera.

It was *L'Italiana in Algeri,* Rossini's whimsical romance about an intrepid Italian girl captured by Turks. If Julian had not already known the plot, he would have found it impossible to follow, since the audience around him went on taking seats and chattering throughout the opening scene. He gazed his fill at the magnificent scenery and costumes, then scanned the boxes above. But his eyes were dazzled by the light from the stage, and at first he could make out only hollow shapes, like empty eye sockets, with here and there a twinkling candle to illumine a game of cards.

A hush fell on the audience as the tenor stepped out to sing *To sigh for a beautiful woman.* The theatre had been fortunate enough to secure the great Rubini for this role. He stood with his bullish head thrown back and his hand clapped over his heart in what, for him, passed for acting. But his voice was sweet and flexible, his range extraordinary. He excelled at fioriture, the trills and other vocal embellishments improvised by singers. Indeed, he indulged in them to excess, or so Julian thought. He found himself mentally excising some and rearranging others.

When the aria was over, there was mad applause, screaming, stamping of feet, and beating of canes on the floor. Julian's thoughts went to Orfeo, whom Lodovico Malvezzi had thought to launch in this same theatre, perhaps even in this same role. He would never know now what it was to be the object of a Milanese audience's adoration—or the butt of their derision, if his efforts failed.

During the duet that followed, Julian noticed the spectators around him staring and pointing up at the boxes toward the left. His eyes had adjusted to the dimness, and he could now see figures in the boxes: two ladies or a lady and gentleman seated at the front, with more shadowy forms sitting or moving about behind them. But one box in the fashionable second tier had its curtains closed, screening its occupants from view.

"Pardon me, signori," said Julian in the Milanese dialect to the middle-aged couple seated on the bench beside him, "whose box is that?"

The couple exchanged glances. They looked like prosperous tradespeople, instinctively friendly, yet wary of a foreigner who, by his clothes and manner, seemed to belong up in the boxes with the nobility. At last the husband said, with the aloof courtesy of a Milanese uncertain of his bearings, "That's Marchesa Malvezzi's box, signor."

"Lodovico Malvezzi's widow?" said Julian, as off-handedly as he could.

"Yes, signor."

The tradesman's wife could not resist adding, "She's been here every night since the news came out about the poor marchese's murder."

"And why shouldn't she come to the opera if she likes?" demanded a woman from the bench behind them. "Holy Virgin! She's been widowed nearly five years!"

"She's kept the curtains of her box closed since she learned of the murder," the tradesman reminded his wife. "So it isn't as if she'd flaunted herself in public, for everyone to see."

"It's still not right," his wife insisted. "She ought to show more respect for her husband's memory. He was a great man, and he was murdered in cold blood by that English singer."

"What can you expect of the English?" broke in another man, throwing up his hands. "They don't believe in God, you know. They're all Freemasons."

The trademan's wife ignored him. "So what I say is, she should be at home praying for her husband's soul, not enjoying herself here."

"She's had masses enough said for his soul," declared the

strident woman behind her. "She even built him a great tomb out of her own money—and him old enough to be her father!"

"Her own money!" scoffed the tradesman's wife. "She hasn't a soldo of her own. Everything she has, the marchese left her in his will. That very opera box she's sitting in now—that was his."

Their argument was so loud it annoyed even an audience used to noisy distractions. Their nearest neighbours hissed at them. The Austrian soldiers scattered through the pit looked around at them ominously. Julian interposed one last question. "What else did he leave her?"

The tradesman blinked in mild surprise at his ignorance. "Why, the villa, signor. The one where he was murdered."

Julian spent the next few days gathering news about the investigation. It was not difficult: at the afternoon parade of carriages on the Corso, at the opera in the evening, and in all the cafés, the murder was on everyone's lips. Julian was thankful that the Milanese dialect had come back to him so readily. It was the language of everyone in Milan from duchesses to street vendors, and foreigners who spoke only the elegant Italian of Dante missed a great deal.

Nothing new had come to light about Orfeo. The police were looking high and low for Lucia Landi and Tonio Farese, but so far the search had been in vain. The Director-General of Police had just appointed Alfonso Grimani, an ambitious young commissario, to head the renewed investigation. Julian was surprised that an Italian rather than an Austrian should be entrusted with such an important, politically delicate case. Grimani must be both a first-rate investigator and a man of staunch and proven loyalty to the government. The stakes would be high for him: an assignment like this could make or break his career.

Julian soon began running into acquaintances from other

parts of Italy, who had come to Milan for the autumn season at La Scala and other diversions. They procured him introductions to the Milanese aristocracy, who were curious to meet the famous man of fashion. English dandies were not very well understood here: to be passionate about grooming and dispassionate about love was inexplicable to an Italian. But many young gentlemen seemed to pride themselves on following in Julian's footsteps, although their long hair and fantastically looped cravats would have astonished St. James's Street.

When it was discovered that Julian could not only dress but sit a horse, flirt, play cards, and talk intelligently about music, his success in Milanese society was assured. At the opera, he soon had the entrée to half a dozen patrician boxes. Each box held about ten guests, but they changed constantly in the course of the evening. The etiquette was inflexible: whenever a new visitor arrived, the one who had been longest in the box must take his leave, whereupon everybody else moved up one seat. In this way, each guest eventually reached the front of the box, where the hostess sat with her husband, a woman friend, or, most often, her recognized lover.

For Julian, the advantage of all this shifting of seats was that he met so many people, most of whom had known Lodovico Malvezzi and were well acquainted with his family. He learned that Lodovico's two relatives now in Milan were his widow, Marchesa Beatrice, and his younger brother, Conte Carlo, who had come from Parma on learning that his brother's death was murder. He was now acting as head of the family in the absence of Lodovico's son and heir, Marchese Rinaldo. Rinaldo was away on a journey, and it was not known if he had heard yet about his father's murder. "Hasn't anyone written to him?" Julian asked.

"Who knows where he is?" shrugged one of the would-be dandies.

"Poor Rinaldo!" sighed a pretty contessa. "He's always away travelling in Austria or Russia or some awful place. As soon as he returns, he's off again."

"It's the pain in his head that makes him restless," the young dandy said knowingly.

"What pain in his head?" cried an elderly duchessa.

"Why, the one that comes from wearing horns for so long, dearest Aunt."

Loud laughter greeted this sally. But the pretty contessa shook her head seriously. "It isn't good for his children, being dragged all over Europe. He ought to leave them here. Beatrice would see that they were well looked after, even if they aren't her own flesh and blood."

They all looked toward the Malvezzi box, where the curtains remained closed. The old duchessa smiled cannily. "It isn't his stepmother he's worried about."

"For the love of Heaven, Aunt," said the would-be dandy, "you can't mean he thinks Francesca would swoop down and carry the children off? I don't believe she's given them a thought these six years."

"You don't know anything about it," retorted the duchessa. "Before Lodovico died, she came from Venice with Valeriano and stayed in a villa just across the lake from Lodovico's. Well, why would she have done that, if not to persuade him to let her visit the children? And after he died, she went to Rinaldo and begged for at least a glimpse of them. I would have thought he'd relent—after all, keeping the children from her was Lodovico's idea, not his. But even from beyond the grave, Lodovico rules him. He turned Francesca away—practically had the servants throw her out! And now he doesn't dare let the children out of his sight, for fear she'll get at them."

A newcomer arrived in the box, reshuffling the guests. When they had all changed seats, Julian remarked, "Marchese Rinaldo must have been greatly shocked by his father's death."

"I expect he was like a little dog that had lost its master," laughed the would-be dandy. "But none of us saw him. He was off chasing Beatrice around Piedmont."

"Chasing her?" Julian lifted his brows. "Was she so difficult to catch?"

"She's impossible to catch!" the dandy lamented. "All Milan knows I've tried!"

"Don't pay any mind to him, Signor Kestrel," cut in the duchessa. "Beatrice was in Turin when the revolt broke out, and she thought it best to leave. And I don't know how it happened, but somehow she was lost on the roads, and Rinaldo went looking for her, and they were both missing for days."

Missing for days, thought Julian. Could people of such exalted rank disappear without a trace? Because if they could, then it seemed that neither Lodovico's wife nor his son had an alibi for his murder.

On his third morning in Milan, Julian heard of a new wrinkle in the murder enquiry. He had been pondering how to offer his services to the Malvezzi family—now he saw an opportunity. He wrote a letter to Lodovico's brother, Conte Carlo:

Bella Venezia Inn
27 September 1825

Signor Conte,—

I hope you'll forgive this abrupt approach from a stranger and impute my boldness, not to impertinence, but to an excess of good intentions. I considered asking a mutual acquaintance to introduce us, but as I wished to broach a delicate matter to you, I thought it more discreet to write. First I should like to offer my sincerest condolences on the death of your brother. I had the honour to meet him when I last visited Milan, and found him generous and kind to a stranger who shared in some slight measure his remarkable knowledge and love of music. I was on my way to Italy when the manner of his death came to light, and since arriving in Milan, I've heard you're proposing to engage the Bow Street Runners to search for the singer known as Orfeo in England. I have worked with the Runners in solving several murders, and if I can be of assistance in providing information about them, or in any other capacity, I hope you won't hesitate to call on me. I should be very glad to be of service to you and to the investigation.

Believe me, Signor Conte, your obedient servant,

Julian Kestrel

He gave the letter to one of the inn servants to deliver to Casa Malvezzi, the family's ancient palace in the Contrada delle Meraviglie. Although the palace presumably belonged to Rinaldo, Beatrice lived there, and Carlo was staying there during his sojourn in Milan. The palace was only a short walk from Julian's inn, and he had strolled by it several times, surveying its imposing Baroque façade and wondering what went on behind it.

Once the letter was gone from his hands, and the die was cast, he felt a need to take his mind off the murder. Surely he had earned a day of sightseeing, after all his researches. So he went to the Brera Academy, with its superb collection of paintings and frescoes. He strolled in the public garden, where Napoleon had built an immense arena that was still used for chariot races or filled with water for mock naval battles. And because this was a rare sunny day, in a city nearly as famed for its fogs as London, he climbed the five hundred and twenty steps to the roof of the cathedral, where he stood amid lofty white-marble spires as delicate as filigree, and looked out across the red-tiled roofs of Milan to the fields, farms, and rivers of the Lombard plain, and beyond to the dreamlike, snow-covered Alps.

He recalled the last time he had stood on this spot, before there was a famous dandy Julian Kestrel—before he had firmly decided to return to England at all. How, having once found Italy, could he ever leave her? Yet he knew now he had done right to go back. Years of Continental travel could mould and polish him, but could not pull up his roots. As long as he turned his back on England, he might be happy, but he would never be whole.

When he returned to the Bella Venezia late that day, he found that the waiters had become extraordinarily obsequious. One begged to be allowed to polish his boots, a task he entrusted only to Dipper, while another offered to run his errands at any hour of the day or night, and a third promised to become his devoted slave if only he would help him obtain a passport to visit his sister in Modena. "I seem to have risen in the world," Julian observed to Dipper.

"It's on account of these, sir." Dipper handed him two letters. "They come for you while you was out. The waiters didn't want to fork 'em out to me without a *buonamano*"—he rubbed his fingers together to signify money—"but I said if they didn't, you'd be glim-flashy, and your bigwig pals'd darken their daylights."

"I should have liked to hear how that translated into Milanese." Julian surveyed the letters. One was written on fine parchment and bore a blood-red seal of a serpent coiled around a sword. The other letter was sealed with the imperial eagles of Austria. "Conte Carlo certainly hasn't lost any time. No wonder the waiters were impressed."

He broke the seal on the first letter and unfolded it. Although he had written to Carlo in Milanese, Carlo had responded in English:

Casa Malvezzi
Tuesday morning

My dear Mr. Kestrel,—

Please do not suppose for a moment that your boldness, as you term it, has offended me. On the contrary, I admire your candour and directness and am grateful for your offer to assist my family in this appalling crisis.

I know little of the Bow Street Runners except such news of their exploits as filters through the formidable barrier between our countries.

Julian suspected that the barrier he meant was not the Alps or the English Channel, but the Austrian censorship, which sought to keep foreign books and journals out of Italian hands. Carlo was a notorious liberal, and his participation in the murder investigation must rankle the government. But he was also Lodovico's brother, and in Rinaldo's absence he was head of the Malvezzi family. However much the authorities loathed his politics, they could not deny his rights.

The letter continued:

But the Englishman known as Orfeo may well have returned to his own country, and I thought it logical to request the Bow Street Runners' aid in seeking him there. I make no doubt that your knowledge and advice would be of inestimable value to Commissario Grimani in determining whether, and how, to obtain their assistance. I have an appointment to see him this afternoon, and you may be sure that I will tell him of your considerate offer and urge him to accept it.

I look forward with the liveliest impatience to meeting you and talking of these and other matters. I have so little opportunity nowadays to speak English or discuss foreign affairs that your acquaintance is doubly precious to me.

Till then, believe me your obliged and faithful servant,
Carlo Malvezzi

"Better than I'd hoped for," said Julian. "Almost too easy, in fact." He unfolded the other letter. "No, I spoke too soon."

This letter, too, was in English, but in an anonymous clerkly hand quite unlike Carlo's flowing, elegant script:

Commissariat of Police
27 September 1825
3.15 p.m.

Sir,—The Director-General of Police and the government of His Imperial Highness the Viceroy of Lombardy-

Venetia thank you for your offer to assist them in finding the murderer of His Excellency Marquese Lodovico Malvezzi. It appears probable that the combined forces of the Milanese police and the Austrian army will succeed in solving this case without your help. We will therefore refrain from troubling you further in the matter.

Allow me to express my hope that you will enjoy your stay in Milan. The Brera Academy, the Ambrosian Library, and the Mint appear to be particularly popular with English tourists.

I have the honour to remain, sir, yours respectfully,

Alfonso Grimani,
Commissario

(Translated by Paolo Zanetti, clerk)

"Put in my place, by Jove!" said Julian, amused. "You've made it very clear you can do without me, Signor Commissario: now it behooves me to show that I can manage without *you*."

"How will you do that, sir?" Dipper asked.

"At the moment, I haven't the slightest idea. I shall go to the opera and see if anything comes to me."

Something did come to him at the opera. He had just arrived and was threading his way through the vestibule, exchanging bows and greetings with elegant ladies and indolent rakes, when he heard someone call his name. He turned. An elderly nobleman he knew slightly was elbowing his way toward him, a lady on his arm. As the crowd perceived her, their chatter died away, and they fell back, opening a path for her as if she were royalty.

She was about thirty, perhaps a little older—it was hard to tell with a woman like this. She was not tall, but her slender, high-waisted figure gave an impression of height. Her hands were small and delicate, her waist as dainty as a doll's, but her breasts, hugged and slightly revealed by her white satin gown, were exquisitely curved. Her complexion was a pale, clear ivory, the cheeks just tinged with carmine. Soft, dusky curls fell about her face; her back hair was caught up in a ruby comb. She had high cheekbones, slim arched brows, and a nose worthy of a Canova Venus. But her most glorious feature was her eyes, which were large, black, and brilliant, like diamonds in the dark.

"Ah, Signor Kestrel!" Her escort led her up to Julian. "I'm delighted to have the privilege of introducing you to the loveliest woman in Milan." He bowed formally to the lady. "I have the honour to present Signor Kestrel, the illustrious English dandy. Signor Kestrel—Marchesa Malvezzi."

Lodovico Malvezzi's widow extended her hands. Julian kissed them in the Milanese manner, which was so much more gallant and intimate than a cold English bow over the hand. When he straightened and looked into her eyes, she smiled.

He said to her in Milanese, "I'm deeply indebted to His Excellency for this introduction, but I had no need to be told I was meeting the loveliest woman in Milan."

"Or I that I was meeting the most elegant gentleman in Europe." Her voice was melodic and light.

"I should be the last man to try to dissuade you of that charming absurdity."

"I hope so, Signor Kestrel. I should be sorry to see you fail at anything you set out to do."

Her escort was bowing and backing away, floridly excusing himself. Julian exchanged courtesies with him, then turned back to the marchesa. "I must be Fortune's favourite child tonight," he said, "since I've not only met you but been left alone with you—or as alone as it's possible to be in this crush."

"Fortune had nothing to do with it. I asked Maurizio to present you to me and then leave us. We planned it together before I came here."

"I'm honoured, Marchesa—and intrigued."

"I won't leave you long in suspense. But we can't talk here."

She glanced expressively toward the great staircase that led to the upper boxes. Julian was momentarily taken aback. That staircase was one of the most significant promenades in Milan. When a gentleman escorted a lady of rank up those stairs, all Milan assumed that he was, or soon would be, her lover.

Masking his surprise, he offered her his arm. It would be the height of rudeness to spurn such an invitation. Besides, he wanted to know what lay behind it.

She slipped her little gloved hand into the crook of his arm, turning her bracelet so that the ruby on the clasp would not dig into his sleeve. That ruby was one of the few touches of colour on her white satin gown; another was a red rose fastened to her bodice so that it nestled between her breasts. It took all Julian's self-command not to stare at that rose, or long to change places with it.

He could not but enjoy the black looks from other young men as they mounted the stairs. When they reached the long curved corridor behind the second-tier boxes, people goggled on seeing them together and broke into murmurs the moment they had passed. Julian scanned the coats-of-arms over the doors to the boxes till he found the familiar serpent coiled around a sword. Two footmen in flame-coloured livery stood guard at the door. When they saw the marchesa, they bowed low, and one of them opened the door with a flourish. Julian felt their stares glued to his back as he led her through the small square anteroom into the box.

The box was narrow but deep, lit only by a silver candelabrum on a round table inlaid with mother-of-pearl. The table was set out with silver dishes of nougats and little almond-flavoured confections known as dead men's beans. There was also a pack of the ninety-seven elaborately decorated cards, three times the size of ordinary playing cards, that were used for the complex game of *tarocch.* Several lyreback chairs were drawn up to the table; more chairs lined the box on either side. At the front, commanding the best view of the stage, were two armchairs upholstered in flame-coloured silk brocade, their mahogany backs carved with the Malvezzi device.

Guests were already gathered in the box: a dowager, three young men-about-town, and the elderly nobleman who had introduced Julian to the marchesa. She greeted them all, and the young men kissed her hands, then Julian led her to the armchairs at the front of the box. He held one of them for her to sit down and moved to take the seat behind it. But she laid her hand lightly on his sleeve. "Won't you sit beside me?"

What the devil was she about? he thought. If he sat with her at the front of her box, he might as well announce to the entire theatre that he enjoyed her favours.

"Should you be embarrassed?" she asked, smiling.

"No, Marchesa—only abashed that tomorrow all Milan will credit me with an honour I haven't earned."

"But I should like to put myself in your debt."

"Impossible, Marchesa. One look from you would wipe the slate clean—a smile would pile up debits on the other side."

"I've always heard the English were good at keeping accounts." She went on more seriously, "I do have a reason. This isn't mere caprice. I want to have an uninterrupted talk with you. If people thought we were merely chatting about trifles, they would wish to join in; if they guessed what I really wanted to discuss, they would try to listen. But everyone accepts that new lovers see only each other. They won't eavesdrop or compete for my attention, except to say good evening when they arrive in my box, and goodbye when they go. And you won't be expected to leave or change seats whenever a new guest comes. Now do you see?"

"Yes. It's very ingenious." Though a little hard on a man's vanity, he thought—more than his vanity, if he were not careful. He was no longer in any doubt about what she wanted to discuss, but he would not be the first to broach the topic. He wanted to see how she would approach it.

The overture began. As usual, the audience paid it no heed, but went on with their chatter and card-playing. The empty chairs in the marchesa's box soon filled. Each new female guest eyed Julian curiously, while the male guests glowered. People leaned out of adjacent boxes to gape at him and the marchesa. Ghostly fingers pointed up at them from the darkness of the pit.

"You haven't closed the curtains tonight," he observed to the marchesa.

"No. I only kept them closed for the past few nights because the police requested it." She gave a faint ironic emphasis to the word *requested.* "They feared that, with my husband's murder so recently made public, the sight of me would cause too much excitement. The police don't like excitement. There's no knowing what turn it might take."

"I assumed you didn't wish to be seen."

"But why? I have no reason to hide. Some people seem to expect me to lock myself away and go into mourning. But I've done that already, four and a half years ago, when Lodovico died. He's no more dead now than he was then, merely because we've learned he was killed by a base assassin, rather than by a weak heart. What I owe him now isn't empty pageantry, but vengeance." She lifted her slim brows. "The word surprises you?"

"Most English people would say justice."

"They would mean the same thing."

"Not quite the same. Justice is a principle, vengeance a passion."

"I owe my husband a passion," she said simply. "Anything less would be a poor return for all he did for me."

Julian pondered the paradox of making a decision to feel a passion—weighing it on scales of obligation and gratitude. Yet would such a passion be any less real than a spontaneous desire of the heart? Might it not be all the more powerful for being directed and disciplined, as trained troops are more effective than raw recruits?

He could not pursue the conversation. The tenor Rubini had stepped to the front of the stage to sing his opening air, and his admirers hissed ferociously for silence. At first he did not receive the usual rapt attention; too many gazes were riveted to Marchesa Malvezzi and her new cavalier. Rubini must have perceived this, for he redoubled his efforts, embroidering his song with arpeggios, double scales, and trills, till his feats of strength and breath left the audience gasping. He finished amid a storm of applause so violent that the Austrian soldiers in the pit began shouting for order, and the gendarmes guarding the doors advanced on the audience, brandishing their bayonets.

Marchesa Malvezzi gazed down at the stage like a marble goddess, remote and still. "That's a beautiful air," she said quietly.

Julian wondered what it was like for her to hear a tenor voice, believing as she probably did that a tenor had made her a widow. He supposed it would depend very much on what she had felt for her imperious, much older husband.

She suddenly looked at him and smiled. "Shall we talk of why I arranged to meet you here? My brother-in-law showed me your letter offering to help in the investigation of my husband's murder. He thought we should accept, but Commissario Grimani disagreed. I must tell you, I don't like Commissario Grimani. Indeed, I can't acquit myself of a desire to bring you into the investigation just to annoy him."

"I can understand the impulse. He sent me a letter this afternoon that wasn't calculated to make us bosom friends."

She studied him, her head tilted musingly. "Why do you wish to investigate my husband's murder?"

"In part, because he was kind to me some years ago, when I first visited Milan. But chiefly because solving murders is by way of being my métier. And—I don't wish to sound unfeeling—but this is a particularly intriguing and extraordinary case."

"You wrote to Carlo that you've solved murders before—that you've worked with the Bow Street Runners."

She pronounced these English words so adorably that Julian was momentarily distracted. "Yes. I've solved two murders with a

Runner named Peter Vance and two more on my own—or rather, without Vance. Naturally one never solves a murder alone."

She smiled. "I'm to conclude from that speech that you're extremely modest, and therefore your achievements must be all the more remarkable."

"Modesty alone doesn't prove a man a hero. But it's incontrovertible that immodesty makes him a bore."

"Very true. Tell me: how would you go about solving my husband's murder?"

"It appears to me that it's never been investigated in a thorough and organised fashion. So I should begin by casting my nets very widely. Naturally I should find out all I could about the singer known as Orfeo. But I should also have to scrutinize everyone else who had a motive and can't set up an alibi."

"Everyone?" she echoed.

"Everyone who benefited by his death, or had cause to desire it."

"That might include the people closest to him—even his family."

"If they're innocent, they have no reason to object to answering questions."

Her lip curled. "In England, are the innocent never wrongly accused? You must have a far more perfect legal system than we can aspire to."

"In England it takes a great deal of evidence even to accuse, let alone convict, a member of a family as eminent as your husband's. I don't believe Italy is any different in that respect."

"But it's obvious that Orfeo killed my husband. He quarrelled with him the day before he died, he ran away on the night of the murder, and he had a pistol with him at the villa."

"I grant you, it seems overwhelmingly likely that Orfeo committed the murder. But I should be doing you a disservice by not keeping an open mind."

"A greater disservice than you would by treating my husband's family as suspects?" She added, with calm curiosity, "And will I be among your suspects, too?"

The audience began crying *"Zitti, zitti!"*—their hissing adjuration for silence. The heroine of the opera had just been captured by Turkish privateers, and the audience wanted to hear her sing of how she would outwit them:

"I know from experience the effect of a languishing look,
a little sigh.
I know how to tame men.
Gentle or rough, cold or fiery, they're all alike:
They all hunger for happiness from a pretty woman."

The marchesa listened, the subtlest of smiles playing around her lips. Julian watched her, thinking: At least in Italy men admit that beautiful women reduce us to drivelling idiocy. Englishmen are forever trying to ignore their burning blood and burgeoning trousers. We're determined to walk on water in which Italian men would be happy to drown.

He said with cool composure, "May I answer your question with a question, Marchesa? Where were you and what were you doing on the night of March fourteenth, 1821?"

She regarded him in silence. He had an idea that she wanted to see if she could intimidate him into taking his question back. He met her gaze, testing her mettle, as she was testing his. If she were too proud—or too afraid—to answer his question, she would be of little use as an ally.

Her face relaxed into a smile. "As you may know, in March of 1821 there was a rebellion in Piedmont. I'd gone to the capital, Turin, for a visit while Lodovico was at the Lake of Como with his tenor. My friends urgently advised me to return to Milan, or least to retreat to Novara, which was held by a loyalist garrison. At first I didn't take the warnings seriously. I couldn't conceive that the rebels would try to harm me—they seemed too taken up with squabbling among themselves to fight their enemies. But in the end I was afraid Lodovico would worry about me if I didn't leave Turin. I started for Milan by way of Novara, but on the way I heard that there were rebel forces on the road ahead. I turned north and continued till I reached Belgirate. It's a village on the western shore of Lake Maggiore."

"Yes, I passed it on my way here from Geneva. It seems rather far out of your way."

"There was no agreeable place to stay between the Novara road and Lake Maggiore. And I could easily return to Lombardy by crossing the lake. But I decided to spend a few days in Belgirate first. I found it charming, with spring approaching, the first flowers in bloom, and no social obligations. If Lodovico could enjoy a lakeside idyll, why couldn't I?"

"I believe I heard something of this story," said Julian, as if he had only just recalled it. "Someone mentioned that Marchese Rinaldo had gone searching for you in Piedmont."

"Poor Rinaldo. Yes, he heard I'd left Turin, and when I didn't arrive in Milan, he went looking for me. He meandered about Piedmont in a great deal of confusion, but finally he found me in Belgirate and brought me back to Milan." She finished sombrely, "That was when we learned that Lodovico was dead."

"I'm sorry. Can you remember when you arrived in Belgirate, and when you left?"

"Not precisely. But I know I was there when Lodovico died. It's the sort of thing you think about when you hear that someone close to you is dead: where was I, and what trivial thing was I thinking of, while he was drawing his last breath?"

"His death must have been a great blow to you."

"Oh, yes. I was very fond of him. And he seemed so indestructible—bright as the sun, enduring as the Alps."

"Yes," said Julian thoughtfully, "that was my impression of him, too."

"And yet you can't have known him very well."

He shrugged. "It isn't necessary to know a whirlwind very well, to feel its force."

She seemed to come to a decision. "Signor Kestrel, I have no doubt that Orfeo killed my husband. I don't for a moment suspect anyone else. But I think this thorough enquiry you propose to make may reveal information about him that the police might not discover. Our police have many virtues. They're diligent, thorough, and persistent. But they lack imagination, and I'm afraid that will cripple them in trying to solve a crime like this. It isn't an ordinary street robbery, it has none of the signs of a crime of passion—there isn't even any proof that it was political, though Commissario Grimani seems to take that for granted."

"But surely that's in his interest." Julian sank his voice, mindful of the spies that infested every public gathering in Milan. "Aren't the rights of an accused person greatly curtailed in political cases?"

"I hadn't thought of that," she said slowly. "That would be a great advantage to him in securing a conviction—assuming he ever finds Orfeo. I know he's determined to solve this crime. He thinks it will gain him advancement, and I daresay he's right. But his very ambition may hold him back from posing impertinent questions to important people. Now you, Signor Kestrel, have proved that you don't suffer from that constraint."

Julian bowed.

She smiled. "In short, I accept your offer. And I place myself under your command. Tell me what I can do for you."

Vistas opened before his eyes that had nothing to do with the investigation. "To begin with, will you be good enough to tell me all you know about Orfeo?"

"Certainly. But first excuse me a moment—I've been very remiss about greeting my guests."

While she exchanged pleasantries with the latest arrivals, Julian glanced past her toward the box on their right. A middle-aged priest had been flirting shamelessly with the lady at the front of that box, but now he withdrew, and a young man with bold black brows and a moustache moved into his place. He did not take the coveted seat behind the hostess, but stood leaning over her to look at the stage through a little cylindrical eyeglass. Julian was about to look away—then he noticed something that piqued his interest. Pretending to be absorbed in the opera, he studied the young man out of the corner of his eye.

He was twenty-five or thirty, with artfully tumbled black curls, a dark complexion, and dazzling white teeth. His moustache was thin and well trimmed; Julian suspected he was vain about it. On the Continent, as in England, moustaches were rarely worn by anyone not in the military. But this man's easy, lounging pose had nothing in common with the upright bearing of an officer.

The marchesa turned back to Julian. "You were asking me about Orfeo. I'm afraid I can't tell you very much. I never met him or heard him sing. Lodovico spoke of him from time to time before he took him to the villa, but only to praise his voice and build castles in the air about his prospects."

"He never wanted you to hear him sing?"

"Oh, no. He didn't want to share him with anyone. He was madly in love with him."

Julian's brows rose as high as they would go.

"Do I shock you, Signor Kestrel?" she asked, smiling.

"Extremely, marchesa. I can't conceive that any man who could call you his wife should fall in love with a tenor—or anyone else."

"I didn't mean that he loved him as he would love a woman. But that sort of love was of little account to him. It was merely an appetite to be satisfied, like hunger or thirst. A fine voice moved him to tears—to transports of sweet pain and sweeter ecstasy. There's a phenomenon called melomania—I once heard a doctor speak of it. Lodovico suffered from it. He was truly a little mad when it came to music." She cocked her head thoughtfully. "The curious thing is that he never took a singer as his mistress. His passions for singers were always chaste. He once told me the combination of love and music was dangerous."

"In what way?"

"I don't know. Like chemicals liable to explode."

"Do you think he spoke from experience?"

"If he did, it must have been a very long time ago, before I knew him."

Julian glanced once more at the moustached man in the next box. He had taken the opera glass away from his eye in order to converse with his hostess, and now he shrugged elaborately, spreading out his fingers and turning down the corners of his mouth. The gesture proclaimed his nationality as plainly as a passport. Julian asked the marchesa, "Who is the Frenchman in the box on our right?"

She did not look around. Instead, she casually lifted her ivory fan, which was decorated with mirrored facets. Her eyes lit up, and she smiled in a way that gave Julian a sudden desire to pitch both Frenchman and moustache into the pit. "That's Monsieur de la Marque. He's very charming and has an extraordinary ear for music. He can hear a melody once and tell you exactly what notes were played, and if an orchestra strikes a sour note, he knows what it was, what it ought to have been, and which player was responsible. Why did you ask about him?"

"I had an idea that he knew you."

"He's a friend." The gleam in her eyes suggested that he was, or aspired to be, something more. "I find him very amusing. We speak French, and he gives me news of Paris."

Julian took one last look at de la Marque, whose eye was glued to his opera glass again. Then he asked the marchesa, "Is there anything more you can tell me about Orfeo?"

"No." Her face clouded. "There isn't much hope of finding him, is there? He could be in England, America—he could be dead, for all anyone knows. Surely we're fooling ourselves—you and Commissario Grimani and I. What's the use of looking for a man who is nothing more than a shadow—who hasn't a face or a name—whose past and future are all a blank?"

"I know we seem to be at a dead lift. But consider what we do know: Orfeo is English, he would now be in his mid-twenties, he's a tenor, and he spent six weeks at the Lake of Como in the winter of 1821—which means he won't be able to prove he was anywhere else."

"But where in all the wide world are we to look for him?"

"Conte Carlo's idea of enlisting the Bow Street Runners to find him in England is a good one—though I don't imagine the British will readily give him up to be tried in Milan. But before we go knocking about the four corners of the earth, we ought to begin where the murder occurred, and where Orfeo was last seen: the villa."

"But surely that's the last place he'll ever be found."

Julian smiled wryly. "Unless he has a singular sense of humour and very little common sense. But there may be some trace of him that hasn't been uncovered, or a memory that can be jogged loose from the mind of a fisherman or servant. I believe the villa is yours now?"

"Yes, though it's to return to Rinaldo or his son after I die. Lodovico wanted me to have it, because he knew how fond I was of it, but he wouldn't have let it pass from his family forever."

"Did you know before he died that he meant to leave it to you?"

"Yes, Signor Kestrel," she said calmly. "He told me all about his will." She added, "Shall I send you a map tomorrow, so that you can see how long it would have taken me to travel from Belgirate to the villa on the night of the murder?"

"No, thank you, Marchesa," he said politely. "I have a map already."

A storm of orchestral flourishes marked the end of the first act. The audience in the pit yawned, coughed, quarrelled, stretched their legs, and shouted greetings across the theatre. Above, people leaned out of boxes to wave and beckon to their friends, while footmen ran about fetching ices, delivering notes, and emptying chamberpots.

So many callers flocked to the marchesa's box that she was obliged to devote herself to receiving them. Julian was introduced to those he did not know, and soon found himself in a circle of young men of fashion, all awaiting their chance to kiss the marchesa's hands and beg for the privilege of buying her an ice. They eyed Julian with a mixture of envy and admiration, but the special delicacy that Milanese society reserved for new love affairs forbade any overt allusion to his good fortune.

He was not surprised to find that one of the young men was de la Marque. A monsignore—a sort of half-cleric in purple stockings—introduced him and Julian. "I'm delighted to meet you," said Julian in Milanese. "I've heard of your remarkable musical gifts."

De la Marque smiled, his white teeth gleaming beneath his black moustache. "Hardly remarkable, Signor Kestrel. I have perfect pitch, which is useful for performing parlour tricks."

"Our Gaston is a little more serious than that." The monsignore clapped de la Marque on the shoulder. "He's writing a book about singing."

"That's true," acknowledged de la Marque. "It amuses me to be writing a book—so much so, that I don't suppose I shall ever finish it."

"It amuses him to interview prima donnas about their technique," said another young man slyly.

"Is that what you do?" asked the monsignore, grinning.

"Oh, yes," said de la Marque, "and sometimes we also discuss singing."

There was a general laugh, abruptly drowned out by the orchestra. The ballet that came between the first and second acts of the opera was beginning. The group of young men broke apart, but de la Marque lingered. "I should like to congratulate you, Mr. Kestrel," he said in English. "It's no small achievement to spend the evening by the side of the most beautiful woman in Milan."

Julian bowed. "In return, may I compliment you on your English?"

"You're most kind, but like my perfect pitch, it's a purely fortuitous talent. I spent the first seventeen years of my life in England. The climate in France had become somewhat unhealthy for my parents."

Julian understood what he meant. He must have been born soon after the Reign of Terror, when any French family with *de* before its name lived in fear of the guillotine, and thousands emigrated to Austria, Italy, or England.

"A wonderful country, England," de la Marque went on dreamily. "A place where the practical and the absurd meet—

where men calculate with mathematical nicety at precisely what angle and with what force to tilt with a windmill."

"It's good of you to credit us with so much engineering skill," said Julian pleasantly. "Perhaps it was in England that you obtained the eyeglass you were looking through earlier?"

De la Marque smiled. He smiled a great deal—whether because he was genuinely amused or wanted to draw attention to his moustache, Julian could not tell. "I've had it so long, I really can't recall."

"I'm afraid I stared at it rather persistently earlier. It's a diagonal perspective, isn't it? I saw the gleam of glass at the side. You were pointing it at the stage, but it was giving you a view to your left—of the marchesa and me, in fact. I can hardly blame you. If I were seated in a box next to Marchesa Malvezzi's, I should be tempted to look her way, too."

"Make no mistake, Mr. Kestrel. Marchesa Malvezzi is well worth a man's gaze. But I was watching you."

"May I ask why?"

"My dear Mr. Kestrel." De la Marque smiled more than ever. "One may always *ask*!"

He bowed and withdrew. Julian looked after him with raised brows.

"So you've met Monsieur de la Marque." The marchesa appeared at Julian's side. "I heard you speaking English with him."

"His English is remarkably good. He could pass for a native, if his manner weren't so French. Does he live in Milan?"

"He comes and goes."

"Was he here in March of 1821?"

She caught her breath and gazed at him intently. "I don't know. I hardly knew him in those days. He interests you?"

"Enough to make me wish to improve my acquaintance with him."

Another guest claimed her attention. It was not until the second act of the opera began, and she and Julian were seated once more at the front of the box, that they could continue their conversation. "So you wish to go to the villa," said the marchesa. "What will you do there?"

He shrugged. "Prowl about with a quizzing-glass, frowning enigmatically at trifles. Justify your faith in my ability to ask impertinent questions."

"I should like to see that. I shall open the villa, and you may stay as long as you like. But someone must come with us, to give us countenance." She laid her fan meditatively against her lips. "I don't get on very well with my female relatives. They disapprove of me for reading too much."

Julian was not surprised by her desire for a chaperon. Milanese women were allowed—almost expected—to have lovers, but they must not flaunt them. That was how Rinaldo's wife, Francesca, had transgressed.

"I shall invite Carlo," she concluded. "I'll speak to him about it tomorrow."

"I take it he approves of your plan to ask me to conduct an investigation independent of Commissario Grimani's?"

"He will," she said, smiling, "when he knows of it. I haven't told him yet, because I wanted to meet with you alone tonight, and he would have insisted on coming with me. Men think a woman can't manage anything on her own except a love affair. And Carlo is starved for serious occupation. For the past ten years, he's been nothing but a courtier, and that's hard for a man who was once a high government official. *Sous les français,*" she added discreetly.

"I should like to ask him some questions."

"I'm sure he'd be delighted to tell you anything you wish to know. Will you come to Casa Malvezzi tomorrow?—shall we say at noon? I'll introduce you to him then. And you'll surely want to meet Maestro Donati. He's staying with me as well."

Julian looked at her quickly. "How did that come about?"

"He retired to Pavia after Lodovico died. When Commissario Grimani was put in charge of the investigation, I knew he would want to question him. So I sent a fast courier to Pavia with an invitation for him to stay at Casa Malvezzi. It seemed only right to take responsibility for him, since he's obliged to relive some harrowing memories for my husband's sake." She added, a smile playing around her lips, "I also knew the investigation couldn't go far in any direction without him. So while I have him, I'll always be kept informed of Commissario Grimani's progress."

"Marchesa, I'm honoured to serve you, but in the realm of ingenuity, I hardly think you need an assistant, or could find an equal."

"I know a little about people," she shrugged, "that's all."

Julian sneezed.

"Salut."

"Thank you. Where is Marchese Rinaldo, and when do you expect him back?"

"I'm not privy to his plans. He and I lead very separate lives. He has his wing at Casa Malvezzi, and I have mine, and when he travels, he doesn't tell me where he's going or when he means to return. I imagine he'll come back when he hears that his father died by violence."

"And Marchesa Francesca?"

"She lives in Venice with Valeriano. Do you want to question her, too?"

"I should like to question both her and Valeriano. Is there any chance they would come to the villa if you asked them?"

"I think they might. I've always got on fairly well with Francesca. Of course Rinaldo would be furious at me for receiving her and her lover, but as he isn't here, that would seem not to be a problem."

Julian sneezed again.

"*Salut.* I hope you're not catching cold?"

Julian smiled wryly. "My friend MacGregor would be enchanted to find he was right in his prediction that I would make myself ill, travelling in such villainous weather. It would very nearly console him for my not having been carried off in a flood."

"I didn't know English dandies caught cold. I should have thought it would be too untidy."

"Oh, we're a very delicate breed. Beau Brummell, our patron saint, once claimed to have caught a cold by being put into a room at an inn with a damp stranger."

"I hope you won't be too ill to call tomorrow."

"Marchesa, I promise you, nothing short of the plague will keep me away."

CHAPTER 11

It was nearly two in the morning by the time Julian got back to his inn. Yet he knew he would not sleep until he had consulted his map of the northern Italian states. By the light of a little olive-oil lamp, he located the Lake of Como. Lake Maggiore, further west, ran roughly north to south and formed part of the border between Lombardy and Piedmont. Belgirate was a village on the western, Piedmontese shore.

The quickest way to reach the Lake of Como from Belgirate would be to cross Lake Maggiore by boat, then proceed overland. Julian estimated that the journey would take seven or eight hours each way. Adding on even a minimal amount of time for the marchesa to reach the villa, find Lodovico in the belvedere, and kill him, she would have had to be absent from Belgirate for at least fifteen hours. Surely a lady of her rank—not to mention her beauty—could not have disappeared for so long without exciting remark. At the very least, her servants would have known if she had gone missing. And was it conceivable that this elegant, urbane woman had ridden by night along lonely roads, in imminent danger of being set upon by customs officials or bandits?

Reassured, Julian put the map away and went to bed. But as he lay in the darkness, he was besieged by questions. Why did the marchesa travel so far off her course after leaving Turin? If her concern was to escape from the Piedmontese rebels, why did she not cross Lake Maggiore into Austrian Italy? Finally, even assuming she would not have travelled alone from Belgirate to the villa, could she not have bribed or enticed some man to help her commit the crime?

He could not acquit her, however much he wanted to. Her husband's death had left her a very wealthy woman. No doubt she had lived in luxury as his wife, but she had been dependent on him for every soldo in her purse, and Milanese noblemen were notoriously miserly in everything but public display. A woman like the marchesa—intelligent, cultivated, a product of the enlightened French régime—might well have chafed against the dominion of an arrogant man like Lodovico. Could her show of gratitude and respect toward him be all a blind?

Julian turned over restlessly, pulling free of the bedclothes tangled around his legs. He would not solve these conundrums tonight—and if he did not sleep a little, he would be in no condition to pursue them tomorrow, either. He lay still, resolutely clearing his mind of the marchesa and all his bedevilling thoughts about her. Yet the last thing he saw as he fell asleep was her eyes, diamond-bright against the sable of his closed lids.

In the morning the waiters at the inn clucked sympathetically on hearing Julian's sneezes and ragged voice. One of them procured him a bottle of cold medicine, which he did not take but kept in his dressing-case, as it seemed to consist almost entirely of spirits and would be useful if his brandy supply ever ran short. Liquors other than wine were hard to come by in the Italian states.

At a quarter to noon he fortified himself with handkerchiefs and set out for Casa Malvezzi, in the Contrada delle

Meraviglie. Although it was only a few streets away, he hired a sediola: a light, open, two-wheeled carriage. He wanted the Malvezzi servants to think him a man of means, so that they would cultivate Dipper, who accompanied him in lieu of a groom. No barriers of nationality or language would prevent them from making friends with a servant whose master might be expected to fork out generous tips. And who knew what Dipper might learn from them about the Malvezzis and their murder?

The Contrada delle Meraviglie—the Street of Marvels—lay in the shadow of the Castello, Milan's ancient fortress, now an Austrian barracks. Casa Malvezzi seemed a fortress in its own right, its marble façade bristling with pointed pediments, its roof lined with spiky finials. Dipper rang smartly at the street door, and a porter ushered them in.

They found themselves in a spacious courtyard surrounded by a portico of granite columns. The porter handed them over to a pair of footmen in patched and faded indoor livery. One of them conducted Dipper to the servants' hall for some refreshment, while the other bade Julian follow him into the left-hand wing of the house.

They passed through damp, draughty, ill-lit rooms, hung with sombre ancestral portraits and huge, moth-eaten tapestries of hunting scenes. Each room had a great glass chandelier with a tangle of snakelike branches. Some of the carved wooden doors were off their hinges; a few were missing altogether. Gaunt wooden statues of saints stared from corners; bronze flowers bloomed grotesquely in urns. High-backed chairs stood at attention and defied anyone to sit on them. Julian saw nothing of the marchesa's personality here. This was a Malvezzi stronghold, as the many gilt reliefs of the family coat-of-arms attested.

The marchesa's sitting-room was similar in style, but much better cared for. The walls were freshly painted and gilded, the windows secure against draughts. There were even a few commodious silk-upholstered sofas and chairs. Over the mantelpiece was a massive equestrian portrait of Lodovico, in the style of Velazquez's paintings of Spanish royalty. He sat his horse proudly and well, his head held high, his hazel eyes flashing gold.

Beneath the portrait stood a man who might almost have been Lodovico returned to life. He had the same commanding height, broad shoulders, curly dark hair, and beaked nose. But his eyes were deep brown rather than gold, which softened his expression, and his face was lined about the mouth rather than the brow, as if he were more inclined to smile than to look fierce.

The marchesa sat on a sofa. She was in white again: a simple cotton gown that was, if possible, even more enchanting than last night's silk, because it showed how little her beauty owed to the trappings of wealth and fashion.

Julian kissed her hands. "Good day, marchesa."

"Oh, dear." She smiled in amused sympathy. "I'm afraid you must have encountered at least two damp strangers."

"It's nothing—a touch of catarrh." Julian was sorry to appear before her with his throat rasping and his handkerchief in highly unromantic use, but there was no help for it.

"I'm all the more grateful you should come today, when no doubt you would far rather be home in bed."

"Marchesa, a man who would wish to be anywhere but in your company is more fit for a madhouse than a sickbed."

She smiled. "Allow me to present you to my brother-in-law."

"Signor Kestrel!" Carlo Malvezzi came forward and wrung Julian's hand. "It's a great pleasure to meet you, and an even greater one to learn that you're going to help us investigate my brother's murder."

"I'm honoured that Marchesa Malvezzi should ask for my help in a matter of such importance. I shall do all I can to be worthy of her trust, and yours."

"I don't doubt it, my friend," said Carlo.

"Carlo has kindly agreed to accompany us to the villa," said the marchesa. "I thought we might leave the day after tomorrow, if that wouldn't be too soon for you, Signor Kestrel—and, of course, if you're well enough."

"It's not too soon," said Julian, "and I shall take care to be well enough."

"That's in God's hands," she said, smiling. "I pray He won't disappoint me. Very well: we'll plan to leave on Friday morning. Carlo and I will come for you in my carriage." She added, "I've sent a letter by courier to Francesca, inviting her and Signor Valeriano to join us at the villa. I've also written to Commissario Grimani."

"You haven't told him about Signor Kestrel's investigation?" Carlo's eyes opened wide.

"Why not?" she said tranquilly. "I informed him that you and I and Signor Kestrel will be leaving for the villa shortly, so that if he has anything to communicate to me, he should direct his letters there."

"He'll descend on us within the hour," Carlo predicted.

"I can't help that. He mustn't be permitted to say we did anything behind his back. That would be far too good a weapon to give him."

"I've been rather looking forward to meeting him," said Julian. "Signor Conte, have you any idea when Marchese Rinaldo means to return?"

Carlo shook his head. "He hasn't written to me for some time. I don't even know where he is." He turned to the marchesa. "Would Ernesto know his plans?"

"Ernesto was Lodovico's manservant," the marchesa explained to Julian. "He served Lodovico for nearly forty years, so Rinaldo is obliged to keep him on, though he isn't comfortable with him and doesn't take him on his travels."

"Did Ernesto accompany Marchese Lodovico to the Lake of Como?" asked Julian.

"Yes, but he never saw Orfeo." She added, "He did talk with him once, in Milan, on the night Lodovico met him."

"Then how is it he can't identify him?"

"Why don't I let him explain that himself? Will you ring, Carlo?"

Carlo pulled the bell-rope by the fireplace. A footman came in, and the marchesa told him to send Ernesto to her.

"I should like to speak with you as well, Signor Conte," said Julian.

"When and where you like," said Carlo.

"I'm afraid I shall have to ask some prying and possibly insulting questions."

Carlo smiled wryly. "I'm a liberal in Italy, Signor Kestrel. I'm accustomed to be regarded as a dangerous criminal."

A servant entered and bowed to Carlo and the marchesa. He was about sixty, with stooping shoulders and a face nearly as grey as his hair. In token of his senior status, he wore a sober grey tailcoat in lieu of livery. His linen, though darned and yellowing, was scrupulously clean.

"Ernesto," said the marchesa, "this is Signor Kestrel, the Englishman I told you of. He wishes to ask you some questions about Orfeo. Pray be absolutely candid with him, and hold nothing back."

"Your Ladyship, I would bare my soul to the Devil himself, if it would help bring my master's murderer to justice!"

"I knew I could rely on you," she said warmly, "just as Lodovico always did." She rose. "I'll leave you to Signor Kestrel, who is very far from being the Devil."

Julian bowed and kissed her hands. "Merely his advocate on occasion."

Ernesto led Julian out through a back door to a dark, narrow passage behind Casa Malvezzi. They stood beneath an ivy-grown wall about twenty feet high, forming one side of a little courtyard off the right wing of the house. Ernesto said, "This is where I saw him, signor."

"Orfeo?"

"Yes, signor."

"Tell me how that came about."

"It was a week or two into Carnival, signor. My master had a headache and had come home earlier than usual, claiming that the noise in the streets was making it worse."

Julian nodded. Carnival was the festive season between Christmas and Lent, when there were masked balls at La Scala, and the streets were thronged with revellers at all hours of the night.

"I was helping him make ready for bed," Ernesto went on. "His rooms were up there." He pointed to a row of windows overlooking the courtyard. "When the young man came along and stood where you and I are now, signor, and began to sing, we could hear him quite clearly. At first my master took offence, and told me to send the impudent fellow about his business. But then he called after me to wait. He started moving toward the windows as if he were walking in his sleep, and didn't say a word till the song was over."

"What was the song?"

"To see her in another man's arms." Ernesto hummed a little of it reminiscently. "Cimarosa was the music of our youth—the marchese's and mine. Strange: you'd have expected a young man like that to sing Rossini."

"But that wouldn't have served his purpose so well," Julian mused.

"What do you mean, signor?"

"I mean that he seems to have set out deliberately to captivate the marchese. In this secluded spot, no one else could have heard him. And you say that Marchese Lodovico had come home early that night. Was anyone else in the house?"

"Only a few footmen, signor, to guard against thieves. Even the servants had leave to be out late during Carnival. And Her Ladyship wasn't expected back before dawn."

"Then it was clearly the marchese Orfeo meant to serenade."

"It does seem so, when you put it like that, signor." Ernesto shook his head sadly. "But at the time I didn't think it out. I was deeply moved myself. That pure, clear voice wafting up to us—I can't tell you what it was like. He wasn't a man, signor—he was the very heart of youth and love, singing to us in the night."

Julian was silent for a few moments. "What happened then?"

"The song ended. My master came to himself with a start. He turned around to me, his face all streaked with tears, and said, 'Ernesto, I must see him! Quick, bring him to me, before he goes away!' I ran downstairs in such a hurry that my candle went out, but I didn't dare take time to light another. I came out through the back door. He was still here. I stood as close to him as I am to you now, signor, but I've no idea what he looked like. It was so dark, and he was wearing a long cloak and a hat with the brim turned down to shade his face."

"How tall was he?"

"I think about middling height, signor. But I didn't take much notice. How could I know it would matter so much?"

"You couldn't," Julian reassured him.

"And yet I feel I ought to have, signor! When I think that it was I, Ernesto Torelli, who brought him to my master—the man who would become his murderer! It makes me want to dash my brains out against this wall, signor!"

Julian laid a friendly hand on his shoulder. "I beg you won't do anything of the kind. I'm in enough of a hobble trying to solve this crime, without being robbed of the man who probably knew Lodovico Malvezzi better than anyone else did."

"That's true, signor." Ernesto seemed a little comforted. "I served him from the time we were both eighteen, and there wasn't much he kept from me." He crossed himself. "God and the Madonna forgive me for what I said about dashing out my brains! It's not only a mortal sin—it's disloyal to my master, to think of leaving the world while there's anything I can do to help solve his murder! What more can I tell you, signor?"

"What happened when you found Orfeo here?"

"I told him my master, Marchese Malvezzi, had heard him singing and wanted to meet him. He bowed and said he was honoured, or something of that sort. I asked him to follow me."

"Did he seem surprised?"

"I couldn't say, signor. He wasn't unwilling. I brought him up to my master's room. I suppose he took off his hat then—my master would have been angry if he hadn't uncovered in his presence—but even then I didn't get a proper look at him. There wasn't much light—my master was sparing with candles. And I wasn't there above a minute or two. My master dismissed me, and I went. And that was the last I saw of Signor Orfeo."

"Who let him out of the house?"

"No one seems to know, signor. I expect it was the marchese himself."

Julian thought a moment. "It seems curious he should have received a stranger alone at that hour. The young man might have been a thief or a hired bully."

"My master was brave, signor, and very proud. He wouldn't have believed any man would dare to lift a hand against him. Of course, he usually had servants about him when he received a guest, but that was for the sake of his dignity, not because he was afraid. And after he heard Signor Orfeo sing, he wasn't thinking of his dignity. Music always made him forget everything else. It was the only thing in the world that could even make him forget that he was a Malvezzi."

The only thing in the world that could make him forget he was a Malvezzi. The words seemed portentous to Julian, pointing him toward some truth he was not yet able to grasp.

He asked Ernesto about the last few months of Lodovico's life. Had he quarrelled with anyone, received any suspicious visits or letters, dismissed any servants? Ernesto shook his head. "Except that on the day he died, he gave the rough side of his tongue to Signor Orfeo for fighting with Maestro Donati's servant, Tonio. I don't know much about that—I wasn't there. I do know Tonio got the sack on account of it. But he couldn't have killed my master, because the police say he was dead drunk at the Nightingale all night."

The marchese had been on good terms with his servants, tenants, and neighbours, Ernesto said. Not so his daughter-in-law, Francesca, to whom he had written a letter a day or two before he died. One strange thing had happened on the last morning of his life: a brown-paper package addressed to him was found outside the gate of Castello Malvezzi. Ernesto did not know what it contained and had found no trace of it after his death.

"Did it come through the post?" asked Julian.

"No, signor. There were no government stamps on it—just *for Marchese Lodovico Malvezzi* in large black letters."

"Have you any idea how long it had been there?"

"It wasn't there the evening before. So someone must have left it during the night."

"Who brought it to the marchese?"

"I did, signor, but I didn't stay to see him open it." Ernesto's face darkened. "But I know there was something evil in it, because my master was in a black mood after it came."

"How do you mean, in a black mood?"

"Fidgety and ill-tempered, signor. And he'd been in such fine fettle before! He was so happy, going to the villa every day to hear Signor Orfeo sing." Ernesto drew closer and dropped his voice confidentially. "There was something else putting him in spirits, signor. I never told anyone about it, because he seemed to want to keep it a secret."

"What was it?"

"He was writing a piece of music, signor. Sometimes I'd catch him scribbling on a pile of papers—biting his pen and tearing his hair, just like a real composer. But when I came near, he'd whisk away what he was writing, as if he didn't want me to see it."

"Then how do you know it was music?"

"Because he left jottings lying about, signor. He'd always had a habit of writing or drawing on any bit of paper that came to hand. He had so much life in him, he never could sit still. After we came to the lake, it was always musical notes. He'd scribble them on anything—newspapers, wrappings of packages, bills. They seemed to haunt him, signor. So I feel sure he was writing music—perhaps something for Signor Orfeo to sing."

"Did you keep any of these jottings?"

"No, signor. I had no reason to. My master just threw them in the rubbish, and when I found them, I did the same."

Julian pondered briefly. "What became of this piece of music after he died? Did it turn up among his papers?"

"I don't know, signor. It wasn't my place to look at his papers."

"Who would have looked at them?"

"I think they went to Conte Carlo, signor. He was my master's executor."

Julian found this curious. "I thought Marchese Lodovico and his brother didn't get on."

"They fought about politics, signor. But my master trusted Conte Carlo in matters of money and family. And he always said Conte Carlo had a good mind, even if he put it to bad uses."

"So they got on personally, despite their political differences?"

"I wouldn't go so far as to say that, signor. But—well, blood is thicker than water."

Julian thought the Malvezzi blood might well run thinner than most. Family feeling had not prevented Lodovico from tyrannizing over Rinaldo or robbing Francesca of her children. If he had trusted his brother and longtime political enemy to be his executor, it could only be because, as Ernesto had said, he did not expect anyone to have the effrontery to injure him. And a man who believed himself invulnerable was very vulnerable indeed.

❀ ❀ ❀

"Do you play *tarocch*?" Carlo asked, pouring Julian a glass of Valtellina wine.

"Yes. Thank you." Julian held up the glass to one of the tall, narrow windows, which formed twin slits of white light in the little wood-panelled study. There was no sun today, but even the palest illumination struck jewel-like glints from the wine's red depths.

Carlo raised his own glass. "Your health, Mr. Kestrel—no idle toast just now, I'm afraid. You don't mind if we speak English? I have so little chance to practice."

"Not at all. But you hardly seem in need of practice, Signor Conte."

Carlo bowed. His English was indeed very fluent, though he spoke with an accent.

Julian tasted the wine. "This is very good."

"I'm glad you like it. These Valtellina reds are our best local wines. Please sit down." Carlo beckoned him to a pair of upright wooden chairs, their leather backs pricked with iron studs. "My question about *tarocch* wasn't mere small talk. The card of the Wheel of Fortune sums up my life—and, in great measure, my relationship with Lodovico."

"I should like to hear about that."

"It's no secret that we were at odds politically. From our earliest youth, he accused me of going over to the rabble, which is to say that I believed in parliamentary government and scientific progress. Of course, while the Austrians ruled Milan, it was hopeless to press for either. But when the French came—those were heady days, Mr. Kestrel! I suppose it's a waste of breath to praise Napoleon to an Englishman. But you English, who've enjoyed the privilege of representative government for centuries, can hardly begin to understand what it meant to us to have even a taste of it. We had a senate and council of state composed of our own people—which is more than can be said of our legislators now—and much of the day-to-day routine of government was left in their hands. We had a written legal code, by which all the people might know and understand their rights. We had new schools, public gardens, flourishing arts and sciences. If it hadn't been for the incessant war that drained away our money and destroyed our young men, we would have thought ourselves living in a new Golden Age."

"And for you, the Wheel of Fortune took an upward turn?"

"Indeed. For many years it seemed I'd chosen the winning side, as well as the right one. I held high government office, married, raised a family. During all that time, Lodovico would have nothing to do with me. I must admit, I exacerbated the trouble."

Julian stifled a sneeze with his handkerchief. "In what way?"

"I acquired the villa—the one where he was murdered. He wanted it for himself, you see. It was owned by a family named Delborgo, who were longtime rivals of ours. Lodovico always claimed it belonged by rights to the ancient Malvezzi fiefdom, and his legal wrangling over it helped ruin the Delborgo. They were obliged to sell the villa, but I believe Ottavio Delborgo would have set fire to it before he would have let it fall into Lodovico's hands. He sold it to me purely to spite him."

Julian sat back, stretching out his legs and crossing one booted ankle over the other. Not that this or any other position could make him comfortable in such a chair—it might have been designed to discourage long conversations. "To me, the question of why the Delborgo sold it to you isn't as interesting as why you bought it. You must have known that would infuriate your brother."

"Our relations could hardly have got much worse. But, really, I didn't give much thought to what Lodovico felt or wanted. I was born on that part of the lake—I grew up there. My earliest memories are of seeing the sun rise over those hills and learning to manoeuvre a boat on those waters. Were there other country properties I could have purchased? Of course. But once I knew the villa was available, my heart became set on that.

"I spent years rebuilding and renovating—turning that decaying shell of a villa into a jewel of classical art. I redid the gardens, too, in the English style. I should like to show them to you when we go—Beatrice says they aren't much changed. I went there often, first to superintend the improvements, then later to enjoy the results. Meanwhile Lodovico sulked—there's really no other word for it—at his castle on the cliff above. So you had the ludicrous spectacle of two brothers living a stone's throw from one another, but not speaking.

"You know the rest. The Wheel of Fortune turned full circle. The French were driven out, the Austrians returned, and all hope of a united Italy turned to ashes. I was a particular target of Austrian reprisals, because they'd somehow got the idea I was hiding munitions from them." Carlo smiled enigmatically. "You'll understand if I don't go into the question of whether they were right in that."

Julian inclined his head.

"I was obliged to leave Milan," Carlo resumed. "I took refuge in Parma, where my wife became a lady-in-waiting to the Archduchess. We lived like courtiers, but we were as poor as rats. I had to sell both the villa and my house in Milan. Lodovico was resolved not to let the villa slip through his fingers a second time. He offered by far the best price, and so the villa came to him at last."

And death found him there, thought Julian. Was that what Carlo was thinking? And did he feel some satisfaction that the villa—his creation, the object of his love and pride—had proved so fatal to the brother who wrested it from him? Impossible to tell: his face expressed only sadness.

"What were your relations with him after he purchased the villa?" asked Julian.

"Oh, they improved considerably." Carlo smiled wryly. "Lodovico was a man who always had to win, but having won, he didn't hold grudges. We weren't close, and we rarely saw each other. But on my visits to Milan, I stayed at Casa Malvezzi, and we met and conversed on civilised terms.

"When Francesca left Rinaldo, I offered to mediate between them. I was sorry for the boy—between Francesca's desertion and Lodovico's contempt, his life was a misery. Lodovico preferred to handle that matter in his own way, but Rinaldo and I became better friends. More recently, I've tried to influence him to do some good with all the wealth that came to him from his father. There's so much he could do to improve the living conditions of his tenants, and to modernize their farming methods."

"I suppose he had the most to gain from his father's death," Julian mused.

Carlo withdrew into polite, patrician reserve. "He inherited his property. That was to his advantage, yes."

"His very considerable advantage, I should think. In England, the heir to a great estate generally has an income settled on him in his father's lifetime. Here, young men like Marchese Rinaldo are apt to remain dependent on their fathers until they come into their inheritance."

"It doesn't follow that Rinaldo killed his father on that account!"

"No, hardly. I'm not accusing anyone, Signor Conte. I'm merely trying to understand how Marchese Lodovico's death affected those around him."

Carlo looked grave. "Beatrice warned me that you would consider our family as suspects in the murder. I must tell you that I find it both painful and offensive to have it suggested that any of my relatives shed Malvezzi blood."

"I understand that, Signor Conte. I'm all the more grateful that you should cooperate so fully in answering my questions."

"I have no choice, Signor Kestrel. Quite apart from all that Beatrice and I know of your experience and acumen in solving murders, you are really the only person we can turn to to conduct a private investigation. Not many Italians would be willing to risk treading on the toes of the Austrian army and the police. Even for you, the endeavour isn't without its dangers."

"Are you warning me off, Signor Conte?"

Carlo broke into a laugh. "If I am, I hope with all my heart that I've failed! Come, it's profitless to talk in this vein. You've kindly agreed to assist us, and you are going about it in the manner you think best. When I was in government, I knew better than to consult an expert and then refuse to be guided by him. *Allora,* what more can I tell you?"

"As long as we're confronting delicate issues, where were you on the night your brother was killed?"

"Ah." Carlo sat back slowly. "At the time Lodovico went to the Lake of Como with his tenor, I was in financial straits. My debts had far outstripped my resources. I had three sons and three daughters to provide for, and the eldest were of an age to marry or be launched in a profession. In short, to use your slang expression,

I was in Queer Street. I could have asked Lodovico for money, but I must confess, my pride rebelled at the thought. So my only recourse was to sell whatever property of value remained to me.

"I still owned a box at La Scala, which I'd been leasing since I left Milan. With that, two horses, and the last of my wife's jewelry, I might keep our heads above water. Early in March—or perhaps it was late in February, I can't remember—I came secretly to Milan to arrange the sale. If I'd sold so much property in Parma, our creditors would have discovered how hard up we were and descended on us *en masse.*

"I'd been in Milan for about a fortnight when I heard of Lodovico's death. I stayed on to make myself useful to Rinaldo and Beatrice any way I could, and to meet with our family lawyer, Palmieri, about Lodovico's will."

"What were you doing on the night of the murder itself?"

"That was four and a half years ago, Mr. Kestrel. I assume I was at home in bed—there's no opera during Lent, and I hadn't come to Milan to carouse in cafés."

"Is there anyone who might remember where you were that night?"

"I shouldn't think so. I was living a very retired life. I'd taken apartments on the outskirts of the city and was keeping my movements very quiet. So there's no one to swear I didn't slip away in the night, unless perhaps my servant remembers. He was the only person I took with me to Milan."

"Is he still in your service?"

"Yes. His name is Guido Gennaro. He's here with me in Milan, if you wish to speak to him."

"Thank you. I shan't trouble him at present." Julian preferred to leave the servants to Dipper, unless any of them had something particularly extraordinary to relate. "Since you were Marchese Lodovico's executor, I should like to ask you how he left his property."

"The entailed property went to Rinaldo. That includes this house, the castle, and the land surrounding it. Beatrice inherited the villa and its contents for her life, with reversion to Rinaldo or his heirs. Lodovico also left her his opera box, and virtually everything else that wasn't within the entail, apart from some bequests to servants and the Church."

"And you, Signor Conte? Did you receive a bequest?"

"A trifle." Carlo smiled his wry, resigned smile. "A few thousand lire to buy masses for his soul. What you would call in English 'a shilling for candles.'"

"Did you know before he died how he meant to dispose of his property?"

"Oh, yes. He told me several years earlier, when he asked me to be his executor."

Then bang goes any theory that Conte Carlo killed his brother in order to put his own affairs to rights, Julian thought. "Did Ernesto tell you about the anonymous package that was left for Marchese Lodovico outside the castle gate?"

"Yes. He told both Beatrice and me. Neither of us has an inkling where it came from or what could have been in it."

Julian put his handkerchief to his nose and sneezed. "Do you know if Marchese Lodovico was composing a piece of music before he died?"

"No. Why do you ask?"

"Ernesto thought he was."

"I know he tried to write music when we were young, but he hadn't any talent for it. It was a bitter disappointment to him. I never heard he'd turned his hand to it again."

"I thought something might have turned up among his papers."

"I wouldn't know. I only really looked at the legal documents—deeds, contracts, that sort of thing. His letters and other private papers I sealed up and gave to Rinaldo." He knit his brows. "Do you think it's important?"

"It's a dangling thread, which I dislike in an investigation nearly as much I do in a coat." He regarded Carlo thoughtfully. "Signor Conte, who do you think killed your brother?"

"Orfeo is the obvious suspect. But, having an affection for lost causes, I often find myself taking his part."

A footman darted into the room. "Excellency, Her Ladyship sent me to ask you and Signor Kestrel to come to her at once!"

"Softly, my boy!" said Carlo. "What's happened?"

"Commissario Grimani is here, Excellency. And he looks like a thundercloud!"

CHAPTER 12

Commissario Grimani wasted no time on preliminaries or social graces. He walked rapidly into the sitting-room and, ignoring Carlo and Julian, made for the sofa where the marchesa sat. After the briefest of bows, he rapped out, "I understand Maestro Donati is staying here."

"How delightful to see you, Signor Commissario. Yes, Maestro Donati is my guest."

"Why was I not informed?"

"My dear Commissario, it would have been an insult to inform you, when you're so eminently capable of informing yourself of whatever you need to know. May I present you to our friend, Signor Kestrel?"

Grimani ran a disparaging gaze over Julian, with eyes as cold and colourless as ice-water. He had a narrow head, thin lips, and a wiry, spare frame. His brown hair grew very neat and straight. Julian supposed it would dare do nothing less.

"How do you do, Signor Commissario," said Julian.

Grimani looked unpleasantly surprised—perhaps at finding that Julian was fluent in Milanese. "Marchesa Malvezzi wrote to me about you. I gather you think yourself more capable of solving this crime than the Milanese police?"

"By no means. But since your quarry is English, I thought my assistance might be of some use."

"What exactly do you mean to do?"

Julian explained his plan to explore the villa and its environs, and to question all who had been at odds with Lodovico Malvezzi before his death, or had benefited from it. Grimani heard him out with rising impatience.

"This broad investigation of yours is a waste of time," he declared, "and an insult to the marchese's family and friends. We know that on the night of the murder an unsavoury young man was left all but alone with Marchese Lodovico, and afterwards fled from the house. I suppose you wish to absolve Orfeo because he's English?"

Julian shrugged. "There have been as many Englishmen who were born to be hanged as men of other nations. But to all appearances Orfeo had nothing to gain from the crime and a great deal to lose. With one pistol shot, he transformed himself from the promising protégé of a powerful and influential patron into a fugitive who could only sing in public at the risk of betraying himself, and who would pay with his life if he were caught."

"This was either a crime of passion or of politics," Grimani said shortly. "The considerations you describe don't enter into it." He turned to the marchesa. "When are you leaving for the Lake of Como?"

"On Friday morning," she replied.

"You will allow me to join your party. I wish to examine the villa and the belvedere, and to discuss the murder with the local officials who first investigated it. And although I consider Signor Kestrel's enquiries frivolous and misguided, it's conceivable he may unearth evidence useful to me, and I cannot risk its being mishandled or lost."

"But my dear Commissario," protested the marchesa, "I should never forgive myself if our frivolous and misguided efforts took you away from your serious duties in Milan."

"I have nothing to keep me in Milan at present, Your Ladyship. I've sent agents out searching for Lucia Landi and Antonio Farese; any news they have to impart can reach me at the villa as easily as here. I consider the matter settled. If you have any complaints, you may take them up with the Director-General of Police. Now I wish to question Maestro Donati. Be good enough to send for him."

"As always, Signor Commissario, your charm sweeps everything before it." The marchesa looked around at her brother-in-law, who was leaning against the mantelpiece, arms folded, regarding Grimani with unabashed dislike. "Carlo, will you please ring?"

Carlo bowed, making plain that he was complying with her request and not the commissario's order. He rang; a footman answered, and the marchesa bade him summon Maestro Donati.

"While we're waiting, I have something to show you." Grimani reached into an inside pocket of his coat and brought out an object wrapped in faded brown paper. Julian's interest quickened—especially when he caught a glimpse of Lodovico's name in block capitals on the side.

"Is that the package?" Carlo asked quickly. "The one that was left at the castle on the night before my brother was murdered?"

"How do you know about it?" Grimani demanded.

Carlo smiled mirthlessly. "By your tone, Signor Commissario, one would never guess you were concerned not to insult my brother's relations. We know about the package because his manservant told us about it."

Grimani parted the wrappings, revealing an inner lining of silver tissue paper and a lady's elbow-length glove. He handed the glove to the marchesa. "Have you ever seen this before?"

She turned it over a few times, running her fingers over the embroidered myrtle leaves and the ruby heart pierced with a diamond shaft. Carlo and Julian came to look as well.

"It's very old," she mused. "At least a quarter-century, I should think. And the workmanship is lovely. No, I've never seen it before."

"And you, Signor Conte?" Grimani proceeded.

The marchesa deliberately passed the glove to Julian rather than Carlo. Grimani's eyes narrowed angrily. She ignored him. "What do you think, Signor Kestrel?"

Julian examined the glove. "It's obviously a relic of some *affaire de coeur*—decorated with symbols of love. And if these gems are as real as they seem, the giver was a man of means." He looked at Grimani. "I take it Conte Carlo is right: this is the anonymous package left for Marchese Lodovico?"

"Yes," said Grimani curtly.

"Was there anything in it besides the glove?"

"Yes." Grimani handed a folded paper to the marchesa.

She read aloud: *"I know who owned this glove and how she came by it. Unless you wish all the world to know her story, meet me on the night of 14 March, after 11.00, at the Moorish belvedere at Villa Malvezzi."* She drew in her breath. "That's why he was in the belvedere alone at that time of night! Then whoever left this package—"

"Is almost certainly the murderer," Grimani finished. "Yes."

"How did the package come into your hands?" asked Julian.

"Conte Raversi made a search of Marchese Lodovico's apartments at Castello Malvezzi after the murder. He found the glove and note locked in a claw-footed chest."

"Why weren't we told about them at once?" exclaimed Carlo. "Even if there were some justification for concealing the murder—which you know I consider an outrage—"

"The police are aware of your opinions on a variety of subjects, Signor Conte," Grimani said.

"It would be extraordinary if they weren't," Carlo flashed back, "since they watch me like hawks whenever I step over the border into Austrian Italy. At all events, those closest to Lodovico ought to have been shown this glove from the first. Some light might have been cast on his murder."

"Conte Raversi determined to keep the glove and note secret, along with the other evidence of murder. I believe that, in addition to his fear of provoking a rebellion, he was reluctant to expose a possible scandal involving Marchese Lodovico, who had been his friend."

"What in the name of God gave him the right to make that decision?" Carlo fulminated. "Surely it was for Lodovico's family to judge whether it was more important to avenge his murder or protect his name?"

"It happens that I agree with you," said Grimani. "If I had been in charge of the initial investigation, I wouldn't have let scruples or squeamishness hold me back from pursuing the murderer with all the force at my command. But what's done is done. Do you recognize the glove?"

"No." Carlo shook his head regretfully.

"Do you know of any scandal in Marchese Lodovico's youth, involving a love affair?"

"No," said Carlo. "Nothing out of the common, at all events."

"It wouldn't have been a scandal in any case," Julian reflected. "This woman's story wasn't known—that was how whoever sent the glove was able to use it to blackmail Marchese Lodovico."

Grimani eyed him with cold satisfaction. "There's no need to speak vaguely of 'whoever sent the glove,' Signor Kestrel. We know who sent it."

"Who?" asked the marchesa quickly.

"Exactly the person Your Ladyship would expect—Orfeo."

Two men came into the room. One was a lean youth of about twenty, with curly dark hair, a bluish upper lip, and dark eyes looking out guardedly from under thick, straight brows. The other was a fragile-looking elderly man with sightless eyes. His circlet of white hair was transparently alight, as if he had been granted a halo a little early. He walked with slow, tremulous steps, leaning heavily on his companion's arm.

Julian pushed forward a chair for him. His attendant grunted by way of thanks and settled him in it, straightening his coat and plumping his pillows with a brusque energy that was not without tenderness. His task finished, he retired into a corner, glowering impartially at everybody.

"My dear Maestro," said the marchesa, "thank you for joining us. You know Conte Carlo, of course, but you haven't met Signor Kestrel, the famous English dandy, who as I told you is conducting an investigation for us."

"It's a great honour to meet you, Maestro," Julian said.

Donati inclined his head in Julian's direction. "You're most kind, Signor Kest-er-el. I'm sorry—your name is a little difficult."

"It's of no consequence, Maestro."

"I'm afraid you're unwell," Donati went on courteously. "I know a great deal about coughs and colds—singers live in deathly fear of them. Have you tried putting medicine into boiling water and breathing the steam? There's a device called an inhaler—Sebastiano could lend you one. He's my pupil and servant—my Eyes, I call him."

Sebastiano looked alarmed at being singled out for attention, and glowered more than ever.

"We're not here to discuss Signor Kestrel's health," said Grimani. "Maestro, I am Commissario Grimani. I've come to question you regarding Lodovico Malvezzi's murder."

Donati sighed. "I'll answer as best I can, Signor Commissario."

"You may go," said Grimani to Sebastiano.

"Commissario Grimani is dismissing your Eyes, Maestro," Julian told Donati.

"I don't need you to interpret for me, Signor Kestrel," Grimani snapped.

"It wasn't for you I was interpreting, Signor Commissario."

"Thank you, Signor Kestrel," said Donati hastily. "Sebastiano, go and practise your *messa di voce.* I'll hear you a little later."

"Yes, Maestro." Sebastiano went out.

"I don't see any need for you to remain, either, Signor Kestrel," said Grimani.

"Not the least in the world," Julian agreed. "I'm more than willing to speak with Maestro Donati privately after you've gone."

Grimani glared. They both knew very well that he would not want Donati questioned about the murder in his absence.

"It seems most efficient for you to stay," Grimani said at last. "But be good enough not to drag this enquiry into irrelevancies. All right, Maestro, let's begin."

Donati patiently recounted how Lodovico had persuaded him to come to his villa on the Lake of Como and train a young English tenor whose identity was shrouded in mystery. Grimani interrupted to ask, "Did Orfeo ever tell you where in England he came from?"

"No. He never spoke of England."

"How long had he been in Milan when you met him?"

"I don't know. Perhaps not very long when the marchese first brought him to sing for me, because he was still learning Milanese. He'd become quite fluent by the time we left for the Lake of Como a few weeks later."

"Where had he come from most recently?"

"I had the impression he'd been in France."

"What makes you think so?"

"I'm trying to remember." Donati furrowed his brow. "Ah, yes. I told him his accent sounded more French than English, and he said he'd learned French before he learned Italian. So I supposed he must have spent some time in France."

"You didn't report this after the murder," Grimani said accusingly.

"No one asked me about it, Signor Commissario," Donati pleaded. "And it never occurred to me that it was important. So many Englishmen visit both France and Italy."

"Are you quite certain he *was* English?" Grimani asked. The marchesa's eyes widened. She looked intently from Grimani to Donati.

"The marchese seemed sure he was," said Donati slowly. "I never thought twice about it, after that first conversation. Though

I must say, he had none of the arrogance of the English—I beg your pardon, Signor Kestrel."

"Guilty as charged, Maestro," said Julian, smiling.

Grimani gave him a withering look. "Maestro, do you think Orfeo deliberately avoided telling you about himself?"

"He was very reserved," Donati allowed. "I think he felt his dependence on the marchese. The English seem much more ashamed of poverty than we are. Most of the time we talked about music. He was very interested in vocal training, and talked with both the marchese and me about what sorts of exercises were most beneficial. He also liked to discuss ornamentation: how much is appropriate, and whether composers ought to write it themselves or leave it to singers to improvise—"

"What about politics?" Grimani cut in. "Did he ever talk about different forms of government, or about the rebellions in Naples and Piedmont?"

"Not that I can remember, Signor Commissario."

Grimani told Donati to describe the last day of Lodovico's life. Donati said Lodovico had come to the villa for Orfeo's morning lesson, and announced he would spend the night there and would not bring any servants. He had seemed nervous and short-tempered, and taunted Orfeo about his visit to the castle the previous night. Orfeo had admitted getting in through the gate with a key he had found at the villa, but denied having an assignation with Lucia.

"I don't doubt he was telling the truth," said Grimani. "We know now why he went to the castle: to deliver the package containing the glove and note."

"But Signor Commissario," said Julian, "the package was found outside the castle gate. Orfeo went *inside,* and in fact stole a key for the purpose. Why should he have done that?"

"It's quite simple, Signor Kestrel," said Grimani. "Orfeo planned to make an attempt on Marchese Lodovico's life that night, but Marchese Lodovico balked him. So he fell back on his alternative scheme of using the glove and note to lure the marchese to the belvedere the following night. He left the package outside the gate rather than inside so that the marchese wouldn't guess it had come from him."

"That's very plausible," Julian admitted. "Is this visit of Orfeo's to the castle the only evidence linking him to the package?"

"It's evidence enough. No one else is known to have gone to the castle that night. Continue with your story, Maestro."

Donati described the fight between Orfeo and Tonio, then recounted in a shaking voice how he had found the marchese's body in the belvedere the following day, and how Conte Raversi had made everyone promise to keep the murder secret. At Julian's request, Grimani grudgingly gave some particulars about the condition of the body.

"Was there any indication of how the murderer arrived or departed?" Julian asked.

"He had no need to arrive," said Grimani. "He was already at the villa. As to how he departed, the police found hoofprints and droppings outside the garden gate, suggesting that a horse had been tethered there. It wasn't the marchese's horse—that was stabled at the Nightingale. So Orfeo must have had a horse waiting for him to make his escape."

Carlo's brows drew together. "Couldn't someone else have come to the villa on horseback and killed my brother?"

"He couldn't have got into the garden," said Grimani. "The gate was kept locked at night."

"Was it locked on the morning after the murder?" asked Julian.

"No," Grimani owned. "Orfeo must have unlocked it so that he could get out of the garden after the murder."

Julian mused, "But isn't it more likely the marchese unlocked it the previous night?"

"Lodovico?" said the marchesa. "Why?"

"Because he had a rendezvous at the belvedere with whoever sent the note and glove. And since there's no reason to believe he suspected the rendezvous was with Orfeo, he would have assumed his visitor had to enter the garden from outside."

"I see!" said the marchesa. "How clever you are, Signor Kestrel! But perhaps Lodovico was expecting his visitor to arrive by boat."

"Can the belvedere be reached by boat?" asked Julian, interested.

"Not directly," she replied. "It's set on an embankment, some fifteen feet above the lake. But there are places where the embankment is crumbling. Someone could have landed a boat on the shingle and climbed up the loose stones."

"With all due respect to Your Ladyship," said Grimani, "this speculation is pointless. It doesn't matter who left the gate unlocked, or how Marchese Lodovico expected his visitor to arrive at the villa. The glove and note came from Orfeo, who was already there, and who used a horse to make his escape after he killed the marchese."

"But, Signor Commissario," Donati ventured, "couldn't it be a coincidence that Orfeo ran away when he did? The marchese had grievously insulted him after he caught him fighting with Tonio. Orfeo might have been unwilling to demand satisfaction, in light of the marchese's generosity to him and the difference in their ages, but at the same time he might have felt he couldn't endure any more."

"Would he have left without saying anything to you?" Grimani countered.

Donati's shoulders slumped. "I own, I find it hard to imagine. I was fond of him, and thought he returned my feelings. I can't help but think that, if there were nothing wrong about his departure, he would have said goodbye."

"Perhaps he didn't kill Lodovico," suggested Carlo, "but ran away because he feared to be accused of the murder."

"No," said Donati positively, "with respect, Signor Conte, that's impossible. Orfeo wouldn't have left me alone, knowing there might be murderers or bandits close by."

"This murder wasn't committed by a troop of brigands," said Grimani. "It was a silent, efficient crime. Maestro, did Orfeo ever receive or send messages while he was at the villa?"

"I don't know," said Donati. "I have very little idea what he did when he wasn't with me."

"He saw to that, no doubt," said Grimani.

"It isn't a crime for a man to guard his privacy," Carlo declared.

"On the contrary, Signor Conte," Grimani said sternly, "no one within the realm of His Imperial Majesty Francis the First of Austria is entitled to keep his name, activities, or opinions secret."

"But Signor Commissario," Donati remonstrated, "the secrecy surrounding Orfeo's identity was the marchese's idea."

Grimani was unmoved. "While Orfeo was under the protection of a man of Marchese Lodovico's rank and unquestioned loyalty, he needed no name of his own. Now his patron is dead, by his hand, and that protection is gone."

Julian understood now why Grimani's enmity toward Orfeo was so personal. The young man was an offence against Grimani's whole political philosophy. He had had the effrontery to come out of nowhere, veil his activities in mystery, and disappear without a trace. He had thumbed his nose at law and authority—and for that, as much as for the murder, Grimani wanted him punished.

"Why do the police have so little information about what Orfeo looked like?" Julian asked. "Didn't the gardener and his daughter describe him?"

"They were asked for a description," said Grimani, "but it's clear from the statements they gave that they were being deliberately obstructive."

"That's too harsh, Signor Commissario," Donati protested. "They were peasants. They couldn't read and weren't accustomed to describing things in words."

"If they'd been pressed harder, they would have found the words. Conte Raversi meant well, but his whole enquiry was grossly mishandled. That's what comes of entrusting criminal investigations to amateurs."

Julian understood that this was partly directed at him. "Have your professionals had any luck finding Lucia and Tonio?"

"Not yet," Grimani admitted. "But the investigation was officially given into my charge only a few days ago. I expect to make progress very soon, particularly with Lucia. She's a peasant—she won't have settled far from the hills and lakes she knows."

"Does she have any family?" Julian asked.

"Not that I've been able to discover," said Grimani.

"I never heard of any," Carlo contributed. "Her father was my gardener originally, when the villa was mine. He was a good man, God rest his soul. Lodovico did well to keep him on."

Grimani eyed him narrowly. "Have you seen or heard from Lucia since you sold the villa?"

"No," said Carlo.

"I'm ready to conclude this interrogation," Grimani announced. "If I need you to swear out a statement, Maestro, I'll send a clerk. Is there anything you wish to add?"

"Only that I can't believe Orfeo was a murderer. He might not have been candid, but he was fundamentally good. Surely an evil soul couldn't sing with such sweetness, ardour, and beauty. He might have lied in his words, but could he lie in his art? My heart always answers: No."

The marchesa lowered her eyes—but not before Julian saw, to his astonishment, the glitter of tears.

"When I asked if you had anything to add," said Grimani, "I meant anything useful. Good day to you all. Marchesa, I'll join you on Friday morning to depart for the lake."

The marchesa lifted her eyes—amused, serene, a little too bright. "I shall strive to endure your absence until then, dear Commissario."

Grimani bowed stiffly and went out.

"Well, Signor Kestrel," said the marchesa, "what do you think of our commissario?"

"I think he has a good mind, and would have a first-rate one if only he were willing to open it a little." Julian turned to Donati. "I hope we haven't tired you, Maestro."

"I am a little tired," Donati confessed. "It isn't the long conversation, but the subject. The more I think on the murder, the less I know what to believe, or even what to wish for. I want it to be solved, yet dread to know the solution."

"A little wine will restore you," said the marchesa.

Carlo rang for a footman. The marchesa told him to bring them some refreshment.

Julian brought his handkerchief to his nose and sneezed. "What's become of Conte Raversi?"

"He's here in Milan," said the marchesa, "crusading against the Carbonari, as always. He was very active in the arrests and trials a few years ago. The government think him a little mad, but useful."

"I should like to speak with him," said Julian.

"I'll try to arrange an interview before we go to the lake," she promised. "I think he'll see you if I ask it. He feels very guilty about having concealed Lodovico's murder from me. He's told me he never expected the secrecy to last so long. I believe that, but even so I find it hard to forgive him." She broke off, studying Julian's face. "You look pensive."

"I was thinking, Marchesa, that you seemed very moved when Maestro Donati spoke of Orfeo's voice."

"Why should I not have been moved?" she asked easily. "Did you think I was made of stone?"

"Of nothing so earthly, Marchesa." Yet he did not believe she was a woman to weep lightly—she was clearly ruled by her head rather than her heart. What was Orfeo to her, that he should be honoured with her tears?

Julian spent the evening indoors as a concession to his catarrh. Dipper gave him a report of all he had learned below stairs at Casa Malvezzi. He had quickly made friends with the Malvezzi servants, and found that they took a keen interest in their late master's murder. Some of them had been with him at his castle on the lake before he died, but none had got a look at Orfeo. The marchese had ordered them to keep away from the villa, and they dared not disobey him. Strange to say, they had been afraid of Lodovico, but they had liked him. He would brook no insubordination, but he was generous to those who served him well. His power could hurt them, but it protected them, too. Whoever wore his livery could do more or less as they liked in Milan; even the Austrian soldiers respected it. The servants obviously did not have the same regard for their new master. Julian was a little sorry for Rinaldo. How could he hope to fill Lodovico's shoes?

The following day Julian received a note from the marchesa, telling him that Conte Raversi was expecting him at four o'clock. He duly presented himself at Raversi's *palazz* in the Contrada di San Maurillo. It proved to be a smaller, more modest residence than Casa Malvezzi. Its outer walls were painted a dull yellow ochre, with long, doleful grey shutters. Inside, the house was ravaged by neglect: the paint peeling, the gilding chipped, the family portraits sinister with soot. The servant who ushered Julian into Raversi's private parlour was hard put to find a chair that retained all four legs and a smattering of upholstery.

Raversi himself might have stepped from a painting by El Greco. He was very pale, with long, gaunt hands and fevered dark eyes. His straight black hair fell about his face in heavy, untidy locks. He sat at a writing-table scored with scratches and strewn with official-looking papers. Above his head was a grisly, blood-daubed crucifix.

"It's easy now to talk of what might have been done to investigate the murder," he said. "No one seems to understand the position I was in—the danger we all faced. Lombardy was honeycombed with traitors eager to plunge us into anarchy and ruin. The ensuing arrests showed how widely the contagion had spread. Carbonari were found in all ranks of life: the nobility, the peasantry, even the clergy. I am sorry, with all my heart, that Orfeo escaped, but I cannot regret the measures I took to prevent his crime from serving as a clarion call to revolution. If people must blame someone, they may blame me. I know in my heart that I've done right. Sometimes a man has nothing else."

He lifted his eyes to the crucifix, with a trusting gaze that Julian found oddly moving. Raversi's enthusiasm for the recent persecutions was repellent, yet there was an ardour and sincerity about him that were worthy of a better cause.

"Do you believe Orfeo was a Carbonaro?" Julian asked.

"It's beyond question. What other reason could he have had for killing my poor friend? He stole nothing—gained no advantage from his crime. His concealed name, his clandestine movements, his choosing the time of the Piedmontese revolt to kill Lodovico—all mark him as a radical incendiary."

"But he was a foreigner."

"The Carbonari are everywhere, Signor Kestrel. They have lodges in Paris and London—followers in Spain, Greece,

Russia, and the German states. There's a miscreant named Buonarotti who lives abroad and recruits young men like Orfeo from all over Europe. He leads a sect called the Sublime Perfect Masters—impious wretches who plot to overthrow governments and abolish religion and private property."

"What other Carbonaro sects are there?"

Raversi's eyes shone with the eagerness of a man in love with his subject. "The first Carbonari came from Naples. Some of them were charcoal-burners, which explains their name, but many were the sort of bandits and cut-throats who infest that region. They originally banded together to drive Bonaparte out of Italy, but after they'd succeeded, they turned on their legitimate rulers and demanded republican reforms. Educated men, who ought to have known better, joined their ranks. Anybody may be one of them—your servant, your mistress, your friend.

"Naples is still a hotbed of Carbonari, but now sects have sprung up all over Italy. At the time of my poor friend's murder, our Milanese Carbonari were plotting uprisings to coincide with the Piedmontese revolt. Many of the ringleaders are now in prison, thank God and the Madonna, but there's a sect who blasphemously call themselves Angeli—though the police call them devils—whose conspiracy was never fully uncovered. It's to be feared that many of them are still at liberty."

Julian leaned back in his chair. Its timbers made a faint splintering sound, and he decided it would be the better part of valour to get up and walk about. "Signor Conte, if Orfeo killed Marchese Lodovico in order to foment a rebellion, wouldn't he have found some means to make the murder public? What does a political incendiary gain from an act of violence, if no one knows of it? The very motive that led you to conceal the murder would prompt the Carbonari to trumpet it to the skies."

"What are you suggesting?" Raversi's eyes narrowed. "That the murder wasn't political?"

"I'm suggesting that, if it was, the motive can't have been merely to spark a revolt or frighten the Austrians. No: the Carbonari must have believed Marchese Lodovico could do them some specific harm. And what could that harm be but exposure of their identities or plans?"

Raversi grew, if possible, paler. "How could Lodovico have had it in his power to do that?"

"If we knew that, we might be within an ace of solving his murder."

Raversi came slowly to his feet. "Young man, I wonder if you have any idea what you're meddling in—how dangerous these secret societies can be. Do you know they take oaths to kill in cold blood any traitors within their ranks, or enemies outside them? For your own sake, I urge you not to cross swords with them. Leave that to the police."

"I'm grateful for your warning, Signor Conte, but I should be breaking my faith with Marchesa Malvezzi if I ignored the forces that both you and Commissario Grimani believe are behind this crime."

"You would hazard your safety—perhaps your life—fighting an enemy you can't see?"

Julian regarded him curiously. "You fight the Carbonari, Signor Conte. Aren't you afraid of their vengeance?"

"I do my duty, Signor Kestrel. My conscience demands no less."

"My honour is equally importunate. I've pledged myself to solve this murder, and solve it I will."

Julian walked home by way of the Contrada Santa Margherita, past the imposing palace where the Milanese police had their headquarters, and where political prisoners were kept until convicted and sentenced. The church bells were sounding the half-hour after five when he entered Piazza San Fedele, where the Bella Venezia stood. As he approached the inn, he saw that there was a commotion in the portico. Waiters and porters were talking animatedly and waving their hands, while out in the piazza two muddy itinerant friars, a fruit-seller trundling a wheelbarrow, and a peasant with a basket of live roosters had gathered to see what the fuss was about. The roosters added greatly to the din, but over it Julian made out a voice he knew:

"Kestrel. K-E-S-T-R-E-L. He *is* here? Well, why didn't you say so? Slow down, can't you? I can't understand a word you're saying. He's out? When will he be back? *Quando*—er—*quando viene*—Here, what are you about? I haven't said you could take that! I don't know yet if I'm staying! Leave go, or I'll call a constable! Lord knows there are enough of 'em about!"

One of the waiters caught sight of Julian and cried out in relief. The group broke apart to reveal Dr. MacGregor, red-faced and dishevelled, playing tug of war with a burly manservant over his portmanteau.

"My dear fellow," said Julian blankly, "England is in the other direction."

"I know that!" MacGregor exploded. "Don't you think I've been reminding myself of it ever since I left Geneva?" He shook his head helplessly. "I just couldn't stop thinking about what Dipper said—that you'd got yourself over head and ears into something really dangerous. I felt responsible for you. If nothing else, I could never face Philippa again if anything happened to you, and I'd let you go alone."

Philippa Fontclair was the fearsomely precocious daughter of a country squire in MacGregor's neighbourhood. Julian and she were fast friends, and kept up a lively correspondence.

"Don't ask me what I expected to do for you," MacGregor finished. "I can't see that I'll be any earthly use. I've come all this way, and eaten more rice than any self-respecting Briton should have to in a lifetime, and for what? Can you say in all honesty that you're glad to see me?"

Julian would have liked to keep MacGregor out of any danger that might exist. Yet he answered from the heart, "My dear fellow, I've missed your common sense and stubborn scepticism ever since I embarked on this investigation, and now that you're here, I can't conceive of how I ever expected to succeed without you."

MacGregor stared. "Do you really mean that?" he asked gruffly.

"You shall see, when I inflict an account of all my adventures on you and demand to know your impressions. Have you dined?"

"No. I only arrived an hour ago, and enquired for you at the police office. They seem to know everything about everybody. So I came here, and now this rascal's trying to make off with my trunk."

"Perhaps you ought to let him," Julian suggested mildly. "You do need a place to stay tonight."

He said a few words in Milanese. The servants scattered. A porter bore away MacGregor's trunk, and several bowing waiters promised that a room would be ready for him in a twinkling. Julian saw him settled there, then went to his own room to dress for dinner. Afterward, he sent Dipper to see if he could be of any help to MacGregor. He soon had cause to regret this act of kindness: MacGregor marched into his private parlour and accosted him. "Dipper says you're ill. Why didn't you tell me at once?"

"It's nothing—the merest touch of catarrh. I'm nearly over it."

"I'll be the judge of that. Sit down and open your mouth."

"My dear fellow—"

"Do as I say."

Julian resignedly took his seat at the table and opened his mouth. MacGregor peered down his throat. "I don't see any inflammation," he said grudgingly. "But you'd better go to bed early tonight and wrap a piece of flannel around your throat."

"I'm afraid I'm obliged to go to the opera."

"Obliged, fiddlesticks!"

"I have to see Marchesa Malvezzi, to tell her you've arrived—present you to her, if you care to come with me. You see, tomorrow morning I leave for the Lake of Como with her and her brother-in-law—"

"Upon my soul! You certainly haven't wasted any time!"

"—and I want to give her an opportunity to invite you to go with us."

"Why should she? She doesn't know me from Adam."

"I shall tell her that you are my invaluable partner, and that without your bracing influence I should never get up till midafternoon, and should spend the rest of the day admiring my reflection in my boots."

"Hmph! It's probably no more than you do in London." MacGregor added curiously, "What is she like—the marchesa?"

To Julian's annoyance, he found himself looking off airily, exactly the way Dipper did when asked to talk about a girl he fancied. "She's beautiful, elegant, and charming. She has great confidence and courage. She's devilish clever, and would probably be an accomplished liar if the need arose."

MacGregor regarded him keenly. Julian restrained himself from fidgeting, and even leaned back in his chair with an appearance of ease.

"She hasn't married again?" said MacGregor.

"No. And as far as I know, she hasn't a lover."

"Well, you'd hardly expect to know about a thing like that!"

"Oh, love affairs are more or less open secrets in Milan, at least among people of the Malvezzis' rank. And gentlemen allow their wives equal licence, which is at least more fair than forcing them to condone their husbands' infidelity, while they themselves can take lovers only in secret, at the risk of a 'crim con' lawsuit and eternal disgrace."

"What you're saying is, the Milanese solve the problem of vice by having twice as much of it!"

"I can see we shan't see eye to eye about this. Why don't I tell you about the murder?"

They sat down to a dinner of veal shank, saffron rice with truffles ("Rice again!" grumbled MacGregor. "Don't these Milanese eat anything else?"), and asparagus in browned butter. There was also a relish made from wild rose bays, which the Milanese called *grattacuu*—"arse scratchers"—because of the thorns. The meal finished with cheese from nearby Gorgonzola and fruit with *panera,* the thick local cream. MacGregor complained that it was all too heavy and spicy, but Julian noticed that he ate a good deal all the same.

He summarized for MacGregor all he had learned about the Malvezzis. MacGregor was too well fed to pace about as he usually did when they discussed a murder, so he contented himself with sitting back in his chair and knitting his brows in fierce concentration. At length he said, "Orfeo still seems the most likely suspect. But I can see why you're troubled about the family. Rinaldo came into a title and a fortune when his father died, and freed himself from Lodovico's domination into the bargain. The marchesa inherited the villa—though it's hard to see her killing her husband just for that. And if she'd fallen in love with another man—well, from all you've told me, being cuckolded is no more than a flea-bite to husbands in this benighted country."

"Milanese men aren't lacking in pluck or passion in matters of the heart. They simply don't waste jealousy on women they aren't in love with, which is why they wink at infidelity in their wives, but cut up savage if their mistresses so much as glance at another man. If Lodovico Malvezzi happened to be in love with his wife, he wouldn't have tolerated her having a *cavalier servente.*"

"He certainly got on the high ropes when his daughter-in-law took up with one."

"Francesca left her husband outright, which is breaking the rules of the game. What's more, she threw herself away upon the most common of commoners. By all accounts, Valeriano's mother was a Venetian prostitute, and his father could have been anybody."

"You've said he was a singer. Is there any chance he might have known Orfeo?"

"I shall certainly ask him about it. But Orfeo was a complete unknown, while Valeriano is one of the most renowned singers of his generation. Before Lodovico Malvezzi drove him from the stage five or six years ago, he was the only male soprano besides Velluti who could still command major roles and major salaries."

"Male soprano?" MacGregor started, then shook his head sombrely. "I didn't realize he was one of those poor creatures."

"Those poor creatures, as you call them, have been the greatest singers in history."

"Do you mean to say that you—a humane man, I know, and a Christian, I hope—approve of mutilating the human body just to create a *voice*?"

"I don't say I approve. But the castrati deserve better than to be spoken of as cripples or victims. They're the undisputed masters of their art—bred up to singing from childhood, and possessed of an instrument unrivalled in power and range." He added, "If it's any comfort to you, even in Italy there's a revulsion of feeling against them. When Velluti retires, there won't be anyone to take his place."

"And a good thing, too," MacGregor declared. "Now, what about Carlo Malvezzi? He had nothing to gain from his brother's death, but every reason to hold a grudge against him. They were political enemies, and Lodovico's side had come uppermost. Lodovico was rich; Carlo was poor. To crown all, Lodovico had possession of the villa Carlo'd taken such pride in. Carlo was in Milan at the time of the murder, just a few hours' journey from the Lake of Como. Couldn't he have killed his brother in a fit of resentment?"

"I can't see him going to the trouble and risk of committing a murder out of pure spite. He's practical, for all his idealism. Throwing in his lot with the French when he did may have been altruistic, but it was also very astute. France's star was rising in Milan—and Carlo's rose with it."

Julian went on to recount his interview with Raversi. "I must admit," he finished ruefully, "I have little idea how to probe the possibility that a secret society killed Lodovico. Such a society may not exist anymore, and if it does, how are we to find out who its members are? The only avenue I can see to pursue is to consider how Lodovico might have become dangerous to a secret society. That means examining his close connexions to determine who among them might have betrayed information to him, either intentionally or inadvertently. But this is a line of enquiry I can only discuss with you or Dipper. Raversi is right in one respect: I'm fighting this battle blindfolded. You and Dipper are the only people I can be certain aren't Carbonari yourselves."

MacGregor pronounced himself in no mood to be dragged off to the opera, from which Julian deduced that his friend was worn out and wanted his bed. He arranged to meet MacGregor for breakfast early the next morning, preparatory to their departure for the lake. MacGregor felt Julian's forehead and pulse, and reluctantly owned he did not seem feverish. Julian made himself scarce before MacGregor could do violence to his evening clothes by wrapping a piece of flannel around his throat.

Since this was his last night in Milan, he was obliged to call at all the boxes where he had been made welcome, to take his *congé.* From one of these boxes, he had a good view of the marchesa's box across the way. The seat beside her was innocuously taken by her brother-in-law. Just behind her sat Gaston de la Marque, the Frenchman with the trick eyeglass. He was leaning very close to her, and even across the theatre Julian could read desire in his manner and his eyes.

He felt his own hackles rise. He tried to tell himself it was no concern of his whether there was anything in the nature of a love affair between them. Once before he had felt—if not love, some stirrings of tenderness—for a murder suspect, and the results had been disastrous. He would not, must not repeat the experiment.

Even so, there was one thing he could not resist. He extricated himself gracefully from the box where he had been conversing and made his way around to the marchesa's box. His entrance, of course, obliged the guest who had worked his way furthest to the front of the box to depart. De la Marque saw who had ousted him, and a smile spread across his face.

He and Julian bowed to each other with great civility. Then de la Marque took his leave of the marchesa, kissing her hands as lingeringly as courtesy allowed.

After de la Marque had gone, the other guests moved up one seat and resumed their gossip, flirtation, and occasional comments on the performance on stage. The rotation of guests propelled Julian forward, till at last he reached the seat behind the marchesa's.

Tonight she had forsaken her favourite white for a black satin gown with sleeves of transparent black tulle, caught at the wrists with bracelets. Julian had already observed that she liked bracelets. The one on her left wrist varied, but the one on her right was always the same. It consisted of strands of tiny seed pearls and a heavy gold clasp set with a large ruby.

She and Carlo greeted Julian warmly and congratulated him on his mending health. Julian told them of the unexpected arrival of his friend Dr. MacGregor, who had been of immeasurable help to him in solving two previous murders. The marchesa at once invited MacGregor to join their party at the villa. Julian put up the requisite polite resistance, then accepted.

"Maestro Donati is coming as well," said Carlo.

Julian frowned. "Do you think that's wise? He seems frail, and this murder has already put him through a considerable ordeal."

"Our friend the commissario insisted on it," said Carlo. "He said he wanted someone at the villa who was there at the time of the murder, so that he could ask him about any evidence he finds. That does seem sensible."

"Monsieur de la Marque is coming, too," said the marchesa calmly. "I've just invited him."

Carlo's brows shot up. *So it's like that between you, is it?* his eyes conveyed.

Julian felt torn. As an investigator, he was elated at the prospect of finding out more about the mysterious Frenchman. As a man, he would like to put a continent between de la Marque and the marchesa. The investigation must come first, of course. He wondered how often, in the days to come, he would have to remind himself of that.

Julian returned to the Bella Venezia at about one in the morning. Dipper was busy preparing for their departure on the morrow: inspecting Julian's linen for rents and smudges, brushing his coats, and polishing his silver-handled razor, comb, and nail scissors. No matter what hour Julian came home after a night out—and in London it might be any time from midnight to mid-morning—Dipper was always awake and at work. He slept in short naps, at odd moments, like a cat.

All the while he helped Julian undress and prepare for bed, he could talk of nothing but the Gerolamo puppet theatre, where he had gone tonight with some of the Malvezzi servants. "Them puppets dresses so flash, sir, it's like the Lord Mayor's parade! And they plays the drums and capers about and sings a rum chant, just as if they was alive! One of 'em was cutting jokes, and I didn't twig much of what he was saying, but just to see him wink and flash his ivories 'most made me fall off the bench with laughing."

Julian listened indulgently. At length Dipper paused, then said, "I was thinking, sir, as how you might like me to make friends with the marchesa's maid, Nina."

"She wouldn't happen to be uncommonly pretty?"

Dipper looked meditatively at the ceiling. "Now you come to mention it, sir, she's dimber enough."

"It's noble of you to offer to cultivate her on my behalf."

"She could be useful, sir. She's been with Her Ladyship for nigh to five years—since before Marchese Lodovico was hushed."

"Has she?" Julian's interest quickened. The maid was indeed a promising source of information about the mistress. Yet it repelled him to think of invading the marchesa's privacy by coaxing her maid to betray her secrets. And the very strength of his revulsion determined him to nip this partiality in the bud.

He said briskly, "I should like to know more about the marchesa's trip to Belgirate: how long she stayed, what she was doing, whether she had any visitors. If Nina was her maid at the time, she must surely have accompanied her. So by all means improve your acquaintance with her. I give you *carte blanche.*"

And Julian retired to bed, never dreaming that this permission would very nearly cost him his life.

Part Three

SEPTEMBER–OCTOBER 1825

With all its sinful doings, I must say,
That Italy's a pleasant place to me...

George Noel Gordon,
Lord Byron
Beppo

Next morning a cavalcade set out from Casa Malvezzi for the Lake of Como. At its head was the Malvezzis' grand barouche, its top let down to give the occupants a view of the countryside. The carriage was painted a brilliant black, with the Malvezzi crest blazoned on either door. The wheels were picked out in flame-red, and a cloth of the same colour, embroidered with the family crest in black and gold, was draped over the box. The horses were a pair of splendid bays, their heads held high, their harness spotless. Whatever economies a Milanese aristocrat might practise behind closed doors, his belongings meant for public display were always dazzling.

The marchesa rode in the barouche, a white silk parasol shading her face, an ermine-lined cloak resting lightly on her shoulders. With her were Carlo, Julian, MacGregor, and de la Marque. Since there were only four passenger seats, Julian and de la Marque took turns riding on the box with the coachman.

Behind the barouche came a smart yellow chariot bearing Maestro Donati, his "Eyes" Sebastiano Borda, and Lodovico's manservant Ernesto. Because the marchesa had no other carriage to place at Grimani's disposal—a fact she conveyed to him with mock solicitude—the commissario rode in a hired chaise with Paolo Zanetti, a police clerk he had brought with him. Zanetti was a short, square man of about thirty, with a face perpetually glistening with sweat, which he mopped with a limp white handkerchief the size of a small table-cloth. He obviously lived in abject terror of Grimani. Julian wondered why his name seemed familiar, then recalled the notation, *Translated by Paolo Zanetti, clerk,* on Grimani's dismissive letter a few days ago. Evidently Grimani did not speak English and had brought Zanetti to remedy that lack.

At the rear of the procession were two waggons drawn by mules, their necks draped with garlands of late-blooming flowers. These waggons carried luggage, together with any servants the marchesa had not sent on ahead to prepare the villa for her arrival. Among the servants were Dipper and the marchesa's maid, Nina Cassera. Dipper was devoting himself to Nina, and Julian readily understood his enthusiasm for the task. She was a slender, fairy-like girl, no more than two-and-twenty, with large brown eyes and hair of the deep, rich auburn common in Milan.

Julian noticed one servant who kept apart from the others. He was a robust man of about sixty, big-boned and sinewy, with narrowed dark eyes that gave nothing away. His skin was swarthy, his hair black with only a sprinkling of grey. He was not in livery, but wore a brown coat and waistcoat almost too fine for his rank, a sleek top-hat, and gold rings in his ears.

"Who is that?" Julian asked Dipper, when they were both walking about to stretch their legs while the procession was halted at the Porta Nuova, Milan's northern gate.

"That's Count Carlo's servant, sir—Guido Gennaro. I've only just met him today—he don't mix much with the other slaveys. They don't cotton to him, but that could be 'coz he's a foreigner. He comes from Naples."

Julian was amused to find that Dipper had picked up the local habit of considering Italians from other states as aliens and enemies. "How does Carlo come to have a servant from so far away?"

"I dunno, sir."

"Find out what you can about him. He's the servant Carlo claims to have brought with him to Milan, when he came to sell off his property at the time of Lodovico's murder. I should like to know what he remembers about their stay."

"I'll have a go, sir."

"But be careful. Neapolitans are a dangerous breed—hot-tempered and prone to settle their disputes with steel."

They rejoined the others. The procession left the city behind and set out across flat, fertile cropland, pleasantly green but wearying in its sameness. Then hills appeared in the distance: lofty grey ridges dotted with houses and draped in wisps of cloud. Gradually the grey slopes turned to green and were seen to be heavily wooded. Further off, drifting in and out of view as the clouds thickened or dispersed, were the solemn, snowcapped peaks of Monte Bisbino and Monte Generoso.

The Lake of Como ran from wild Tyrolean regions south to the Lombard plain. Halfway down its length it divided, pointing one long finger southeast and another southwest. At about two o'clock, the marchesa's party reached the fortified gates of the town of Como, at the tip of the southwestern prong. Austrian soldiers in uniforms of white or sky-blue and silver eyed the crested carriages with cautious approval. Custom-house officials requested the travellers' passports, and retired with beaming faces and generous bribes.

"Why is this town so closely guarded?" MacGregor asked Julian. "It's worse than Milan!"

"Smuggling," said Julian under his breath. "We're only a few miles from the Swiss border."

"And they need all these soldiers and customs men to stop it?"

"No," murmured Julian, "they need them to appear to stop it. To stop it in reality would require twice as large a force, all incorruptible, and with eyes in the backs of their heads."

Once through the gates, the marchesa's party found themselves in a confusion of narrow, filthy streets, overhung with crumbling brick upper stories that all but blocked out the sun. Houses, shops, and even churches were dilapidated and soot-stained. Half-naked urchins gaped at the parade of carriages; black-clad crones gloomily crossed themselves. MacGregor looked about him in disgust at the dirt, and dismay at the poverty. Then, all in a moment, the houses looming over them fell away. MacGregor gasped, and even Julian, who had known what he would see, caught his breath.

Como harbour lay in a bowl of wooded mountains, their lower slopes spread with white, pink, and yellow cottages, their upper reaches crowned with ancient shrines. Reflections of clouds danced on the deep-blue water. The pier teemed with slim, agile rowing boats, each with a canopy of three or four curved wooden strips and a piece of canvas wrapped around a pole at the top, ready to be pulled down as a shelter against the sun or rain. Some boatmen slumbered beneath these awnings, while others plied for trade along the shore. When the marchesa's party came in view, they shouted with delight, for the lakeside roads were poor, and the marchesa and her companions would have to proceed by water.

A fleet of boats was quickly engaged. The marchesa, as if determined to keep Julian and de la Marque in maddening equilibrium, invited them both to share her boat, while MacGregor went with Carlo, whose command of English and interest in science had quickly led to a rapport between them. Donati and Sebastiano accompanied them, and the others disposed of themselves as best they might.

The boatmen pushed off, standing in the bows of their boats and plying their long oars expertly. Como grew more beautiful the further they left it behind, its drab houses gleaming white against the dark green hills, its boats bobbing gaily, its church roofs catching the sun. Then the town shrank to a speck, and the marchesa's little flotilla proceeded jauntily up the lake.

This arm of the lake was a narrow, irregular sweep, alternately pierced by promontories or swelling into bays. Cliffs rose on either side, their bald, bleak summits draped in mist, their lower slopes mantled with oaks, chestnuts, and wild cherries. On some of the hillsides peasants had built small, fragile terrace farms planted with mulberries and vines. Villages hugged the shore, their ancient belfries rising over the trees. An occasional villa, white and elegant, nestled amid rosebushes or myrtle and orange groves. The marchesa pointed out Villa Garuo, where Queen Caroline, estranged wife of the present King of England, had lived with her Italian lover.

Some eight miles north of Como, a lofty crag jutted out from the western shore. On its summit, a grey castle perched, its walls bristling with stone teeth, doubled-pronged like the tuft of an arrow. "That is Castello Malvezzi," the marchesa said.

At the base of the crag was the villa, gleaming like a pearl against the dark cliffside. In front was a semicircular terrace, with a marble balustrade over the lake and a diminutive pier beneath. Several boats, gaily decorated with ribbons and flowers, were tied to slender poles.

The marchesa was not looking that way. Her enigmatic gaze was fixed on a nearer object, linked to the villa by an avenue of plane trees along the shore. It was a tiny octagonal building, painted white and blue, with Moorish windows, a blue dome, and a balcony over the water.

Julian did not need to ask what this building was. De la Marque likewise surveyed it in silence. The boatman crossed himself as he rowed past it and muttered a prayer for *"i poveri morti"*—the poor dead ones.

As the boat drew near the villa, servants' heads appeared at the grey-shuttered windows. Footmen streamed out of discreet doors beneath the imposing double stairway that led to the formal entrance. They ran across the terrace and down to the pier, where they stood waving handkerchiefs and waiting to help the marchesa ashore.

De la Marque turned to Julian, a gleam of amusement in his eyes. "Your heart must beat faster on seeing this place, Mr. Kestrel."

"Why should you think so?" Julian enquired.

"Because this is to be the scene of your triumph—the stage on which you'll conjure up Orfeo, when no one else has the slightest idea where in the wide world he's concealed himself."

"I can't promise to make him rise up from the floorboards," said Julian. "But the logical place to begin looking for someone who's gone missing is wherever he was last seen."

"Observe the English mind at work," said de la Marque to the marchesa. "It's like a well-kept lodging-house: whether amply or sparsely furnished, it's always orderly."

"You seem to doubt Signor Kestrel's ability to solve my husband's murder," the marchesa remarked. "Perhaps the two of you would like to wager on it?"

De la Marque bowed. "Marchesa, I must decline. My English friends have acquainted me with Signor Kestrel's prowess at solving crimes, and, far from doubting his abilities, I am firmly convinced that if he can't find Orfeo, no one ever will." De la Marque slanted a speculative gaze at Julian. "I will propose another wager, Mr. Kestrel. I'll stake three thousand francs that if you do find Orfeo, you'll regret it."

Julian's interest quickened. "Why?"

"*C'est évident.* Since Orfeo is almost certainly the murderer of Marchese Lodovico, he's likely to object strongly to being found, and we know that his objections can be of a rather violent nature. On the other hand, there's always the chance he may be innocent, in which case I should think it would trouble your English conscience to turn him over to the police. Do you suppose they'll consider anyone else as a suspect, once Orfeo falls into their hands?"

The boat bumped gently against the pier. Julian and de la Marque both moved to pay the boatman, but Julian was quicker. De la Marque revenged himself by alighting first and giving the marchesa his arm. She watched their manoeuvres serenely, a smile playing around her lips.

The other boats docked and discharged their passengers. MacGregor found Julian looking after de la Marque and the marchesa. "What do you make of that Frenchman?" MacGregor asked.

"He doesn't wish me to like him, and I'm obliging him in that regard. When a man tries so hard to be provoking, it would be ungracious not to be provoked."

"Why should he want to provoke you?"

"I think provoking me is only for his own amusement. His paramount goal is to warn me off." Which makes three people, thought Julian, who've tried to warn me off this investigation: de la Marque, Raversi, and, more subtly, Carlo.

Just then he heard Carlo's voice. "Fetch my trunk, Guido. I want to dress for dinner."

Guido was sitting on the edge of the marble pier, dicing with one of the boatmen. He must have heard Carlo's summons, but he did not look around.

"Guido," Carlo repeated, in the silky tone of one determined not to lose his temper.

Guido threw the dice once more before slewing his gaze around to Carlo. "Master?"

"Bring my trunk to my room. I'm going to dress."

Guido grudgingly heaved himself up and swung Carlo's portmanteau effortlessly onto his shoulders. He set his tall hat at a defiant angle and trudged away, his gold earrings swinging against his heavy jaw. Carlo lifted his eyes heavenward, as if asking for patience, and followed.

"That's a brazen-faced fellow!" MacGregor exclaimed. "Are servants allowed to be so saucy in this country?"

"Not generally. Perhaps Carlo didn't engage him for his virtues as a servant."

"For what, then?"

Julian shrugged. "Guido is from Naples, and as Raversi pointed out, Naples is a hotbed of Carbonari."

All the bedrooms at the villa were on the upper floor. The marchesa's foreign guests were favoured with rooms at the front, overlooking the lake. Julian's was in the southeast corner,

MacGregor's was next to his, and de la Marque's was on the other side of MacGregor's. Then came the main staircase, and finally the marchesa's little suite in the northeast corner. A broad corridor, its walls covered in red silk and hung with paintings and tapestries, ran between the front and back rooms. Grimani's room was in the southwest corner, opposite Julian's. Carlo's was next to his; then the row of rooms was broken by a balcony overlooking the garden behind the villa. An unobtrusive servants' staircase followed; then came Donati's room in the northwest corner, opposite the marchesa's. It did not escape Julian's notice that de la Marque was placed closer to the marchesa than he was himself, and that the only person even closer was blind and would not be able to see anything that might go on between them.

In other respects, the location of Julian's room was one of its charms. It had two balconies, one commanding a panorama of the lake, the other overlooking a charming orchard garden on the south terrace. The wallpaper was white, splashed with blue, green, and purple birds and flowers in the Chinese style. The bed was hung with blue damask curtains and crowned with gilt finials of mermaids.

Julian dressed for dinner, then went downstairs to the great square salon known as the Hall of Marbles. It had a grey and black mosaic floor and a replica of the Parthenon frieze running around the upper walls. Busts of Italian statesmen and poets stood in each corner; fragments of Roman columns were ranged along the walls. But the room's chief glories were two life-sized marble groups by Canova. One showed a grave and lovely Minerva subduing the Centaur with her wisdom; the other, in startling contrast, swooningly depicted Cupid embracing Psyche, both of them naked, their lips about to meet in a kiss.

Somewhat to Julian's chagrin, the marchesa caught him contemplating this work. His face grew hot, but he kept his manner cool. They discussed the sculpture's merits with a dispassion that Julian, for one, was far from feeling; then the marchesa offered to show him more of the house.

That was when the ghosts came out in force. Impossible to explore the villa without thinking of its former inhabitants. Julian could picture them all so clearly: Lucia, the bright, brisk peasant girl; sullen, skulking Tonio; Lodovico, arriving for Orfeo's lessons and filling the villa with his imperious presence. And of course there was Orfeo, absorbed in his music, his other passions known only to himself.

The marchesa explained that the ground floor of the villa was given over to kitchens and storerooms, the first floor to public rooms, the second floor to bedchambers, and the attic to servants' quarters. She and Julian began their circuit of the first floor in the library, which was lined with exquisitely bound books but conspicuously lacking in tables or chairs for reading them. Julian supposed it was only to be expected that, in a musical household like Lodovico's, literature would get rather short shrift.

They passed through a frescoed parlour to the billiard room, which was gaily if grandiosely painted with scenes of Greek and Roman sporting events. From there they crossed the Hall of Marbles to the elegant dining room, where servants were busily laying the cloth for dinner.

Next door was the drawing room, with cream marble walls and turquoise hangings and upholstery. Julian's interest was caught by a magnificent family tree hanging on the wall. The branches bore golden apples, each with a name and date of birth. An inscription above the tree read *VIVA CASA MALVEZZI ANNO 1742,* but some apples had been painted in later, including those bearing the names of Lodovico, Carlo, Rinaldo, and Rinaldo's children, Niccolò and Bianca.

"Conte Carlo's children aren't mentioned," Julian noticed.

"There wasn't room," said the marchesa coolly. "He has six, you know."

She walked on abruptly. Julian looked after her intently for a moment, then followed.

The music room was at the front of the house, looking out on the terrace and the lake. It was a dainty white and gold confection, decorated with motifs of lyres and laurel wreaths.

Glass-fronted cabinets displayed antique violins and wind instruments. At one end of the room was a harp, with a gilt music stand beside it. At the other was an English piano in an elegant marquetry case. The piano attracted Julian irresistibly.

"Should you like to try it?" the marchesa asked.

"If I may." He swept his coat-tails from under him and sat down, running his fingers experimentally over the keys. Their beautiful, rich tone swelled through the room. He launched into Weber's sparkling *Invitation to the Dance.*

The marchesa listened with dawning surprise and pleasure. When he had finished, she said, smiling, "I see I have a great deal to learn about you. That you should understand music, I would have expected of a man so civilised. But that you should prove a virtuoso in your own right, I wouldn't have guessed."

"Hardly that, Marchesa."

"Who is that playing?" asked a voice from the doorway.

Julian and the marchesa looked around. Maestro Donati stood leaning on Sebastiano's arm, his sightless eyes straining toward the source of the music.

Julian rose. "It's I, Maestro—Julian Kestrel."

Donati seemed surprised. "You have a sensitive touch, Signor Kestrel. It was a pleasure to hear you." He hesitated. "Forgive me, but I thought it was uncommon for men to play the piano in your country."

"It is," said Julian lightly. "I had an eccentric education." He moved away from the piano. "I should far rather hear you, Maestro. Would you be good enough to play—perhaps one of your own compositions?"

Donati furrowed his brow, as if some disturbing train of thought had been loosed in his mind. But he bowed politely, and signed to Sebastiano to lead him to the piano. He played an air from *The Return of Ulysses*, an opera he had written long ago. To Julian's mind, his restrained, effortless mastery knocked spots off his own more superficial skill.

The other guests began to appear, and the bell rang for dinner. The marchesa gave her arm to Donati, thus obviating any need to choose between Julian and de la Marque. The dinner combined French delicacies like *foie gras* and *béchamelle* chicken with veal *alla Milanese* and the ubiquitous saffron rice. After the meal, everyone retired from the table; Milanese ladies, unlike their English counterparts, did not leave the gentlemen to their port. Chairs had been set out on the terrace, both around the central lily pond and along the balustrade. Some of the company drank coffee or liqueurs there, while others strolled in the gardens. As twilight fell, lamps were lit on the terrace, their warm light contrasting with the cold, dusky blues of the lake and hills.

Julian looked over the balustrade, pondering the possibility that Lodovico's murderer had arrived by boat. If so, it seemed unlikely that he had landed at the villa pier. The villa was far too conspicuous at night: with even a few lamps lit, it glowed like a beacon in the blue-black stillness. No: the murderer would have left his boat on the shingle and climbed up the embankment into the gardens. The marchesa had said the embankment was worn away in places and might have afforded footholds to an intruder. Julian determined to see whether there were any such places near the belvedere, while there was still enough light to make investigation worthwhile.

He set off down the flagstoned path that led south from the terrace along the shore. To his right, the landscape garden stretched away, its greens and browns fast fading in the gathering dusk. To his left, the lake was partially screened from view by a row of magnificent plane trees. Julian passed between two of these trees and peered over the edge of the embankment. At its foot was a pebbly strip of shingle, broken by jagged rocks and clumps of bushes.

He walked along the edge of the embankment, his body bent at a precarious angle to examine the embankment wall. Sure enough, he found several spots where the wall was worn away, and one where entire stones had been dislodged. There was even a straggly row of bushes where a boat could be concealed.

Very well—it was possible the murderer had come or departed by boat. But was it likely? Even assuming the embankment wall had been sufficiently eroded four or five years ago, when Lodovico was killed, the idea of an approach by boat was pure conjecture. In contrast, very real hoofprints and droppings had been found outside the garden gate. Was it not far more probable that the murderer had used a horse?

Having walked this far, Julian decided to have a look at the belvedere. He followed the shore path to the little Moorish pavilion. Every other of its eight sides had an entrance with a set of blinds that could be let down for privacy. Three of these entrances fronted a small gravelled yard; the fourth led to a white-railed balcony overhanging the lake. Each of the intervening sides had a narrow, pointed window.

Julian went in through the nearest entrance. In the ebbing light, he made out pale grey walls and a floor tiled in black and white marble. White stucco designs in fanciful Moorish patterns surrounded the windows and doors. Two low marble benches were the only furnishings.

The place had nothing to say to him. It was charming, tranquil, a little absurd—a trifling toy of a Moorish palace on an Italian lake. The idea of hatred, betrayal, violence erupting here seemed ludicrous.

He went out onto the balcony. All around him was a slate-blue mystery of restless waters and towering hills. On the farther shore a few lights twinkled, one perhaps marking the villa where Francesca and Valeriano had stayed.

A bell chimed somewhere across the water. Another answered on Julian's side, and soon a lovely chaotic chorus resounded from shore to shore. Julian knew that peasants all around the lake would be laying aside their work or amusements to say their evening prayer. He prayed himself, asking for guidance. But did God listen to prayers wrung from people who never thought to address Him when they were not in need?

The bells died away, till only a single chime lingered on the air. "B-flat," said a meditative voice.

Julian turned. Gaston de la Marque was lounging on one of the marble benches inside the belvedere. "I trust I don't disturb you?" he said in his flawless English, always startling in a man so thoroughly French.

"On the contrary." Julian came in from the balcony and took a seat on the opposite bench. "I've been hoping for a chance to speak with you."

"How opportune. Perhaps you called to me in some mystic fashion, and I answered."

"And perhaps you followed me to see what I was about."

"Mundane," shrugged de la Marque, "but within the realm of possibility. What did you want to talk with me about?"

"I should like to ask where you were in March of 1821."

De la Marque's eyes widened with interest, curiosity—a touch of wariness. "I was in Piedmont—Turin, to be precise. I remember quite well, because a most tedious and inconvenient revolt took place there at about that time."

"How long were you there?"

"I believe I went there for Carnival, which would mean I arrived the previous December. I remained until the end of March or the beginning of April—I can't recall precisely."

"May I ask why, if you found the revolt so tedious and inconvenient, you remained in Turin throughout the time it was taking place?"

De la Marque's glance strayed off reminiscently. "I believe I had a particular reason for remaining, but I no longer remember who she was."

"Can you recall anything about her?"

"My friend, can you remember every woman you were pursuing four or five years ago?"

"If I had braved a rebellion in order to be near her, I probably should."

"Your orderly mind again! I stand abashed."

"Did you see Marchesa Malvezzi while you were in Turin?"

"Was she there? Then I must have seen her—La Beatrice is nothing if not conspicuous—but unluckily I hadn't the honour of a close acquaintance with her at that time."

Julian regarded him wryly. "Would it do any good to ask what game you're playing?"

"Not the least in the world," de la Marque said, smiling. "You never said yea or nay to my wager."

Julian thought back. "Three thousand francs that if I find Orfeo, I'll be sorry. That seems rather vague. How will you know for certain if I'm sorry or not?"

"Let that be my look-out. Is it a wager?"

"Done." Not having their betting books with them, they shook hands.

They walked back to the villa in a strangely companionable silence. Night was falling in earnest; the mountains on the farther shore looked black against the sky. Ahead, the villa terrace seemed an oasis of light, with figures gliding about as if in a magic lantern show.

When they reached the terrace, de la Marque immediately made for the marchesa. Julian dutifully sought out MacGregor, who was sitting by the balustrade, watching a night fisherman at his work. The fisherman leaned over the side of his boat, deftly harpooning fish as they came to the surface, dazzled by the light of the lantern hanging in the prow.

"We could try that some night if you like," said Julian. "It's something of a sport on the lake."

"I'll stick to angling," said MacGregor. "This pouncing with a harpoon looks like a good way to take a header into the lake. He's a rare hand at it, though."

A strain of singing came through the open windows of the music room. It was a basso cantante voice—a light, lyrical bass—with a piano accompaniment. The voice was youthful, imperfectly controlled, but full of promise:

"Che invenzione, che invenzione prelibata!
Bella, bella, bella, bella in verità!"

"I know that tune!" said MacGregor. "It's from one of those Figaro operas."

"*The Barber of Seville*," Julian confirmed. "It's one half the duet between the barber Figaro and the hero Count Almaviva."

Donati had grasped the gist of their conversation. "It's Sebastiano," he explained. "He uses that duet to exercise his voice."

"It's a pity we don't have a tenor," said Carlo.

"As far as we know," murmured de la Marque.

"What do you mean by that?" Grimani demanded.

"Why, my dear Commissario," de la Marque said suavely, "only that our friend Orfeo may be anywhere."

"Che invenzione, che invenzione prelibata!" sang Sebastiano.

"What does that mean?" MacGregor whispered to Julian.

"'What an idea, what a marvellous idea.'"

The night air grew colder, and the company began drifting indoors. Julian contrived to give his arm to the marchesa.

"I noticed you out walking with Monsieur de la Marque," she observed.

"Yes, we were becoming better acquainted. Tell me, did you see him in Turin in the winter of 1821—in particular during the period leading up to the revolt?"

"Is that where he says he was?" she mused. "No, I don't remember seeing him. But we didn't know each other very well in those days."

"Yes, so he told me."

She studied his face. "You didn't believe him?"

"Marchesa," he said lightly, "naturally I see rivals everywhere."

She smiled, and waved away some gnats with her fan. "If Monsieur de la Marque was in Turin in March of 1821, he can't have been here killing my husband."

"Did you suspect him?"

"Did you?"

They held each other's gazes, saying nothing.

"Even if he was in Piedmont," Julian said at last, "he could have crossed the border into Lombardy long enough to commit the murder."

"Anyone could have crossed the border."

"Yes, Marchesa," he said steadily.

"Of course, it would be easier from Belgirate than from Turin. One would merely have to cross Lake Maggiore and land at some secluded spot."

"But de la Marque wasn't in Belgirate. Was he?"

She paused on the stairs leading up to the villa doors, looking at him with laughing eyes, the lamps shedding gold on her hair. "Not that I noticed."

Is she daring me to suspect her? he thought. Does she merely want to know if I do? Or is she trying to divert suspicion from someone else?

He was tired of these little taunting shafts—first from de la Marque and now from her. They both enjoyed tweaking the lion's tail, but when the marchesa did it, it hurt.

Above her head, a moth flew suicidally into one of the lamps. Julian took heed of the warning, and led her indoors.

CHAPTER 15

On his first morning at the villa, Julian was served a breakfast of eggs, ham, sausages, toasted bread, and polentina, a cornmeal porridge. He much preferred the Continental habit of eating lightly in the mornings, but the marchesa took such delight in offering him and MacGregor an English breakfast that he felt compelled to do it justice. MacGregor, for his part, declared that it was the best breakfast they had had since they left England.

At mid-morning, the marchesa received a ceremonial call from Benedetto Ruga, the podestà ("part mayor and part magistrate," Julian explained to MacGregor). He was in his fifties, with several chins and a broad expanse of waistcoat spanned by a gold watch-chain. Julian gathered that he owned a large silk mill and boasted the grandest house in the village. His fulsome speech of welcome to the marchesa was cut off by the arrival of Don Cristoforo, the parish priest, a tall, gaunt, silver-haired man with a gait like a dignified crow. He talked with the marchesa at some length about the festival of Santa Pelagia, Solaggio's patron saint, which was to take place in a week. Julian did not hear much of this conversation, but judged from Don Cristoforo's increasingly unctuous manner that Marchesa Malvezzi had promised a generous donation.

The next caller was Friedrich Von Krauss, commander of the Austrian garrison barracked near Solaggio. Julian found him polite, urbane, and far more respectful toward the marchesa and Carlo than Grimani was. "Grimani is an Italian," explained Carlo in English, a little apart from the others. "Those whose power is unquestioned can afford to make concessions. Grimani must be more German than the Austrians he serves."

He broke off. Grimani's English-speaking shadow, Zanetti, had sidled up behind them. Carlo shifted smoothly into a conversation in Milanese about boating.

After Von Krauss had presented his compliments to the marchesa and her guests, Grimani bore him and Ruga away to discuss deployment of the local gendarmes and soldiers to search for clues and question the lake dwellers. Julian was not invited to this conference and did not much care. He trusted Grimani to handle the gathering of physical evidence with the dogged persistence and thoroughness for which he was known. As for questioning the local people, Julian would rather pursue that on his own, free from any alliance with the hated army and police.

Left to his own devices, Julian proposed to MacGregor that they walk to Solaggio. "How will we know our way about?" MacGregor objected.

"I gather we've only to follow the lakeside path to the end of the garden and go through the gate. Solaggio will be directly before us."

They set off down the shore path, stopping briefly at the belvedere so that MacGregor could see it. Beyond the belvedere, there were no plane trees to cut off their view of the lake. They watched fishermen, two or three to a boat, expertly casting nets or wielding fishing lines heavy with hooks and sinkers. It was warm work, for the sun was out, after a fashion, shining whitely through a veil of mist. To the right of the path, the garden offered enticing views of green hillocks and shaded pools, winding paths and mysterious rough-hewn stairs.

The path terminated in an elegant wrought-iron gate with a letter *M* in the centre and serpents entwined around swords along the top. The gate was set into a stone wall some twelve feet high, running along the south end of the garden and swelling into a round bulwark at the brink of the embankment. Julian and MacGregor passed through the gate and continued along the shore till they reached Solaggio.

The village had a tiny harbour all but enclosed by breakwaters of masonry and rubble. A row of whitewashed houses, all different heights, ran along the shore. The more substantial houses had balconies overlooking the water, with flowering shrubs spilling from wood-frame balustrades.

Julian and MacGregor walked around the harbour, drawing curious stares from the peasants, their children, and even their dogs. At the far end was a commodious house composed of blocks of assorted heights, haphazardly stuck together and criss-crossed by lines of fluttering linen. Each block had its own red-tiled roof and a scattering of green-shuttered windows. The front door opened on a small, vine-covered terrace at right angles to the lake. A sign outside the door bore a crude painting of a bird.

A girl of about eighteen came out on the terrace. When she saw the strangers, her black eyes lit up, and she sauntered to the balustrade. She wore a white blouse with the sleeves pushed up to her elbows, a bright blue skirt, and a white cap from which several black ringlets had been artfully allowed to escape. Her scarlet bodice was tightly laced beneath mouth-watering breasts.

Julian doffed his hat and addressed her in the clipped Milanese of the lake dwellers. "Excuse me, popola, is this the Nightingale Inn?"

"What else should it be, signor?" She leaned toward him over the balustrade. "You'll be one of Her Ladyship's guests, I suppose?"

"I am Julian Kestrel, and this is my friend, Dr. MacGregor."

"Rosa!" A middle-aged woman erupted from the inn. Her snapping black eyes and handsome figure were very like the girl's, but her face was all sharp angles, her features haggard, as if wrecked by emotional storms. Her iron-grey hair was scraped up into a knot and pierced by a wicked silver hairpin. "What do you mean by idling with gentlemen—*foreign* gentlemen," she added, after a keener look at Julian and MacGregor—"when there's work to be done indoors? Holy Madonna, but you're a useless cow! In with you at once!"

Rosa tossed her head. "This gentleman asked me a question, Mamma. What was I to do, cut him dead?"

"There's no need to get so close to a gentleman to answer a question! Foreign gentlemen!" she exclaimed, flinging up her hands. "As if the soldiers weren't bad enough!"

"I beg your pardon, Signora Frascani," Julian interposed soothingly. "I didn't mean to distract Popola Rosa from her work. I only wished to know if this was the inn I'd heard praised so often."

"This is the Nightingale, signor," nodded the woman, a little mollified. "Come in for a glass of wine any time you like. But remember, wine and food are all that's sold here!" She took Rosa by a hank of her black curls and drove her indoors.

Julian looked after them wryly. "No man should ever offer for a girl without meeting her mother. Would you marry Rosa, after seeing what she may become in ten or twenty years?"

"I wouldn't marry a girl that forward, whatever her mother was like," declared MacGregor.

They turned inland and ascended a steep, crooked flight of stairs to the piazza, the local equivalent of an English village green. It was roughly rectangular, with a crude stone fountain at the centre, around which women in brightly coloured shawls stood chatting and filling pitchers. At one end was an ancient church of grey-brown stone, with a pointed roof and a tall, square belfry whose slit windows showed it must once have been a defensive tower. Opposite the church was a handsome two-story house that was probably the podestà's.

Julian and MacGregor were making a circuit of the piazza when a great sound shook the very earth beneath their feet. The bells in the church tower were pealing out their mid-day hymn. The women at the fountain left off gaping at the strangers to cross themselves and pray. MacGregor regarded them askance. "Tomorrow is Sunday," he said abruptly. "I suppose there's no chance of finding a church of our own hereabouts?"

"I shouldn't think so."

"I thought as much. I'll have to stay home and read my Bible, which is more than these papists are allowed to do."

"Should you mind very much if I went to mass with the Malvezzis?"

"If you want to have a priest mutter over you in Latin, that's between you and your conscience!"

"I don't wish to be muttered over in any language. But I should like to hear the music. Country musicians here are often very good."

"If you thought less about music and more about your immortal soul, you'd be the better for it."

"I'm never so aware of my immortal soul as when I hear music."

Their conversation had attracted the attention of a dapper little man with large spectacles and Macassar-oiled hair. He came forward, bowing, and said in heavily accented English, "Sirs, I hope I do not intrude. Permit me the honour to introduce myself. I am Dr. Curioni."

Julian introduced himself and MacGregor in Milanese, but Curioni begged they would speak English. He had been to London, he informed them proudly, and subscribed to several British medical journals. When he learned that MacGregor was a surgeon, he was overjoyed, and at once invited him and Julian to his house for some refreshment. Julian was delighted. It was the first time in their Continental journey that he had been included in an invitation for MacGregor's sake, rather than the other way around.

Curioni ushered them into his tidy house on the piazza and offered them wine and panettone, a porous yellow cake with raisins and bits of candied orange. He and MacGregor were soon deep in conversation about contra-stimulation and other Milanese medical theories. Julian would have liked to broach the subject of the murder, but he did not want to remind MacGregor that Curioni was the doctor who had perjured himself about the cause of Lodovico's death. MacGregor would not have understood the pressures brought to bear on Curioni, or the general despair that induced Italians to submit to occasional outrageous demands by the government, in the hope that the rest of the time they might at least be left alone.

The two doctors' conversation was so completely over Julian's head that he finally took his leave, confident that MacGregor would get on famously without him. As he retraced his steps through the village and along the shore, he noticed a number of boats left carelessly on the shingle or outside the doors of cottages. Were the boats chained up after dark? He rather doubted it—crime was so infrequent on the lake. That meant Lodovico's murderer could easily have borrowed a boat and approached the belvedere by water.

Julian stopped at the gate to the villa garden. Here a horse's hoofprints and droppings had been found on the morning after the murder. Grimani believed that Orfeo had killed Lodovico, then used the horse to make his escape. But where would the horse have come from? The villa had no stables, and no horse hereabouts had gone missing. Whether Grimani realized it or not, his theory presupposed that Orfeo had had an accomplice.

The sun was burning ever more brightly, banishing the mist to the mountaintops, its last place of retreat. Julian's close-fitting wool tailcoat began to feel uncomfortably sticky. He took off his hat and let the breeze from the lake run through his hair. The cool gardens beckoned invitingly. He decided to take Carlo up on his offer to show him around them. That would give him a prime opportunity to talk with Carlo about other matters.

"Of course it's patterned on an English landscape garden," said Carlo.

"Yes, one sees that at once." Julian gazed around him. Just as in a Capability Brown garden, the villa grounds presented a series of views as finely arranged as painted landscapes. Every bend in a path yielded fresh surprises: a Chinese footbridge arching over a pond full of goldfish, a breathtaking glimpse of the lake from the top of a rock-hewn stair, a secluded clearing presided over by a lion-headed Egyptian goddess. But the narrow compass of these grounds, compared with those of an English country house, caused the paths to wind more tightly and tortuously, giving the garden a labyrinthine quality wholly Italian.

Carlo added, smiling, "If we'd taken this walk before I acquired the villa, it would have been much more perilous. It used to be full of little traps set by Achille Delborgo, who owned the villa some two centuries ago. There were several spots where the pressure of a foot would cause concealed jets to spray water on the person's legs. And there's a wonderfully frightening *trompe-l'oeil* effect in the grottos, underneath the caves at the north end of the garden."

"I should like to see that," said Julian.

Carlo bowed. "Allow me to take you there."

They made their way north as directly as the twisting paths would allow. Presently Julian said, "Your servant seems rather out of the common."

Was it Julian's imagination, or did Carlo stiffen momentarily? "Yes, I suppose he is. I'm so used to him, I don't notice."

"How did you come to engage him?"

"It was the merest chance. I told you how I went to Milan shortly before Lodovico died, in order to sell some property on the sly. I needed a servant to take with me, but I'd greatly reduced my domestic staff, and I was reluctant to deprive my wife and children of any of the servants we had left. At about that time, Guido came seeking work, as itinerant peasants are apt to do. He agreed to accompany me to Milan in exchange for little more than his keep. We rubbed along well together, so I took him back with me to Parma."

"His circumstances seem to have improved since then," observed Julian, thinking of Guido's fine clothes and gold earrings.

"As have mine, thank God and the Madonna," said Carlo.

"How did he come to be so far from Naples?"

"I don't know. He's never said much about his past, and I'm not of a prying disposition."

Unlike some of us, Julian inferred wryly. "I wondered if perhaps he found it awkward to return to Naples in March of 1821."

"People have had their suspicions about that. But he's never given me any cause to think he had anything to do with the revolution there."

"I thought, since it was suppressed at about that time—"

"Quite so. But I understood from Guido that he'd been absent from Naples for many years."

"Did he have any references?"

"No. But that didn't concern me, because I originally thought our association would be very brief. And by the time I decided to keep him on, I was satisfied with him and didn't think to ask him for a character."

"He seems rather insubordinate."

"I daresay he does, to an outsider. But that's just his way." Carlo looked straight ahead, his face set. "In important matters, he's never failed me."

Julian acknowledged to himself that some successful master-servant relationships had incongruous beginnings. He himself had taken as his valet a young urchin he had hauled before a magistrate for stealing his watch. But could it be merely a coincidence that Carlo—a notorious liberal and opponent of the Austrians—had engaged a Neapolitan servant to accompany him to Milan, just when the revolt in Naples was inspiring uprisings in Piedmont and Lombardy? Had Carlo and Guido served as links between the Neapolitan Carbonari and Lombard conspirators?

Julian and Carlo had reached the lake shore north of the villa. The promontory loomed up before them, with Castello

Malvezzi baring its double-pronged teeth at the summit. A few minutes' walk brought them to the foot of the crag. There was no path to the caves, but a trail of trampled grass and exposed earth showed the way.

The cave mouth was narrow and pointed, as if some giant had slit the base of the crag with a knife. Scarlet creeper spilling across the entrance added to the impression of an open wound. Carlo led Julian inside. "This cave is known as the Salon, because it's the largest—the others are little better than rabbit-holes."

Julian turned slowly about, letting his eyes adjust to the dimness. The Salon was some thirty feet wide and almost perfectly round, with high walls of pockmarked stone. In the centre of the packed earth floor was a trapdoor in the form of a padlocked iron grating. There was also a little marble pool, its rectangular basin hollowed out of the ground and its back, some three feet high, set into the cave wall. A nozzle protruded from the mouth of a grotesque face, but no water emerged, and the basin contained nothing but grit and dead leaves.

"There used to be a pipe running down to the lake to feed this pool," said Carlo. "That was in the time of Achille Delborgo, who as I told you was fond of water tricks. It was he who built the grottos beneath this cave. Before his time, wine had been stored in the cave itself, where it was vulnerable to thieves. The lake was a lawless place in those days—swarming with pirates and mercenary soldiers. They would hide their boats on the other side of the crag and climb over the rocks at its base to the cave mouth. So Achille had grottos dug under the cave and used them as wine cellars. They still serve that purpose, though nowadays no one bothers to keep the trapdoor locked when the owner is in residence."

He drew up the trapdoor, which moaned faintly on its rusty hinges. A long ladder led down into near-darkness. Carlo waved his hand for Julian to precede him.

What most struck Julian as he backed down the ladder was the silence. The breeze, the birdsong, the mournful plashing of the lake, were all stilled. The smells of the living world—grass, flowers, fish—were left behind as well. He might have been descending to the realm of the dead, like Aeneas, or Orpheus.

He felt firm ground under his feet and stepped away from the ladder. All at once he seemed to be under water; even the faint light was bluish green. He was in an oval room about fifteen feet long, its floor, walls, and low, vaulted ceiling covered with mosaics of under-sea life. It was their vivid hues that gave the light filtering down from the cave its uncanny colour.

Carlo joined him. "You can see that Achille built far more than a wine cellar! There really are wine racks, though—you can just make them out along the walls."

"Yes, I remember Orfeo and Tonio broke a wine bottle when they fought here."

"I'd forgotten about that." Carlo smiled indulgently. "I expect they came down here for a tipple on the sly, and got into a row while they were in their cups. Now then: if you'll permit me, I'll do the honours of the place. We ought to have a lantern, to get the full effect. But we can always return another time."

He led Julian to one end of the room, where the wall gave way to a dark, low-ceilinged passage. "There's another grotto here, but without a lantern you'll hardly be able to see it at all. It hasn't any source of daylight from above. But as it's much like this room, you aren't missing a great deal. Now I'll show you Achille Delborgo's joke."

They turned about and crossed to the opposite end of the grotto. Here was another passage, barely high enough for a man to stand upright. Carlo waved Julian inside.

Julian had taken no more than a few steps when a dark figure sprang up before him. He halted, then cautiously extended his walking-stick. It tapped against glass. "A mirror."

"Yes," chuckled Carlo. "Achille used to bring guests down here and show them the two grotto rooms, then send them into this passage, telling them there was a third grotto. But in reality the passage is blocked off, with a mirror at the end, so that anyone entering seems to see someone coming out at him.

At night, by torchlight, and in a more credulous age, it must have been quite frightening."

Julian examined the mirror. It was full-length, hanging on pegs driven into a wall of hard, seasoned wood.

"The grottos weren't much used for entertaining after Achille's death," Carlo went on. "Sinister legends grew up around them: it's said that some erring Delborgo wife was imprisoned here and left to starve, and boatmen claim they can still hear her screams at night when they round the promontory. The local peasants give the place a wide berth, and servants who come to fetch wine cross themselves and say a prayer before entering."

The two men retraced their steps to the principal grotto room and the ladder to the upper world. Carlo stood back to let Julian ascend. But Julian was gazing thoughtfully around him. "Signor Conte, would you be good enough to go up and wait for me outside the cave? I shan't keep you more than a minute or two."

"But why?"

"I should like to try an experiment."

"As you wish."

Carlo climbed the ladder and disappeared through the narrow opening in the grotto ceiling. For a time his body blocked off the light from the trapdoor above, throwing the grotto into chilling darkness. Then the light returned. Julian waited another half-minute, then called out as loudly as he could, "Signor Conte! Signor Conte!"

His cry reverberated against the walls and the low, vaulted ceiling, like a live thing trying to escape. He waited a few heart-beats, then ascended the ladder and emerged from the cave. His hand went to his eyes. The sunshine was dizzying, unreal, as if he had spent a lifetime underground.

Carlo looked at him enquiringly.

"Did you hear me call out?" asked Julian.

"No."

"You heard nothing at all?"

"I didn't even know you'd called out till you told me just now." Carlo searched his face. "What was this in aid of?"

"Musical knowledge," said Julian lightly. "The march of science. A possible future career designing opera houses."

Self-indulgence, chided a voice in his head. You will get yourself into trouble, Julian Kestrel.

As he was dressing for dinner late that afternoon, Julian told Dipper about his visit to the grottos and his conversation with Carlo. "It whetted my appetite to learn more about Guido."

"I've been trying to pump him, sir. But he's old for me to be making a pal of—he must be sixty if he's a day. And he's a close file—keeps himself to himself, except to play at dice and cards."

"Then take up gaming. And let him win, to a modest sum. I'll be your banker."

"Yes, sir." Dipper took up a clothes-brush and walked around his master, brushing his coat. "I did want to tell you, sir: Nina and me, we was piking around the garden, and we had a confab about Her Ladyship's trip to Belgirate. It took a long time—"

"I can well imagine," said Julian, who knew a little about Dipper's strolls with maidservants.

"On account of the lingo, sir," Dipper clarified patiently. "She don't patter no English, and I ain't such a dab at Milanese as to twig all she says, first go. Anyhow, she was with Her Ladyship in Turin in '21 when the rebels kicked up a combustion. Her Ladyship lit out for Milan with Nina and two menservants. They travelled out of twig, in a plain rattler and prads."

It did make sense for the marchesa to have left Turin incognito, Julian thought. Her usual retinue of liveried servants and carriage blazoned with the Malvezzi crest might have attracted unwelcome attention from the rebels. But her anonymity would also have made it difficult for anyone to find her, or to reconstruct her movements afterward.

"They pushed off at lightmans, sir," Dipper went on, "and took the high pad to Novara. But at mid-day Her Ladyship said she'd heard there was rebels on the road, and they'd have to change course in order to tip 'em the double. Nina hadn't heard anything about any rebels, but she didn't like to ask questions. So they drove like smoke, and reached Belgirate that same night."

"Why did they go all the way to Belgirate?"

"Nina didn't know, sir."

"How long were they there?"

"All the next day and night, sir. Then a party of slaveys sent by Marchese Rinaldo smoked 'em out, and Marchese Rinaldo came that night, and next morning they all piked back to Milan."

"The night Rinaldo and the marchesa were in Belgirate: was that the night of the murder?"

"No, sir, the murder was the night before."

"Which would have been the marchesa's second night in Belgirate," Julian calculated. "I assume Nina can vouch for her whereabouts?"

"That's just what she can't do, sir. She came over queer the first night they arrived, and Her Ladyship had her bled. She slept most of the next day and night. And she don't know nix-my-doll about what Her Ladyship was doing, meantime."

"The devil! And of course the inn servants won't remember after all this time. The marchesa could have retired to her room, saying she didn't want to be disturbed, then travelled here, committed the murder, and been back in Belgirate in fifteen hours, while the servants thought she was merely resting after her long journey."

Dipper left off brushing the back of Julian's coat and came around to look at him encouragingly. "She'd have had to plan all that, wouldn't she, sir?"

"Probably."

"Well, sir, she couldn't have counted on her maid being took ill and not knowing what she was about."

"No," said Julian, with cold composure, "not unless she was responsible."

Dipper's eyes got very round. "You mean she might've hocused her, sir?"

"It's possible. Nina's illness was remarkably convenient, if the marchesa was up to some devilry." He relented. "Of course there's a good deal to be said in the marchesa's favour. To begin with, she would have been taking an extraordinary risk. She had no alibi for the murder, and no way of knowing that the authorities would hobble their investigation by keeping it a secret, or that they would fasten so firmly on Orfeo as the murderer. Then, too, it's hard to imagine a woman so refined journeying alone at night across a countryside infested with smugglers and soldiers."

He leaned thoughtfully against the mantelpiece. "If I were Commissario Grimani, do you know what I would say? I would say: it's most unlikely the marchesa killed her husband herself. If she had any hand in his death, it must have been as an accomplice to the real murderer—Orfeo. When Orfeo fled the villa after the murder, his first concern would be to escape from Austrian Italy. The Swiss border at Chiasso is close by, but very well guarded. So perhaps he crossed Lake Maggiore into Piedmont, where the marchesa was waiting for him with horses, provisions—whatever he might need."

He smiled quizzically. "It's not a bad theory. The marchesa would make a first-rate accomplice: clever, adroit, quick-witted, able to keep a cool head in a crisis. But if she was an accomplice—whose was she? Rinaldo is the only person we know for certain joined her in Belgirate. Can it be that she deliberately made herself scarce so that he could wander about the countryside on the pretext of searching for her? If he were caught at the villa, he could have pretended he had come to report that the marchesa was missing. —Where are my gloves?"

Dipper presented them. Julian drew them on, pursuing his train of thought. "Then there's de la Marque. He admits he was in Turin at the same time as the marchesa, though there's nothing to indicate he followed her to Belgirate." Julian looked up from doing up a glove button. "How long was the marchesa in Turin?"

"About a month, sir, Nina said."

"Why was she there?"

"I dunno, sir."

Julian pondered. There were three significant facts about Turin in the first months of 1821: the marchesa had gone there, de la Marque had gone there, and the rebellion had occurred. The more he thought about it, the more certain he felt that at least two of these events were linked. Could the marchesa or de la Marque have had some connection with the revolt, on either the government's side or the rebels'? Or had they merely gone to Turin to be well out of the way of the marchesa's autocratic, perhaps jealous husband? Julian hoped that politics and not love had sent them to Turin. But there was no denying that, especially in Italy, it could be both.

CHAPTER 16

Next morning the villa party disembarked at the pier in Solaggio and strolled up to the church. The marchesa walked arm-in-arm with Carlo, Nina following with a cushion of scarlet velvet and cloth-of-gold for her mistress to kneel on at mass.

The congregation filing in at the church door was large—perhaps swelled with people from outlying neighbourhoods, come to see the marchesa and her guests. Everyone made way as the Malvezzi party swept into the church. De la Marque dipped his fingers in the font and held them out to the marchesa, smiling into her eyes as she touched her fingers to his to receive the holy water. This pretty ceremony annoyed Julian exceedingly. If de la Marque was anything more than a nominal Catholic, he would be much surprised. Yet he was not enough of a hand at self-deception to believe his indignation was religious.

The cold and gloom of the church contrasted starkly with the sunshine and gaiety outside. The frail tapers and dimly burning lamps did no more than add a gold fringe to the darkness. Don Cristoforo took his place before the high altar, droning the time-honoured Latin words amid clouds of incense and the meek, muttered responses of his flock. Julian excited great superstitious dread by being the only person there who did not take Communion. As he had hoped, the music was very fine. No one seemed scandalized to hear airs from Rossini's operas mingled with the liturgical strains.

After mass, the villa party made their way back to the harbour. As they approached the pier, Julian heard a little cry behind him. He turned. Nina was standing stock still, gazing toward the pier with stricken eyes. He followed her gaze. Dipper was sitting on one of the stone breakwaters, his feet dangling over the lake. Beside him, talking and laughing, her face close to his, was Rosa, the black-eyed temptress from the Nightingale.

Dipper caught sight of Nina. He sped to her side, telling her in his mixture of broken Milanese and eloquent gestures that he had come to escort her back from church. At first she shrank from him, but after a good deal of coaxing she consented to take his arm. Rosa looked after them with hands on hips and narrowed, glinting eyes. Julian perceived that war had been declared.

Life at the villa soon settled into a pattern. During the day the party dispersed. The marchesa went boating, walked in the garden, called at neighbouring villas, or visited beauty spots. Frequently Carlo escorted her, sometimes Julian or de la Marque.

Carlo spent a great deal of time on the lake. He was a first-rate boatman, understanding the lake's many moods as well as any of the local peasants. Yet Julian wondered if he went rowing so often in part to escape from the villa. Though he gave no sign of grudging it to Beatrice, it must surely bring him painful memories.

Grimani's time was taken up with supervising the local gendarmes, who were methodically combing the villa and gardens and the surrounding area for clues. He was frequently absent from the villa, but the constraint he created was never wholly dispelled, because he or his shadow Zanetti had a way of turning up unexpectedly.

Donati's pupil, Sebastiano, talked very little, scowled a great deal, and practised his singing every day. His *Che invenzione, che invenzione* soon became a collective joke, with people rolling their eyes in tolerant exasperation whenever they heard it.

Julian continued his explorations in the neighbourhood. He talked with a number of people about the murder, including Ruga and Curioni. He ascended the crag and circled the grim, grey walls of Castello Malvezzi, though in Rinaldo's absence he could not go inside. Sometimes he went up into the hills, rambling through forests bright with autumn berries or along rocky gorges cut by sparkling streams. Climbing higher, he watched eagles wheeling or caught dazzling views of the Lombard plain and the snow-dappled peaks of the Alps.

At first he worried that he was neglecting MacGregor, but when he looked for him to invite him on these expeditions, he often could not find him. MacGregor would have gone out fishing with Carlo, or to visit a patient with Curioni, or to watch the fishermen at work and listen to the songs of their wives mending fishing nets.

"You've discovered *dolce far niente*," Julian told him one day, finding him seated on the terrace of the Nightingale, with the inevitable cup of bad tea.

"Dolce far—what?"

"It's an Italian saying—'Sweet to do nothing.'"

"I'm not doing nothing!" MacGregor bridled. "I'm learning how they make wine here." He pointed to a spot on the shore, where two naked little boys were cavorting in a vat of grapes and splashing each other with the juice.

"I beg your pardon," said Julian, eyes dancing. "It must have been all my fancy that you were asleep when I came upon you just now."

"Hmph!—well, I might have nodded off for a minute or two." MacGregor rallied. "Not much else to do, now that your wild scheme of trying to solve a murder that's none of your business has pitched us into the Land of the Lotus-Eaters."

It dawned on Julian that being effectively stranded in Italy had set MacGregor free. As long as he had had it in his power to go back to England and his patients, he had fretted after them. But now that he was pledged to remain at the villa till the murder was solved or the investigation abandoned, leisure was forced on him. Italy had done the rest.

On Julian's fourth day at the lake, he was out on one of his rambles, following the twisting path of a mountain stream, when he saw a man's hindquarters protruding from under a holly bush. He asked in English, "Have you lost something?"

The man scrambled out from under the bush. "No, not exactly. I was trying to catch a lizard, but they run confoundedly fast." He got to his feet, vigorously brushing off the knees of his trousers. "How did you know I was English?"

"Not many Italians wear English twill, and those who do don't hazard it crawling about under bushes."

"I see." The man grinned. "Very scientific. I approve."

He was about Julian's age, big-boned and lanky, with wiry brown hair and a countenance that looked as if it had been put together at random with rejected features from other faces. The effect was surprisingly pleasant, though it might have been the young man's cheerful brown eyes and wide grin that made it so.

He retrieved his hat from the depths of the bush and started to put it on. "Oh, dash it!" He took it off and ran his fingers through his hair. "Holly prickles!" he pronounced, as if it were a curse. He gave the hat a good shake and cautiously put it on again. "That's better! How do you do, sir? I'm Hugo Fletcher."

He thrust out his hand, and Julian shook it, "Your servant, Mr. Fletcher. I am Julian Kestrel."

"No—are you really?"

Julian smiled. "So my passport says, and in Italy one should never be at odds with one's *documenti*."

"Are you staying hereabouts?"

"Yes, at Villa Malvezzi."

"This is the most extraordinary piece of luck. Should you mind if I used you as a diversion?"

"What do you mean?"

"I'm tutor to the Honourable Beverley St. Carr. He's on the Grand Tour, and his parents sent me with him in the fond delusion that I could keep him out of trouble. He got into some scrapes in Milan, so I brought him here, and already he's bored to distraction. But when he finds out you're here, he'll be in high feather—he has horrifying pretensions to be a dandy, when he remembers. But you mustn't on any account let him meet you straightaway. Angling for an acquaintance could keep him harmlessly occupied for weeks."

"You don't seem overfond of your work," Julian observed.

"I don't know if you've ever had charge of a rich young man with little sense and less discipline, let loose in a country where the wine runs too fast, and the women not fast enough. Perhaps you've tried to carry a swarm of bees about in your pocket—it's much the same thing." Fletcher grinned ruefully. "I talk too much. It's just that it's been so long since I had a civilised conversation."

"Are you a tutor by profession?"

"I'm a naturalist. I used to work with a German naturalist in Berlin, helping him with a book he was writing about arachnids—spiders, you know. But I had to return to England when my father died. He was Lord St. Carr's steward, and the St. Carrs have done everything for me—sent me to university and helped me to get on in the world. When they asked me to take their son abroad, I couldn't refuse."

"Hugo!" a young male voice shouted. "Hugo, where are you?"

"Over here, Beverley!" called Fletcher resignedly.

The Honourable Beverley St. Carr erupted around a bend in the stream, hat in hand, his light-brown hair in a tangle. He was in his early twenties, all coltish legs and wide blue eyes. His coat was a parody of the latest fashion, with sleeves absurdly padded at the shoulders and half covering the hands. Coat, hat, and trousers were spattered with water and mud.

"Good Lord!" said Fletcher. "What have you done now?"

"I haven't done anything! I was walking by the stream, and some girls came along with baskets of linen to wash, and I went behind some bushes—so as not to be in their way, you understand—but they saw me and set up the deuce of a hue and cry."

"That's odd," said Fletcher.

"Not really," Julian murmured. "The women here do their washing with their skirts kilted up above their knees."

"Oh, Beverley." Fletcher shook his head reproachfully.

"Well, I didn't ask them to show me their legs, did I?" St. Carr retorted in an injured tone. "If they go about like that in public, they can't expect a fellow to close his eyes."

"They didn't know they were in public," said Fletcher. "No wonder they cut up rough when they found you skulking there."

"I wasn't skulking! I was only—well, it doesn't signify what I was doing. Hugo, they threw stones at me! They ran after me and splashed me with water and shouted at me, and I don't know what they were saying, but it sounded like the most frightful abuse. And then my hat fell off, and I trod on it, and they just stood there with hands on hips and laughed at me." He glared at Fletcher. "This would never have happened in England!"

"In England, you'd have had better manners."

"No, I wouldn't! I mean—I don't think I did anything ill-mannered. I was only taking a stroll." He kicked a pebble disconsolately. "What else is there to do in this poky place? We might as well be in Hampshire!"

Julian glanced around at the stream threading its way through wooded cliffs and dropping in a crystal cascade to the lake. "Hampshire must have attractions I've missed."

"This is all very well if you like scenery," said St. Carr. "When I came to the Continent, I thought I was going to *do* things."

"You *have* done things," said Fletcher. "That's just the problem. Should you like to be introduced to this gentleman, or should you rather go on talking at him as if he were a lackey?"

For the first time, St. Carr looked a little ashamed of himself. "I beg your pardon, sir," he said to Julian. "I didn't mean to be rude. It's just that I was a little rattled, on account of being set upon like that."

"Shall we begin over?" Julian suggested. "Your servant, sir. Julian Kestrel."

He held out his hand, but St. Carr only gaped at him. "Oh, I say! How—how simply—Hugo, why didn't you tell me who this gentleman was?"

"I wanted to," said Fletcher, "but *somebody* would go on talking."

St. Carr looked in dismay at his ruined clothes. "I'm not usually all of a muck like this, Mr. Kestrel. Those women—"

"I quite understand, Mr. St. Carr. Any gentleman may meet with a mishap."

"That *is* good of you!" St. Carr brightened. "You ought to see me when I'm got up properly. I cut quite a figure."

"I can imagine," said Julian, who could all too well.

St. Carr cast a triumphant look at his tutor. Then he peered more closely at Fletcher's trousers. "You're all of a muck yourself, Hugo! What have you been about?"

"I was trying to catch a lizard."

St. Carr rolled his eyes. "You're not taking that up again? Hang it, Hugo, you've been at Oxford! Thanks to my father, you're very nearly a gentleman. I should think you could find something better to do than cutting up lizards and collecting leaves." He appealed to Julian. "You've no idea how ghoulish his dissection is, Mr. Kestrel. At home after shoots, he used to take a bird or rabbit to his room and cut it open and study it. I caught him at it once—bent over the corpse of his dismembered victim, and up to his elbows in blood!"

"You've been reading Monk Lewis again," sighed Fletcher. "Tonight you'll be jumping out of your skin whenever a floorboard creaks, and getting up every hour to renew the priming of your pistols."

Julian thought these two had been spending far too much time together. "Should you care for a little society? I should be delighted to procure you an introduction to Marchesa Malvezzi."

St. Carr's eyes lit up. He started to speak, but Fletcher cut him off. "That's very good of you, Mr. Kestrel, but we don't want to intrude on a private party."

"I don't doubt the marchesa will be delighted to meet you." He cocked an eyebrow at Fletcher. "Can you sing?"

Fletcher looked blank for a moment. Then he laughed. "Not without creating a public nuisance. Why? Are you getting up a concert?"

"No," said Julian, "actually, I'm investigating a murder."

St. Carr's jaw dropped. "A murder? Oh, but of course, you've solved several murders, haven't you? I read all about it in *Bell's Life in London.* Who's been killed? How was he killed? When did it happen?"

"It's Marchese Malvezzi's murder, I suppose," said Fletcher slowly. "We heard a little about it in Milan. It was years ago, wasn't it?"

"Four and a half years," said Julian. "But it's only recently come to light."

"Four and a half years?" said St. Carr, disappointed. "Then the killer will have made himself scarce long since."

"Not necessarily, Mr. St. Carr. Sometimes the safest hiding place is in plain sight."

"Do you mean—somewhere close by?" St. Carr shot a thrilled, uneasy glance around him.

"Mr. Fletcher has already searched the holly," Julian advised.

"A murderer in the neighbourhood!" Fletcher shook his head in comical dismay. "And to think I brought Beverley here to keep him out of trouble!"

Julian told the marchesa about Fletcher and St. Carr, and she promptly sent them an invitation for coffee tomorrow evening. She remarked that, at the rate things were progressing, the English would soon outnumber the Italians at the villa. But, touching on the subject that evening, she seemed pensive. She and Julian had the music room to themselves, a balmy night having tempted the others to remain outdoors.

"Don't you think it curious that two young Englishmen should turn up almost on our doorstep?" she asked.

"Not necessarily. Don't a good many foreigners visit the Lake of Como?"

She sighed. "I suppose it would be too much to expect Orfeo to walk into our waiting arms."

"I don't think anyone expects him to do that, except perhaps de la Marque."

"That's odd, isn't it?" she mused. "Why do you think he's so confident Orfeo will be found?"

Julian shrugged. "Monsieur de la Marque's conversation is

three parts mockery to one part mystification. One can't infer anything of what he thinks from what he says."

"You don't like him," she remarked.

"I might like him more, Marchesa, if you liked him less."

She smiled. "But I only invited him for your sake, because you said you wanted to improve your acquaintance with him." She touched his arm lightly. "Come, will you play something for me?"

She went to the piano and took a sheaf of music from a rack underneath it. "Here." She drew out Beethoven's *Appassionata* sonata. "Lodovico admired this piece, though as a rule he didn't like German music. If you'd care to play it, I'll turn the pages for you."

He sat down at the piano. She stood beside him, bending close from time to time to turn a page. This disrupted his concentration but greatly increased the ardour of his playing. When he finished, the marchesa clapped her hands. *"Bravissimo!"*

Julian bowed. She reached out to remove the sonata from the music stand—then bent to look at it more closely. "How strange. Look."

She pointed to the bottom of the page, where the ruled lines of the staff extended a little way beyond the final notes. The same pair of eighth notes had been scribbled there three times with a blue pen: *F* and *B*.

"That's Lodovico's writing," she said.

"Are you certain?"

"Yes. I often saw him take down snatches of new pieces."

Julian frowned at the notes. At length he asked, "Did Ernesto tell you he thought Marchese Lodovico was composing a piece of music before he died?"

"Yes. I remember I was a little surprised that it was never found. But in all the shock of Lodovico's death, I didn't give it much thought."

"He also said Marchese Lodovico had taken to jotting down musical notes on any paper that came to hand. These could be some of those jottings." He glanced at the rack of music under the piano. "Was all this Lodovico's?"

"Yes. Do you mean that we might find more jottings?"

"We ought to look," he said.

They sat side by side on the piano bench, each leafing through a pile of music. At last Julian said, "I've found something."

The marchesa leaned toward him to look, her soft dark hair brushing his cheek. *"C—F-sharp,"* she read. "The same two notes, three—no, four places on the page, wherever there's space left in the staff. It's definitely Lodovico's writing. What is the piece?"

"In vain I call for sweet forgetfulness of my sorrows, from Rossini's *Mohammed II.*" He turned to the title page. "First performed in December 1820. So Marchese Lodovico must have jotted down these notes between December of 1820 and his death in March of 1821."

"Exactly the period when he knew Orfeo," the marchesa said quietly.

They looked through the rest of the music, but found no more jottings. "Why should he have written the same two notes over and over on one page?" the marchesa wondered.

"Perhaps he was struggling with a difficult passage in his composition, and those notes were part of it."

She smiled reminiscently. "He did have a habit of absently writing down things that were on his mind. I once found out the name of his latest mistress, because he'd scribbled it on a bit of wrapping paper from Ricordi's."

"Did you have a row?"

"Heavens, I never quarrelled with Lodovico about his mistresses. He was very vigorous—he would naturally have them. I twitted him about them sometimes. He took it in good part."

She unfurled her fan and waved it lightly back and forth. "Talking of names, I like yours better in Italian: Giuliano. I should like to call you that sometimes, when we're alone."

"I beg you won't do it too often—not more than once or twice of an evening."

"Why is that?"

"Because of the effect it has on me. People will think I've broken into the wine cellar."

She laughed. "Tell me something, Signor Kestrel—"

"Giuliano?" he suggested.

"For a man so wary of being intoxicated," she teased, "you seem very eager to uncork the bottle. Very well, Giuliano—solve me this riddle. You flirt like a Frenchman, reason like a German, and understand music like an Italian. How is it that in spite of all that, you're so thoroughly English?"

"National character is hard to eradicate. I lived on the Continent for some years and acquired a veneer, as oak tables dress themselves up as tulip-wood or tortoiseshell. But the underlying material remains the same."

"You remind me more of my mahogany night-table. It's exactly the same colour as your hair. And it has beautiful legs."

Julian felt himself blush like a schoolboy.

She asked, "What is Beatrice in English?"

"Spelled the same, but pronounced differently." He said it for her. It sounded clipped and harsh, compared with the Italian *Bay-ah-TREE-chay.*

"I prefer the Italian."

He looked into her great, dark, sparkling eyes. "So do I."

There was a short, sharp clatter. Her bracelet had come unfastened and dropped on the floor. It was the one she always wore on her right wrist, made up of strings of seed pearls attached to a large oval gold clasp set with a ruby. Julian bent to retrieve it for her, and saw for the first time what was on the inner side of the clasp. It was a miniature portrait of a young man with dark eyes and a black moustache. He wore a green uniform with red facings and gold epaulettes, and a brass helmet with a leopard-skin turban and a black crest. Julian had seen that uniform in paintings of battles—seen it, too, patched and ill-fitting, on veterans begging in the Paris streets. The portrait that Lodovico Malvezzi's wife kept hidden against her wrist was of an officer in Napoleon's elite company of lancers.

Julian looked up and found her regarding him with a

faint, inscrutable smile. She was not a whit disconcerted. He wished he could say the same for himself. "Who is he?"

"He is Major de Goncourt, my first husband."

"I didn't know you'd been married before."

"It's never spoken of now. He was one of Napoleon's officers. He came on a mission to Milan and fell in love with me, and my father took that opportunity to make a French alliance. Napoleon had held Milan for so long that even patricians like my father were becoming resigned to his rule. Of course Lodovico, who was a close friend of my father's, violently opposed the marriage."

"For political or personal reasons?"

"Oh, only for political reasons in those days. I was the merest child to him. Even if he had been in love with me, Isotta, his wife, was still alive, and he would never have been so dishonourable as to seduce me before I was married. No, it was simply that he hated the French and all they stood for. But my father was determined on the match, and so on my eighteenth birthday I became Madame de Goncourt."

Julian looked again at the major. He was very handsome, or at least the painter had made him so. He hardly appeared old enough to have commanded a regiment, but of course many young men had advanced rapidly in the Grande Armée. "You loved him," he said.

"How romantic you are. I was fond of him. And he loved me, though there was someone else he loved more."

"Who was that?"

"His emperor. Philippe wasn't one of those aristocrats who embraced Napoleon out of necessity while secretly despising him. He worshipped Napoleon. He asked nothing more than to be allowed to die for him, and he had his wish. He was killed at Waterloo."

"I'm sorry." After a pause Julian asked, "How did you come to marry Lodovico?"

"After Philippe died I returned to Milan, and found my father frantically trying to ingratiate himself with the Austrians.

My French marriage was a terrible embarrassment to him. At first he hid me away—even tried to persuade me to take the veil. Then he saw how the Austrian officers flocked around me, and began to push me forward. I saw that he was disposed to force an Austrian husband on me as he'd once forced a French one. I liked Philippe, but I wasn't sure I would like the next foreign alliance so well. So I determined that this time I would choose for myself.

"I had no lack of admirers, but none of them spoke of marriage. I was poor, you see. Philippe had given all he had to the Emperor's cause, and my father would do nothing for me unless I married as he wished. But now that I'd been a married woman, I could take a lover if I liked. Since my return from France, Lodovico had made it unmistakably clear that he no longer saw me as a child. He wanted me; I liked him and needed a protector. It was very simple. Some months later, Isotta died, and he made me his wife. It was generous of him. There was no reason why my being his mistress should have obliged him to marry me."

Julian was moved by her story—all the more by the matter-of-fact way she told it. He sensed a profound loneliness in her—the solitary vigil of the cynic watching over her vulnerable heart, lest anyone surprise it into trust or tenderness. But had she always been so wary? Or had she learned from bitter experience not to open herself to love?

He asked, "Why do you still wear de Goncourt's portrait on your wrist?"

"Isn't it better than wearing it against my heart?" Seeing him so in earnest, she went on more gently, "Philippe gave me the bracelet soon after we were married. He was often away on campaign, and he said he wanted me to have his portrait always by me, so that I wouldn't forget him while he was gone. I think he would want me to go on wearing it, now that he's gone so much longer." She held out her right hand, palm upward. "Will you put it on for me?"

He complied. As he was doing up the clasp, MacGregor came in. He stopped on the threshold in some confusion, seeing Julian holding the marchesa's hand.

The marchesa rose, unruffled. "Thank you, Signor Kestrel. I think the clasp will hold now. Good evening, Signor Dottor. I'll leave Signor Kestrel to you, shall I? I've been too long away from my other guests."

She glided out. MacGregor gazed after her, a little nonplussed, then looked tartly at Julian. "Was that some new form of interrogation?"

"That was a courtesy to a lady, whose bracelet had fallen off." Julian sat down at the piano and began playing the *Appassionata* again. "I'd just been interrogating her."

"You had, had you?" said MacGregor sceptically. "What have you found out?"

"I've found out she had a husband before Lodovico Malvezzi. His name was Philippe de Goncourt, and he was a loyal officer of Bonaparte. She spoke of him with great detachment, but I wonder if she cared more for him than she admits."

"Is that important to the investigation?"

"It is if she feels any sympathy for the cause in which he died. In England, we think of Bonaparte as a despot and conqueror, but here he symbolizes liberation and the unifying of Italy. If the marchesa loved de Goncourt and blamed Bonaparte's enemies for his death, she might have been tempted to throw in her lot with the Carbonari."

"But she married Lodovico Malvezzi, who hated the Carbonari and the French."

"Thus placing herself above suspicion, and gaining an entrée to the highest government circles, where she could pick up information useful to the secret societies."

"Do you think she was in league with Orfeo?" MacGregor asked eagerly. "That trip she made to Belgirate—it might have been in order to help him escape!"

"I'm more inclined to link that with de la Marque, who was also in Piedmont at the time."

"You think there was something hole-and-corner between them?"

"In the way of a love affair, or a murder?" Julian asked.

"Well, the one might lead to the other."

"Not in Italy. Why should it? An *amica* is expected to have a husband—he gives her countenance. De la Marque would have had no reason to kill Lodovico unless he wanted to marry the marchesa." Julian left off playing to consider this. "That's actually a likely ambition for de la Marque, who strikes me as something of an adventurer. The marchesa is beautiful and of high birth, and Lodovico's death left her well provided for. The trouble is—he didn't marry her. Is it possible he offered, but she refused?"

Neither of them knew the answer. Julian went back to playing the piano. "What piece is that?" MacGregor asked.

"Plaisirs d'amour."

"Pleasures of love, eh? I might have known it would be some frippery thing."

The words ran through Julian's mind. *The pleasures of love last only a moment; the pains of love last all your life.* He shut up the piano and went over to the window.

MacGregor looked after him with misgiving. "This flirtation between you and the marchesa—"

"—is nothing to be concerned about. I have a tight rein on my feelings. I must. Because if I didn't, that woman could do anything she liked with me."

CHAPTER 18

Julian had solved the problem of being served large English breakfasts at the villa by eating a little less of them each day, until by the fourth morning, the kitchen was sending him a typical Italian breakfast of coffee and rolls. Dipper brought it to his room with his shaving-water at eight o'clock. Julian, who was not yet out of bed, eyed Dipper's broad grin disapprovingly. "You know that I object to high spirits at this hour. If you don't immediately put on a face suitable for a funeral, I shall draw the bed-curtains and sleep until noon."

"Yes, sir." Dipper looked so grave that Julian could not help laughing, and resigned himself to getting up.

As Dipper was helping him into his dressing-gown, he said, "I suppose I have Nina to thank for this unseemly elation of yours?"

"No, sir—Guido."

Julian's brows went up. "I've never known your affections to range quite so widely as that."

"I mean, sir," said Dipper patiently, "I've smoked out something about him for you. You know I've been trying to suck his brains, but he ain't been come-at-able."

Julian nodded. Even losing to Guido at dice and cards had failed to loosen his tongue.

"So I've been touting what he keeps about him," Dipper went on. "He's got a gold watch and some rum booze, 'most as good as his master drinks. In his pocketbook there's a roll of banknotes as thick as your fist, a couple of wafers, a pencil, and some papers with writing on 'em."

Julian stared, then asked in a dangerously soft voice, "How do you know what Guido keeps in his pocketbook?"

Dipper's gaze strayed off. "I might've eased him of it, sir, just to twig what was in it, then left it for him to find, so he'd think it fell out of his pocket."

"Hell and damnation! Didn't I warn you to go gingerly to work with Guido?"

"But, sir—"

"Do you realize what would have happened if he'd caught you out? A Neapolitan attacked by a thief wouldn't trouble a magistrate to deal with him—he would simply draw his dagger and stab him out of hand."

"It ain't as if I was going to be caught, sir," said Dipper, a little hurt.

"I can't afford to take that chance. I haven't time to hunt up a new manservant because the one I brought with me had daylight let into him unexpectedly. So you will oblige me by not trying such a trick again. Do you understand?"

"Yes, sir."

Julian's face relaxed. "Still, as long as you've hazarded life and limb to find out what was in Guido's pocketbook, we may as well make what we can of the information."

He went to the washstand and splashed his face with water, then scrubbed it vigorously with a towel. Emerging from behind it, he said, "Let's begin with the cache of banknotes. Guido might have won it at dice or cards, though with such a run of luck as that, his fellow players would do well to look up his sleeves. Then again, Carlo may be paying him uncommonly generous wages, in which case we have to wonder what extra duties he's performing to earn them. A third possibility is that he's working on the sly for someone else."

"The Carbonari, do you mean, sir?"

"Possibly. But I should think the government of one or other of the Italian states would pay him better. Carlo is a noted liberal and Bonapartist. Perhaps the Austrians planted Guido on him to keep them apprised of his activities. But it's hard to believe that Carlo would be taken in by such a ruse. He must be able to recognize a spy as readily as you would a Bow Street Runner."

He draped the towel around his neck, over his bottle-green silk dressing-gown. Opening his shaving box, he took out his silver-handled razor, touching the blade lightly to be sure it was sharp enough. He always shaved directly he got up, because he felt the world had him at a disadvantage if it caught him with a night's coating of stubble on his face. He worked some soap into a lather and applied it to his face with his shaving brush. Then he carefully scraped the lather from his cheeks with the razor, speaking only between passes of the long, wicked blade.

"Guido's writing implements are actually more interesting than his money. Not many Italians of his class can write, particularly in Naples. Literacy would be a great boon to a Carbonaro, because he wouldn't have to entrust his communications to the village scribes who write letters for peasants here. Do you know what the papers in his pocketbook said?"

"Some of 'em looked like scores of card games. The rest was in some h'Italian lingo I ain't flash to—Neapolitan, I expect. But he writes a neat hand, as if it come easy to him."

"It's all Lombard Street to ninepence he once occupied a higher station in life." Julian lowered the razor abruptly. "Confound me for a blockhead! I'm overlooking the most obvious possibility." He smiled and lifted the razor again. "Don't on any account let Guido know you've perceived he can write. That might interfere with a little experiment I mean to try."

At mid-day, Nina brought Julian a message from her mistress, asking him to join her in the music room. He found her seated on a white and gold scroll sofa, reading a letter. She wore a simple white morning frock, and a cap with a soft black bow on the top and a fall of white ruffles on either side of her face. Philippe de Goncourt's bracelet was in its usual place on her right wrist.

She looked up when Julian entered. "I've just received Francesca's answer to my invitation. She accepts on behalf of herself and Valeriano, and expects to arrive before the end of the week."

"I'm glad to hear it. Does she say anything about the murder or the investigation?"

"She mentions Lodovico." The marchesa read from the letter: *"I know I was not a good or obedient daughter to him, but please believe I am sorry with all my heart for the way he died if only because of the shock it must be to you and others who loved him."*

"She's very frank."

"She can't help that. She's always been as transparent as water. Valeriano is more opaque. Lodovico always found him an enigma."

"In what way?"

"Most singers courted Lodovico's favour, knowing he would go to great effort and expense to aid those he admired. But Valeriano seemed to want nothing to do with him. I don't mean that he was rude or haughty—he has exquisite manners. He simply held aloof. Lodovico could never be denied anything he coveted, especially when it involved a beautiful voice. The more elusive Valeriano proved, the more determinedly Lodovico pursued him. He invited him to Casa Malvezzi, and here as well. He lavished attention on him. That was how Valeriano came to know Francesca so well. Ironic, isn't it? Of course, after he ran away with her, Lodovico hated him in proportion as he had adored him before. And he hated Francesca twice over: because she had brought down ridicule on the Malvezzi name, and because she had stolen Valeriano from him."

"How did you get on with Marchesa Francesca?" Julian asked curiously.

"Tolerably well," she said with a shrug, "but we weren't close. Francesca is a very simple soul, and I—" She smiled quizzically. "I'm not simple."

"No," he agreed, mirroring her smile. "What was your relationship with her after she left Marchese Rinaldo?"

"I had none, really. I only saw her once, before she and Valeriano left Milan. I tried to persuade her to return to Rinaldo."

"What prompted you to do that?"

"I thought someone ought to reason with her. Lodovico's threats weren't working, and of course Rinaldo could do nothing but bite his nails and peep out from behind Lodovico's coat-tails. I told her I wasn't asking her to give up Valeriano. She could see him as often as she liked—be everything to him that she wished to be—or could be, given what he is. Why should she have to live with him? It only enraged Lodovico and made a *cause célèbre* of what might have been a charming and agreeable love affair."

"How did she respond?"

"She listened meekly and thanked me for my concern, but she wouldn't budge an inch. I hadn't much sympathy for her after that. I know it was hard on her to lose her children, but she could have recovered them at any time by coming back to Rinaldo. She would have sacrificed little and gained much. But she couldn't compromise. She must needs wallow in her martyrdom. I wished her joy of it. But I thought she was a fool."

"Why are you so angry with her?"

The marchesa rose abruptly and went over to the piano. She stood half-turned away from him, her hand resting on the instrument, her face darkly reflected in its polished surface. "You think me cold, I suppose. Your English sensibilities are shocked. You're romantic—I told you so last night. But you judge me a little harshly." She turned back to him, her eyes stretched wide with pain, yet meeting his steadily. "If I had two beautiful children, as she does, I would not have left them."

He was silent, feeling the inadequacy of anything he might say. Finally he asked gently, "Have you never had a child?"

"No. Never even the promise of one. After two husbands, I can only conclude I'm quite barren. You don't like the word. But it isn't an insult—merely a fact. That Canova Cupid and Psyche you like to look at when you think no one is watching you is barren—that doesn't mean it isn't beautiful."

"Can you, with your intellects, your charm, your courage, your exquisite, living loveliness—can you seriously mean to compare yourself to a block of stone?"

She said wistfully, "I wish I had known you some years ago. I think you might have been good for me."

"And now?"

"Now I shall probably be bad for you." She touched his cheek lightly. "If you'll let me."

The imminent arrival of Francesca and Valeriano posed a problem: the villa's seven bedrooms were all occupied. Maestro Donati volunteered that the stairs were difficult for him, and he would gladly give up his bedchamber for a room on the entrance floor. The marchesa offered him a small parlour to the left of the foyer, known as the Parnassus Room because it was frescoed with scenes of the Muses pursuing their various arts on Mount Parnassus. At Donati's request, she arranged for Sebastiano, who till now had been sleeping in the servants' quarters, to share this room with him.

This freed one bedchamber but did not end the dilemma, since the conventions forbade giving Francesca and Valeriano a room together, however known and accepted their relationship might be. Julian took MacGregor aside and suggested that they give up their adjacent rooms overlooking the lake and share the back room being vacated by Donati. MacGregor agreed, and they offered this solution to the marchesa. "How very kind of you both," she said, and went away to confer with the servants.

De la Marque had been leaning against a nearby wall, unabashedly following their conversation. Now he sauntered over, saying to Julian, "Allow me to compliment you on your adroitness, *mon vieux*."

"What do you mean?" MacGregor demanded.

"But my dear Doctor, how can you ask? Your friend has very neatly killed two birds with one stone. He's contrived to provide La Francesca and Signor Valeriano with adjacent rooms, which is only common courtesy to a lady travelling with her lover. And he has graciously relieved what would have been the marchesa's and my solitude on the other side of the floor."

MacGregor rounded on Julian. "You didn't tell me we were giving up our rooms so that those two could creep into each other's beds at night!"

"That was *sous-entendu*," said Julian.

"Well, it wasn't understood by me! Do you think I'd have gone to the trouble of changing rooms in order to aid and abet adultery? I thought we were just being courteous, giving up the best rooms to the newest guests, and one of them a lady."

"My friends, I am desolate to have provoked a quarrel between you." De la Marque looked thoroughly pleased with himself. "You mustn't distress yourself, Doctor. Consider what a very *theoretical* adultery this must be. How far can a castrato impinge on the sanctity of marriage? I daresay he goes to her room at night and sings to her."

"Maestro Donati is blind," murmured Julian, "but he can find his way across a room."

"Well, what of that?" said MacGregor impatiently. "His hands substitute for his eyes—Oh, I see what you're saying." His voice grew gruff with embarrassment.

"Castrati have a long history of love affairs with women," Julian added. "They must have something to offer."

"It's not natural," MacGregor insisted.

"Que voulez-vous?" shrugged de la Marque. "Love is unnatural. If we followed nature, we would mate indiscriminately, like rabbits. Which reminds me, my dear Doctor, as you've undertaken to be guardian of our morals, you may wish to tie a string between Mr. Kestrel's wrist and your own at night. The room you'll be sharing is just across from that of a lady who would bring out the rabbit in any man."

He went away laughing. MacGregor glared at Julian. "Is he right? Did you want that room so that you could sneak out of it at night to see the marchesa?"

"By no means, my dear fellow. But it did cross my mind that my presence might deter de la Marque from sneaking out of his."

Donati's belongings were duly moved down to the Parnassus Room, and Julian's and MacGregor's transferred to the bedchamber he had vacated. When all the fetching and carrying was finished, Julian went to have a look around his new room, which was in the northwest corner of the house. It was large and well furnished, but lacked the light and warmth of the south-facing bedchamber he had relinquished, not to mention the magnificent view of the lake. The walls were covered in dark-gold silk with a pattern of laurel wreaths. The bed and windows were hung with forest-green curtains fringed with gold tassels. The furniture was of veneered oak, with bronze mouldings of nymphs and fauns and, of course, serpents coiled around swords.

Donati was out on the balcony, leaning dreamily on the balustrade, the breeze ruffling his coronet of white hair. Sebastiano was prowling about the room, peering into corners and opening drawers. At the sound of Julian's entrance, Donati turned toward him.

"It's I, Maestro," said Julian. "I'm sorry to disturb you. I thought you'd gone."

"I'm afraid it's I who disturb you," said Donati, with the quaint, courtly air that always reminded Julian of the powdered wigs and minuets of Donati's youth. "This is your room now. Sebastiano just wanted to have a last look around and make sure none of my things was left behind."

"Pray take your time," Julian told Sebastiano. "I'm in no hurry to take possession."

Sebastiano muttered some acknowledgement and went on with his inspection. Julian would have withdrawn, but Donati came forward, feeling his way with his light rattan cane. "You seem to have got over your cold, Signor Kestrel."

"Yes, Maestro, long since. Should you like to sit down?"

"I would, thank you."

Julian helped him into an armchair and set a footstool before him. Again he would have taken his leave, but Donati lifted a veined, transparent hand. "Have you a moment to talk with me, Signor Kestrel? I should like to ask your advice about something."

"Of course, Maestro." Julian sat down opposite him.

"I'm told you've investigated murders before, in your own country."

"Yes."

"Don't you ever worry about the danger?"

"What do you mean?"

Donati looked grave. "I'm beginning to worry myself. You see, I'm the only one who can identify Orfeo, apart from Lucia and Tonio, who can't be found. It's true I would only know for certain it was Orfeo if I heard him sing—speech and manner are so easily disguised, and may even change naturally in the course of five years, especially at Orfeo's age. All the same, he might see me as a threat. I know what you will say: he isn't here, and why should he come to the very place where's he's most in danger?" Donati smiled. "Between you and me—and not for Commissario Grimani's ears—it wouldn't surprise me if Orfeo did the very thing one would least expect of him. He was a most unaccountable young man."

"Maestro," Julian asked point-blank, "is there anyone you suspect?"

Donati hesitated, then said with a sigh, "Half the time I tell myself Orfeo is in England, or dead, or anywhere but here. The rest of the time, I think I recognize him in every male voice around me and every footfall or opening of a door. You cannot know what a knife-edge I live on—of anticipation and dread, hope and despair."

"Maestro—"

"No, Signor Kestrel," Donati said quickly, "you mustn't be alarmed on my account. I didn't mean to make such a drama of this. I only wanted to say that I feel very torn about Orfeo. My heart tells me he didn't kill Marchese Lodovico and would never harm me. But I may be duped by the purity of his voice. If he is a murderer—" Donati smiled sadly, shaking his head. "You can imagine how easy I would be to kill."

"Is that why you wanted Sebastiano to share your room?"

"You're very quick. Yes. I have asked him never to leave me alone."

Julian looked at Sebastiano, who had left off searching the room and was leaning back against the wall, arms crossed, listening with his usual scowl. "Do you know how to use a gun?"

Sebastiano looked hard at Julian for a moment, then said, "Yes."

"Good. I advise you to keep a loaded pistol about you at night, and whenever you and Maestro Donati go anywhere alone."

"Do you think me in as much danger as that?" asked Donati, startled.

"I don't think you in any danger, Maestro. I merely hoped to set your fears at rest by providing you some protection."

"Ah." Donati sat slowly back in his chair and smiled. "I see. That was most kind of you, Signor Kestrel. Indeed, I feel safer already."

"I'm glad to hear it. You are the last person I should wish to see suffer on account of that pestering mountebank Orfeo."

"You mustn't speak so harshly of him."

"You must own that, murderer or not, he's been an infernal amount of trouble."

"If I can forgive him, Signor Kestrel, surely you can as well?"

Julian smiled ruefully. "I daresay he must have some redeeming quality, Maestro. Else how could he be so lucky in his friends?"

That evening Julian's new acquaintances, Fletcher and St. Carr, joined the villa party for coffee and liqueurs on the terrace. Fletcher was much taken with the villa at dusk, with its white marble terrace and balconies gilded by lamplight. St. Carr appeared impervious to scenery and architecture alike, but the merest smile from the marchesa reduced him to a state of tongue-tied idiocy.

The two young Englishmen were introduced all around, and the marchesa took pains to draw them out. It helped that Fletcher spoke a little Milanese, though with an execrable accent. St. Carr relied on Fletcher to interpret for him, but Julian perceived he could follow any conversation that interested him. He seemed most disposed, however, to attach himself to Julian, whom he peppered with questions about clothes.

"Young fellows here make such quizzes of themselves," he complained, "with their long hair and their cravats looped up in bows. I should be ashamed to look such a Miss Molly."

"A man has to be extremely confident of his courage to dress like that," observed Julian mischievously.

"Do you think so?" St. Carr appeared much struck. "I never thought about it that way before." He looked doubtfully at his own formidably padded shoulders. "Of course one wouldn't want to seem as if one had something to *prove*—"

Julian made a wager with himself that the next time he saw St. Carr, the boy would be curling his hair and wearing rings on the outside of his gloves. He was already asking Julian how to tie his cravat in the *Sentimentale* style when Carlo kindly came along and took him off Julian's hands.

Fletcher and MacGregor joined Julian. "You're a trump to let Beverley tease you like that," Fletcher said.

Julian shrugged. "When one can't get out of the way of a storm, it's better to enjoy the spectacle than to curse the rain."

"And Lord knows, no one has more of a knack for making a spectacle of himself than Beverley!" Fletcher added more gravely, "It's a great relief to me to settle him somewhere away from Milan. We were only there a fortnight, and during that time I had to pluck him out of a dishonest gambling house, fish him out of a canal he fell into during a drunken carouse with some soldiers, and save him from being arrested for eating watermelon in the street."

"Why in Heaven's name would anyone be arrested for that?" MacGregor asked.

"It's red, white, and green," explained Julian, "like the tricolour of Bonaparte's Kingdom of Italy."

"Well, of all the preposterous—!" MacGregor shook his head in disgust. "You'd think the police would have something better to do than persecute people over a piece of fruit!"

"They're frightened," said Julian. "They've eliminated all overt dissent, and the result is, they no longer know where their enemies are. So they strike out randomly, even hysterically, at anyone who seems in the least suspicious."

"Makes you grateful to be English," said MacGregor.

"I don't know about that," Fletcher mused. "My mother was Irish, and to her people, I don't suppose there's much to choose between the English and the Austrians."

"Very perceptive, Mr. Fletcher." Carlo had joined them unnoticed, along with St. Carr and de la Marque. "There's a tedious sameness about tyranny—"

He broke off. Grimani had appeared out of nowhere, as he often did, his shadow Zanetti with him. Carlo changed course. "I hope you mean to come to our festival. This Saturday is the feast day of Santa Pelagia, Solaggio's patron saint."

"Santa Pelagia?" St. Carr stumbled over the name. "Who was she?"

"She was a virgin of Antioch," said Carlo. "When she was fifteen, soldiers came to her house to seize her for being a Christian, and she leaped from the rooftop to save herself from rape."

De la Marque laughed aloud.

"How dare you, monsieur?" snapped Grimani. "I might expect these English schismatics to laugh at the saints, but you are a Catholic. From you, such conduct is an outrage."

"A thousand pardons, my dear Commissario," de la Marque said suavely. "But, really, have you—has anyone—ever met a girl who would dash out her brains sooner than open her legs?"

"I believe I have," MacGregor said sternly.

"Ah, but I meant outside the pages of Walter Scott!" de la Marque rejoined.

"I defer to your greater experience," said Julian. "I've never been obliged to give a woman that choice."

There was a general laugh. De la Marque's eyes glinted, acknowledging the hit and promising a riposte.

"None of this excuses your blasphemy against the saint," Grimani told de la Marque.

"I assure you, Signor Commissario, I meant no disrespect to Santa Pelagia. I was only pointing out her uniqueness. If I ever meet a young lady capable of jumping off a roof to preserve her virtue, I vow here and now to light a hundred candles at Santa Pelagia's altar. Now, if you'll excuse me, gentlemen, I promised to copy out some French verses for Marchesa Malvezzi in exchange for the flower in her hair, and I want to finish before it wilts."

De la Marque bowed and sauntered off. Everyone looked at Julian to see how he took this parting sally. His rivalry with de la Marque for the marchesa was becoming all too public. But it was an unequal contest, Julian thought, because de la Marque could pursue her actively and openly, while he himself was shackled by his need to maintain some semblance of objectivity about her, as long as she was a suspect in the murder he was trying to solve.

He remained conversing on the terrace until Fletcher and St. Carr took their leave, and the others began to retire indoors. He and MacGregor were the last to leave the terrace. As they were ascending the majestic double stairway to the villa entrance, a shadowy male figure emerged from one of the servants' doors below. Julian saw the glint of gold earrings, and laid a detaining hand on MacGregor's arm. "Guido!" he called softly.

Guido turned sharply and clapped a hand to his right trouser pocket—where he kept his knife, no doubt. He peered up at Julian and MacGregor, his own face fully illumined by a lamp at the foot of the stairs. "Signor?"

Julian said, very clearly and deliberately, *"Homicidae linguam Latinam intellegunt?"*

Guido started violently and crossed himself. His upturned eyes were wide with comprehension and alarm. "Si-signor?" he repeated.

"It was a joke," Julian explained.

Guido began backing slowly away. Just before he was swallowed up in the darkness, he pointed the fore and little fingers of one hand at Julian and made stabbing motions.

"What is he doing?" MacGregor asked.

"He's making the sign of the cuckold's horns," said Julian, "calling down bad luck on me."

"He's brazen enough!" MacGregor marvelled. "Well, are you going to tell me what this little drama was all about? Why did you ask him if murderers understand Latin—in Latin?"

"For the obvious reason, my dear fellow: to see if he understands it himself."

"Why did you want to know that?"

"Because I wanted to find out just how educated he is. Dipper discovered he can read and write, which I thought very rum in a Neapolitan servant. Now it seems he's conversant with Latin as well."

"Couldn't he have guessed at your meaning, given the resemblance between Latin and Italian?"

"Perhaps he could, but he didn't. He grasped what I said without having to puzzle over the words."

"And he got in a fair pucker when you asked him what you did," MacGregor pointed out eagerly.

"Yes. But I don't think we can infer much from that. My question sounded like an accusation, and accusations frighten even the innocent. That he's well educated—and would rather no one knew it—is tolerably clear. Whether he's a murderer is something else again."

CHAPTER 19

On Thursday it rained, and the lake was unutterably dreary. The mountains were all in shades of grey: dark woods, bald patches of granite, summits bathed in billowy mist. The villa servants went about shivering and muttering, *"Brutt temp!"* while the fishermen frantically made for shore, leaving the lake to the screaming, swooping gulls.

Grimani seemed, perversely, to thrive in such weather. He spent most of the day collecting reports from the gendarmes and soldiers who had been making enquiries and searches in the neighbourhood. In the late afternoon, he sought out Julian in the billiard room, where he was having a game with MacGregor. "Would you like to join us?" asked Julian pleasantly.

"I would like to speak with you about what you are pleased to call your investigation. I'm going to Como tomorrow with Comandante Von Krauss to make a report to the prefect, and I require a full report of your progress, in the unlikely event you have made any."

"Why should you assume he hasn't made progress?" MacGregor demanded, when Julian had translated this for him.

"Because I haven't seen him do anything practical. Oh, I know you've interviewed a few people, Signor Kestrel. My men have kept track of your activities. But I've interviewed them as well, and they have nothing to add to the statements they gave four and a half years ago. You've done nothing else but daydream and roam about the gardens. Can you claim to have discovered anything useful?"

"No, Signor Commissario. I cannot claim that." At all events, thought Julian, not without showing far too much of my hand so early in the game.

Grimani's lip curled as if to say, *I thought as much.*

"You can't expect Kestrel to solve the murder in a week," protested MacGregor, "when no one else has been able to do it in four and a half years! I haven't heard that you've accomplished anything to the purpose, either."

Julian tactfully translated this in milder terms than MacGregor had used. Grimani said, "I've at least learned there's nothing new to be discovered here. Now I intend to concentrate on finding Lucia Landi and Tonio Farese."

"Do you know anything further of what's become of them?" asked Julian.

Grimani's cold, colourless eyes appraised him. Finally he appeared to conclude that Julian was not worth concealing such matters from. "About Lucia, we have some leads, which my men are pursuing. Tonio's trail still ends with his departure from the Nightingale on the morning of the marchese's murder. We've found no one who's seen or heard anything of him since."

"Which suggests that his disappearance was intentional," said Julian, "although whether the intent was his own or someone else's remains to be seen."

"He left the Nightingale of his own accord," said Grimani. "Marianna and Rosa Frascani were clear on that point."

"They said he seemed alarmed and in a great hurry to be gone," Julian recalled. "That suggests he was in danger, and knew it."

"Perhaps he guessed that Orfeo was a Carbonaro," said Grimani, "and ran away for fear Orfeo's cohorts would kill him to ensure his silence. It's also possible that he and Orfeo were fellow Carbonari, and plotted the marchese's murder together."

"Then why would they have been fighting tooth and nail?" MacGregor objected.

"Tonio needed an excuse to leave the villa so that he could assist in Orfeo's escape after he killed Marchese Lodovico," Grimani replied. "So he and Orfeo counterfeited a fight in order to get him dismissed, and at the same time mask their connexion by appearing to be enemies. Tonio made preparations for Orfeo's escape—for example, obtaining the horse whose hoofprints were found outside the gate—then gave himself an alibi for the actual killing by shamming drunkenness all night."

"That's quite ingenious," Julian admitted. Not for the first time, he reflected that it would be a great mistake to underestimate Grimani. There were, on the other hand, advantages to letting Grimani underestimate him.

Grimani remained closeted with his police reports for the rest of the day. Next morning, he departed for Como to see the prefect, which was how he came to be away from the villa when Francesca and Valeriano arrived.

They disembarked at the villa pier at mid-day, under a sky as blue and clear as the previous day's had been bleak and stormy. Servants conducted them to the drawing room, where the marchesa, Carlo, and Julian awaited them. The other guests had taken advantage of the improved weather to go off on excursions. Zanetti hung about in a corner, mopping his face with his handkerchief as always, and no doubt storing up all that was said to report to his chief when he returned. The marchesa scorned to take sufficient notice of him to exclude him.

Francesca came in on Valeriano's arm. She was in her late twenties, of medium height, round and womanly without being plump. She had green eyes, a face sweet rather than pretty, and soft brown hair unfashionably braided and wound about her head.

She hung back shyly when she saw the marchesa, but Beatrice came forward, embraced her, and kissed her on either cheek. Carlo followed suit, then presented Julian, who bowed and kissed her hands. "It's a great pleasure to meet you, Marchesa Francesca."

"The pleasure is mine, signor. But please, will you call me by my family name? Just Signora Argenti."

"If you wish."

"You see," she said, blushing a little, "I don't live with my husband. So it wouldn't be fair to use his title or his name."

Meanwhile, Valeriano was exchanging greetings with the marchesa. From his speaking voice alone, it would have been hard to identify him as a castrato: by keeping it low and a little husky, he was able to approximate a light tenor rather than a soprano. Like many castrati, he was long-limbed and extremely tall. It was as if the bodily energy that should have gone into growing whiskers and begetting children spent itself in a senseless, slightly grotesque display of height. He had brown hair, streaked gold here and there by the sun, but his eyes were dark. His features were beautiful. At first glance, he appeared to be quite young, yet when Julian exchanged greetings with him he perceived grey hairs at his temples and the finest of lines at the corners of his eyes. No doubt his smooth cheeks contributed to the impression of youth, but there was something more—a childlike wistfulness that had nothing to do with innocence. Why grow up, his face seemed to say, when you can never become a man?

"Beatrice," said Francesca, "is—is—have you heard anything—"

Valeriano spoke for her: "Is Marchese Rinaldo here?"

"No," Beatrice assured them. "We've heard nothing from Rinaldo in weeks."

Francesca let out a long breath, then cast down her eyes, as if ashamed of her relief. A woman less suited to be a notorious adulteress, Julian had never seen.

He said, "I'm very grateful to you both for coming. As you may know, Marchesa Malvezzi has asked me to enquire into her husband's murder, and it will be of great benefit to me to speak with you—in particular about his last days."

Francesca looked at Valeriano as if for encouragement, then said, "We would be happy to talk with you, Signor Kestrel. We want to be as helpful as we can. But at the time Marchese Lodovico was—was—"

"Murdered," supplied the marchesa quietly.

Francesca coloured. One little hand reached out for Valeriano, who clasped it in his. As if it were he who had been speaking all along, he proceeded, "At the time Marchese Lodovico was murdered, we hadn't seen him for more than a year. And we never saw the singer known as Orfeo. So I'm afraid we may not be of very much help to you."

"At this stage of an investigation," said Julian, "it's difficult to tell what may be of use. So you may find my questions ranging rather widely. I beg your pardon in advance if I appear to pry."

"I understand," said Valeriano. It was evident to Julian that he did. He had read between the lines that, however offensive Julian's questions might appear, Julian would require answers.

"When do you wish to question us?" Francesca asked.

"I shall wait upon your convenience. When you've been shown to your rooms and have quite recovered from the journey, perhaps you'll be good enough to send me word." He added, to hurry them along a little, "Of course, if you wish to wait until this evening, Commissario Grimani will have returned from Como and can be present as well."

"Oh, I don't want to see a police officer," said Francesca quickly. "I would rather just speak to you."

Julian felt compelled to point out, "Commissario Grimani may wish to question you as well. But his concern is primarily with Orfeo."

"We know nothing of him, as I told you," said Valeriano in his quiet, level voice. "May I ask why, when the police are content to look for Orfeo, you feel compelled to extend your search beyond him?"

"My dear Valeriano," said the marchesa, "I've engaged Signor Kestrel to investigate Lodovico's murder precisely because he will do what the police will not."

Julian looked at her more closely. He knew that tone: she wrapped up her voice in silk when it would otherwise have an edge to it. She spoke to Grimani in just this way. But what did she have against Valeriano? Was it merely that he had come between Rinaldo and Francesca? Or was there some ill will between them that had nothing to do with Francesca at all?

Within half an hour after Francesca and Valeriano had been shown to their rooms, Valeriano's servant brought Julian word that they were ready to be questioned. At Julian's behest, they joined him in the drawing room. Zanetti, who had declared he must be there to take notes for Grimani, sidled in and sat down in a corner with a battered wooden secretary, which he opened to reveal a stack of paper, an inkwell, and a bundle of pens.

"Which of you would like to be questioned first?" asked Julian.

"Can't we stay together?" pleaded Francesca.

"I'm afraid not. It's important that I determine what each of you remembers, unaided by the other."

"Then I'll be first," said Valeriano.

Francesca said nothing, only lowered her eyes ever so slightly. But Valeriano at once asked, "Or would you rather be first, my love?"

"I—I own I should like to have it over."

Julian was more firmly resolved than ever to separate them. Two people who could communicate by such subtle means should not be interrogated together.

"Then I'll retire," said Valeriano. "I shall be in my room if you need me, Francesca. Signor Kestrel, I am at your service whenever you're ready for me."

He bowed with the weary, instinctive grace that marked

his every gesture. But of course, he had been on the stage for years. He would have been cut at an early age, before his voice could change, and from then on he would have been schooled to stand, walk, and move for an audience. All that was natural in him after he had lost his manhood would have been slowly but surely refined away. And yet, when he turned to give one last encouraging look to Francesca, his beautiful eyes softened, and a man looked out from behind the mask. How did she do it—this timid, unassuming woman, who next to the marchesa was positively plain? Julian could only judge of her power by its results.

"Please sit down." Julian motioned toward a turquoise and white striped sofa facing away from Zanetti's corner. It was bad enough that the clerk's pen would be scratching throughout their interview. At least Francesca need not be intimidated by the sight of him.

She sat on the edge of the sofa, her fingers laced tightly together. Julian pulled up a chair opposite and began, "Signor Valeriano said you and he hadn't seen Marchese Lodovico for more than a year before his death. Is that your recollection, too?"

"Yes," she answered in a small voice.

"When and where did you last see him?"

"It was while Pietro and I were still in Milan. So it must have been early in 1820—perhaps January?" She looked at Julian as if for confirmation.

"Was it Carnival?" he suggested.

"Yes," she said gratefully. "So it was January."

"Pietro is Signor Valeriano?"

"Yes. His real name is Pietro Brandolino—Brandolin, in Venetian."

Julian nodded. Most castrati went by stage names. "Under what circumstances did you and Marchese Lodovico meet that last time?"

She looked down, plucking at her skirt. "I'd been trying to see him for weeks. You see, I came to Casa Malvezzi one day while he was out, to see Niccolò and Bianca. When he found out, he was furious. He gave orders that I was never to be admitted again, and any servant who spoke to me of my children would be turned into the street without a character. I went to see him, to beg him not to cut me off from my children, but he wouldn't receive me. I went day after day, and his servants always turned me away."

Her lips trembled. "Finally I was admitted to see him. He wasn't unkind at first. He thought I had come to ask for forgiveness and return to Rinaldo. When he found I hadn't, he was furious. He shouted at me. He called me every terrible name a woman can be called." She lifted the back of her hand to her eyes, as if to shut out the memory.

"What happened then?" Julian prompted gently.

"I pleaded with him not to punish my children by making them motherless. He said no mother at all was better than a mother like me. I left, because he threatened to have the servants throw me out if I didn't. Soon after, Pietro and I went to live in Venice."

"What did Signor Valeriano make of the quarrel?" Julian asked curiously.

"He was very upset. It was an agony to him that I should be separated from my children on his account. He was always trying to make me leave him. But I couldn't do that." Her eyes appealed to him to understand.

He did not. As Beatrice had said, Francesca might have easily have gone on living with Rinaldo, while taking Valeriano as her lover. "You disliked your husband?"

"It wasn't that. Rinaldo wasn't kind to me, but I didn't blame him for that. No one had ever been kind to him except his mother, and even she didn't dare defend him from Lodovico. He ought to have had a wife like Beatrice—one who would guide and instruct him, and help him to make his mark in the world. I didn't know anything about society or politics or love affairs. I was useless to him, except to give him children. I don't suppose he missed me at all when I left him—it was only the humiliation he minded."

"Then why not return to him?"

"Because it wouldn't have been enough to see Pietro from time to time—to drive with him on the Corso or sit beside him at the opera." She blushed deeply. "To let him into Casa Malvezzi at night when Rinaldo was out, and force him from my arms before morning, for fear we should be caught together. Any woman could do that much for him. At the time we fell in love, he had never known what it was to have a home. He just travelled, singing now in one city, now in another. He was so famous and admired, and yet in all my life I had never known anyone so alone. I wanted him to know that, wherever he went, there was always someone who loved him waiting for him—someone who was all his. Do you see?"

"Yes." He saw a good deal now—and never again would he make the mistake of dismissing this woman as timid or weak. "How did you come to be at the Lake of Como in March of 1821?"

She lowered her eyes and plucked at her skirt again. "Rinaldo was away travelling when Lodovico forbade me to see my children. About a year later Pietro and I heard that he'd returned to Milan, and that Lodovico had gone to the lake with a young tenor he was training for the opera. I hoped against hope that if I appealed to Rinaldo, he might be kinder than Lodovico and let me see Niccolò and Bianca, or at least send me some word of them. They were so young—Niccolò was only four, and Bianca not yet two. If they fell sick, if they hurt themselves, if they missed me and asked for me, no one would have told me—" Her voice died away.

Julian half rose. "Would you like me to ring for a glass of water, some wine—"

"No—no, thank you, I'll be all right." She looked at him apologetically "It's just that it's hard, having to remember."

"I'm sorry. If it weren't of the greatest importance, I wouldn't ask you to relive all this."

"I believe you, Signor Kestrel." She touched his sleeve reassuringly. "I know you don't wish to be unkind."

How the devil had it come about that she was comforting him for his having to hurt her? "Thank you, Signora Argenti. I wish I could make your task as easy as you've made mine. Please go on. You were telling me how you hoped Rinaldo might relent towards you and allow you to see the children."

"Yes. It was foolish of me—I ought to have known he would never defy his father. But I wanted it so badly, I persuaded myself it was possible. I told Pietro I wished to go to Milan and see Rinaldo. He agreed at once, but he didn't think we should stay in Milan, where I was so well known, and our elopement had caused such a scandal. He was afraid I would be shamed and taunted, and I feared the same for him, so in the end we borrowed a villa on the Lake of Como from one of his friends."

"Did you know that villa was just across the lake from Villa Malvezzi?"

"No. I—we didn't know exactly where it was."

"Had you any thoughts of seeing Marchese Lodovico while you were at the lake?"

"I didn't want to see him. And I knew it wouldn't have been any use."

"And Signor Valeriano—did he ever attempt to see him?"

"No."

"Are you certain?"

"Oh, yes. He would have told me. He keeps nothing from me. We keep nothing—" She broke off.

"From each other?" Julian suggested. But Francesca could not say it.

He asked, "What did you do after you got to the lake?"

"I sent Rinaldo a letter begging him to let me see the children, and asking if I might come to Milan to plead with him in person. I was on thorns every moment, waiting for the answer. Finally it came—not from Rinaldo but from Lodovico. Rinaldo had sent my letter on to him. He wrote that if I didn't return to Rinaldo, I would never see my children again. He said they would be as dead to me as if I had buried them with my own hands."

"Do you still have that letter?"

"No. Pietro burned it."

"Why?"

"Why?" she echoed on a high note of fear. "Because it made me unhappy. Because it haunted me. Why should he not have burned it?"

"No reason," said Julian mildly. "I merely wondered. When did you receive the letter?"

"A day or two before we heard of Lodovico's death."

"How did you come to hear of it?"

"I don't know. Suddenly everyone was talking of it."

"Did you and Signor Valeriano leave the lake?"

"No, not for a few weeks." She hung her head. "I tried to be sorry for Lodovico's death, but to me it meant one thing above all—that Rinaldo might be kinder to me, now that his father wasn't egging him on to punish me. I wrote to him again, as humbly as I could. I offered to do anything, short of leaving Pietro, if he would only give me one glimpse, even from a distance—" She shook her head. "It was all in vain. He rebuffed me just as Lodovico had."

"What happened then?"

"There was nothing left to happen. Pietro and I returned to Venice."

Julian pondered. "There's one thing I don't understand. You said you received Lodovico's letter a day or two before his death. Why didn't you return to Venice then and there?"

Francesca avoided his eyes. "I didn't want to leave yet. I hoped Rinaldo might be kinder than his father, or Lodovico might soften towards me."

"That wasn't very likely, surely?"

"I was desperate. I went on hoping."

"And Signor Valeriano? What did he think?"

"He didn't try to persuade me to leave. He knew how much it meant to me in those days to see my children."

"In those days?" said Julian. "Not now?"

"Now a great deal of time has gone by," she said carefully. "I've come to accept that I shall never, never see my children again. They're part of a life so distant from me that it's as if another woman had lived it."

"It must be a relief to you," he said, "not to miss them anymore."

She looked at him swiftly, with such anguish in her eyes that his heart smote him. "I'm sorry." He laid his hand on hers. "I wished to know your true feelings. Why did you try to hide them?"

"I always hide them now. It has nothing to do with you. I don't want Pietro to know how much it still matters. It's taken me years to convince him I've recovered from the loss. Please don't betray me. I don't know what he would do if he realized how I grieve for my darlings—how I always will."

"I shall say nothing to anyone, unless the investigation demands it. And I can't at present see why it should."

"Are we finished?" she asked hopefully.

"Not quite. I should like to ask you about the night of March fourteenth—the night Lodovico Malvezzi was murdered. Where were you?"

"At home—at the villa where Pietro and I were staying."

She held her breath, braced for the next question. But Julian only regarded her expectantly, brows raised. He had learned from experience that this was often more effective in provoking a flow of speech than interrogation. Sure enough, she plunged nervously on.

"I went to bed—I don't remember when, but it was probably before midnight. Pietro—he had gone out riding. He has trouble sleeping. When he sang in the opera, he was accustomed to be up most of the night—first on the stage, and then at cafés or parties. Some nights he can't fall asleep as early as I do, and then he goes walking or riding or plays music softly so as not to disturb me. The night Lodovico died was one of those nights." She brightened. "But I remember he was out the night before, too, so there was nothing strange or special about the night of the murder."

Now this was extremely interesting, Julian thought. Because it was likely that whoever had killed Lodovico had been to Castello Malvezzi the previous night in order to leave the package containing the glove and the note appointing the belvedere rendezvous. Yet if Valeriano had been gone on each of those significant nights, this begged another question. "While he was out riding, were you left alone?"

"Of course." She was as ruffled as any wife whose modesty was called in question. "Who should have been in my room if Pietro wasn't?"

"I didn't mean to imply anything improper. I only wondered if perhaps you kept your maid with you."

"No, she slept upstairs."

"Have you ever seen a lady's elbow-length glove sewn with green myrtle leaves and a ruby heart pierced by a diamond shaft?"

"No." She looked bewildered.

"Do you know of anyone who ever had such a glove?"

"No. Why do you ask?"

"Someone delivered a glove of that description to Marchese Lodovico on the night before the murder, along with a note threatening to reveal some truth about the glove's owner unless he came to the belvedere on the following night."

"How strange."

"Yes. On the night of Marchese Lodovico's murder, did you go out at all?"

Her face flamed. "I—yes—I—I did. It was quite late—after midnight—close to two o'clock. I woke up and found that Pietro hadn't come back. I was worried. I put on my shawl and went up and down the halls looking for him. He wasn't in the villa. I dressed, took a lantern and went outside, calling his name and looking for him in the grounds."

"Didn't you wake any of the servants to assist you?"

"No. I was silly. I wasn't thinking clearly. I just got into a fright and wanted to find him. They did wake up when they heard me calling for him, and came out to see what was the matter."

"Why were you so afraid for him? You say he often went out at night."

"But he didn't usually stay out so late. And he didn't know the neighbourhood very well. He might have been thrown from his horse, or—I don't know what."

"Had he ever been thrown from his horse before?"

"I don't think so," she whispered.

"Did it cross your mind he might have gone to see Marchese Lodovico, in the hope of persuading him to relent towards you?"

"No! Why should he have done so? Lodovico hated him as he did me. Why should he have listened to anything he could say?"

"Then perhaps Signor Valeriano might have quarrelled with him, challenged him—"

"He didn't kill him! He would never do such a thing. He's gentle and honourable. That singer must have done it."

"Apropos of Orfeo, have you any idea at all who he might be?"

"I know nothing about him. I know Lodovico often made friends with singers. That's how Pietro and I met."

"Let's go back to the night of the murder. Did Signor Valeriano eventually return?"

"Yes, quite soon after I went out looking for him. He was very upset to find me outside—I suppose he thought I would take cold. It was damp and windy, and my gown was sodden, and my shoes were all over mud."

"Did he say where he had been?"

"I don't think he had been anywhere, particularly—just riding."

"Is that what he told you?"

"I don't remember what he told me," she said piteously, "or if he told me anything."

"We're nearly finished." Julian knew he ought to have kept her in suspense about this, so that she would remain tense and anxious and talk volubly in an effort to end her ordeal—though the truth was, the more a suspect talked, the more questions there were to ask. But as happened so often, his chivalry trumped his investigator's instincts. "Do you know whether Signor Valeriano brought a pistol to the lake?"

"He always travels with pistols. Everyone here does."

That was true, Julian acknowledged. The roads were plagued with bandits and smugglers. "Did you know where he kept his pistols?"

"I don't think I ever thought about it. I hadn't fired a pistol in years."

His brows went up. "How did you come to fire a pistol at all?"

"I had five brothers." She smiled reminiscently. "We ran a little wild when I was young. They taught me to ride and row and climb trees and fire a gun." She heaved a small, resigned sigh. "Of course none of them will speak to me now."

Julian regarded her in silent sympathy. Yet at the same time he reflected that a woman who could row a boat and fire a gun would have been well able to cross the lake secretly to the belvedere and kill Lodovico. Her servants could presumably confirm that they had found her out searching for Valeriano on the night of the murder, but who could say when she had actually left the house, or how long she had been gone? True, it was hard to imagine her cold-bloodedly shooting anyone. But she was a woman ruled by her heart—swept up by her passions like a leaf in a gale. Who knew what she might have been driven to do to the man who had robbed her of her children?

One thing was clear, and it complicated Julian's enquiry considerably. Francesca might be ingenuous and clumsy when it came to defending herself, but Julian believed she would say anything, tell any lie, to protect her lover.

CHAPTER 20

Julian escorted Francesca upstairs after their interview. She seemed grateful for this attention, which made him feel a little guilty, since his principal goal was to prevent her from conferring with Valeriano before Julian questioned him. He walked her to the door of her front corner room, which had formerly been his. Valeriano at once emerged from his room next door. He said nothing to Francesca—only took her hand and looked at her intently. She smiled up at him more cheerfully than Julian would have thought possible after what she had been through, but Valeriano clearly was not taken in. The gaze he turned on Julian was cold. "If you'll permit me, Signor Kestrel, I should like to make sure Signora Argenti is all right before you and I talk."

"I'm fine, Pietro," Francesca assured him. "You mustn't worry about me."

Valeriano reluctantly parted from her and accompanied Julian down to the drawing room. Zanetti sat in his corner as before, energetically sharpening quills. Valeriano was drawn to the elaborately painted and gilded Malvezzi family tree hanging on the wall. He contemplated it in silence. Julian wondered what such a display might mean to a Venetian prostitute's son, who had no known father and could have no descendants. When he turned to Julian, his eyes were veiled. "Signor Kestrel, I wait upon your pleasure."

"This will seem a strange way to begin an interrogation," said Julian, "but I've never had the privilege of hearing you sing. I'm told you still perform in private, and I wondered if you would be good enough to sing for us while you're here."

Valeriano bowed. "I should be honoured."

"Thank you. I shall look forward to it eagerly. Please sit down."

Valeriano disposed his long limbs elegantly in a chair. Julian sat down opposite, saying, "I should like to ask you about your first acquaintance with Marchese Lodovico. I've heard he was eager to cultivate you, but you hung back. Why was that?"

"I didn't need a patron. I'd been on the stage for fifteen years."

"Surely the backing of a man like Lodovico Malvezzi could only have benefited even an established career like yours."

Valeriano's gaze turned inward. "Singers are superstitious, Signor Kestrel. This may sound fanciful to you, but I knew somehow that he would transform my life. He did—first by introducing me to Francesca, then by driving me from the stage. You might say that he gave me my heart and took away my soul."

"Was it a fair exchange?"

"Oh, yes. It's better to be sincerely loved by one person than acclaimed by countless strangers. My career would have ended soon in any event. I'm forty years old, and I know that I'm an anachronism. I have been from the first. At the time I made my debut, it was already clear that castrati belonged to another era. Only the best of us would still find work on the operatic stage."

"But you were one of the best."

Valeriano inclined his head, acknowledging a fact. "I was very fortunate. But I can't complain that the inevitable end came a little sooner than it need have. Signora Argenti has given up far more for me than I have for her, and received far less in exchange."

"I don't think she would say so."

"That's because she's the most generous soul on earth," said Valeriano quietly, "and has no idea what she means to me."

Julian could only hope that neither of these lovers was his murderer. He did not like to think what the guilt and punishment of one would do to the other.

He said, "I've heard you take pupils occasionally."

"Yes," said Valeriano. "It allows me to keep my hand in professionally. And I take great pleasure in their success."

"Have you ever run across an English tenor in his early twenties during the past, say, half a dozen years?"

"You're thinking of the young man known as Orfeo. No. My pupils are mostly women. I'm not best suited to train a tenor or a bass."

Julian thought briefly. "When did you last see Lodovico Malvezzi?"

"I ran into him at a *conversazione* given by a friend of his. It would have been in the autumn of 1819, on a Friday evening, when there was no opera. I remember that I was disturbed at meeting him, because Signora Argenti had already made up her mind to leave his son, and I had been trying to dissuade her—not, I admit, with a very whole heart."

"Did you speak with him at all?"

"If I did, it was inconsequential. He probably asked me if I was going to sing at the party, and I said I would if I were asked. But I left almost immediately afterward."

"You never saw or spoke with him after Signora Argenti placed herself under your protection?"

"You will oblige me by not speaking of Signora Argenti as if she were a courtesan. No, I never saw him. He would have nothing to do with me directly. He blackened my name to impresarios and exerted all his influence to see that I obtained no further engagements. But he didn't deign to notice me personally."

"Did you ever attempt to see him?" Julian asked.

"No. If I'd thought I might persuade him to soften toward Signora Argenti, I would have made my way into his presence somehow. But I had no hope of that, and feared that seeing me would only make him more angry with her."

"In March of 1821 you and Signora Argenti went to the Lake of Como. Did you know that the villa where you were staying was just across the lake from the Malvezzi villa and castle?"

"Yes. But I had a friend who allowed us to borrow that villa on short notice. That was a great convenience."

Julian sat back in his chair and surveyed him with lifted brows. "Signora Argenti says it was Marchese Rinaldo's return from his travels that prompted her to make another attempt to see her children."

"Yes."

"Yet you and she went to stay at a villa miles away from Rinaldo's home in Milan, and only a stone's throw from where you knew Marchese Lodovico to be staying. Forgive me, Signor Valeriano, but it looks very much as if at least one of you was more concerned to see Lodovico than Rinaldo."

"If you've been to Milan, Signor Kestrel," said Valeriano, wearily, "you must know that the aristocracy to which Signora Argenti belongs is small, idle, inquisitive, and ruthless in its ridicule. If we had gone to stay there, we would have been recognized: she might have gone about veiled, but I am extremely conspicuous. I didn't want her mocked or tormented. So we determined to take up residence some miles from the city."

"Did you think her approach to Marchese Rinaldo would be of any use?"

Valeriano steepled his fingers. "I thought, Signor Kestrel, that they would probably be reconciled. I tried to be glad of that for her sake. I knew she missed her children a great deal."

Julian briefly reviewed with him how Francesca had written to Rinaldo, and how Marchese Lodovico had sent her a stinging rebuff. "Why did you and Signora Argenti remain at the lake after that?"

"I didn't think we should give up yet. It was too important to her. So I persuaded her to remain and try once more to approach Rinaldo or Lodovico."

"How did she respond to that?"

"She had no hope. But she acquiesced because I wished it."

"Would it surprise you to learn that she says it was she and not you who wanted to remain?"

He did look surprised. But he said quite levelly, "Her memory is playing her false. It was my idea."

They were a difficult pair of suspects, Julian thought. Francesca stammered and blushed so much that everything she said appeared to be a lie, while Valeriano's poise and calmness gave all his statements the ring of truth. But of course he was a performer by profession. Many singers were content to stand stock-still on the stage, emitting beautiful music without regard for the characters they were portraying. But Valeriano's acting had been known to bring operas to a halt, because the orchestra could not play through their tears.

Julian said, "I understand from Signora Argenti that you went out riding on the night Marchese Lodovico was murdered."

"That's correct."

"Where did you go?"

"Anywhere and nowhere. I only wanted to tire myself."

"Weren't you afraid you might be lost?"

"One can't be lost in this neighbourhood as long as one keeps in sight of the lake."

"Did you ride north or south along the lake?"

Valeriano hesitated, but only briefly. "South, I think."

"Sooner or later you would have rounded the tip of the lake and reached Villa Malvezzi."

"Perhaps I would have, Signor Kestrel," said Valeriano politely, "but I didn't."

"You had been out riding the previous night as well?"

"Yes. I was extremely troubled after Marchese Lodovico's letter came. It was very hard, knowing I had brought grief and humiliation on the being I loved most in the world. I knew I wouldn't sleep, and if I lay awake beside her, she wouldn't, either. And she needed sleep desperately—her eyes were bruised with exhaustion, like a little girl's. So I went out."

Julian leaned toward him, saying softly, "The author of her suffering was just across the lake. How could you resist the temptation to go and see him—to persuade or force him to relent towards her?"

Valeriano's head went back a little, as if he wished to withdraw his gaze from Julian's but could not. "It was a temptation," he whispered. "I did not give in to it."

Julian waited expectantly, giving him a chance to go on. But the silent technique did not work on him. So Julian proceeded, "I understand you'd been to Villa Malvezzi before?"

"Yes. Marchese Lodovico invited me to sing there during the summer of 1819."

"Did you go into the Moorish belvedere?"

"I believe so. I know that I was shown around the gardens."

"On the night Marchese Lodovico was murdered, you didn't by any chance tether your horse outside the garden gate?"

"I've told you, I kept well away from the villa—precisely because I might otherwise have been tempted to try to see him."

"There was no danger of that, surely? He was living at the castle and only came to the villa during the day."

Valeriano hung fire a moment, then said carefully, "I had no way of knowing that. It was his property. He might have been there."

"Have you ever seen a lady's elbow-length glove decorated with green silk myrtle leaves and a ruby heart pierced by a diamond shaft?"

"No." Valeriano lifted his brows in mild surprise. "Why do you ask?"

"I'll tell you another time. On the night of the murder, did you see anyone approaching Villa Malvezzi, either on land or by boat?"

"No. But it was dark, and I wasn't looking out for such a thing."

"How long were you out riding?"

"A few hours, I should think."

"And when did you return?"

A kind of preternatural alertness settled on Valeriano. He watched Julian like a fencer anticipating his adversary's next thrust. "I don't remember. Quite late."

"What happened then?"

"I went to bed, Signor Kestrel."

"And was Signora Argenti in bed?"

"Yes," said Valeriano, after the briefest of pauses.

"She remembers this night quite differently, Signor Valeriano. She says she woke up and found you gone, and was so worried that she dressed and went out looking for you."

Valeriano's gaze strayed off, as if the memory were coming back to him. "Yes. She's right. I had forgotten." He lifted his shoulders apologetically. "It was four and a half years ago."

Very well done, thought Julian, but I don't imagine you forget a great deal, and certainly not that night. "She says you were upset when you came home and found her outside. Why was that?"

"Again, I don't rightly remember. But I believe she was very cold, and her dress was wet. I feared she would be ill."

"It didn't perhaps occur to you that she'd been across the lake? She told me she can handle a boat."

"The thought never crossed my mind."

"That, at least, you seem to remember very clearly."

"I trust Signora Argenti, Signor Kestrel. I believe in her as I do in God."

"Then why did you hold back information to protect her?"

"I beg your pardon, but I didn't. Though if I had," he added in a low, deliberate voice, "it would be because innocence isn't a sufficient protection in itself. If it were, there would be no martyred saints, no wronged women—" He paused, then added with a faint, sad smile, "No castrati. So don't speak to me of innocence. If that were our only clothing, we would freeze."

"You seem in a brown study," Julian observed to Dipper, as the lithe little valet was helping him dress for dinner.

Dipper hesitated, then came closer and asked in a confidential whisper, "Signor V., sir—what did they cut off him? Both barrel and shot pouch?"

"Only the shot pouch. It would have been done when he was no more than seven or eight, after putting him into a hot bath and giving him a drink to dull his senses."

Dipper shuddered.

Julian went down to the drawing room and found that Grimani had returned from Como. The commissario was angry that Francesca and Valeriano had been questioned in his absence, but as Julian had predicted, they did not much interest him, once he had ascertained that they knew nothing about Orfeo.

At dinner, the talk was all of tomorrow's festival. The marchesa and her guests planned to go to Solaggio in the morning to see the grand procession through the village and attend the Festival of Baskets, when baskets of food prepared by the local women and girls would be auctioned for the benefit of the church. Fletcher and St. Carr, who were dining at the villa, reported that all the church silver was being polished for the occasion, and half the village had turned out to decorate the church with crimson hangings, flowers, and pictures of miracles. Moreover, to the great delight of the villagers, the podestà had obtained leave for a firework display.

"How fortunate that permission came in time," said de la Marque. "I remember a cold winter in Milan when the Viceroy wanted to fill the Arena with water, so that the children could skate. Permission arrived from Vienna—in July!"

Grimani eyed him coldly. "No doubt you would have preferred us to go on sending our requests to Paris."

"It's nothing to me either way," de la Marque said, smiling. "But I think the couriers would have enjoyed it more."

After dinner, the company went out on the terrace. Looking south, they could see the harbour of Solaggio hung with coloured lanterns in honour of Santa Pelagia, while all along the shore were tiny twinkling lights, which Carlo explained were snail shells that the local children had filled with oil and set afire.

The marchesa's servants brought out coffee, liqueurs, fruit, and little cylinders of mascarpone cheese sprinkled with sugar. When all the guests had partaken to their liking, the marchesa asked Valeriano to sing. Donati offered to accompany him at the piano, and the party adjourned to the music room.

Valeriano gave them *Parto, parto*, Mozart's tour de force for castrato, in which the young Roman hero Sextus took leave of his beloved Vitellia:

"I go, I go, but you, my love,
Make peace with me.
I shall be whatever pleases you;
Whatever you wish, I shall do..."

At the first sound of his voice, MacGregor, Fletcher, and St. Carr jumped in their chairs. Julian was not surprised. Most English people were not used to castrati, and to hear such a voice from a man over six feet tall was bound to startle them. Too chill for a woman's voice, too powerful for a boy's, it was eerily brilliant, not quite human—repugnant yet sublime. Valeriano's range and technical prowess were unmatched. His voice effortlessly spanned three octaves: each single note crystalline and perfect, yet following in such rapid succession that just listening made one breathless. Then Valeriano began to improvise, letting the melody flower into scales and cadenzas, trilling for a minute or more without a breath, now fast, now slow, swelling his voice till the hearer felt it in every nerve end, then letting it die away to a lover's sigh. Francesca's eyes shone with quiet pride, while Valeriano turned to her at all the most tender passages, as if singing for her alone.

When he finished, he was showered with applause. But MacGregor muttered to Julian, "I still don't like it. I know he's a fine singer—as a physical feat alone, his performance is a marvel. But every note reminds me of how his body was mutilated to produce that sound. To applaud him feels as if I were encouraging what, as a medical man and a Christian, I think is sacrilege."

"At least audiences no longer call out *'Hooray for the knife!'* as they did a few generations ago. We have more conscience now—or more shame. Civilisation's aesthetic sense called castrati into being; now civilisation's moral sense is stamping them out. But in the meantime, what is left to these men but the admiration their training and discipline merits? Think of yourself as applauding the hard work that made Valeriano an artist, not the surgery that made him a soprano."

"I suppose you're right." MacGregor joined in the applause with more enthusiasm. "You know, he must have hated Lodovico Malvezzi for taking that away from him."

"Lodovico didn't stop him from singing, only from performing in public."

"Well, isn't that an important part of being a singer?"

"I daresay," Julian mused. "To me, it would be like appearing naked before a crowd of strangers."

The marchesa next asked Julian to play *Invitation to the Dance.* He complied. The others applauded warmly. Fletcher and St. Carr, who had not heard Julian play before, were impressed.

"That's quite a difficult piece," said St. Carr knowingly, "on account of all the sharps."

Julian's brows went up. "Do you play, Mr. St. Carr?"

"No. Why?" added St. Carr anxiously. "Do you think I ought?"

"*I* don't think so," said Fletcher decidedly, "considering that it's I who'd have to listen to you practice." He explained to Julian, "Beverley learned to read music so that he could turn pages for ladies in low-necked evening frocks."

St. Carr glared. Julian thought it like him to study music for such a reason. Yet he also reflected, not for the first time, that

St. Carr had a very good mind, on the rare occasions he chose to use it.

Grimani took advantage of this lull in the musical entertainment to make an announcement. "I've decided to return to Milan the day after tomorrow. I would go tomorrow, but it would be impious not to stay for the feast day of Santa Pelagia. Signor Kestrel may, of course, pursue his vagaries here as long as it pleases Marchesa Malvezzi to tolerate them. But for my part, I consider this whole sojourn at the villa a waste of time."

"What more progress are you likely to make in Milan toward solving the murder?" Carlo wanted to know.

"I have no obligation to detail my plans to you, Signor Conte."

Carlo's eyes flashed. "Lodovico was my brother, and in Rinaldo's absence I am head of this family! Who in the name of all the saints are you to thumb your nose at me?"

"I am the loyal servant of His Imperial Majesty Francis the First of Austria," said Grimani impassively, "engaged in the task to which I was assigned by the Viceroy. If you wish to be of use to me, I respectfully suggest that you pray for my success."

"I will," snarled Carlo, "since nothing short of a miracle seems likely to bring it about."

"If you must quarrel," interposed the marchesa, "will you be good enough to go out on the terrace? Else I shall have to ask Signor Kestrel and Signor Valeriano to drown you out."

"I beg your pardon." Carlo bowed to her, swallowing down his anger. "I have a proposal to make to you, Signor Commissario, if you'll hear it."

"What is it?" said Grimani.

"The same one I made before we left Milan, and before Signor Kestrel undertook to assist us: that we search for Orfeo in England and ask the Bow Street Runners to help us."

Grimani frowned. "These Bow Street Runners are not police. As I understand it, they work for hire, and their power is greatly restricted."

"If you mean that they can't make a search or arrest without cause, that's true," said Julian.

"Our police are more efficient," said Grimani. "They make the search or arrest in order to find the cause."

"All the same," said Carlo, "the Bow Street Runners are considered to be expert investigators. What do *you* say, Beatrice?"

The marchesa's slim brows drew together. "I should be sorry to see the investigation move so far away from me. But I can't see anything to be gained by our remaining here. I should like to know what Signor Kestrel thinks."

Everyone looked at Julian. He leaned back in his chair, regarding them all thoughtfully. "I think there's far more to be learned here, where the events leading up to the murder took place, than in England, where we should find ourselves combing the country for a singer of whom we know almost nothing, and who could be anywhere."

"It may be a waste of time," said the marchesa, "but it has the great virtue of not having been tried. Let Commissario Grimani go to England—let Carlo go too, if he wishes, since he speaks the language so well—and let the rest of us go on with our lives as best we may. Signor Kestrel may stay here if he likes, and pursue the investigation in his own way." She smiled at Julian. "Perhaps I'll even visit you occasionally."

"I wish to point out," said Grimani, "that I require the permission of no one here to conduct an investigation to England. I'll take it up with my superiors in Milan and advise Your Ladyship of their decision—as a courtesy."

"How delightfully novel that will be, Signor Commissario," said the marchesa.

"I'm going to Milan with you," Carlo told Grimani. "I have a right to know what you're doing to solve my brother's murder."

"To my knowledge, there are no restrictions on your movements in Lombardy-Venetia," Grimani said coolly. "As yet."

"May Signora Argenti and I return to Venice?" asked Valeriano.

"It wasn't my idea to bring you here in the first place," said Grimani.

It was agreed that the whole party would stay for the festival tomorrow, and disperse the following day. "I must say, this has been a disappointing visit," sighed de la Marque. "Not that you all haven't been enchanting company, but when one expected high drama and blood-curdling revelations—" He shrugged disconsolately.

"You're very quiet, Signor Kestrel," the marchesa observed.

"I've had a thought, Marchesa. Signor Commissario, you can't approach Bow Street until you've obtained the approval of your superiors in Milan—perhaps of officials in Vienna as well. It may be days or weeks before you're able to leave for England. In the meantime, I could write to Peter Vance, my friend among the Bow Street Runners, and ask him to begin making enquiries about Orfeo informally, as a favour to me. That would speed your investigation when you do arrive, and in the meantime you won't have overstepped your authority, because I and not you will be responsible for whatever Bow Street has done."

Grimani thought this over. "That's a sensible plan," he allowed. "Very well, you may write to this Vance. But leave my name out of it. And keep the request personal and unofficial."

Fletcher nudged St. Carr, who was fiddling with his neckcloth, which, ever since Julian's remark about the courage it required to dress effeminately, he had taken to wearing in an extravagant bow. He and Fletcher rose to take their leave. Julian and MacGregor offered to walk with them to the end of the garden and lock the gate after them.

"I won't say goodbye," Fletcher said when they came to the gate, "since I daresay we'll see you at the festival tomorrow."

"Shall you go to Milan after that," asked St. Carr, "or to England to help the Runners find Orfeo?"

"If Bow Street finds anything but a mare's nest, I shall be much surprised."

"Then why did you offer to set Vance hunting for Orfeo?" MacGregor wondered.

"Because if there must be an investigation in England, it had best be got over as quickly as possible." Julian looked out across the lake, with its rippling reflections of gold boat lanterns and silver stars. "Depend upon it, if the solution to the murder is anywhere under Heaven, it's here."

CHAPTER 21

Next morning a fleet of garlanded and beribboned boats brought the marchesa and her guests and servants to Solaggio for the festival. Even MacGregor had overcome his aversion to Catholic rites sufficiently to attend. A glorious day, so clear that hardly a trace of mist clung to the mountaintops, had attracted visitors from all around the lake, and even from as far away as Bergamo, Brescia, and Milan. The harbour was so full of boats that the marchesa's party could hardly find a place to disembark, though the podestà ran about the pier frantically adjuring people to make way for them.

Once on dry land, they were swept up into the crowd surging toward the church. Many young women carried baskets adorned with ribbons and silk flowers, and filled with meat pasties, game birds, fruit, cakes, wine, and even live rabbits. These would be placed in the church to be admired, then sold at auction.

"You'll be expected to bid on one of them, you know," the marchesa murmured to Julian, as they walked arm-in-arm. "And to bid quite high, because the English are reckoned rich."

"May I give the basket to the poor afterward, or would that be a slight to the young lady who prepared it?"

"It would be a very graceful gesture, and only insulting if you were the girl's sweetheart."

"You aren't contributing a basket?" he asked, smiling.

"No, but Nina is." She glanced behind her to where Nina was walking happily, one arm in Dipper's, the other bearing a dainty little basket decorated with sky-blue ribbon and silver lace.

"I shall make sure Dipper is aware of his duty," Julian promised.

As they neared the church, Julian caught a glimpse of Fletcher craning his neck above the crowd and elbowing his way now in one direction, now in another. Julian guessed he had lost St. Carr, and not for the first or last time today.

The marchesa's party entered the church. It was transformed, its austere columns swathed from top to bottom in red damask, its archways hung with gold festoons and pictures from the life of the virgin saint. Santa Pelagia's shrine could hardly be seen amid the flowers, candles, and gold-paper decorations. The aisles were lined with baskets of every size. Nina placed hers among them, lovingly spreading out the blue bow and arranging the ribbon ends.

There was a commotion in the shuffling, gazing throng behind the marchesa's party. Rosa, the girl from the Nightingale, fought her way through. She looked luscious, her black hair done up with silver pins, her crimson and gold bodice pushing up her magnificent breasts so that they pointed like artillery. She came to a stop before Dipper, her lips parted, her eyes lit up alluringly.

Nina abandoned her basket and hurried to Dipper, slipping her arm through his. Rosa glared. Then her black eyes travelled to Nina's basket. She laughed, tossed her head, and shoved her own basket in beside it. Her basket was immense, covered with scarlet ribbons and silk roses. Beside it, Nina's looked like one of the tiny baskets carried by pedlar dolls.

Nina's lip trembled. Dipper gave her waist a reassuring squeeze. When Rosa saw that, she turned on her heel in a fury.

Her foot shot out and knocked over Nina's basket, spilling out apricot tarts and almond biscuits.

Nina jumped at her. "You did that on purpose!"

"I didn't!" Rosa's mocking eyes belied her words. "How is anyone to notice such a poor little dab of a basket as that? No wonder you're such a scrawny thing. Perhaps if Signor Dipper asks me nicely, I'll give him something to feed you from my basket, to put some flesh on your bones."

"He wouldn't need a basket to feed *you*!" exclaimed Nina in a trembling voice. "He could just take you to the meadow to graze!"

"How dare you?" shrieked Rosa. "Slut!"

"Cow!"

"Bitch!"

They flung themselves at each other, kicking and pummelling. Rosa got her hands well into Nina's hair and pulled for all she was worth. Nina screeched and tore off Rosa's necklace, scattering garnets all over the aisle.

Dipper and Julian got hold of Nina, while other onlookers pried Rosa's hands from Nina's hair and dragged her back. Don Cristoforo, resplendent in his holiday vestments, came thundering down the aisle. "Fighting in the church!" he cried. "And on Santa Pelagia's day!" He looked imperiously from one girl to the other. "Are you not ashamed?"

Nina hung her head contritely. Rosa sullenly shuffled her feet.

"I shall expect to see you both in church before the end of the day to confess and receive penance," said the priest. "In the meantime, I won't sully our festival by taking any more notice of you—unless you give me cause!"

He stalked back to the altar, leaving Nina to put her basket to rights, while Rosa gathered up the garnets from her necklace, stealing little melting glances at Dipper from time to time.

Julian prudently removed him a short distance. "Did you think things weren't lively enough, and it might be amusing to cause a second murder?"

"*No,* sir. I'm knocked acock—blow me if I ain't! I never knew Rosa was so took with me."

"I wonder you can have missed it. You talk with her often enough."

"That's just being civil, sir."

"The devil it is. No one has made so many conquests in Italy since Napoleon. But never mind: fortunately—or perhaps unfortunately—it isn't I you'll have to convince."

"You love her!" Nina wailed.

"I don't," said Dipper.

"You think she's prettier than I am."

"She can't hold a candle to you."

"You think I'm little and scrawny, just as she said!"

"That only means a cove can get his arm around you proper." He suited the action to the words, in case she failed to understand his pastiche of English and Milanese.

She sobbed into her handkerchief. Dipper could see that her tears were very real. These Italian girls certainly took things to heart.

"Come," he coaxed, "all's well as ends well, ain't it? The church was rigged out to the nines, the auction was bang-up, and we've got the fireworks come nightmans." He reached into her basket, for which he had paid an extravagant price. "Have a biscuit. You ain't ate nix-my-doll since we come back from church."

"I'm not hungry. How can I bear to eat, knowing you may be thinking of her this very minute, and wishing you were with her instead of me! And after I gave you what I never gave any man before!"

Dipper's experience of women told him this was not true, but he thought it a lie that girls were entitled to tell, and men ought to pretend to believe. "Who'd want to wrap his arm round a great swinging gal like that, when he could have one as light-timbered as a willow, with hair like silk, and eyes as soft as velvet?"

She nestled a little closer to him and looked up in his face. "Swear that you love me."

"I love you." Dipper had said this to many girls and often meant it, as he did now.

"But swear by the Madonna—no, no, swear by your God, the God of the heretics."

"I swear."

He gathered her into his arms and kissed her. She flung her arms around him, pressing her lips and body ardently to his. "You must keep your word!" she breathed. "You must! Because if you were untrue to me, I don't know what I'd do!"

The marchesa did not return to Solaggio for the evening celebrations, preferring to watch the fireworks and hear the music from the terrace of Villa Malvezzi. All the servants had the evening free and quickly made off for Solaggio. The marchesa gave her guests *carte blanche* to follow suit, but most of them declined. MacGregor wanted no part of an Italian village carouse, Donati would not have felt safe, and Grimani took no interest in such foolery, except to warn the local gendarmes not to let the revels get out of hand. Carlo, Francesca, and Valeriano likewise elected to remain with Beatrice. Only de la Marque had other ideas.

He stopped Julian in the Hall of Marbles at nightfall, just as Julian was on his way to join the rest of the party on the terrace. "A word, *mon vieux*. What would you say to coming with me to the village to see what sorts of primitive pleasures are to be found?"

"I'm afraid I'm obliged to decline. I still haven't written that letter to my friend at Bow Street, and I want to be in time for the next post."

"Write it in the morning."

"You seem to have in mind the sort of evening that would leave me in no condition to write it in the morning."

"Then the devil with it. You know it's all nonsense anyway."

"What do you mean?" asked Julian curiously.

"Oh, *mon vieux.*" De la Marque looked at him with fond reproach. "They will never find Orfeo in England. They will merely be wasting their time, as you are wasting this magnificent night scribbling rubbish and hobnobbing with men too old and bloodless to appreciate those black-eyed goddesses I saw in the crowd today. Now, you and I are young enough to worship them with the vigour and thoroughness they deserve. Surely you don't mean to let them languish for want of a cavalier?"

"I have great confidence in your ability to console them. Why are you so convinced that Orfeo won't be found in England?"

"What I think about Orfeo," said de la Marque succinctly, "is that he is becoming a bit of a bore. So I can't persuade you to come with me?"

"Are you afraid I might find it tiresome here, with nothing to do but talk with the marchesa all evening?"

A smile spread across de la Marque's face. "One of many things I find both delightful and disconcerting about you is that one can say so little to you, and convey so much. Ah well, I shall have to leave La Beatrice to you for the evening. Bacchus and Venus are calling to me irresistibly."

They went out onto the terrace. De la Marque took leave of the marchesa and went off down the shore path. Julian and the others stood along the balustrade, looking expectantly toward the village harbour where the fireworks were to take place. The night was perfect for such an entertainment: the sky a soft sable flecked with stars, the breeze caressing, the air deliciously warm. Skeins of music from all around the lake were woven in a wild, sweet symphony.

All at once a rocket sailed into the sky, flinging a shower of sparks down to the lake. Another and another followed. A great Catherine wheel erected on the pier began to spin, throwing out tongues of fire. The marchesa laughed and clapped her hands. Julian had never seen her so unguarded and carefree.

He hated to leave her when the fireworks were over. He had never wanted so much to be alone with her. The investigation came first—the damned investigation, which was always thrusting itself between them. He had a duty to do, and must discharge it.

He excused himself and went inside. In the Hall of Marbles he took an oil lamp from a cabinet and lit it at one of the wall sconces. On his way to the library, he passed Cupid and Psyche, locked in their breathless, eternal embrace. He averted his eyes.

He seated himself at a writing-table by the library window, overlooking the terrace and the lake. The glass panes caught the glow of his lamp and threw it back, increasing the light but blocking out the view. He found a sheet of writing-paper, sharpened a quill, and commenced:

Villa Malvezzi
8 October 1825

My dear Vance,—

I hope this finds you as well as you deserve to be—in other words, in a deal better health than could be expected in a London autumn. But don't suppose me basking in sunshine here. The mist that hangs over these mountains would put a London particular to shame.

I am writing to ask a favour of you, and in that connexion, to give you an account of the most remarkable murder case I've ever encountered...

After the fireworks, MacGregor lingered by the balustrade, watching the revellers come out on the lake in boats. Some drifted dreamily, while others laughed, sang, drank, and called to friends across the water. Occasionally a quarrel broke out, and there was much shaking of fists and shouting of obscenities, but no blows. MacGregor had long since observed that in minor matters, the bark of Italians was worse than their bite.

He was enjoying watching the villagers enjoy themselves. Of course it was a scandalous way to celebrate a religious holiday. A whiff of brimstone borne on the soft south wind from the scene of the fireworks reminded him of the fate reserved for idolatrous papists. He did not want to think about that now. He liked these people. And he admitted to himself in moments like this that he was not sure he believed in eternal damnation, anyway. If that made him a bad Christian, so be it.

He glanced around to see what his fellow guests were about. Kestrel was inside writing his letter; MacGregor could just make him out at a table by the library window, a lamp lighting his work. Francesca and Valeriano had gone for a walk in the garden. The marchesa and Carlo were seated a short way back, beside the little rectangular lily pond at the centre of the terrace. Grimani had drawn a chair up to one of the lanterns and was reading reports. Donati sat near MacGregor at the balustrade, and seemed to take as much pleasure in the sounds of the revels on the lake—the laughter, snatches of song, and rhythmic plash of oars—as MacGregor did in the sight of them.

"You seem so contented," MacGregor stammered to him in very bad Milanese.

"I beg your pardon," said Donati apologetically, as if it were his hearing rather than MacGregor's speech that was at fault. "I don't understand."

Carlo came over to them. "Allow me to interpret for you."

"Thank you," said MacGregor, and continued in English, "I was wondering how you manage to keep in such good temper, when the rest of us are never satisfied for two minutes together."

"Old and blind as I am, do you mean?" said Donati, smiling. "I suppose I expect less of life, and so enjoy what pleasures I do find all the more. And I feel I still have something of value to offer—my music, my teaching. I can never be lonely while young singers seek me out for guidance and encouragement. Of course, I'm not as fortunate as you. Even in Italy, there will never be as much need for a singing teacher as for those who can heal the sick."

"But—" MacGregor broke off, his tongue tied by embarrassment. Yet what did it matter what these people thought of him? He would probably never see them again after he returned to England. "I sometimes wonder what will become of me when I'm too old and infirm to work any longer."

"I trust that day will be long in coming," said Donati. "But when it does, it will simply mean that it's no longer God's plan for you to do the work of the world."

"But why should it be God's plan for me to be useless?"

Donati smiled gently. "Perhaps because He wishes to bring you closer to Him, and He can't get your attention any other way."

A figure came onto the terrace from the lakeside path. MacGregor could not tell who it was until he stepped into the light of the lamps along the balustrade. "Do you need anything, Maestro?" he asked gruffly.

"No, Sebastiano, I'm fine. Go to the village and enjoy yourself."

"I'd rather practise my singing."

"Of course you may if you like. But you've worked hard for weeks. You deserve a holiday."

"I'd rather practise," Sebastiano said stonily.

Donati shook his head. "Do as you will."

Sebastiano went inside.

"He's not very happy here," Donati told MacGregor and Carlo. "He's accustomed to town life. And he left a sweetheart behind in Pavia."

"That's hard on a boy his age," said MacGregor.

"Yes," said Donati. "And her husband is so jealous, she doesn't dare write to him."

MacGregor shook his head over the extraordinary morals of this country. "Why can't he find a girl who isn't married?"

"You would have him ruin a virgin?" said Donati, horrified.

"No, no!" expostulated MacGregor. "I would have him marry one!"

"He hasn't any money to marry on," said Donati.

"Then he can stay celibate," grumbled MacGregor. "Your priests do."

Carlo laughed out loud. "Who told you so?"

From inside the villa came Sebastiano's voice:

"All'idea di quel metallo
portentoso, onnipossente..."

It was that duet from *The Barber of Seville* again—the one Sebastiano had been practising ever since they came to the villa. MacGregor knew by now what it was all about: Figaro the barber was instructing the hero, Count Almaviva, to disguise himself as a drunken soldier in order get into the house of his beloved Rosina. Sebastiano sang Figaro's part and used the piano for Almaviva's.

"Do you think he'll make a success of it as a singer, Maestro?" MacGregor asked.

"He shows great promise," said Donati. "His voice is warm and flexible, he works hard, and he has the temperament."

"The temperament?" said MacGregor.

"Endurance, single-mindedness, vanity. The courage to hold his own with impresarios and rivals, and the humility to defer to patrons and the public. Now, Orfeo—" Donati's voice softened. "He had the more remarkable voice, but he didn't have the temperament. Not at all."

"Che invenzione, che invenzione prelibata!" sang Sebastiano. *What an idea, what a marvellous idea!*

"I liked that tune once," said MacGregor, "but after hearing it every night for a week—"

"Hush!" Donati started up. "Listen!"

MacGregor listened. At first he heard only the same confounded "Che invenzione, che invenzione." Then he caught his breath. Above Sebastiano's jaunty baritone was another voice, soaring and sweet. Someone was singing the tenor part.

Sebastiano broke off. The tenor voice was heard alone, but only for a moment. Then it began again in a different strain—ardent, beguiling, languorous:

"Un'aura amorosa
Del nostro tesoro
Un dolce ristoro
Al cor porgerà..."

MacGregor, Donati, Grimani, Carlo, and the marchesa listened, transfixed. Sebastiano came out of the house and stood protectively beside Donati. MacGregor looked about for Kestrel, then saw his tailcoated figure on the library balcony, silhouetted against the light behind it. He was looking to his right, along the façade of the villa toward the south terrace. MacGregor realized the voice was coming from there.

"Un'aura amorosa
Del nostro tesoro..."

"He always did like Mozart," said Donati quietly.
"Who?" demanded Grimani.
"Orfeo, Signor Commissario. That is Orfeo."

CHAPTER 22

The spell was broken. Grimani and Carlo tore across the terrace toward the south side of the villa. The singing stopped. MacGregor shouted, "Kestrel! Maestro Donati says it's Orfeo!"

The figure on the balcony vanished. The next minute, Kestrel joined MacGregor on the terrace. He sprang agilely onto the balustrade, unhooked a lantern from a column at one end, and jumped down again. MacGregor started to run toward the south terrace, then saw that Kestrel was running the other way, along the lake shore to the north. "Where are you going?"

Kestrel did not answer. MacGregor ran after him. "There's no gate on this side for him to get out," he panted.

"He could have left a boat on the shingle," said Kestrel. "Or he could hazard his chances and swim."

They slowed their pace and looked over the side of the embankment, Kestrel holding the lantern aloft. There was no boat on the shingle, and no sign of a swimmer. Further out on the lake, the holiday boats still bobbed, the revellers laughing and singing. It would have been child's play for Orfeo to lose himself among them.

Kestrel and MacGregor had nearly reached the caves that bounded the garden on the north side, when Kestrel stopped before a small, stunted tree at the edge of the embankment. By the lantern-light, MacGregor saw a strip of white linen tied in a bow around one of the branches. Kestrel surveyed it briefly, then untied it and put it in his tailcoat pocket.

"Does it mean something?" MacGregor asked.

"It may. I daresay Commissario Grimani would have liked to see it *in situ*, but I couldn't count on its being still here by the time he came to see it."

"Why would anyone remove it?"

"That depends very much on why anyone put it here at all."

"You think Orfeo, running for his life and about to jump off the embankment, stopped to tie a bit of rag to a tree in a neat little bow? Why in blazes should he do that?"

"My dear fellow, I don't know. Perhaps Orfeo didn't put it here at all. He may have run south, toward the garden gate. He may be taking coffee in the villa drawing room. But if he did escape this way, he might have left this as a signal to someone that he got away safely."

MacGregor shook his head, at a loss. "What shall we do now?"

"Continue as far as the caves, then turn back and see if the others have fared any better. I can't see any point in wandering aimlessly about the garden. Orfeo might have concealed himself temporarily, but sooner or later—assuming he doesn't mean to give himself up—he'll have to escape, by land or water. So it's the shore and the garden gate that should be watched."

"That's sensible, I suppose."

A brief walk brought them to the caves. "Do you think he could be hiding in them?" MacGregor asked.

"He would be asking to be trapped. But we'll look."

Kestrel lifted the curtain of scarlet creeper and went into the large round cave known as the Salon, his lantern held before him. MacGregor had been shown this cave before, but on a sunny morning. Now it was perfectly dark, the lantern light cutting a narrow swathe through the gloom to reveal patches of scarred grey wall. When the light fell on a pallid, openmouthed face, MacGregor jumped. But it was only the little grotesque head carved on the back of the disused pool against the cave wall. The nozzle protruding from its mouth gave the impression it was about to play a tune.

Kestrel shone the lantern all around, but there was no one hiding in the cave. He went to the trapdoor in the centre of the floor. "Locked. I thought as much. Stealing wine from the cellar would be too much of a temptation on a night like this."

"You don't suppose Orfeo could have kept a key to it?"

"Whether he did or not makes no odds, since we haven't one. Come, let's see if Grimani's turned up a trump."

On their way back to the villa, they ran into Francesca and Valeriano. They were strolling arm-in-arm, she nestled close to him and clasping his arm with both hands. In his free hand, he carried a dark lantern, the shutter open to light their way. When they saw Julian and MacGregor, they stopped abruptly.

"Have you seen anyone in the garden?" Julian asked.

"Seen anyone?" said Valeriano. "Whom should we have seen?"

"A young man," said Julian. "A tenor."

"A tenor?" Francesca's eyes widened.

"Yes. Orfeo has reappeared, in a manner of speaking. He serenaded us a short while ago."

"Madonna!" marvelled Valeriano. "Where is he now?"

"We don't know. We're on our way back to the villa to see if he's been found."

Valeriano and Francesca joined them. As they hastened along, Julian asked, "Did you see or hear anyone in the garden?"

"No," they both said.

"Were you together all the time?"

"Of course," said Valeriano. "Even in a walled garden, I wouldn't have left Signora Argenti alone on a festival night."

"Did you leave the garden at any time?"

"No," said Valeriano.

They reached the villa terrace. Grimani was pacing tensely. Carlo was downing a glass of some liqueur. Donati sat where he had been before, Sebastiano standing sentinel beside him. The marchesa stood by the balustrade, turned away from the others and looking out on the lake.

"Where have you been?" Grimani snapped.

"North to the caves," said Julian. "We thought Orfeo might have gone that way, but we didn't find him."

Grimani resumed his pacing. "We went as far as the garden gate. But he had the start of us. Curse him! On this night of all nights, I'll be lucky to find a sober gendarme within five miles to chase him. Even Zanetti is at the festival—the devil take him!"

He stopped walking and clenched his fists, his body quivering with the effort to control his rage. "I'm going to the barracks to find Von Krauss and have him send out soldiers to look for Orfeo. Not that I think it will do any good. He'll have got well away by now—or resumed his real identity."

The marchesa looked around at that. "His real identity?" she asked, in a strange, light voice. "What do you mean?"

"I mean that there are two young Englishmen in Solaggio. I want them brought here for questioning." Grimani's eyes narrowed. "And that Frenchman, who knows so much about music, and who according to Zanetti speaks English like an Englishman. I want to know if they can account for their whereabouts at the time Orfeo was singing."

"What time *was* that?" asked Carlo. "I wasn't paying attention."

"About ten," said Grimani. "That's an estimate—I didn't look at my watch immediately."

"It's a very good estimate," said Julian. "It was ten exactly, by the library clock."

Grimani's eyes sparked. "I don't need to have my observations confirmed by amateurs!"

MacGregor nudged Julian. "Show him what you found!"

Julian took out the strip of white linen and explained how it had been tied in a bow to a tree branch along the embankment. Grimani looked it over and pocketed it. "It may be nothing. But it could be some sort of Carbonaro signal. At any rate, it's the only clue we have." He nodded at Julian grudgingly.

"Have you searched the south terrace?" asked Julian.

"I know how to conduct a criminal investigation, Signor Kestrel. Yes. But it will have to be done again by daylight. I'll have the whole garden combed at first light tomorrow. If that insolent blackguard left so much as a thread or a button behind him, I'll find it."

The marchesa said, a throb of urgency in her voice, "Hadn't you better go to Solaggio, Signor Commissario? The longer you tarry here, the greater the chance he'll get away."

"I'm going, Your Ladyship. But nothing much will be accomplished tonight. Orfeo chose the perfect moment to mock us with his song: the height of the festival, when we won't be able to mount a concerted search for hours. It was a clever trick!"

"Che invenzione prelibata!" Julian murmured.

Grimani rounded on him. "You think this is funny?"

At that moment, Julian did. He suddenly missed de la Marque, who he felt would be the only other person to appreciate the humour in an entire barracks being called out to look for a lone serenader. "You think Orfeo did this to mock us?"

"He's obviously drunk on his own villainy," said Grimani, "taunting us for our failure to solve his crime."

"He wouldn't do that," said Donati gravely. "I feel sure he must have had a good reason for this."

"If he did," said Grimani, "I mean to find out what it was. I'm going to Solaggio. In the meantime, no one is to leave the villa grounds, and no one is to enter—except Monsieur de la Marque, should he return. I'll be sending a party of soldiers to see that my orders are obeyed."

"You've no call to turn this house into an armed camp!" Carlo declared.

Grimani's voice was like ice. "I will do whatever must be done to trap Orfeo, Signor Conte. If I have to put a soldier at every window and under every bed, so be it."

He strode off in the direction of Solaggio. The marchesa looked out on the lake once more. Carlo offered to escort her inside, but she declined. Julian would have liked to try his own luck, if only to find out what lay behind her separateness and self-containment. It was as if she carried herself in an over-brimming vessel and had to concentrate all her faculties on ensuring it did not spill. But first things must come first.

He turned to Sebastiano. "You were in the music room when Orfeo was first heard singing."

"Yes, signor." Sebastiano straightened and looked at Julian warily.

"The windows of that room face the south terrace. Did you look out?"

"No, signor. I came here to find Maestro Donati."

"You didn't stop to see who was singing?"

"It was dark in the garden, signor. Anyway, it wasn't my business to look for the singer, but to protect Maestro Donati."

"Did you think the singer might be Orfeo?"

Sebastiano shrugged. "Orfeo was a tenor, signor. This man was a tenor. Maestro Donati thought Orfeo might be in the neighbourhood, and might mean to do him some hurt. That's why he told me never to leave him alone. So my business was to see that he wasn't alone, and to stand by him. That's all."

"Thank you, my boy," said Donati, touched.

Sebastiano made a brusque movement, like an animal unwilling to be petted. "It's my job, Maestro."

"Yes," said Donati, smiling. "I understand." He turned his sightless eyes appealingly toward Julian. "Signor Kestrel, why do you think Orfeo did this?"

"I can think of several reasons, Maestro. He may have wanted to alert someone at the villa that he was in the neighbourhood. He may have been trying to distract our attention from someone or something else." Julian paused. "But the best way to determine the purpose of an act may be to look at its results."

"Its results?" MacGregor began counting them off on his broad, flat fingers. "We know now that Orfeo is here. We know he's a saucy fellow, if we didn't already, and not behindhand in courage. We know Grimani is as angry as a hornet and means to look for Orfeo under every blade of grass in the neighbourhood." MacGregor shook his head. "It looks to me as if Grimani is right, and Orfeo did it out of sheer devilry. What would be the point of signalling to someone at the villa that he's here? We were all leaving tomorrow, anyway."

Julian lifted his brows suggestively.

"By George!" MacGregor slapped his forehead. "We *were* leaving, but now Grimani will stick here till Doomsday, sooner than let Orfeo slip through his fingers! And *you'll* stay, which means I will, too—I expect everybody will stay. Is that why you think Orfeo did it—he didn't want us to go?"

"It's possible."

Julian translated this exchange into Milanese for Donati and Sebastiano. "Now if you'll excuse me, I should like to have a look at the south terrace."

"I'm coming with you," said MacGregor.

"By all means." Julian took up the lantern again, and they made their way toward the south side of the house.

MacGregor asked, "But why should Orfeo care a pin if we go or stay?"

"Because we amuse him? Because he wished to do his country a service by keeping Grimani out of it?"

"Be serious, man!"

"If I were serious, Doctor, I should have to make the rather melodramatic suggestion that Orfeo didn't kill Marchese Lodovico, and that he thinks one of us did."

"Good God. You know, if that's the case, Orfeo may well be Fletcher, St. Carr, or de la Marque. They all knew we were planning to leave the villa tomorrow." MacGregor stopped walking abruptly and stared at Julian. "Do you realize how lucky you are that you came out on that balcony while Orfeo was singing? Grimani suspects every other young Englishman in the neighbourhood of being Orfeo—he even suspects de la Marque, who isn't English. If he hadn't seen you on that balcony with his own eyes, he'd be suspecting you, too!"

"I'm surprised he allows a trifle like that to prevent him."

They ascended three broad stairs to the south terrace. It was about twenty feet square, planted with fruit trees and crisscrossed by paved paths. At the back was a brick wall with a walkway at the top, reached by a narrow flight of stone stairs. An archway in the centre of the wall led behind the villa.

Julian crossed to the archway, "Orfeo must have escaped this way. If he'd left by the stairs at the front, he would have run straight into Grimani's and Carlo's arms." He let his lantern play over the archway and the ground on either side. "No telltale buttons or scraps of cloth. And the night is too dry for him to have tracked mud or grass stains on the paving stones."

"There's no sense hunting about for clues at this hour of the night," said MacGregor. "I'm for bed. Are you coming?"

Common sense drew Julian inside, toward rest and calm reflection. The Italian night tugged back, and won. "Not yet. I think I'll go for a walk."

"Why?" MacGregor's eyes narrowed. "What are you up to?"

"I'm not up to anything, my dear fellow. It's merely that I'm not sleepy, and there won't be many more nights this mild. Here." He handed MacGregor the lantern. "I don't need this to walk in the garden. I know the paths well enough to see by moonlight."

"Well, don't stay out too long," MacGregor grumbled.

They descended the terrace steps. Just as they were about to go their separate ways, MacGregor said, "You know, he really does have a beautiful voice."

Julian was taken aback. MacGregor was not given to volunteering opinions about art or music—yet here he was commending Orfeo, of all singers. "Do you think so?"

"Don't you?"

"I wasn't in the best position to hear him. Anyway, I prefer women's voices."

"Oh, well, it may have been partly the time and place. Instead of sitting in a hot, crowded theatre watching people in trumpery costumes strut about the stage, we were in a garden by night, hearing a singer we couldn't even see. Come to think of it, Lodovico first heard Orfeo under those same conditions. No wonder he was so struck by his voice."

Julian was silent for a moment. "Tell me, what did Marchesa Malvezzi do when Orfeo sang?"

"I don't know." MacGregor knit his brows. "I wasn't paying attention. Why?"

"I merely wondered."

"Wondered, fiddlesticks! What do you suspect?"

"I don't care to suspect anything more tonight. I want a holiday from questioning and being questioned. Look around you:

"*'The moon shines bright: in such a night as this...*
Troilus methinks mounted the Troyan walls,
And sigh'd his soul toward the Grecian tents,
Where Cressid lay that night.'"

MacGregor stared. "What has got into you?"

"Italy has got into me. If it isn't out by morning, you may extract it with one of those ghoulish instruments you carry about in your medical bag. Till then, *buona sera, mio signore*!"

"Mad as a hatter," said MacGregor gloomily, "or worse, in love." He stumped off toward the villa entrance.

Julian struck out into the garden. The night remained wondrously clear. The breeze was warm and cajoling, the air thick with scents of ripe fruit. From the south, the bells of

Solaggio chimed: ten, eleven, twelve. Midnight—the feast-day of Santa Pelagia was over. But when Julian came to the lake shore, near the garden gate, he found that there were still many boats out, though the revellers were quieter now, their laughter low, their voices husky, amorous. Their boats bobbed aimlessly on the water, the oars unattended. Somewhere on the lake a guitar began to play, and men's and women's voices rose in songs of enticement and desire.

Julian wanted to be a part of this night, this country. He had forgotten for so long—had willed himself to forget, perhaps—what Italy had meant to him when he first came here. His senses, starved for beauty, had been richly, gloriously sated, and he had felt grateful as he would to a lovely woman who relieved him from a long and agonizing celibacy. Suddenly he no longer knew what had possessed him to return to England—to forsake this air, this luxuriant growth, this music, this ardent, artless people, for London's damp and fog and its population of affected patricians and money-hungry tradesmen. Ambition: that was what had driven him back—that and old loyalties, old dreams, old grievances. *They've shackled you all your life*, said a voice in his head. *You were old at ten, worldly-wise at twenty. When have you ever done anything simply and solely because it made you happy?*

He walked south along the shore path, not meaning to return to the villa, but too possessed by music and the night to keep still. All at once he saw a flicker of light ahead. Eyes straining to penetrate the darkness, he made out the belvedere silhouetted against the sky, its windows lit from within.

His thoughts scattered like chaff in the wind. He moved forward slowly and silently, thankful he had not brought a lantern to betray him. When he reached the patch of ground in front of the belvedere, he stepped aside to avoid crunching the gravel and crept up along the narrow grass verge by the lake. The belvedere doors were dark; their blinds must be let down. He tiptoed to one of the narrow Moorish windows and stole a look inside.

The marchesa sat on one of the marble benches, a lantern beside her. Her ermine-lined cloak hung loosely on her shoulders and pooled about her on the floor. Her head was uncovered, and a few diamonds shone in her dusky hair. Earlier she had been wearing a spray of flowers at her breast, but now the low neck of her white satin gown was bare, and there was a carpet of petals around her feet.

Julian went to the nearest doorway and tapped on the blinds. He heard her footsteps and the swish of her skirt as she approached. "Who is it?" she called, a little breathlessly.

"Julian Kestrel. Am I disturbing you?"

There was a short pause. Then the blinds at the door began to rise. He saw her skirt, her waist, her breasts, and finally her face. He stepped in, and she dropped the blinds again.

"I saw your light," he said. "Why are you here alone?"

"I wanted to be alone. I thought this was the place people were least likely to look for me."

"Shall I go?" he asked.

"No. I don't feel the same need for solitude now."

"When I knocked, and you asked who it was, I almost thought you expected someone else."

She smiled. "Are you asking as a jealous lover, or as an investigator?"

"Both."

"The only person I expected—or rather feared—to see was Lodovico."

"Are you superstitious?" he asked in surprise.

"Not very. But I know that if he were ever to return to earth, it would be tonight, to hear that voice."

"What rubbish," he said involuntarily.

She looked surprised, then shook her head. "You don't understand."

"I know that if I were Marchese Lodovico, and could struggle back to earth for a single night, it would be only to see you."

"My poor Giuliano, you *are* in a bad way."

He pulled himself together. She was a suspect. He would treat her as such. "There's something I should like to ask you."

She looked at him quickly, hearing the change in his voice. "What is it?"

"In Milan, I saw your eyes fill with tears when Maestro Donati spoke of Orfeo's voice. Now you've heard it for yourself, and I find you alone in the small hours of the night, your flowers torn to shreds. What is Orfeo to you?"

"To me, nothing. But I own, his voice did move me. It was Lodovico's last love. And it is beautiful—pure yet passionate, exactly the sort of voice Lodovico adored. The voice of an angel and the hand of a killer—unlike Maestro Donati, I don't see why they shouldn't exist in one man."

"But we don't know that they do. If Orfeo killed Marchese Lodovico, why should he have advertised his presence here, when we never would have known of it?"

She smiled. "You like to defend him. I understand why. For him to have killed Lodovico is too simple. You want a dazzlingly difficult solution—a killer no one would ever suspect." Suddenly she grew serious. She came close, laying her hand on Julian's arm and looking up into his face. "You're the cleverest of us all. If you would only concentrate on finding Orfeo, instead of casting your nets in all directions as you have, I know you would succeed. Find him, Giuliano." She shook his arm. "Find him!"

"Why? Why do you want him so badly?"

She backed away, drawing a long breath. "I want him brought to justice. Lodovico wasn't a good man, but he was my husband, and he was kind to me. He trusted Orfeo, and Orfeo betrayed him as only a singer he loved could."

"I think you believe what you say," he said slowly, "but it isn't the truth, or not the whole of it. I wanted an answer, and you've given me a performance."

She stood very still, and looked at him. "You think you know me very well."

"I think in this instance you're not being candid with me."

"Candid?" Her slim brows went up derisively. "Candour—a subject on which you are an expert, I know. Signor Kestrel, who gives nothing away—who is as careful of his heart as a singer of his voice. Shall I hold up a mirror to you? You are one of the clever cowards, who see into everyone, and let no one see into you. You can be hurt, but nobody will ever see it. You only know how to bleed inwardly, though those wounds take much longer to heal—if they ever heal at all."

"When you held up that mirror," he asked quietly, "which way was it pointing?"

Her breath caught. "Both ways, of course." She laughed unsteadily. "Can you conceive how absurd we should be as lovers? We should do nothing but play hide-and-seek with one another."

He said, "I would rather search for you than find any other woman."

"Oh, Giuliano," she whispered.

He went to her and took her in his arms.

For a moment she stiffened. Then he felt her yield, her head tipping back, her lips opening under his. Her arms went around his neck. He kissed her lips, her throat, the hollow of her neck. Her soft hair tickled his face, her pearls got between his teeth, he would have been in heaven if it had not been for this driving need to have *more* of her—to crush her to him until there was no longer any knowing where he ended, and she began—

"Giuliano," she whispered. "Giuliano, stop."

He groaned, pulled her to him all the more urgently.

"Giuliano!" She twisted in his grasp.

He stepped back. She was flushed in the lamplight, her hair tumbling over her shoulders, her gown askew. "I'm sorry," she said, wide-eyed. "I remembered where we were. I thought of Lodovico stretched out on the floor with a bullet in his heart, and I couldn't do it."

"No. No. I understand." He was actually incapable of understanding much of anything. He picked up her cloak, which had dropped on the floor, and draped it around her shoulders.

"I've lost some hairpins," she said.

He took up the lantern, and they hunted about the floor for them. Since they were tipped with diamonds, they were easy enough to find. She twisted her hair up behind her head and thrust the pins through it. He drew up the blinds at one of the doorways, and they went out.

The night was chilly now. Julian offered Beatrice his coat, but she said she was warm enough in her cloak. With the tacit complicity of lovers, they returned to the villa by a roundabout route through the garden, avoiding the shore path, which was too exposed to the gazes of anyone still on the lake. The path was dark and secluded. It occurred to Julian that they might stop, spread his coat on the grass—

But of course he would not propose any such thing. He had been mad, back in the belvedere, and now he was in his right mind again. If he became the marchesa's lover, his investigation would be all to pieces. Honour, which now demanded that he find the truth at all costs, would clamour even more compellingly for him to protect his mistress, whatever she might have done. He had to solve the murder, if only to remove the doubts and secrets between them. Then, perhaps, if she were innocent, and he were lucky—

They came in sight of the villa. "You had better go in before me," he said. "The servants may be back from the festival, and be up and about."

She thought a moment. "I think we should pretend this never happened between us. Until Orfeo is found, and the murder is solved, everything is uncertain and wrong."

"I agree," he said with a wry smile. "But somehow I wish *you* hadn't thought so."

She held out her hand. "We never met in the belvedere, and you never kissed me."

They shook hands. But when she would have withdrawn hers, he held it back. "You must know that I am desperately in love with you."

"Then find Orfeo." She clasped his hand in both of hers. "It's he who stands between us."

Julian entered the room he shared with MacGregor as quietly as he could, but even so MacGregor's nightcapped head popped out from under the bedclothes. After years of being summoned at all hours to extract gallstones and deliver babies, he had a great capacity for starting wide awake at the slightest sound, and falling asleep as soon as the disturbance was over. "What o'clock is it?"

"Nearly two."

"What have you been up to?"

"Walking in the garden. I ran into the marchesa in the belvedere. As long as you're awake, I think I'll ring and see if Dipper's returned from the festival."

He pulled the bell-rope. MacGregor sat up in bed, saying tartly, "Heaven forbid a man should have to take off his own clothes at night."

"Quite so," Julian agreed.

"What was the marchesa doing in the belvedere?"

"Not a great deal."

"Didn't you want to know why she was there?"

"I asked. She said it seemed the last place people would be likely to look for her. She wanted to be alone. Hearing Orfeo sing had disturbed her."

"You mean, because she thinks he killed her husband?"

Julian set his candle on a table and sat down, stretching out his legs before him. "I think there's more to it than that. She begged me to find Orfeo, and I don't think it was simply to avenge her husband's murder. There was a passion behind her request that I don't understand."

"Sounds as if she knows more about Orfeo than she's telling."

"Or feels more about him. But then again, we may be looking at this the wrong way round. Perhaps she wants Orfeo found and charged with the murder in order to protect someone else—one of Marchese Lodovico's family, or even herself."

"Or de la Marque?" MacGregor suggested.

"Yes," said Julian after a moment, "or de la Marque."

Dipper came in. "I'm glad to see you back safe and sound," Julian said.

"Thankee, sir. But there was nothing to fret your eyelids about. When it comes to larking, this here festival can't hold a candle to Bartholomew Fair or the Westminster Dog Pit."

"Have you heard about our visitation tonight?" asked MacGregor. "Orfeo turned up and sang us a ditty in the garden."

"Yes, sir. Commissario Grimani, he's been in the village rounding up all the *sbirri* as ain't too snuffy to stand upright."

Julian thought it like Dipper to know the Italian equivalent of calling the police *pigs* or *traps* in English. "Did you see Fletcher and St. Carr in the village tonight?"

"No, sir. But I wasn't there long. Nina and me, we got separated, and she went out in a boat with some of the other servants, and I didn't want her to think I was knocking up a lark with Rosa, so I swam out to her boat."

"In this weather?" exclaimed MacGregor. "I know it was a mild evening, but even so, you'll catch your death of cold. Why didn't you take a boat?"

"I thought she'd like this better, sir. H'Italian gals, they likes a cove to cut a dash."

"She won't like it so well when you start snuffling and sneezing," MacGregor warned.

"She took care to see I wouldn't, sir—brought me back here and give me a posset to warm the cockles of me heart—"

"I think," said Julian, "to avoid scandalizing the good doctor, we had better not hear any more about your cockles." He wondered, with some exasperation, why Dipper's love affairs were always so simple, and his own always so complex. "At least if in spite of all this tender care you should take cold, we still have the medicine I brought from Milan."

"Nothing but strong spirits, I expect," said MacGregor.

"I hope so," said Julian. "That's why I kept it."

There were footsteps and muffled male voices in the garden behind the villa. Julian looked out of the window. "Two soldiers have taken up sentry duty at the back door."

"What's the point of that?" said MacGregor. "Orfeo is long gone."

"Unless he's de la Marque, in which case he may return at any time. In fact, what would you wager he's just come back, and the soldiers are here to see that he remains?"

As if on cue, a male voice was heard singing inside the villa, *"Che invenzione, che invenzione prelibata, bella, bella, bella—"*

Julian looked out into the hall. De la Marque appeared at the top of the main staircase, nearly opposite Julian's room. When he saw Julian, he stopped singing and exclaimed, "Ah, *mon vieux*! I've just heard about Orfeo's impromptu serenade! I am desolate to have missed it! Do you suppose he'll return for an encore?"

"I have no idea."

De la Marque beamed at him. "*Mon cher anglais,* have I ever told you how tremendously I admire you?" He staggered to Julian, embracing him and kissing him on both cheeks.

Julian extricated himself and took him by the arm. "Allow me to help you to your room."

"No, no." De la Marque put Julian from him. "I'm half seas over, and there's no telling what madly imprudent thing I might say. Go to bed, *mon très cher camarade.* We'll talk in the morning."

He reeled off to his room, resuming under his breath, *"Che invenzione prelibata, bella, bella, bella—"*

MacGregor shrugged into his old wool dressing-gown and joined Julian at the door. "He's singing that same song—the one Orfeo sang!"

"Yes. But either he isn't Orfeo or he's not so foxed as he appears. Because he's singing it in the baritone range."

Next morning the villa party gathered on the terrace, drinking coffee before embarking for Sunday mass. De la Marque was the last to appear. His dark face was a pale, sickly olive, and he winced at the sunlight. The marchesa was all solicitude, settling him in a chair out of the sun and sending servants for cushions and strong coffee. Julian was exasperated. How, after last night, could she make so much of de la Marque under his nose? Was she merely trying to throw dust in people's eyes about her feelings for Julian? Or did she repent of the encouragement she had given him, and was this her way of putting a damper on his hopes?

Grimani strode up to de la Marque. "I wish to know where you were at ten o'clock last night."

"And good morning to *you*, Signor Commissario."

"You refuse to answer?"

"I should be grateful if you would defer your questions until I can only see one of you."

"I have no time to wait upon your convenience. Either you will answer my questions here and now, or I shall obtain a warrant from the podestà to commit you to the village gaol until you are more tractable."

De la Marque sat slowly back in his chair, his eyes on Grimani's face. "Very well, Signor Commissario. Ask away."

Zanetti placed a chair for Grimani opposite de la Marque's, then took a seat further back, his portable writing-desk open on his lap.

"Where were you at ten o'clock last night?" Grimani commenced.

"At the festival."

"I know you claim to have gone to the festival. But where were you at precisely ten o'clock?"

"I really have no idea. My best guess would be that I was out in a boat."

"For what purpose?"

De la Marque's lips curved into a smile. "I ran into a most charming woman from Milan, who had somehow got separated from her husband. As she was feeling rather forlorn, I took her out on the lake to console her. We moored in a hollow in the rocks south of Solaggio."

"How long were you there?"

"Perhaps two hours."

"What were you doing?"

"Oh, talking," said de la Marque mockingly.

"About what?"

"About the remarkable probity and efficiency of the Milanese police."

Grimani glared. "You may be under the impression, monsieur, that being a foreigner, you are not subject to Milanese justice. It may interest you to know that your countryman, Monsieur Andryane, is now serving the second year of his life sentence in the prison fortress of Spielberg for conspiring against the government of Lombardy-Venetia."

De la Marque withdrew his gaze for a moment. "May I ask what I've done to be threatened with a prison fortress?"

"I am asking the questions. Where is this woman you say you were with last night?"

"I don't know. We parted company on the pier. I assume she rejoined her husband."

"What was her name?"

"We thought it more prudent not to exchange names, Signor Commissario."

"I see. Did anyone else see you out on the lake with her?"

"I shouldn't think so. We took care not to be seen."

Julian glanced at the marchesa, wondering how she felt about this adventure of de la Marque's. She was listening intently, but without the slightest appearance of shock or jealousy. Either she did not care about de la Marque's relations with other women, or she did not believe his story.

"Of course," said Grimani, "you realize this gives you no alibi at all?"

"No alibi?" De la Marque widened his eyes. "Whatever can you mean, Signor Commissario? Has there been another murder, and am I the last to hear of it?"

"Don't be disingenuous, monsieur. I mean that you can't prove you weren't singing in the garden last night."

De la Marque's black eyes gleamed with amusement. "So you think that *I* am your elusive nightingale?"

"You fit the description. You're about the right age, to begin with. How old are you?"

"Twenty-eight."

"Near enough. Orfeo claimed to be twenty-one four and a half years ago. What's more, you read music—in fact you have perfect pitch, and I understand you're writing a book on singing."

"I scribble at it from time to time." De la Marque spoke easily, but his eyes never left Grimani's.

Grimani went on, "You speak English extremely well, according to Zanetti."

"That's hardly surprising. I grew up in England."

"But you are also French, and Maestro Donati thought Orfeo's accent sounded more French than English."

"Did he?" de la Marque responded brightly.

Grimani turned to Donati. "Maestro, does Monsieur de la Marque's voice remind you of Orfeo's?"

"No, Signor Commissario," said Donati. "His voice is deeper and has a different tone."

"Could a tenor like Orfeo feign a deeper voice?" Grimani pursued.

Donati looked troubled. "I suppose so."

Grimani's gaze returned to de la Marque. "Where were you in the first months of 1821?"

"In Turin."

"Can you prove that?"

"I shouldn't think so."

Grimani rose. "Monsieur de la Marque, I must ask you not to leave the neighbourhood until I give you leave. If you do, you will be hunted down and brought back. One word more: if you are Orfeo and a Carbonaro, you would do well to confess it before you are exposed. Your only hope of leniency is to cooperate with the police—in particular by giving us the names of any secret society colleagues of yours who remain at large. We know there are many Angeli, in particular, who plotted against the state in '21 and were never caught."

"Worse and worse!" laughed de la Marque. "You accuse me of being a tenor, a murderer, and now a revolutionary! I should like to see my family's faces at the thought—especially my great-aunt Mathilde, who was lady-in-waiting to Marie Antoinette, and still powders her hair and calls her little house in the Faubourg St. Germain *le petit Versailles*."

There was a sudden movement on the lake. A boat was cutting swiftly toward the villa, bearing a young gendarme. He leaped out the moment the boat touched the pier, ran up the stairs to the terrace, and presented himself before Grimani. "Signor Commissario, I have dispatches from my sergeant, who begs you will read them at once and send me back to him with instructions."

"Come inside." Grimani turned briefly to the marchesa. "I'll follow Your Ladyship to mass as soon as I'm at liberty."

He and the gendarme went inside. Nina brought the marchesa's veil and parasol, and the marchesa, Carlo, Francesca, Valeriano, Donati, and Sebastiano prepared to depart for mass. MacGregor went inside to observe the Sabbath in his own way.

"Are you coming to mass?" the marchesa asked de la Marque and Julian.

"I must beg you to excuse me," said de la Marque. "I'm still recovering from last night's religious excesses."

"I'll stay and bear you company," said Julian.

The marchesa smiled as if she would have liked to witness this tête-à-tête. "Then good morning to you, gentlemen. Monsieur de la Marque, I shall pray for your recovery."

"Then, Marchesa, I count myself cured already, since no prayer of yours could possibly be refused."

The marchesa smiled a little wryly. She and her party embarked for Solaggio, and Julian and de la Marque had the terrace to themselves.

De la Marque looked dolefully into his empty cup. "*Mon vieux*, would you be kind enough to ring for more coffee?"

"I should recommend soda water."

"As you will." De la Marque leaned back in his chair and closed his eyes.

At Julian's bidding, a servant brought a bottle of soda water and two glasses and set them on a little wicker table before de la Marque. Julian drew up a chair for himself. "Allow me," he said, pouring them each a glass.

De la Marque took an experimental swallow. "Ugh. It's certainly insipid enough to be wholesome." He glanced in the direction Grimani and the gendarme had disappeared. "What do you suppose that's about?"

"To judge by the state of the gendarme's boots and the way he walks as if he still felt the saddle under him, he's come a long distance in a hurry. But why he should have ridden like thunder to see Grimani on a Sunday morning, the devil only knows."

"If the devil knows," said de la Marque, "then Grimani will find a way to make him talk." He began to laugh. "Fancy his taking me for Orfeo! It's outrageously droll."

"You aren't alone. He also suspects Fletcher and St. Carr."

"But not you, my enigmatic friend?"

"No, not I. You see, I was there when Orfeo sang."

De la Marque blinked at him. "*Mon dieu.* How very fortunate for you."

"Well, it's convenient. I should have found it a nuisance to be dogged at every step of the investigation by suspicion of being Grimani's mysterious singer."

"So instead it's I who'll have my life plagued out by his persecutions. Heavens know, I should be delighted to tell him more about that enchanting little vixen I picked up, but I don't suppose he would be interested in those sorts of details. He's distressingly un-Italian."

"Conte Carlo says he strives to be more German than the Austrians he serves."

"That's not surprising. It's very common for a prisoner to identify himself with his captors."

Julian looked at him more closely. "I wasn't aware you had political views about Austrian rule in Italy."

"I don't. But I know something about the effects of being a prisoner. A cousin of mine was arrested during the Reign of Terror, and fell so under the sway of his captors that by the time he was released, he was waving the tricolour and calling everyone *'Citizen.'* He was a great embarrassment to the family." He shrugged. "The weak always ape the powerful, as servants in England take their masters' names and assume their privileges below stairs. Grimani finds it ill-convenient and restrictive to be an Italian, so he becomes an Austrian in every way he can, and in the end he convinces himself—but he will never quite convince the Austrians."

"If you're not careful, Monsieur de la Marque, I shall begin to think you profound."

"*Mon vieux*, I am French. My nation's greatest talent is to appear cleverer than we are."

Julian smiled. "I've been meaning to ask you something. Did you know Philippe de Goncourt?"

"La Beatrice's first husband? No, I never met him. He was an aristocrat who went over to Bonaparte, which made him *persona non grata* in my family's set. I must say, I envy him. Imagine being the man to introduce the divine Beatrice to the art of love! At least I assume he was the first. For all the licence granted to married women in this country, young virgins are very closely guarded."

"No doubt you've made attempts."

"No doubt."

Grimani and the gendarme came out onto the terrace again. "What news, Signor Commissario?" de la Marque hailed him.

"Nothing I can discuss at present," Grimani flung at him as he passed. He and the gendarme descended the stairs to the pier, presumably to catch what remained of mass.

Julian and de la Marque exchanged foreboding looks. "This is very ominous," said de la Marque.

"Yes," agreed Julian. "Grimani was smiling."

Soon after the marchesa and her party returned from mass, half a dozen soldiers brought Fletcher and St. Carr to the villa for questioning. Grimani received them in the drawing room, with Zanetti to act as scribe and interpreter. The marchesa requested that Julian and she be allowed to attend as well. Grimani acquiesced with a fairly good grace. Julian wondered more than ever what was in those dispatches the gendarme had brought.

The soldiers marched the two young Englishmen in and brought them to stand before Grimani's chair. They both looked extremely rattled. Fletcher rallied first.

"What the deuce is happening?" he appealed to Julian in English. "When Beverley and I came back from the festival early this morning, there were soldiers all around our inn. They let us in, but they wouldn't let us out. Signora Frascani, the landlady, was in a ferocious taking, threatening to chuck us out for bringing the soldiers down on her house. Then we heard that this singer everyone is looking for turned up here last night, and the police suspect he's one of us!"

Zanetti translated this for Grimani. He was a first-rate interpreter, smooth and swift, and so self-effacing that he seemed a mere appendage Grimani used for speaking, like a tongue or a larynx.

Grimani turned to the sergeant in command of the soldiers. "Have you secured their passports?"

"Yes, Signor Commissario." The sergeant presented two well-worn documents stamped with assorted visas.

"That's another thing," said Fletcher to Grimani. "If you take our passports, how are we to go anywhere?"

"I don't wish you to go anywhere," said Grimani. "If and when I determine that neither of you is the Englishman I am seeking, your passports will be returned."

"But you can't do that!" Fletcher expostulated. "We're British subjects!"

"My father knows the British consul in Milan," bleated St. Carr.

"Then I suggest you take this up with the British consul," Grimani rejoined.

"We can't," said Fletcher, seething. "We don't have any passports. We couldn't go one posting stage without being stopped. But we'll write to him, never fear—or do you mean to stop our correspondence, too?"

"You have only to satisfy me of your innocence," said Grimani, "and the police will take no further interest in your affairs."

"What about Monsieur de la Marque's passport?" the marchesa murmured to Grimani. "Do you mean to take that as well?"

"Yes," said Grimani. "I've obtained warrants from the podestà to detain all their passports."

Julian did not suppose this had been very difficult. The obsequious Ruga would not oppose any wish of a commissario who was rumoured to stand in high favour with the Director General of Police.

Grimani opened one of the passports and perused it. "Hugo Patrick Fletcher, born July eighth, 1799." He looked up at Fletcher. "You are precisely the age Orfeo claimed to be."

"I can't help that," said Fletcher.

"Where were you from December of 1820 to March of 1821?"

"Oh, Lord." Fletcher ran a hand through his wiry brown hair. "Let me think. I'd been helping a natural scientist in Berlin with a book he was writing. It was finished at the end of 1820, and I knocked about France and the German states for about six months."

"You never came to Italy?"

"Not then, no."

"But you have been here before?"

"Yes, afterward. I was living in Berlin, teaching English and studying natural science. During school holidays I travelled. I came once to Italy—no, twice. I returned to England last December, when my father died."

"Why are you in Italy now?"

"Because Lord and Lady St. Carr, whose steward my father was, asked me to take their son on the Continent." He added with an edge to his voice, "They were under the impression that Italy was a civilised place, and that every gentleman ought to see it."

"You will find Italy most civilised and hospitable toward those who come with benign intentions. Can anyone vouch for your whereabouts in the first months of 1821?"

"I shouldn't think so. I was mostly on my own. I suppose if I thought hard, I might remember someone." He spread out his fingers helplessly. "It was so long ago."

"If I were you," said Grimani, "I would attempt to remember. Where were you last night at ten o'clock?"

"At the festival."

"That is not sufficiently precise."

"It's the best I can tell you. I was moving about all the time, looking for—" He broke off.

"Yes?"

"For all the different things there were to see—singing, dancing, and so on."

"Were you alone?"

"Yes." Fletcher grinned. "Sometimes even a tutor has to slip his leash for a bit."

"Now, that's too bad, Hugo!" protested St. Carr. "First you blow me up for going off on my own and making you hunt for me half the night, and now you say you wanted to be alone anyway!"

"Beverley," said Fletcher in a strained voice, "I think you should let me answer the questions."

Grimani turned his icy gaze on St. Carr. "When you went off on your own last night, where did you go?"

"Oh, anywhere and everywhere. I was getting on quite famously with everybody, especially the soldiers."

"It's wonderful what stumping up for a few bottles of wine can accomplish," muttered Fletcher.

Grimani's eyes remained fixed on St. Carr. "Where were you at ten o'clock last night?"

"Look here," stammered St. Carr, "I don't think—"

"Answer the question. Where were you at ten o'clock?"

"I don't know. I never think about what time it is."

"Can anyone swear to your whereabouts at or about that time?"

"I don't see how. I was always running into new people, and I don't know who they were, or where they came from. I say, I don't like above half what you're implying!"

"Beverley!" broke in Fletcher. "Think before you speak!"

"But, Hugo, he's making me out to be a liar! He thinks I was skulking about here last night, *singing* to people!"

"For God's sake, Beverley!" Fletcher threw up his hands. "He's making you out to be a murderer! If you're this singer Orfeo, then it's all Lombard Street to an eggshell that you killed Marchese Malvezzi!"

St. Carr's jaw dropped. "*I* killed him? I never even met him!"

"It's ridiculous to think Beverley is Orfeo," Fletcher argued to Grimani. "He's too young."

Grimani opened St. Carr's passport. "Beverley Percival Stanhope St. Carr," he read, stumbling a little over the English names. "Born April ninth, 1803." He looked up at St. Carr. "You would have been nearly eighteen in the first months of 1821. That's old enough for your voice to have changed. And it would have been very natural for you to give your age as twenty-one, to reassure Marchese Malvezzi that you weren't a minor and could take responsibility for yourself."

"But I *didn't*!" exclaimed St. Carr. "I wasn't here! I've never been to Italy before! And I'll tell you something: I'm not ever coming back! I'd no notion a fellow could be pulled about so."

"You can read music," Grimani went on, "and I gather that in your own country you pass for a gentleman."

"Pass for one!" St. Carr sputtered. "No, really, that's—"

"Take a damper, Beverley!" Fletcher caught his arm.

"Where were you from December of 1820 to March of 1821?" Grimani pursued.

"Do I have to answer that?" St. Carr demanded of Fletcher.

Fletcher looked uneasily at Grimani.

"If you don't answer," said Grimani, "you will be taken into custody. The gaol in Solaggio is somewhat primitive. The roof leaks, and the prisoners sleep on straw and are sometimes troubled by rats. But if you choose to go there, it's no concern of mine."

"Can he do that?" St. Carr asked Fletcher in a small voice.

"Why do you keep appealing to him?" Grimani snapped. "You were brought here at my command. I've taken your passports. Can you have any doubt that, if I order these soldiers to take you away and lock you up—for a day, for a week, for however long it takes to bring you to heel—it will be done?"

St. Carr swallowed and said nothing.

"For the last time," said Grimani, "where were you in the first few months of 1821?"

"I was living in Canterbury, with a grinder."

Zanetti broke off interpreting. "A grinder? What is that, please?"

"It's a tutor. An old quiz who hammers knowledge into your head before you go off to university, so that you won't make too much of a cake of yourself when you get there."

"You lived in this man's house?" asked Grimani.

"Yes. He had three of us living with him, muzzing over Latin verbs and that sort of thing."

"How long did you live there'?"

"I don't remember exactly. From about the autumn of 1820 to the summer of 1821."

"What was this grinder's name?"

"Hawkins. And the other pupils were Whitfield and Noyes."

"What were their Christian names?"

"I don't remember. We didn't call each other by them."

"Have you any proof you were in this Can-ter-bury with this grinder at the time Orfeo was here?"

"No, of course not. The other fellows could vouch for me, but—they aren't here."

"No," said Grimani, "they aren't."

"Oh, for the love of God!" broke in Fletcher. "You can't suppose he ran away from the grinder and came all the way to Italy?"

"I have no way of knowing if he was ever with the grinder to begin with. And nor do you. You say you weren't in England at the time."

"But I would have known if he'd disappeared for months! His parents would have written."

"Perhaps they were embarrassed," said Grimani. "Or they didn't know. The grinder may have been afraid to tell them their son had disappeared. Or perhaps he sent Signor St. Carr to Italy deliberately, as a Carbonaro agent. The Carbonari have recruiters everywhere, including England."

"Of all the preposterous—!" Fletcher started to walk about, but found himself hemmed in by the soldiers. He turned back to Grimani, his anger giving way to entreaty. "Signor Commissario, you must see that Beverley isn't your man. He's too young and feather-headed to be a Carbonaro, much less an assassin. He can't sing, and he only learned how to read music so that he could look down the front of ladies' dresses—I beg your pardon, Marchesa."

Beatrice inclined her head with the faintest of smiles.

"So give him back his passport," Fletcher urged, "and let him cross into Switzerland. I'll stand surety for him."

Grimani waved this aside. "Why have you come to Solaggio?"

"We were looking for rural peace and quiet," said Fletcher wryly.

Grimani rose. "This interrogation is concluded. You may go about your business. When I need you again, I'll send for you."

"And you expect us to cool our heels here until you're convinced that neither of us is Orfeo?" said Fletcher. "How the deuce do you prove you can't sing? You can croak a few lines off-key, but you may be play-acting. The fact is, this is a stalemate, and I don't see any end to it."

"It may end sooner than you think." And for the second time that day, Grimani smiled.

He signed to the soldiers that they might go. Fletcher hung back, apparently wanting to speak to Julian. Zanetti drew near, to overhear whatever they might say. "Oh, hang it!" said Fletcher, and tramped out, St. Carr with him.

Grimani tucked the two passports into an inside pocket of his coat. "You've been remarkably quiet, Signor Kestrel."

"I shouldn't think you would object to that," said Julian.

"I don't. I approve. I'm told that in England people go to the magistrates' courts as if they were theatres, to watch the interrogations. I can tolerate you on those terms."

He went out, Zanetti scurrying after him. Julian was left alone with the marchesa for the first time since last night. She had taken off the black veil she had worn to church, and her soft hair was uncovered. Only some twelve hours ago, his hands had run riot through that hair and scattered the pins on the floor of the belvedere—

Her thoughts were evidently far from the belvedere. "Grimani is right, Signor Kestrel. You didn't question Signor Fletcher and Signor St. Carr at all."

Julian marked how formally she addressed him. He assumed a cool, calm manner mirroring hers. "I could have added little to Grimani's interrogation, and would have forfeited a great deal."

"I don't understand."

"Some people, Marchesa, will confide in a friend far more readily than they will submit to an enemy. At present, Fletcher and St. Carr are inclined to see me as their ally rather than Grimani's. Why should I do anything to dispel that view?"

"Ah, yes, I see." Her face cleared. "Giuliano, I should have trusted you." She held out her hand. "Will you forgive me?"

He took her hand, but only to bow over it and let it go. "It seems to me, Marchesa, that I wax and wane in your regard in proportion as you find me useful."

"We've agreed that Lodovico's murder must be solved before we can think of anything between us. So why should I not be glad when you come closer to solving it?"

He searched her face. He wanted so much to believe her. "The murder may be solved sooner than we expected—or at all events, the investigation is about to take a decisive turn. Ever since that gendarme arrived, Grimani has been smiling like a spider with its web nearly complete. He's turned up a trump, and is only waiting his opportunity to play it."

Grimani's secret did not come to light until late that day. The villa party had dined early. Francesca and Valeriano had gone walking in the garden, as they often did, while de la Marque, as if in defiance of Grimani, had sauntered off without leaving any word where he was going. The rest of the company were taking coffee on the terrace. The sun, low in the western sky, streaked gold gleams on the lake, and cast long shadows across the white marble floor and balustrade.

The villagers, recovered from last night's celebrations, were out on the lake in force, savouring what remained of this fair, bright Sunday. All at once a larger boat cut a swathe through their lazily drifting craft. It made determinedly for the villa, a little knot of gendarmes aboard.

Grimani rose and watched it approach, his gaze fairly raking the air. At length one of the gendarmes moved, and disclosed a woman seated among them. Grimani let out his breath in satisfaction. "Now you'll see this investigation speedily brought to an end. My men have found Lucia Landi."

Beatrice, Carlo, Julian, MacGregor, and Grimani surged to the balustrade to have a look at the girl—perhaps the only person on earth—who could identify Orfeo by sight. She was about twenty, dressed in a blue skirt, a white blouse, and a blue bodice with red laces. Her hair was dark, her skin brown and satiny. Her proud head and coronet of silver hairpins gave her the air of a captive queen.

Her eyes travelled over the elegant company ranged along the balustrade. She stared longest at Julian, then seemed to ask a question of the others in the boat. The boatman, a veteran of the lake who had ferried guests to and from the villa before, leaned down and spoke to her, jabbing a finger in Julian's direction. Her eyes blazed up at Julian again, and her face hardened.

"She was discovered last night," said Grimani, "in the town of Brescia, about seventy miles from here. She's been a servant there for the past three years, since her father died."

"Why has it taken so long to find her?" asked Julian.

"Her employers, out of a misplaced desire to protect her, delayed in telling the police where she was. But in the end they did their duty, and my men travelled to Brescia to collect her. The gendarme who came this morning brought me word that she was on her way."

Lucia's boat bumped against the pier. Two gendarmes sprang out and helped her to alight. Julian saw that her wrists were handcuffed behind her. He turned sharply to Grimani. "Half a dozen gendarmes, and they needed to put her in irons?"

"They followed proper procedure," said Grimani. "She grew up on this lake and no doubt swims like a fish. They couldn't risk her jumping overboard to escape."

"I wouldn't blame her if she did!" exclaimed Carlo. "Blood Of Diana! She's only a slip of girl, and a witness, not a criminal!"

"My men had their reasons," was all Grimani would say.

Lucia walked meekly up the stairs to the terrace, the six gendarmes forming a phalanx around her. At the top, she broke from them so suddenly that they were caught off guard. She rushed up to Julian. "The boatman told me who you are! You're the Englishman who's come to capture Orfeo! But you will not do it! I tell you, you will not touch him!"

Julian was so taken aback that for a moment he could not reply.

"The boatman said you've come all the way from England to help the police trap Orfeo," she stormed. "Bah! You know nothing about him!" She looked around fiercely at the others. "None of you knows anything! Only *I* know."

"And you will tell what you know," said Grimani.

"Signor Commissario—" Julian began.

Grimani cut him off. "Lucia Landi, I am Commissario Grimani, of the Milanese police. I've had an account of you from my sergeant. I understand that when you heard my men were coming for you, you ran away into the mountains, and they had to pursue you and bring you back." He glanced toward Carlo. "That, Signor Conte, is why she's in handcuffs. She isn't merely a witness, but Orfeo's accomplice."

"You can take the handcuffs off now," said Julian. "There's no longer any danger of her swimming away. And in any event—"

Lucia rounded on him. "You keep the hell out of this! I can fight my own battles!"

"Softly, softly!" said Carlo. "My dear little girl, let me look at you. What a beautiful woman you've grown!"

"Thank you, Excellency," she said more gently, and curtsied. Julian realized that she and Carlo must remember each other from the days when the villa was his, and her father was his gardener.

Carlo turned to Grimani. "Signor Commissario, it's absurd to speak of this girl as Orfeo's accomplice. We know she had nothing to do with my brother's murder. She was at the castle all that night, looking after a sick maidservant."

"That doesn't prevent her being an accessory after the fact," said Grimani. "She resisted giving information about Orfeo after the murder, and last night she ran away sooner than help the police identify him." He bent a hard, intent gaze on Lucia. "You are in serious trouble. If you are charged as an accessory, you could spend your youth, perhaps your life, behind prison walls. But you are young, and obviously were in love with this scoundrel you protected so foolishly. So I'll give you a chance to atone. Tell all you know about Orfeo, and I can save you. Conceal anything, and you are lost."

"Oh, yes," said Lucia quietly, "I'll tell you about Orfeo. I'll tell you all you need to know."

Julian drew a long breath. The marchesa hardly seemed to breathe at all. Grimani smiled his tight, cold smile and said to the sergeant of gendarmes, "Remove her handcuffs."

The sergeant obeyed. Lucia flexed her wrists in relief, then began, "I met Orfeo when Marchese Malvezzi brought him and Maestro Donati to live at the villa." She looked at Donati, who was seated a little way away. "It's good to see you again, Maestro."

"And to hear your voice, little Lucia," Donati said.

"Go on," ordered Grimani.

"Orfeo was stuck at the villa all day, with no young people to talk to but Tonio and me. Tonio was a cur and a lout, and no sort of friend for him, so there was only me. He would walk with me in the garden, or fetch and carry things for me about the house. He was always wanting to help me with my work, even when it wasn't fit for a gentleman. It was partly that he was kind, and partly that he was bored. He worked hard at his music, but it couldn't take up every minute of every day."

"What did you and he talk about?" asked Grimani.

"He would talk to me about singing, or ask me about things I knew more about than he did, like gardening and fishing. But oftentimes we wouldn't talk at all."

Grimani's lip curled.

She lifted her chin. "I know what you're thinking, but you're wrong. He never touched me. Oh, sometimes he looked at me and thought of it. A girl knows when a man is thinking that way. But I was very young and had never known a man, so he was careful of me. You wouldn't understand. We were friends, so far as a peasant girl can be friends with a man of his quality. He called me Barbarina."

"Barbarina?" said MacGregor, who had been following her peasant's Milanese with great difficulty.

"Barbarina is the gardener's daughter in *The Marriage of Figaro*," said Julian in English.

Lucia whirled toward him. "What is he saying? Signor, what did you say just then?"

Julian repeated it in Milanese.

"I don't trust you," she muttered, glaring at him. "You might try to trick me by talking your language behind my back. If you do it again, I won't say a word more—not to you, not to anyone."

"You will speak when I require it," Grimani told her, "and to me, not to Signor Kestrel. Did Orfeo ever talk to you about politics?"

"No, Signor Commissario."

"Did he ever express any feelings toward Marchese Malvezzi?"

She lowered her eyes. "In words, only gratitude."

"How do you mean, 'in words'?"

"His eyes showed he had other feelings. How could he help it? Maestro Donati loved him, called him 'my son.' But to the marchese, he was only a voice. He felt that. It was one of the things he had dark thoughts about."

"One of the things? What were the others?"

"I don't know, Signor Commissario. I only know he had dark thoughts, and sang to keep them away."

"This is all fancy," said Grimani. "Tell me about his fight with Tonio in the grottos. It was you who found them fighting and summoned your father to stop them."

"I didn't find them fighting. I was there from the beginning. The fight was about me."

The others exchanged startled glances. Donati said in amazement, "About you, Lucia?"

"Yes, Maestro. Tonio had been wanting me for a long time. He never spoke of it, but I knew by the way he stared at me—followed me with his eyes. And Orfeo knew. He wanted me to keep away from Tonio, and on no account to be alone with him. But I didn't pay enough heed to his warning. I thought so little of Tonio, I couldn't be bothered to be afraid of him.

"On the day the marchese died, God rest his soul, I went to the grottos to fetch some wine. Tonio followed me and came down after me. At first he was tongue-tied and more afraid of me than I was of him. But when he realized he had me trapped down there, he grew bolder and bolder. He grabbed me, and I couldn't get away.

"Orfeo came. He'd known I was going to the grottos, and when he couldn't find Tonio, he got worried. He pulled Tonio away from me, and they went down grappling and punching and beating each other's heads on the floor. Orfeo was faster and smarter, but Tonio was much bigger, and he was furious. I ran for help. Thank the blessed Madonna, I found my father nearby, and he came and broke up the fight."

"Orfeo and Tonio told Marchese Malvezzi they were fighting over a game of cards," Grimani objected.

"Orfeo made that up on the spur of moment," said Lucia. "It was for my sake. He knew it would look bad for me if people found out two young men had been fighting over me in the grottos. Everyone would think I was the mistress of one or the other."

"But why did Tonio hold his tongue and let Orfeo lie about the cause of the fight?" asked Carlo.

"What would you have had him say, Excellency? 'Excuse me, but it wasn't a card game. I was trying to attack the virtue of this girl, and Signor Orfeo prevented me.' That wouldn't have helped him."

"Her story does have the ring of truth," said Carlo to Grimani.

"It's exactly like Orfeo," Donati put in.

"It's a drama out of some opera or ballad," Grimani scoffed. "You expect me to believe that, with political rebellion threatening on all sides, and only hours before he killed Marchese Malvezzi in cold blood, Orfeo was rushing about rescuing damsels like some trumpery Tancred?"

"I only know he rescued me. I was never so afraid in all my life as I was down there in the dark, with Tonio slobbering on me and pushing me against the wall and forcing his hand up my skirt. Orfeo came and saved me, at the risk of his own life—because Tonio was so angry, he might have killed him." She lifted her head and looked Grimani straight in the eyes. "And that is why I will never tell you what Orfeo looked like, or anything about him that might help you find him. I have a right to protect him, as he protected me! If he were here, he would understand."

"If he would let any harm come to you on his account," said Julian, "he wouldn't be worth protecting."

"No harm has come to me yet, signor," she urged. "There would be time enough for Orfeo to interfere if I were really in danger. In the meantime, he wouldn't break my heart by giving himself up for nothing."

"He will never give himself up for you or anyone else." Grimani advanced on her, his words clear and cutting as glass.

"Like every foolish peasant girl tumbled by a gentleman, you cling to the benighted notion that your lover is a hero. But your lover is a murderer—probably a Carbonaro as well—who made use of you and forgot you, and would laugh up his sleeve if he knew of the sacrifice you wish to make for him. I shall give you a taste of just how great a sacrifice it is. Sergeant, put on her handcuffs again, and attach a rope to drag her by. We'll exhibit her to the village, and then lock her in the gaol."

"That won't make me talk!" Lucia flung up her head defiantly, though her voice trembled.

"Listen to me," said Grimani softly, his face close to hers. "Before I am finished with you, you will wish you were back in the grotto with Tonio."

Julian stepped between them. "Signor Commissario, this has gone far enough—"

"Wait." Marchesa Malvezzi glided among them. "You're too harsh with her, Signor Commissario." She turned Lucia gently to face her. "You know that my husband was murdered, don't you, Lucia?"

"Yes, Your Ladyship."

"Can you conceive what a grief it is to me that he died in the prime of life, unshriven, with all his sins upon him?"

Lucia stared in horror and crossed herself. "I'm sorry for it, Your Ladyship, with all my heart!"

"You must see that the one thing we can do for him now is to avenge his murder. And you may be the only person in the world who can help us."

"But Your Ladyship, that's just what I can't do," Lucia pleaded. "I don't know anything about His Excellency's murder, except that Orfeo didn't do it. He never would have! Please believe me."

"My dear, I believe that *you* believe it." The marchesa turned to Grimani. "Grant me this favour, Signor Commissario. Give Lucia a few days to reflect quietly on the course she's chosen. Her own good sense and conscience will do more to persuade her than all your threats and punishments."

"You expect me simply to let her go?" said Grimani. "She'll only run away again, and my men will have to bring her back."

"I'm not suggesting that you let her go," said the marchesa. "I only wish you to find a more comfortable lodging for her than the gaol. Signor Ruga has the largest house in Solaggio—I'm sure he could spare a room for her, and would guard her well, if only out of fear of you. And Don Cristoforo could come and pray with her and remind her of her duty under man's law and God's."

Grimani looked from Lucia to the marchesa and back again. "Very well. I'll give you three days to repent of your obstinacy. But if at sundown on Wednesday you still refuse to help the police identify Orfeo, it will be worse for you than if I had never given you this respite. Do you understand?"

"Yes, Signor Commissario." Lucia turned gratefully to the marchesa and curtsied. "Your Ladyship has been so good to me! Thank you."

"Don't thank me, Lucia," the marchesa said kindly. "Only consider whether you can find it in your heart to help me."

"I only wish I knew something that could help Your Ladyship. If I did, I would tell it. I swear by all the saints!"

Lucia was taken inside the villa to wait while Grimani sent a soldier to summon Ruga from Solaggio. Julian turned to the marchesa. "Thank you for intervening as you did. You may have prevented another murder."

"Another murder?" she said, startled. "Do you mean that Orfeo would have killed to protect her?"

"I mean that I was within an ace of strangling Grimani."

"Oh." She smiled. "Grimani uses the weapons he knows. He lacks imagination, as I told you from the first. The last thing to do with a girl of her spirit is to make her a martyr—she'll glory in the role. What was it you said?—some people will confide in a friend more readily than they will submit to an enemy. So I've become Lucia's protector. We'll see whether a gentle tapping may not open her heart more quickly than a battering ram."

"Do you feel nothing for her?" Julian asked.

"I feel for her," the marchesa said seriously. "I think she loved Orfeo, that she was another victim—" She stopped. "And I feel for you," she went on, smiling. "I could see that you were outraged to the depths of your chivalrous English soul by Grimani's methods." She looked gravely toward the door through which Lucia had disappeared. "She had better make good use of the next three days to wean herself of her loyalty to Orfeo. Grimani accedes to my wishes in small matters, because it suits his Austrian masters to show respect for Italians of my rank, but I have no power over him. And neither for your sake nor for mine will he spare her, after those three days."

Next morning MacGregor ran into Carlo on the terrace. "Ah, Doctor," Carlo greeted him. "I was just going out on the lake for some fishing before the weather changes."

MacGregor squinted at the sky. "It doesn't look like rain."

"I can tell by the wind. Winds on this lake are creatures of habit. The Tivano blows down from the north until noon, then the Breva blows from the south. This morning the winds are unsettled. It's a sure sign of rain."

"Had you better go out?"

"Oh, it won't come till late in the day—perhaps not till tonight. Trust me: I know the moods of this lake as I do the faces of my children. Should you like to come with me?"

MacGregor was tempted. He enjoyed fishing, and it would be a relief to get away from the tensions at the villa for a few hours. He said reluctantly, "I'd better not. I want to find out what's become of Kestrel. He went out first thing in the morning without saying where he was going."

"He's probably off on one of his famous walks in the hills."

"Kestrel never willingly goes anywhere at that hour. He didn't even stop for breakfast—just took a few swallows of coffee and bolted." MacGregor shook his head forebodingly. "I think it's something to do with that girl."

"Lucia?" Carlo shook his head. "*Poverina!* To fall into the hands of the Milanese police is a grim enough fate for anyone. But what chance has a peasant girl against them?"

"She seemed to look after herself pretty well," said MacGregor.

"She's a gallant girl. But that will only make Grimani all the more determined to break her. Our police show mercy to the craven and submissive—the brave must be made an example of."

"Good God!" said MacGregor. "Better by far for the poor girl to tell what she knows of Orfeo, and let him take his chance."

"I agree." Grimani came up to join them. "Any of you who can persuade her to that course are welcome to try."

Carlo translated this for MacGregor, who said, "It isn't as if she's told you nothing. At least you know now what Orfeo and Tonio fought about."

"I know what story she's chosen to tell," said Grimani.

"There's no doubt that the fight was about Lucia, Signor Commissario," said a cool, rather bored voice. "That was evident even before she was found."

They all turned. Kestrel was approaching from the direction of the shore path, his walking-stick tucked under his arm.

"What do you mean?" Grimani asked sharply.

Kestrel turned to Carlo. "Do you remember, Signor Conte, when you showed me the grottos, and I asked you to go up before me and wait outside the cave mouth? I shouted from the grottos as loudly as I could, but you didn't hear me."

"Well," said Carlo, mystified, "what of that?"

"We'd been given to understand that Orfeo and Tonio were fighting in the grottos, and Lucia heard them and ran to fetch her father. But that was impossible, because however much noise they made, it wouldn't have reached her outside the caves. It was far more likely she was with them in the grottos from the beginning. And when two young men come to blows in the presence of the only female in their midst, the odds are very good that she is the cause."

"Why didn't you tell me this?" Grimani demanded.

"I beg your pardon, Signor Commissario. I didn't suppose my opinions were of any interest to you."

"That's never stopped you expressing them before."

Kestrel regarded him with a faint, enigmatic smile. "As far as you know, Signor Commissario."

Grimani's eyes blazed. "If you're keeping anything else from me, Signor Kestrel, you had better out with it! I won't be trifled with!"

"I'm not trifling," Kestrel said calmly. "I've never been more in earnest."

"You would be well advised not to make an enemy of me."

"I won't if I can avoid it. But nor will I flee from the honour if it's thrust on me."

"Take a damper, man." MacGregor slipped a hand under Kestrel's elbow to lead him away. He had not understood all their conversation, but the tone alarmed him. They had had skirmishes before, but this was different. Kestrel was really angry, and MacGregor knew now why it was a phenomenon Dipper was afraid of. Who would have thought that anything so quiet could have such force?

He and Kestrel crossed the terrace and strolled into the garden. At one time MacGregor would have peppered Kestrel with questions about why he was in such a wayward humour, and what had possessed him to put Grimani on the high ropes. But he had picked up a grain of his young friend's subtlety. Instead of using his tongue, he used his eyes and wits. "You've been to see Lucia."

"I tried. I ran the gauntlet of gendarmes about Ruga's house and spoke with his wife. She assured me that Lucia has a comfortable room, ample food, and no greater annoyance than frequent harangues by Don Cristoforo about her religious duty. I asked to see her, but she sent back a refusal on no uncertain terms. I could have insisted, but what would have been the point? No one—least of all I—will persuade her to talk, when loyalty and conscience bid her be silent."

"Loyalty and conscience?" MacGregor said sceptically. "Say love, and be done with it."

Kestrel did not reply, only slashed at the shrubbery with his walking-stick.

"Do you think Orfeo seduced her?" MacGregor asked.

"No. By which I mean to imply nothing in his favour, and everything in hers."

"You're very taken with her."

Kestrel shrugged. "I admire her courage and dislike Grimani's bullying in equal proportions."

"She certainly took against you."

"She doesn't trust me. I wouldn't either, in her place." He made a small, decisive movement, as if shaking off his brooding. "You must forgive me, my dear fellow. It's rattled me, realizing how little time I have left to solve this murder. In less than three days Grimani will call Lucia to account. She won't give in, and the devil only knows what he'll do to her."

"So we have to find the murderer by Wednesday night."

"The murderer—or Orfeo."

MacGregor frowned. "You think Orfeo is innocent, don't you?"

"Of the murder, yes."

"If you hand him over to Grimani, it'll most likely be the finish of him, innocent or not. Doesn't that trouble you?"

"Yes," owned Kestrel wryly. "But Orfeo has got himself into this fix, with his hole-and-corner appearing and disappearing. If it comes to a choice between him and Lucia, I shall hand him over to Grimani trussed and ready for roasting."

MacGregor felt a shiver down his back. "What are we going do now?"

"I've been standing too close to this puzzle—looking at the parts instead of at the whole. I need to take stock of what we know so far, and what we need to find out." Kestrel smiled. "In short, my dear fellow, there's nothing I should like so much as to talk it all out with you."

"Well, I'm here." MacGregor clapped him on the shoulder. "You talk, and I'll listen."

"We can't talk as freely here as I should like. This garden is a paradise for eavesdroppers, and there are too many English-speaking people about. Do you remember we talked of visiting Villa Pliniana?"

"The place with the intermittent spring? Yes."

"I think it's time we had a look at that spring."

"Lead on," said MacGregor.

"We can't hide in our room all afternoon," said Fletcher.

"I'm not hiding," rejoined St. Carr. "I just don't like being stared at."

"People stared at us before we were ever suspected of being Orfeo."

"Well, it's got much worse. And they point and cross themselves and mutter. You'd think we were Hottentots."

"I should have thought you'd be glad to get out for a bit," coaxed Fletcher. "Only yesterday you were complaining that the fire smoked, the windows banged, and the landlady's geese were so loud, you were sure they were penned up under your bed."

"I don't want to go out. I want to go back to England. This place is detestable, the people gibber like monkeys, and the police are raving mad. This is all your fault. When we left Milan, you said—"

There was a violent knocking at their door. Fletcher opened it and found Marianna Frascani, arms akimbo, eyes snapping, a pair of long, wicked hairpins stuck through her iron-grey topknot like crossed swords. She launched into a tirade in Milanese.

"Slower!" pleaded Fletcher. "I can't understand a word you're saying."

"That commissario from Milan is here with a troop of soldiers! He wants to see you and the young signor at once." She shook her fist under Fletcher's nose. "For two days I've had the police in and about my house on your account—I, who never had a speck of trouble with them before!"

She stormed off. Fletcher and St. Carr had no choice but to follow. They made their way through the maze of corridors surrounding their room, and descended to the dark, bare foyer of the inn. Here they found Commissario Grimani, his aide-de-camp Zanetti, and four soldiers in the sky-blue and silver uniform of Austria. A little way off, half in shadow, Gaston de la Marque lounged against the wall with his usual insouciant smile.

"What do you want now, Commissario?" said Fletcher.

Grimani said, signalling to Zanetti to interpret, "You may have heard that Lucia Landi has been found. I require you and Signor St. Carr and Monsieur de la Marque to come with me to see her."

"But that's splendid!" said Fletcher. "Beverley, she's the girl who knew Orfeo when he was at the villa four or five years ago. She can tell the police he's neither of us."

"Actually," murmured de la Marque, "by all accounts she's shown no disposition to tell the police anything. That's why the commissario has arranged this little drama—to see if the girl will lose her mind and fling herself into the arms of one or another of us. As she's rumoured to be uncommonly good-looking, I hope you'll permit me to stand in front."

"Do you mean to say she could set us right with the police, and she won't?" exclaimed St. Carr. "I call that monstrous selfish!"

"We're losing time," said Grimani. "Sergeant, take them out."

The soldiers herded Fletcher, St. Carr, and de la Marque together and marched them out, Grimani and Zanetti bringing up the rear. They ascended one of the steep, narrow flights of stairs to the piazza. The villagers scattered before the soldiers like frightened birds, only to gape at the procession from a distance.

"Confound it!" St. Carr fumed. "Hugo, it was your idea to come here—to keep me out of trouble, you said! Can't you do something about this?"

"Signor Commissario," said Fletcher, "where is Mr. Kestrel? Does he know about this?"

"To my knowledge," said Grimani, "no one has appointed Signor Kestrel to a position with the Milanese police—or indeed to any official post at all. This is no affair of his."

They entered the piazza and made for Ruga's tall, whitewashed house. The gendarmes standing guard outside the door parted to let them through. Ruga received them with fulsome greetings and assurances of his vigilance, which Grimani cut short by demanding to see Lucia. Ruga conducted them upstairs.

Lucia had a room under the eaves, with one low window beneath the slanting ceiling. The only furnishings were a plain wooden bedstead and a small chest of drawers with a ewer and basin on it. Two cushions on the floor, with a crucifix hanging above them, formed a rough prie-dieu. Lucia was kneeling there, her back to the door, when Grimani and his party filed in.

She started up and turned, staring at the group of men who all but filled her room. Grimani made a sign, and the soldiers stepped back, leaving Fletcher, St. Carr, and de la Marque exposed to her view. Her eyes travelled slowly over them, then came to rest on Grimani.

"Do you recognize any of these men'?" he asked.

She looked back briefly at the three of them. "Perhaps. Perhaps not."

De la Marque smiled. St. Carr eyed Lucia indignantly. Fletcher's lips parted, and he gazed at her with all his eyes.

"This isn't a child's game!" said Grimani. "Answer me! Is any of these men Orfeo?"

Lucia stared straight ahead, saying nothing.

Grimani turned to Zanetti, who was sitting on the end of the bed, his writing-desk on his knees. "Translate all that passes between us. I don't want these gentlemen to miss a word."

"Yes, Signor Commissario."

"Lucia," said Grimani in a cold, quiet tone, "I want you to understand precisely the danger you face. At present, you have it in your power to help me. You have only to give me Orfeo, and I'll show my gratitude by letting you go. The longer you resist, the greater the risk that I may find him on my own. Maestro Donati may suddenly recognize him by some trick of manner or speech. My men may track down Tonio. If that happens—if Orfeo is in my hands, and you haven't helped me find him—your fate is sealed. Don't delude yourself that Marchesa Malvezzi can protect you. In less than three days, you will be mine, and no one and nothing shall come between us."

He walked slowly, deliberately toward her. "You will come back to Milan with me and be put in the women's prison. You will be the only girl of your stamp there. The other women are all harlots and thieves. You will live with them day by day, and week by week. How long do you suppose it will be before you become like them?"

Lucia backed away before him until she bumped against the wall behind her. He stood over her, continuing in the same soft voice, "I am thirty-six years old, Lucia. In the ordinary course of nature, I can expect to live twice that long. And while I live, you will not come out of prison. You will never see another festival, never marry, never be a mother—unless of such bastards as may be got on you behind prison walls. We try to enforce chastity within the prison, but we don't always succeed."

Lucia's chest heaved. She flattened herself against the wall to keep from brushing against him.

Fletcher sprang forward. "This is inhuman! I won't stand by and see it!"

Two soldiers pulled him back and held him by either arm. Grimani regarded him coolly. "Have you something to confess, Signor Fletcher?"

Fletcher looked at Lucia helplessly, then at Grimani. "I'm not Orfeo. I wish to God I were!"

St. Carr half stepped forward, opened his mouth, closed it again. De la Marque made no movement, only watched Lucia intently, and no longer smiled. Lucia glanced quickly at Fletcher, then averted her eyes from all three men.

Grimani turned back to her. "Tell me what I want to know, and you'll be released. The police will never trouble you again. Is one of these men Orfeo?"

She wet her lips. "Perhaps. Perhaps not."

Grimani's eyes kindled, and he clenched his fists. "Do you doubt I can do all I say, Lucia?"

"No," she whispered.

"It can happen to you, Lucia. It has to many others. Every prisoner weighted down by chains in the Spielberg once deluded himself he would somehow escape—never dreamed he could be immured for the rest of his life in that anteroom to Hell. And yet you go running to meet that fate—and all for the sake of a coward who stands by and lets you suffer, when a word from him might save you!"

"He isn't a coward!" She flung up her head. "Whatever he does, whatever he may seem, it costs him his heart's blood to let me do this for him. He suffers far more than I do. But he understands why I want to do it—he honours me by letting me protect him! I will never betray him—never, never! I don't care *that!* for your threats!"

"Then God have mercy on you, Lucia," said Grimani, "for no one else will." He demanded of Zanetti, "Why does she still have those pins in her hair? They're potential weapons. Take them from her at once."

Zanetti hastened to Lucia and plucked out her silver hairpins. Her glossy brown hair fell down around her shoulders.

"Write her out a receipt for them," said Grimani.

Zanetti sat down once more with his portable desk on his knees. The soldiers eyed Lucia's tumbled hair appreciatively. She looked toward a hook on the wall, where a blue kerchief was hanging, but the soldiers were blocking her way.

De la Marque moved suddenly, took the kerchief, and presented it to her with a respectful bow, as if she were a lady. She curtsied and murmured a word of thanks, but did not meet his eyes.

She tied the kerchief around her head. Zanetti gave her the receipt, which she looked at with blank, illiterate eyes. Grimani went out without a backward glance, Zanetti at his heels. When they had gone, Lucia suddenly lifted her eyes and looked directly at Fletcher, St. Carr, and de la Marque.

Fletcher took a step toward her, then checked himself. St. Carr reddened and looked at the floor. De la Marque bowed to Lucia again, gravely. The soldiers ushered them out.

They emerged into the piazza. The soldiers followed Grimani, leaving the three young men alone. They stood silent, not looking at each other. The piazza was largely deserted, thanks to the intimidating presence of the gendarmes outside Ruga's house. Birds dipped and frolicked around the fountain where the village women usually congregated.

St. Carr asked in a small voice, "What is the Spielberg?"

"It's a fortress in Moravia," said de la Marque, "where the government of Lombardy-Venetia sends eminent poets, philosophers, and other independent thinkers, to be chained by the ankle, sleep on bare boards, and knit greasy, foul-smelling yarn into stockings."

St. Carr stared. "Why would the government want poets to knit stockings?"

"Monsieur de la Marque means they're Carbonari," said Fletcher. "The Spielberg is an Austrian prison."

"Hugo," said St. Carr, "you don't look at all yourself."

"Perhaps Mr. Fletcher is thinking that whichever of us is lucky enough to be chosen as Orfeo may spend the rest of his life in that charming abode. But don't be downcast, Mr. St. Carr—it's far more likely the winning candidate will be hanged out of hand."

"Hugo," said St. Carr shakily, "I should like to go back to the inn."

Fletcher seemed not to hear. "It's a damned outrage, the way Grimani is treating that girl!"

De la Marque shrugged. "Grimani has a good deal at stake. Lucia has the information he needs to solve this murder, and so gain the trust and recognition he needs from his Austrian masters. But she has proved to be a locked chest. What wonder if he will go to any lengths to break her open?"

"You sympathize with him?" said Fletcher, staring.

De la Marque smiled. "To understand is not to sympathize."

"Hugo!" St. Carr urged. "I want to go back to the inn. I want some wine."

"We'll be stared out of countenance there," Fletcher warned. "Everyone will have seen us marched off by the soldiers. And Signora Frascani will be waiting to comb our heads with a three-legged stool."

St. Carr poked the ground with the toe of his boot. "If that girl can bear to be locked up and threatened with prison, and all the rest of it, then I daresay I shan't mind too much being stared at."

Fletcher looked at him in surprise. Then he asked de la Marque, "Will you crack a bottle with us, monsieur?"

"Ordinarily I should be delighted. But just now I have a reckoning at the church."

"A reckoning?" said Fletcher.

"Yes." De la Marque smiled wryly. "I have to light a hundred candles to Santa Pelagia."

"I'm glad to see you in better spirits," said MacGregor.

Julian congratulated himself on seeming so. The truth was, he had never been involved in an investigation that had appeared so hopeless. He had suspects aplenty, but nothing to link any of them to the murder. He had theories, but they were insubstantial—as easily unwoven as spun. The girl he admired was in danger; the woman he loved might be the criminal he sought. He was failing in his task; what was worse, he now felt he had been mad to undertake it. His friend Sir Malcolm Falkland, the classical scholar, would have had a name for what had possessed him. Hubris: the overweening pride that makes a man think he can tilt with gods.

He rose and walked to the parapet of the loggia of Villa Pliniana. From here he could gaze north up the smoke-blue ribbon of water to the frozen summits of the Alps. The villa itself was little better than a ruin. Behind it rose terrace upon terrace of dark cypresses, broken by a waterfall casting itself from the topmost crag into the lake. It was a scene of stark beauty, but not one to lighten the heart.

Julian returned to sit with MacGregor by the famed intermittent spring, which had ebbed and flowed every three hours since the days of ancient Rome. The spring emerged from a cleft in the stone at the back of the loggia. Julian and MacGregor watched the water creep toward Julian's onyx ring, which Julian had placed on the ground. It was a game all travellers played here: waiting for the spring to submerge an object and then withdraw, leaving it dry again. But at present Julian and MacGregor had the place to themselves. It was an ideal spot for the tête-à-tête that Julian had meant to have with MacGregor, but had not yet begun. The devil fly away with all this melancholy, he thought. If I'm to be defeated, at least let it be in a battle and not a rout.

He said, "Do you remember when we discussed the investigation the evening you arrived in Milan, and I said that, if Marchese Lodovico was killed by Carbonari, it couldn't have been merely as an incendiary gesture?"

"Yes. Because if they were trying to set off a rebellion, they would have made the murder public."

Julian nodded. "So Marchese Lodovico must have had it in his power to do them some specific harm—most likely by exposing their identities or plans. The Milanese secret societies were plotting an insurrection to coincide with the Piedmontese revolt. Betrayal might well have meant the end, not only of their rebellion, but of their lives. The question is, how might Marchese Lodovico have come by such dangerous knowledge?"

MacGregor thought it over. "He could have overheard a conversation, got hold of a letter meant for somebody else, been approached by one of the rebels who offered to take money for informing on his friends."

"If he was approached by a complete stranger, we shall have the devil of a time finding out anything about it. But if he came upon the information by chance, through eavesdropping or intercepting a letter, that means someone in his circle was privy to Carbonaro secrets, and thus almost certainly a Carbonaro himself."

"Who do you think it was?"

Julian got up and took a turn about the loggia. "We know from Grimani's interrogation of de la Marque that he suspects Orfeo belonged to a Milanese Carbonaro sect called the Angeli. Raversi told me about them: he said the police call them *Diavoli*, devils, in part because they escaped detection in '21, when so many other Milanese Carbonari were exposed. Let's take a leap in the dark and assume that someone close to Marchese Lodovico belonged to the Angeli, and that this person gave him information about them, whether willingly, unwillingly, or inadvertently."

"Then why didn't Marchese Lodovico go straight to the police with it?"

"I should guess that either he hoped to gain still more information from the same source, or the information he had wasn't complete or clear enough to make use of."

"But it was complete enough for the Angeli to kill him in order to stop him revealing it?" MacGregor said sceptically.

"On this hypothesis, yes. They were playing for very high stakes. They might have been unwilling to take the chance that the information could incriminate them."

"This all sounds like so much whipt syllabub—all froth and no substance. But very well: say Marchese Lodovico had information about the Angeli, and say that for some reason or other he kept it to himself. Who do you think gave him the information?"

Julian leaned back against the wall, looking thoughtfully up at the white and grey puffs of cloud slowly filling the sky. "If our Carbonaro is also our murderer, we should be looking for him among Marchese Lodovico's relations and longtime friends."

"How do you make that out?"

"It's almost certain he was killed by someone close to him. Remember the glove. Whoever used it to summon him to the belvedere knew a secret about him that even his wife and brother claim ignorance of, yet one that exerted such power over him that he came to the rendezvous—he, to whom obedience and submission were as foreign as Mohammedanism. That glove is of the greatest importance. It might be the very thread to lead us through this labyrinth—if only we knew how to use it."

Julian continued, "We also know the murderer was familiar with Marchese Lodovico's property. He found his way to Castello Malvezzi at dead of night to leave the note and glove, and he singled out the belvedere as the place of meeting."

"All right: so we have a murderer who was one of the Angeli and was also on close terms with Marchese Lodovico. What else can you daub into your portrait of this person?"

"As long as we're painting in bold strokes, let's eliminate Marchese Lodovico's servants. Northern Italian Carbonari tend to be educated, international in outlook, with close ties to the French. Now, we know of two people close to Lodovico Malvezzi who fit that description: his brother, who was an official of the French Kingdom of Italy, and his wife, whose first husband was one of Bonaparte's officers. Carlo has no known ties with the secret societies, and one might think that if he were a Carbonaro, he wouldn't espouse republican ideals as openly as he does. But for him, moderate liberalism may well be a better mask for radicalism than a false conversion to orthodoxy. And it seems highly significant that he suddenly acquired a Neapolitan servant a fortnight before his brother was murdered, at a time when Naples was in the throes of a Carbonaro revolt.

"The marchesa never expresses any political views beyond an offhand contempt for the police, and she affects not to have been much attached to Philippe de Goncourt. But she wears his portrait faithfully on her wrist. Was it a coincidence that she was in Turin when the rebellion broke out there in March of 1821? Or was she carrying messages between the Angeli and the

Piedmontese rebels? And what does it mean that de la Marque claims to have been in Turin as well?

"We don't know much about Rinaldo's politics, but we do know that Marchese Lodovico belittled and tyrannized over him. Perhaps, not daring to defy his father openly, he avenged himself by consorting with Lodovico's political enemies."

"And perhaps I'm a Dutchman," said MacGregor. "We've as much evidence of the one as the other."

Julian smiled. "My dear fellow, there's some merit in theorizing without evidence. If we don't have patterns in mind we may not recognize the evidence when it comes. We do have one concrete ground for suspecting Rinaldo: he isn't here. One would have expected him to return to Milan, or at least to write, once it became public knowledge that his father's death was murder."

"That's true," acknowledged MacGregor. "The marchesa and Carlo still haven't heard from him?"

"They say not. But post on the Continent is infernally slow. If Rinaldo is in some far-off country—Russia, for instance—the news of his father's murder may not have reached him yet, or he may still be on his way home.

"Now then: Signora Argenti and Valeriano. They don't seem at all political, but if they'd somehow become privy to Carbonaro secrets, they might have dangled them before Marchese Lodovico as a lure to allow Signora Argenti to see her children."

"If they'd done that," MacGregor objected, "why would they have killed him?"

"Perhaps they kept their part of the bargain, but he didn't keep his. Yes, I know, my dear fellow—another flight of speculation. Let's approach this conundrum another way. If one of these people—Carlo, the marchesa, Rinaldo, Signora Argenti, or Valeriano—gave Marchese Lodovico information about the Angeli, when and how was the information passed? The marchesa had the best opportunity, since she lived with him. Carlo is another possibility: he lived in Parma but says he visited Milan, and when he did, he stayed at Casa Malvezzi.

Rinaldo seems to be out of the running: he was away travelling for months before his father's death, and when he returned to Milan, Lodovico had already gone to the lake with Orfeo. Signora Argenti and Valeriano lived in Venice, but they came to the Lake of Como while Marchese Lodovico was there, and may have offered him the information then."

Julian sighed. "Then again, it's possible that the murder has nothing whatever to do with the Carbonari. Rinaldo may have killed Lodovico to inherit his property and escape from his domination. Carlo may have killed him in a burst of frustration over his own fall from power and Lodovico's wrenching the villa from him. The marchesa may have killed him in order to gain her independence and a beautiful villa in which to enjoy it. Signora Argenti or Valeriano may have killed him in the hope that once he was out of the way, Rinaldo would relent and allow Signora Argenti access to her children."

MacGregor sprang up and started pacing. "We haven't got anywhere!"

"We have got everywhere," Julian amended ruefully. "Which comes to the same thing."

MacGregor stopped walking. "What about Orfeo? If he knows something, you can't afford not to find out who he is. Who do you think he's most likely to be: Fletcher, St. Carr, or de la Marque?"

Julian considered. "De la Marque has the musical knowledge. And the fact that his native tongue is French would explain why Orfeo sounded French to Maestro Donati."

"He certainly doesn't fit Lucia's description of Orfeo," MacGregor declared. "She says Orfeo was so chivalrous, he rescued her from Tonio but wouldn't touch her himself. De la Marque is an arrant rake."

"Or so he would have us believe." Julian pondered. "Do you know what troubles me most about the idea of de la Marque as Orfeo? Musically, his personality is wrong. De la Marque plays half a dozen instruments very accurately, and with no expression whatsoever. Maestro Donati says Orfeo was a thoughtful, sensitive artist. It's actually quite difficult for a good musician to pretend to be a bad one. It would better to pretend to have no musical knowledge at all."

"Like Fletcher," MacGregor said eagerly.

"Yes, like Fletcher, who is exactly the right age to be Orfeo, who was on the Continent when Orfeo was, and who has something of the character that Lucia and Donati ascribe to Orfeo. St. Carr is the least promising of the three: he's too young, and, I think, quite genuinely birdwitted. Though I don't believe he's without intellects: they're merely sluggish from disuse. I should guess he's a much-indulged only child, who has always been treated as if he were unable to look after himself. His parents began it, and Fletcher takes his cue from them."

MacGregor was about to reply, when his attention was diverted. "Look," he said, "the water's covered your ring."

"So it has." Julian picked up the ring, shook the water off it, and replaced it on his little finger. He felt better for this discussion. Yet he could not help asking himself how many more times this spring would ebb and flow before Orfeo was in custody, the investigation was closed, and the real murderer went free. How many days, how many hours—

He resolutely banished these thoughts. Consulting his watch, he said, "It's half-past three. We had better go back to the villa and dress for dinner."

"You'll be very distressed to hear it,," the marchesa told her guests when they met in the drawing room before dinner, "but Commissario Grimani has sent word he won't be joining us. He's dining with Comandante Von Krauss."

A ripple of pleasure ran through the company. The next moment, they heard someone pounding on the front door. "It seems we're not to be free of Grimani, after all," said Carlo. "Only the police knock like that."

"The door isn't locked," said the marchesa. "I told the servants to leave it open for Monsieur de la Marque, because he hasn't returned for dinner."

The knocking stopped. A servant must have answered the door. The next moment, sharp footsteps sounded in the Hall of Marbles, and a young male voice shouted in Milanese, "Where is the marchesa? I demand to see, her at once!"

"Heavens." The marchesa came unhurriedly to her feet. "Rinaldo."

Francesca gave a little cry and ran to Valeriano, who put a sheltering arm around her. The next moment, a man burst into the room. He was about thirty, of middling height, with a reedy figure and round eyes of a pale, watery brown. He had a low forehead and almost no chin, so that his face seemed all eyes, nose, and mouth, like a monkey's. His clothes, though of rich material and extravagant cut, were rumpled and travel-stained, and his brown hair was disheveled.

"My dear Rinaldo!" Carlo sprang forward and embraced him heartily, kissing him on both cheeks. "Thank God and the Madonna you've arrived safe and sound! I've been worried about you."

"Not so worried as that comes to!" Rinaldo flashed back. "While I was away, you could play head of the family. You could take the lead in investigating *my* father's murder—without so much as a by-your-leave from me! Am I Marchese Malvezzi, or are you?"

"You are, of course, Rinaldo. But you were away—no one knew where to find you. Something had to be done at once."

"What business is it of yours? My father never had any use for you!"

Carlo froze, then looked at his nephew steadily, saying nothing. Julian had no difficulty reading his mind: *He had still less for you, my boy, and everyone knew it.*

"Where are the police?" Rinaldo demanded. "I want to know why it's taken them almost five years to tell me my father was murdered. It's an outrage!"

"Yes, Rinaldo," said Beatrice. "We were all very angry about it. But I'm afraid you can't see Commissario Grimani at present. He's dining out."

She came forward, extending her hands for him to kiss in greeting. He looked as if he would have liked to slap them down. "How dare you have all these people here to investigate my father's murder without me? You've never held me of any account! You've always treated me as if I weren't good enough to fill my father's shoes!"

"Don't be silly, Rinaldo." She regarded him with a faint, derisive smile. "Talking of shoes, would you be good enough to go outside and scrape yours off? You're tracking dirt on the carpet."

Rinaldo flushed. "You treat me like a child. You go out of your way to insult me. But what's worse than all the rest—what I never can forgive—you invited *that whore* to stay under your roof!"

He turned, pointing a trembling finger across the room at Francesca.

"For the love of God, Rinaldo," said Carlo, "she is still your wife."

"Yes, she's my wife, God send her to perdition!" Rinaldo bore down on Francesca. "How dare you show your face here, among my family, my friends! Look at me, you cringing slut! You can make a fool of me for six years, but you can't look me in the eyes—"

Valeriano stepped between them. "Signor Marchese, if you must quarrel, I beg you will do so with me."

"*You* speak for her, Signor Gelding?" Rinaldo choked. "You dare speak for her—to me, to *me*?"

"Rinaldo, this is not the time or the place." Carlo laid a hand on his nephew's shoulder. "Consider that we have guests. I haven't even had a chance to introduce them to you. Come."

Rinaldo allowed himself to be led away, though his eyes remained malignantly fixed on Francesca and Valeriano. Carlo said, "I believe you know Maestro Donati."

"Yes," said Rinaldo. "Your servant, Maestro."

Donati bowed formally. "A great pleasure, Signor Marchese."

Carlo shepherded Rinaldo over to Julian and MacGregor. "I have the honour to present Signor Kestrel, the renowned English dandy, and his friend, Dr. MacGregor, an eminent man of science."

Julian bowed. "Your servant, Signor Marchese."

"How d'ye do," MacGregor nodded curtly.

Rinaldo rounded on Beatrice again. "That's another thing! They told me in Milan you'd taken up with this Englishman and got him to mount a private investigation for you. I want it stopped. You've no right to interfere. Leave the investigation to the police."

"With the greatest respect," said Beatrice with delicate irony, "I don't see what authority you have to tell me whom I may receive in my house, or what we may do here."

"Your house!" An unpleasant smile spread over Rinaldo's face. "Perhaps it won't be that for long! You know that my father always believed this villa belonged by rights to the Malvezzi fiefdom, and not to the Delborgos. He fought about it in the courts for years, and only gave it up because the Delborgos sold the villa to Uncle Carlo, who sold it to him.

"When I got back to Milan last night, after travelling all the way from Prague, and I heard how you'd come here with my uncle and my wife and a parcel of strangers to investigate my father's murder, I swore I'd be revenged on you. Before I left Milan this morning, I turned over all the papers about the Malvezzi claim to the villa to Palmieri. He's been the family lawyer for years, and knows all about the case. He thinks he can prove once and for all that this is Malvezzi land. That means it's within the entail, and my father had no power to bequeath it to you. It's mine."

"Rinaldo," Carlo remonstrated, "Lodovico only left the villa to Beatrice for her life. It will come back to you in the end—or if not to you, then to Niccolò. You wouldn't be so ungenerous as to deprive your father's widow of her home—"

"My dear." Beatrice laid her fingers lightly on Carlo's arm. "It's good of you to take my part, but Rinaldo has obviously made up his mind. And it's unkind to deprive him of a weapon, when he has so very few."

"You'll be sorry!" said Rinaldo in a shaking voice. "You think so much of yourself, because my father left you this villa and his opera box, and everything he had that wasn't entailed to me! But the villa is mine by rights! It ought to have been joined with the Malvezzi lands—not left to a widow who couldn't even give my father a child!"

Beatrice's head moved as if he had struck her. With an effort, she collected herself and stood looking at him, taking slow, deliberate breaths.

"You had better go, Rinaldo," said Carlo.

"No." Beatrice glided to Rinaldo and smiled serenely at him. "You're exhausted with travel, and probably as hungry as a wolf into the bargain. Do you mean to go back to Milan tonight or on to Castello Malvezzi?"

"To the castle," Rinaldo said sullenly.

"Here's what I propose. Stay here for the present—rest, change your clothes, have dinner. In the meantime, the castle can be made ready for your arrival. You know how draughty and dreadful it is when no one has stayed there for a long time."

"Why should you want me here?" said Rinaldo suspiciously.

"I don't, particularly," she admitted, "after the way you're been behaving. But I'd as lief not quarrel with you publicly. And you are my stepson."

"You want to change my mind," Rinaldo declared. "You think you can charm me, make me ashamed of myself, so that

I'll let you keep the villa. But it won't work. You may wrap every other man around your little finger, but I'm proof against you."

"Then why are you so determined to run away from me?" she asked whimsically. "Come, you wanted to see Commissario Grimani. He'll be back after dinner, and you can take him to task as much as you like."

Rinaldo said, "If you think I would sit down at the same table with that whore and her tame eunuch—"

"You would not be asked to," Valeriano interrupted quietly. "With Marchesa Malvezzi's leave, Signora Argenti and I would dine in our rooms."

"Signora Argenti!" spat out Rinaldo. "What a farce!"

"I—I thought you would rather I didn't use your name," said Francesca faintly.

"I would rather you didn't *have* my name, you damned bitch!"

"I think we had better retire now," said Valeriano, drawing Francesca's arm through his.

"Monster!" raved Rinaldo. "Shrieking, prancing capon!"

Valeriano looked faintly bored. A castrato in this present age must be a connoisseur of mockery. Rinaldo's efforts obviously did not impress him.

He and Francesca went out, she pale, exhausted, and leaning heavily on his arm. Rinaldo bit his nails and paced in a tense, tight circle.

"Now there's nothing to prevent your staying to dinner," said Beatrice. "Shall I have the servants prepare a room for you to wash and dress?"

"He can use mine," said Carlo.

"Oh, very well," said Rinaldo. "I'll stay, but only to see Commissario Grimani."

"Perhaps in the meantime you might like to talk with Signor Kestrel," Beatrice suggested. "He's the nearest thing to a police official we have at present."

"Oh, I don't think I need trouble Marchese Rinaldo with questions about the murder," said Julian. "I can't conceive he could have anything to add to what I know already."

"What the devil do you mean by that?" Rinaldo bristled. "Do you wish to insult me, signor?"

"By no means, Signor Marchese. I merely meant that Marchesa Malvezzi, Conte Carlo, Signora Argenti, and Signor Valeriano have been so obliging in providing me with information that I have no need to plague you with questions I should think you would prefer not to answer."

"Why shouldn't I wish to answer them?" shouted Rinaldo. "I have nothing to hide! And I should be much surprised if they've told you the truth—especially my wife and her abortion of a lover."

Julian's brows drew together. "I don't think I've been misled in any particular."

"We'll see about that!" said Rinaldo. "We can talk while Uncle Carlo's room is being prepared for me. I warrant I'll have a few things to tell you that will surprise you!"

"As you wish. Perhaps we might go into the library?"

Rinaldo led the way to the door. The marchesa held Julian back a moment. "Oh, very well done!" she said softly.

He smiled back, bowed, and followed Rinaldo out.

In the Hall of Marbles they found two tall, strapping footmen, their flame-coloured livery coated with travel-dust. When they saw Rinaldo, they stood to attention—without much alacrity, Julian noticed. "I'm staying for dinner," Rinaldo told them brusquely. "Get my baggage out of the boat. The servants here will tell you what to do with it."

"Yes, Excellency," they muttered.

The front door opened. De la Marque came in. "Ah, *mon vieux*," he said to Julian, "I'm afraid I've delayed dinner abominably, but—" He broke off and looked at Rinaldo—once, twice, then his eyes stretched wide with something like alarm. Rinaldo looked back without recognition or interest.

De la Marque's gaze travelled slowly to the footmen. They goggled at him and nudged each other. One started forward impulsively, but the other, who looked a few years older, caught him by the skirt of his frock-coat and pulled him back.

De la Marque withdrew his gaze from them and bowed to Rinaldo. "A thousand pardons. I ought to have introduced myself at once. I know I have the honour of addressing Marchese Malvezzi, but you may not recollect me as readily. I am Gaston de la Marque."

"I remember you now, monsieur," said Rinaldo. "You're very often in Milan."

"Often enough, it would seem," observed Julian, "for you to recognize Marchese Rinaldo's footmen."

"As they're dressed in the Malvezzi livery, I can hardly credit myself with any great discernment there," de la Marque said easily. "But in fact, I remember them because they used to be Marchese Lodovico's. They rode at the back of his carriage in the Corso every afternoon and stood guard at the door of his opera box every night. They were one of the sights of Milan: the very type of the picturesque *buli* who a few generations ago attached themselves to great men and disposed of their enemies with a thrashing or a knife in the ribs—"

He stopped short, a little breathless. The footmen exchanged excited looks. Julian was immensely curious to know what this was all about. Yet if he tried to get to the bottom of it now, Rinaldo might wriggle off his hook. He would confront de la Marque later, and set Dipper to pump the footmen in the meantime.

"I'm afraid we're detaining you from dressing," he said to de la Marque. "Signor Marchese, shall we go into the library?"

"I knew you hadn't been told the whole story," said Rinaldo triumphantly. "You know that my stepmother left Turin in March of '21—to get away from the rebels, supposedly. And you know she was lost for two days, till I found her in Belgirate. But what you don't know is that she deliberately set out to bamboozle my father and me about where she was going and what she meant to do. She was lost because she wanted to be."

"Why should she want that?" Julian asked.

"I expect she went to Belgirate to meet a lover. That's what women do."

"So you're not suggesting she came here secretly and killed your father?"

Rinaldo blinked in astonishment. "Why should I think that? That singer killed him. Everyone knows that."

Julian pondered briefly. "What makes you think she deliberately set out to be lost?"

"It shows in everything she did. She travelled incognito, to begin with, in a plain coach, with servants out of livery."

"That seems a sensible precaution. The country was in the throes of a revolt. She might have been taken hostage by the rebels, or robbed and mistreated by brigands taking advantage of the general confusion."

"Was it a sensible precaution for her to send a courier on ahead from Turin to make arrangements for her to stay the night in Novara—then to turn off the Novara road without leaving any word for him where she was going? She hadn't even told him she would be travelling incognito, so that when she didn't arrive in Novara and he went searching for her on the road, he was asking after the Malvezzi coach and servants, which of course nobody had seen. Even after she got to Belgirate, she never tried to send a message to me in Milan or to the courier in Novara. She just plumped herself down at an inn and frittered away two days, while the courier and I and a parcel of servants combed the countryside looking for her!"

Julian had to acknowledge these were ominous revelations. The marchesa must have intended to baffle pursuit when she went to Belgirate. The only alternative was that she had panicked at the outbreak of revolution and acted on irrational impulses for days. And Julian knew her better than that.

He asked, "When did you learn she'd gone missing?"

"At dawn the next day. A message arrived from the courier that she'd disappeared. I was horrified. I collected half a dozen servants and set out for Novara at once."

"Forgive me," said Julian delicately, "but there doesn't seem to be any love lost between you and Marchesa Beatrice. Why were you so worried about her?"

"I wasn't." Rinaldo's eyes screwed up vindictively. "If I'd had my choice, I would gladly have seen her robbed of her last soldo and set loose on the roads in her petticoat. But—" His voice grew hollow. "My father loved her. He would have gone off his head if anything had happened to her. And he would have held me responsible. No matter how it came about, or how she'd brought it on herself, he would have found some way to blame me for it. I had to find her—what was more, I had to do it before he knew she'd gone missing. He would still have found something to upbraid me for—that I didn't do it quickly or bravely or cleverly enough. But if everything had come right in the end, he wouldn't have made too much of it."

Julian began to feel some sympathy—if not for Rinaldo now, then for the frightened, belittled boy he had once been. But he was still that boy, Julian realized. Underneath his bravado and skittish pride, he probably always would be.

"So you set out for Novara with half a dozen servants," said Julian. "What then?"

"The courier met me in Novara. He'd already alerted the Piedmontese police and the loyalist garrison in Novara that Beatrice was missing, but we knew we couldn't count on them to help us much—they had their hands full with the revolt. We mustered as many searchers as we could and set off along the road between Turin and Novara. By the end of the day, we'd found the point where she turned north. We divided into parties of two or three and separated, each party assigned to search a different part of northern Piedmont. I took two servants and went northeast."

"How long did you continue searching?"

"All that night and the next day. We'd arranged to meet in Oleggio—that's a town about halfway between Novara and Lake Maggiore—at the end of the day. Soon after I got there, a message came that one of the search parties had found my stepmother in Belgirate. I set off at once to bring her home. I arrived exhausted and saddle-sore from riding all day and all the previous night. But was she the least bit sorry? Not she! Oh, she apologized prettily enough. But she didn't care."

"Did she give any explanation for leading you such a dance?"

"She's never felt she had to explain herself to me. She actually had the gall to ask if my father had been worried about her—when it was I who'd been searching for her for almost two days! I said he didn't even know she'd disappeared—I'd left orders with the servants in Milan that he wasn't to be sent word unless I gave leave."

Julian wanted to know more about Rinaldo's movements on the night of the murder. "How did you go about searching for Marchesa Beatrice at night? You must have astonished a good many villagers, knocking them up in the small hours to ask after her party."

"We mostly enquired at custom's offices and inns where she might have changed horses. I sent the two servants I'd brought with me to drive along the Ticino—the river on the eastern border of Piedmont—and see if she'd crossed into Lombardy, while I searched the villages further west."

"Alone?"

"Yes. The servants had been driving me to distraction, wanting to know what we should do next, and looking at me as if they expected me to produce Beatrice out of my saddle-bag. They kept whispering to each other, and I knew they were saying they wished my father had been there instead of me. I had to get away from them. Of course they made a fuss about my going off alone, but I told them I had a brace of pistols and could look after myself."

Did Rinaldo grasp the significance of what he was saying? Julian wondered. He admitted to being alone on the night of the murder, armed with pistols, in a region of Piedmont within a few hours' ride from the Lake of Como. Would he have volunteered such information if he were guilty? He might, if he thought Julian would find out some other way. Certainly the rewards for killing his father would have been great. At one stroke, he would have freed himself from Lodovico's domination and made himself one of the wealthiest landowners in Lombardy.

But if Rinaldo had killed Lodovico, did that mean it was he who had left the note and glove at the castle, and so lured Lodovico to the belvedere on the following night? If so, then he had not only killed his father but planned the murder in advance. Yet how could he have known that his stepmother would conveniently go missing, so that he would have an excuse to wander the countryside alone? Could he and Beatrice have been acting in concert? Was their enmity all a blind?

He asked, "Where were you on the night before you learned of Marchesa Beatrice's disappearance?"

"What difference does that make?"

"The rest of your family have been willing to tell me."

"I don't see how the rest of my family can remember. It was years ago. I suppose I was at home." He looked bitter. "I didn't go out much."

"Have you ever seen a lady's glove decorated with green silk myrtle leaves and a ruby heart pierced by a diamond shaft?"

"What has that to do with my father's murder?"

"Have you seen such a glove?" Julian repeated.

"No! If I did, I never noticed it. What do I care about lady's gloves?"

"This one may have belonged to a woman your father knew years ago."

"One of his harem of mistresses?" Rinaldo laughed mirthlessly. "That's just the sort of thing he used to give them."

"Do you know the names of any mistresses he had when you were very young—perhaps before you were born?"

"No. I never wanted to know about them. Why?"

Julian explained how the glove had been left at Castello Malvezzi on the night before the murder. Rinaldo said, "I expect the singer brought it."

"Do you know anything about him?" Julian asked.

"Only that he was English and a tenor. I was away when my father took up with him."

"Did Marchese Lodovico ever write to you about him?"

"He never wrote or talked to me about music," Rinaldo mumbled. "I don't have any ear for it."

"You mentioned that you were away from Milan when Marchese Lodovico met Orfeo. When did you return?"

"A few weeks before my father died."

"Did you see your father during that time?"

"No. He was away at the lake with his tenor and didn't invite me to join them, so I stayed in Milan."

"Signora Argenti wrote to you from the lake, where she had come with Signor Valeriano. But I understand that it was Marchese Lodovico rather than you who answered her letter."

"I sent it on to him to answer."

"Why?"

"Because I wanted her crushed!" Rinaldo walked about rapidly, fists clenched. "Because I wanted the bitch ground in the dust, and I thought he would do it better than I would. Ever since I'd arrived in Milan, everyone had been sniggering at me. I was the man whose wife would rather go to bed with a eunuch than with him. Improvisers made up poems and songs about me. I couldn't go anywhere."

"Did you ever think of coming to the lake to confront your wife and Signor Valeriano?"

"That was just what she wanted—to meet me face to face, so that she could try to cajole me into letting her see Niccolò and Bianca. I wasn't going to give her that chance."

It had nothing to do with the murder enquiry, but Julian could not help asking, "Do you ever mean to allow her to see them?"

"I'll see them damned first, and myself as well! Have you any idea what she's done to me? Do you know what it is to have a wife, and to know that every day, every hour, she's betraying you before all the world?"

"You do have a means of obtaining satisfaction," Julian pointed out.

"Oh, don't taunt me with that." Rinaldo's voice was suddenly tired, quiet, and more wretched than Julian had heard it before. "I know Valeriano will have told you about the duel."

Julian pricked up his ears. Valeriano had said nothing about any duel. Julian felt his way. "I'm willing to hear your side."

"I had to call him out after my wife left me for him. Even if my honour hadn't demanded it, my father would have given me no peace. I sent a challenge I'd written at my father's dictation. Valeriano accepted. We met at the appointed time and place. Our seconds measured the ground and inspected the pistols."

He went to the window and stood with his back to Julian, his hands against the panes. "Valeriano was so—so *tall.* He was quiet and dignified. He wasn't afraid—at all events, he didn't seem to be. But I was ten years younger, and I'd never fought a duel before."

Julian pictured it all very clearly. He knew the strange, lightheaded sensation of proceeding to the place of meeting, not knowing if you would leave it alive or dead—knowing only that you must not seem to care. Because whichever of the combatants showed fear had lost already—lost the battle of nerves, which in its way was as important as the duel itself. It was all too clear who had won the battle of nerves in Rinaldo's case.

"Tell me what happened," Julian said.

"We took our places, the signal was given, and we fired. Valeriano fired into the air. I fired at him and missed." He spun around toward Julian, his face scarlet. "I was nervous! I'd never shot at a live person before—or been shot at by one. I just couldn't hold the gun steady. When I found he hadn't hit me—hadn't even tried—I was so shocked, I came over dizzy. I could hardly stand. My second was looking at me, and I knew he expected me to demand a second shot. I did. Valeriano agreed. We loaded our pistols again."

Rinaldo stood sideways, his body tense, his eyes staring into vacancy, as if he were on the duelling field again. "I knew by the look in his eyes, by the calm way he stood when we took our ground, that he was going to do exactly the same thing—fire into the air. I was more nervous than ever. I could hardly see for the sweat pouring down my face. I had no excuse not to hit him this time, when he wasn't even going to try to hit me."

Rinaldo lifted his hand, his forefinger extended as if he held a gun. "The signal came. He fired into the air. I—I—" He slowly lowered his arm. "I missed him again. It was humiliating. My second looked at me in disgust. He said I had better declare myself satisfied, and I did. Valeriano bowed and went away. I wanted to run after him, say for God's sake kill me, anything would be better than being sent back to face—"

He ended on a gasp that was nearly a sob. Julian asked gently, "What did your father do when he found out?"

"I don't want to remember." Rinaldo passed a hand across his face. "Those were the worst hours of my life. In the end I asked him to let me leave Milan. I had to have his permission—I hadn't any money of my own. He practically threw it at me. He said I was only fit to crawl away like a whipped dog, with my tail between my legs. I went—to Florence, Naples, Spain. It didn't matter—everywhere I went I saw the same thing: Valeriano, tall as a tower, pointing his gun at the heavens and firing—and myself, trying to hit him and failing, always failing."

"Have you any idea why he didn't return your shot?" To Julian, this was the most curious part of the whole affair.

"I don't know. To humiliate me, I suppose."

"He couldn't have known you wouldn't hit him. He could very easily have been killed."

"How can I tell what was in his mind? I'm not a damned eunuch! I don't know how they think! He probably hates all men who aren't mutilated like him. He fired into the air to show how brave he was, and to make me feel it was I who was only a fragment of a man, not he. But I'll make him suffer for it—somehow, some day!"

"He gave you satisfaction," Julian reminded him. "He owes you nothing more."

"Do you think honour is a thing to be totted up on a ledger?" Rinaldo's monkey face twisted. "To hell with your satisfaction! While he lives, and she is with him, I am not avenged!"

CHAPTER 27

His interrogation over, Rinaldo went up to Carlo's room, where he found a hot bath and a pile of white towels smelling of orange-flower water. His silver-handled razor lay gleaming on the washstand in case he wished to shave. Ernesto was waiting to assist him however he might require. Rinaldo sent him to fetch more towels, although there were already plenty. It was their usual struggle, renewed each time Rinaldo returned from his travels: Rinaldo striving to be rid of his father's manservant every way he could, Ernesto clinging on, serving the young marchese as he had served the old.

With Ernesto's assistance, Rinaldo bathed and changed into his evening clothes. The local church bells were chiming the half hour after five when he dismissed Ernesto and took a last look in the glass before going downstairs. All at once the door behind him opened again. "I don't need you anymore—" Rinaldo began irritably. Then he saw in the looking-glass that it was not Ernesto.

He turned. Francesca had closed the door behind her and was sidling along the far wall. She was trembling, and her eyes were fixed on Rinaldo's face.

"What do you want?" he demanded.

Francesca sank to her knees. "Please. Tell me something. Tell me anything—how tall they are, what they like to eat, whether Bianca's eyes are still green, whether Niccolò still loves horses. Oh God, Rinaldo, have pity on me! For six years I've heard nothing! I think of them all the time—their little faces and hands and the way they smiled. I know they must have changed so much, and I'm missing it all."

"Whose fault is that?" Rinaldo retorted. "No one took them away from you. You abandoned them."

"One word, Rinaldo! It would cost you so little, and it would mean so much to me! I'll do anything."

"Anything?" He caught her up swiftly. "Leave your eunuch? Swear by God and the Madonna never to see him again?"

"I can't do that," she whispered.

"Then what does all your whining and begging amount to?" He dragged her up to face him and held her against the wall. "Slut! You miss your children—but not enough to give up your lover! And you expect me to be sorry for you? You want me to let you spread corruption over them—teach Bianca to rut with eunuchs? I'd rather bring them up in a brothel than let you near them—not that it wouldn't come to the same thing! But don't worry—they won't forget you! Every day I'm teaching them to say, *'My mother is a whore'*—"

Francesca twisted in his arms. "I want to go—"

"Oh, you want to go! God forbid you should be shut up in a bedroom with your husband! You filthy drab! You ought to be thanking God on your knees that I'm still willing to take you back. But I expect you only pray with your knees in the air!"

Francesca sobbed and struggled. There was a rustling behind her.

"What's that?" Rinaldo said sharply. "What are you hiding behind your back?"

He let go of her arms. She brought out a package wrapped

in pink tissue paper and offered it shakily. "It's—it's for the children. You wouldn't have to tell them where it came from. You could say it was from you."

He took it and unwrapped it. Inside were a porcelain doll dressed for a ball and a perfect little coach drawn by four grey horses. Rinaldo took the doll by the feet and swung her against the wall, shattering her head and sending the pearl pins in her hair flying. He threw the coach on the floor and ground his heel in it. Francesca swayed and covered her mouth with her hands. "Madonna, help me—"

"Get out!"

She moved unsteadily toward the door. When she reached it, she stopped to dry her eyes and smooth her hair.

Rinaldo jerked open the door. "Get out, I say!"

"Oh, hush, please!" Francesca glanced fearfully toward the room across the way.

"Whose room is that?" said Rinaldo. "The eunuch's? Why don't you want him to know you've been with me? Is he so jealous?"

"No." Her eyes dilated. "No—he—"

Rinaldo sprang forward and caught her by the wrist. "Let's find him and tell him!"

"No!" she cried. "Leave him alone, Rinaldo, please! I beg you—"

He drove her, stumbling and pleading, along the hall and down the stairs to the Hall of Marbles. There were voices coming from the drawing room. Rinaldo half dragged, half carried Francesca to the door and pushed her in. She landed, staggering, almost under Valeriano's nose.

Valeriano steadied her and looked across at Rinaldo with astonishment and dawning anger. Julian, MacGregor, Carlo, and the marchesa hastened forwards ready to protect Francesca at need. Rinaldo looked beyond them to his rival and laughed exultantly. "Do you know where she's been, Signor Gelding? In my room, snivelling and begging for some news of the children! That's how happy *you've* made her!"

Valeriano held Francesca between his hands and tried to

look into her face. His own was very white. "Francesca, is this true?"

"No—no, Pietro—I mean—I did ask him about the children—just because he was here, and I might not have had another chance—"

"Asked me!" hooted Rinaldo. "She grovelled on her knees! 'One word, Rinaldo! Have pity on me, Rinaldo!' You should have seen the spectacle she made! Look at her now—just look at her face—all blotched and tearstained. What can you give her, monster, to make up for what I gave her, and you took away?"

"Francesca," whispered Valeriano, "how could you not have told me? I thought you'd got over the worst of your grief for the children. I thought—Mother of God, what fools love makes of us!—that you were happy!"

"I was! I am!" She tugged at his coat. "I do miss my children and think of them, but it doesn't matter. I choose to stay with you. I love you."

"I see how you were able to deceive me," he said quietly. "I don't know what it is to have children. I don't even have nephews or cousins who might have taken their place for me. I can't hope to understand your feelings. You counted on that."

"I wasn't so cold-blooded. I only wanted to spare you pain. I knew you would be laden with guilt and grief if you knew how I was—" She broke off.

"Suffering?" he finished. "Yes, I would. Thank God it isn't too late to do something about it." He drew a long breath. "Your husband is mistaken, Francesca. I am not a monster. Signor Marchese, if your wife breaks with me, will you take her back and restore her children to her?"

Rinaldo's eyes sparkled. "I've already told her I would."

"No!" cried Francesca. "No, Pietro! What are you saying? I won't leave you!"

"You won't have to, my dearest love. Because I am leaving you."

"No!" She flung her arms around him. "No, I won't let you! You're mad!"

"I am sane, Francesca, and I am resolved. I love you too much to keep you from what you love even more than you love me. Don't you see? As long as you live with me, you'll be torn apart."

"Do you think I won't be torn apart if you leave me?"

"I think your children can console you for my loss better than I can for theirs. And—" His throat closed. "And you can have more children. They'll fill any emptiness I've left." He turned up her face to his. "You would like that, wouldn't you?"

She coloured and tried to look away.

"Yes," said Valeriano sadly. "I thought as much."

He started to move away from her. She clung to him. He was so much taller, he easily detached her. "Why?" she burst out. "Why should I have children when you can't?"

"Why should one man have anything that another would give his heart and soul to gain? A priest knows that, not I. We're taught that in Heaven we shall all be equal." Valeriano lost control of his voice a little, and it wavered into the soprano range. "Perhaps there won't even be any distinctions of male and female there. Have you ever noticed that angels in paintings don't have beards or breasts? When I was a boy, after I was cut, I used to wonder if they were all castrati—"

He closed his eyes for a moment. When he opened them, he was fairly composed. He went to Beatrice and kissed her hands. "Thank you, Marchesa, for your hospitality, and for your kindness to Francesca. I entreat you to remain her friend—she'll need such friends as you. I shan't be staying for dinner—I shall leave as soon as my things are packed."

"Where will you go, Pietro?" asked Francesca in a hollow voice.

"Back to Venice." He went to her, took her hand, and lifted it to his lips. For a long moment he looked into her upturned face. "Goodbye," he said softly. "God keep you, my angel—my one and only love."

He tore himself from her and walked rapidly toward the door. Rinaldo shot out a hand to detain him. "I'll have her breeding again in a month," he promised.

Valeriano permitted himself a single look of white-hot hatred. Then he was gone.

Francesca swayed suddenly. Beatrice was at her side in a moment and helped her into a chair. Julian poured a glass of red wine from a decanter in a corner and brought it to Beatrice, who coaxed Francesca to take a few sips. Rinaldo looked on scornfully.

"My dear Rinaldo," said Beatrice, "after so much upheaval, you can't think of rushing away after dinner. I should be so pleased if you and Francesca would spend the night here. Now that Signor Valeriano is leaving, you may have his room."

"I don't want his room!" Rinaldo retorted. "If I stay, you can put me in with my wife. That's where I belong."

Francesca gasped and covered her face.

Beatrice looked wry. "Of course, Rinaldo, if that's what you wish. You'll stay, then?"

"Yes," said Rinaldo, satisfied. "I'll stay."

"Why don't you rest here for a while?" Beatrice proposed to Francesca. "I'll have dinner delayed another half an hour. I don't think, after all this excitement, anyone is in a great hurry to eat."

Julian realized she wanted to keep Francesca in the drawing room until Valeriano had gone. Francesca was too exhausted to understand. She sat back in her chair, closing her eyes. But the next moment her eyes flew open and looked fearfully toward Rinaldo.

Carlo said to her quickly, "I'll keep you company, shall I?"

"I can keep her company," said Rinaldo.

"My boy, I should be delighted to keep you both company," Carlo said. "It's been so long since I've seen you."

Rinaldo dropped ungraciously into a chair. Francesca closed her eyes again. A more uncongenial family reunion, Julian had never seen.

The marchesa sent word to the kitchen to keep the dinner warm half an hour longer. Then she and Julian walked out onto the terrace. The fair weather of the festival had stolen away. The air was damp, the lake grey and dappled with reflections of cloud. Mist huddled in the hollows between the mountains.

Julian and Beatrice stood looking over the balustrade at a lone swan floating on the leaden water.

"Rinaldo isn't much like his father," Julian said.

"I'm glad you see that. Lodovico wasn't mean-spirited. He had to have his way, but once he'd triumphed, he could forgive and forget. Rinaldo is like his mother, both in looks and in temperament. They were both weak-willed, terrified of Lodovico, cruel and vindictive to others in order to make themselves feel less small and contemptible. I don't envy Francesca. Rinaldo will never let her forget what she did to him. He'll make her pay, not only for her humiliation of him, but for Lodovico's as well. And that's a score she'll never be able to settle, if she lives a hundred years."

"Can you do anything for her?"

She pondered. "I shall try to make him see that mistreating her will only keep the scandal of her infidelity alive, when it's in his interest to bury it. That may have some effect. In the meantime, I'm glad I prevailed on him to stay the night. I was really afraid of what Francesca might do if she were borne away to the castle and isolated with him and his servants."

Her mention of Rinaldo's servants reminded Julian of the footmen. He had set Dipper to find out all he could from them about why they had been so agitated at seeing de la Marque. It was a tantalizing lead, and it could not have come at a more opportune time. This was Monday evening. Lucia had only two days left.

Out of the corner of his eye, he saw Fletcher and St. Carr approaching along the shore path. They came onto the terrace, bowed over the marchesa's hand with proper English stiffness, and greeted Julian, then launched into an account of their visit to Lucia that afternoon. Julian, who had heard nothing of this, cursed himself for his excursion to Villa Pliniana, which had left Lucia at Grimani's mercy. He ought to have known Grimani would have found some way to harass her.

"The man is a devil!" Fletcher said roundly. "He reads her like a book, and threatens her with everything he knows she would fear most. And in spite of it all, she was so brave, so—" He caught himself up short, and looked away.

"Do you think he'll find Orfeo?" St. Carr asked Julian.

"I think someone will," Julian said.

"Do you mean that you will?" asked Fletcher, alarmed. "Because if you do, and you turn him over to the police, Grimani will take his change out of Lucia for not helping him when she had the chance."

"Leave Grimani to me," said Julian. "If I have Orfeo, I can bargain with him—make him release Lucia in return for my giving Orfeo up. He wants Orfeo too much to refuse him on those terms."

"I see!" Fletcher brightened. "Are you likely to find him soon—before Lucia's three days are over?"

Julian had been translating their conversation for the marchesa. When he came to this question, she looked at him intently, awaiting his answer.

"I can't say," he said.

"We've been having the deuce of a time on his account," St. Carr declared. "First Grimani took our passports, then he dragged us off to see that girl, and now Signora Frascani wants to chuck us out of our inn."

"Why is that?" Julian asked.

"She doesn't like her guests being such objects of interest to the police," said Fletcher with a wry grin.

"There isn't another inn in the village," complained St. Carr, "or anywhere else hereabouts. We can't leave the neighbourhood, and we can't stay. Does Grimani expect us to sleep in the piazza?"

"But this problem is easy to solve," said the marchesa. "My stepson has arrived unexpectedly, and Signor Valeriano is leaving, which means I shall have a bedroom free. I should be delighted if you would accept my hospitality until your passports are restored to you."

"We wouldn't dream of imposing on you," said Fletcher.

"It wouldn't be an imposition," the marchesa assured him.

"You've been caught up against your will in the investigation of my husband's murder. The least I can do is to give you a roof over your heads until this tangle is sorted out. Please, Signor Fletcher—will you not let me have my way?"

Her smile was pure enchantment. Fletcher was not proof against it. He glanced at St. Carr, who looked apprehensive but eager. Then he bowed and said in his awkward Milanese, "Thank you, Marchesa. You're very kind, and we're very grateful."

"I hope you won't mind sharing," she said. "I have only the one room."

"Not at all," said Fletcher.

"I'll send a servant to the inn for your things," she said. "Have you dined? We're dining late tonight."

"We've dined already," said Fletcher, "and we didn't realize you hadn't. We'll go at once, and return in the evening."

"I shall look forward to greeting you as my guests." She extended her hand to each of them, and this time St. Carr, blushing fiery red, dared to bring it to his lips.

The villa party dined on the lake fish *missoltitt,* with truffles from the mountains and tiny onions grown along the shore. Francesca ate almost nothing and looked dazed and unbelieving, as if she still could not credit that she was with Rinaldo once more, and Valeriano was gone. He had left quietly by boat, without seeing her again.

Rinaldo was in high feather, refilling his wineglass so persistently that Julian hoped that by the end of the evening he would be in no condition to trouble his wife. Carlo and Beatrice looked on with increasing distaste. Julian had often observed that, for all the wine drunk in Italy, outright intoxication was despised.

With rain threatening, the villa party remained indoors after dinner. Donati played the piano, and Carlo improvised humorous poems, but no one was disposed to be very cheerful. Grimani's return hardly helped to lift the general gloom. He was annoyed to find that Rinaldo had arrived and been questioned in his absence, but since Rinaldo appeared to have nothing to say that would aid in identifying Orfeo, Grimani was in no hurry to interrogate him. This was just as well, because Rinaldo was now three sheets in the wind, and his boisterousness contrasted grotesquely with the dejection around him.

The arrival of Fletcher and St. Carr at least created a distraction. The marchesa exercised all her powers to make them welcome. It fascinated Julian to watch her at work. She slowly but surely drew out St. Carr, delicately flattering his youthful self-love, till she brought him from shy stupefaction to unabashed enslavement. Fletcher she knew better than to charm with coquetry. She adopted an attitude toward him that was friendly without being flirtatious, and listened seriously to his discourses on botany. All the while she did not forget de la Marque, but kept up an amorous banter with him that nettled Julian, though he tried to tell himself that her interest in all three men was driven by her passionate desire to find Orfeo.

Julian was taking his turn at the piano when he caught sight of Dipper peeking in at the music room door. He finished the piece so as not to attract attention by breaking off abruptly, then strolled out to join Dipper in the Hall of Marbles. MacGregor went with him. Zanetti sidled across the music room to a favourable eavesdropping position by the door.

Dipper knew a trick worth two of that. He said to Julian, "The rainbows that come with His Nibs want to cut whids with you, sir, and tipped me a scudo to work it for 'em."

"What do they want to put down to me?" Julian asked.

"I dunno, sir. I tried to smoke it out, but they cutty-eyed me and stood mum. They'll only whiddle the whole scrap to you."

Julian thought briefly. "Bing avast to my lib-ken with them. I'll transnear you."

"Yes, sir." Dipper went off.

"What in blue blazes—" MacGregor began.

"My dear fellow," said Julian, taking his arm and drawing him back into the music room, "did I ever tell you about Rossini's visit to London last year, when I heard him sing duets with the King?"

He led MacGregor past Zanetti, who regarded them with a dropped jaw and a comical look of dismay. Soon after, seeing Zanetti absorbed in eavesdropping on Fletcher and St. Carr, Julian slipped out with MacGregor and started upstairs.

"Now will you tell me what you and Dipper were jabbering about?" said MacGregor.

"He told me that Marchese Rinaldo's footmen want to talk to me, and gave him a scudo to arrange it. I asked what they wanted to tell me, and he said they were wary and would only talk to me. I told him to take them up to my room, and I would follow presently."

"I didn't realize you'd got to be such a rare hand at speaking Dipper's slang."

"It's quite useful sometimes," said Julian, smiling. "I imagine Zanetti will be up half the night looking up words in his English dictionary—and not finding them."

They had reached Julian's and MacGregor's room. Dipper was waiting with the two footmen Julian had seen that afternoon. They had brushed the dust of travel from their flame-red frock-coats and changed into spotless white silk stockings and lavishly powdered wigs. They were both tall and robust, with the broad shoulders and muscular calves so sought after in footmen. One was in his early twenties, with a ruddy face and round, bright eyes; the other was perhaps five years older, sallow and sharp-jawed, his black eyes narrowed appraisingly. They both bowed respectfully to Julian. The younger one opened his mouth to speak, but the elder checked him with a quick shake of the head.

"You wished to see me?" said Julian.

The older footman stepped forward. "Milord, I'm Tommaso Agosti, and this is Bruno Monti. We're in the service of His Excellency Marchese Rinaldo, and before him of Marchese Lodovico, God rest his soul." He crossed himself, and Bruno did likewise.

Julian was amused to find that they had elevated him to

the peerage. He decided not to disturb this impression; no one respected rank more than a great man's servants. "Go on."

Tommaso shot a sidelong glance at MacGregor and Dipper. "With respect, Milord, we wanted to speak to you alone."

"Dr. MacGregor and Dipper are in my confidence," said Julian, "and I can vouch for their discretion." He turned to Dipper. "It might be best if you stood by the door, so that you'll hear if Zanetti turns up at the keyhole."

"Leave me alone for that, sir," Dipper promised.

Tommaso said cautiously, "Milord, we heard you were helping the police investigate Marchese Lodovico's murder."

"Yes," said Julian.

"We liked our former master, Milord," Tommaso went on. "He was good to us—stood by us in his way, as we stood by him in ours. Everybody respected us in those days. No other servants dared cross us. Peasants took off their hats when they saw us coming. Shopkeepers courted our favour—"

"So did their daughters!" Bruno's eyes sparkled at the memory.

Tommaso shot him a quelling look. "Anyhow, we want to do right by our old master. We'd like to help find the son of a whore who killed him—"

"And string him up with our own hands!" Bruno exclaimed.

"Shut your beak," said Tommaso. "As I was saying, Milord, we want the same thing as you: to bring Marchese Lodovico's murderer to justice. Well, there's something we know that might help you. We didn't realize it was important when our old master died, because we didn't know he'd been murdered, see? By the time we found out, we'd all but forgot about this, it was so long ago. But then we came here and—" He broke off.

"And saw Monsieur de la Marque?" Julian supplied.

"What did I tell you?" Bruno pulled down the bottom lid of one eye, signifying, *Watch out, he's smart!*

"That's right, Milord," said Tommaso reluctantly. "That slimy Frenchman! Fancy him having the brass to come here! We thought we ought to tell somebody."

"But we didn't want to talk to the police," added Bruno, "because they might—"

"Because we don't like *sbirri*," said Tommaso shortly.

Julian smiled, took a seat, and lounged back, stretching out his legs. "Might I hazard a guess that this information is of a sort that might get you into trouble?"

Bruno laughed. "No use trying to keep anything from this one, Tommaso! He's no German-head! Milord, you're in the right of it. Tommaso and me, we did something the *sbirri* wouldn't take kindly to. We weren't afraid of them at the time, because we knew if they arrested us, we'd only have to deny it, and Marchese Lodovico would get the charges dropped. He looked after us, just as Tommaso said. But Marchese Rinaldo's another matter. Not the man his father was—not by half! He might not stand up for us against that stiff-rumped bugger, Grimani. As for Conte Carlo, he's a liberal,"—Bruno said this with a sneer befitting Lodovico's loyal footman—"and our old master didn't trust him. And Marchesa Beatrice, she's the finest lady as ever breathed, but she's only a woman. Then we heard about you, Milord—how you were a famous English dandy who solved crimes just for a lark. They told us below stairs that you weren't afraid of Grimani nor any of the *sbirri*. So we thought we'd come to you."

"But we haven't made up our minds yet," warned Tommaso, giving Julian a hard, assessing look. "Milord, if we tell you what we know, will you give us your word not to tell Commissario Grimani?"

"I can't go so far as that," said Julian. "But I swear to you upon my honour not to tell Grimani unless it proves necessary to the investigation. And if I must tell him, I shall do all I can to procure you leniency as informers." He smiled. "Come, Tommaso, you know that Bruno will tell me sooner or later."

"That's so," Tommaso admitted. "All right, Milord. This is how it was. One night we were with our old master in his opera box, pouring wine for him and his friends, when he saw the Frenchman sitting by himself in a box up in the fourth tier, scribbling away at something. My master laughed and said, 'What, has he come to write his letters at the opera?' One of his friends said, 'No, he writes down the singers' fioriture.'"

"That's their ornaments," put in Bruno. "The parts of the songs that aren't in the score, that they add themselves to show off their voices."

"Milord knows that," said Tommaso. "He's not a clod-hopper. Anyhow, when my master heard that, he opened up his eyes very wide and said, 'What, while they're singing?' 'To be sure,' says his friend. 'He can take down music like words from dictation.' My master says, 'I must meet this fellow.'"

Bruno eagerly took up the story. "So he says to me, 'Bruno, go and ask him to wait on me here.' I went to the Frenchman's box. He was still scribbling away, but when he saw me, he stopped and shut up the notebook he was writing in."

"This notebook," said Julian. "What was it like?"

Bruno wrinkled his nose, thinking back. "It was about so big." He sketched in the air an object of some eight by ten inches. "And it had a russet leather cover."

Julian's heart beat quick. He knew he was discovering something of the greatest importance. "I'm sorry I interrupted you. Go on."

"I told Monsieur de la Marque that my master, His Excellency Marchese Malvezzi, requested he come to his box. He didn't show proper respect for the honour being done him. I think he asked what my master wanted. 'He wants to see you,' says I. 'He expects you there before the end of the opera.' I added that last bit myself," Bruno confided. "I wanted him to know my master wasn't to be trifled with."

"What happened then?" said Julian.

"He came," said Bruno. "He wouldn't have dared do anything else. He sauntered into my master's box in the interval between the end of the opera and the final ballet. My master made much of him—invited him to sit down and take some wine, and introduced him to all his friends. He said—my master did—that he'd never met anyone before who could take down fioriture while it was being sung. He said, 'You must have captured all manner of fine performances in that notebook—performances even the singers themselves might not remember.' De la Marque was shrugging his shoulders and shaking his head and being too modest by half for a Frenchman. Then my master said, 'I'd be very grateful if you would let me borrow that notebook for a week or two, so that I could have the pleasure of studying it.' And what do you think the Frenchman said?" Bruno gaped and sputtered at the memory.

"He refused," said Tommaso. "Flouted my master before all his friends. Oh, he tried to put a good face on it—said he was writing a book on singing and didn't want to lend his notes to anyone before it was finished." Tommaso set his jaw. "That was no way to talk to my master. It was an insult. Marchese Lodovico felt it. And we felt it for him—Bruno and me."

Tommaso paused and shifted his feet. He had clearly come to the part of the story that worried him. The voluble Bruno stepped into the breach. "The marchese was in a temper after de la Marque left his box, and told Tommaso and me to make ourselves scarce. We did. Then we got to talking. We said to each other: 'Are we going to let that scurvy Frenchman make a fool of our master? We'll serve him out, or never wear Malvezzi livery again!'

"No sooner said than done, Milord! We didn't see the Frenchman in any of the boxes, so we thought he must have left the theatre. We tore down the stairs to the vestibule and were just in time to see him going out into the street. We followed him at a distance. The neighbourhood was quiet at that hour. The streets and cafés wouldn't fill up until the ballet was over.

"We got closer and closer to the Frenchman. Finally Tommaso said, 'Now!' and we grabbed him and pulled him into a little dark alley off Corsia del Giardino." Bruno leaped forward and seized an imaginary de la Marque. "We pinned him against a wall, me on one side, and Tommaso on the other. We says, 'You have something our master wants. Hand it over.' He says in his satirical way, 'Does he know you've taken it on yourselves to persuade me to give it up?' Tommaso says, 'No, but he'll be glad enough to get it. If you're a good boy, he may even give it back to you when he's done with it.'

"The Frenchman opened his mouth, and I knew he was going to call for help. I fetched him a plug in the pit of his stomach. That stopped his breath, I can tell you! We hit him a few more times. We *had* to," Bruno declared in an injured tone. "He wouldn't give in.

"After we'd knocked him senseless, we found the notebook in a pocket of his cloak and took it. We left him in the alley. He was breathing regular, so we knew he'd come to before long. We were back at La Scala in plenty of time to accompany our master home."

"Did anyone see this encounter between you and Monsieur de la Marque?" Julian asked.

"If they did," said Tommaso, "they kept their distance."

Julian could well believe this. No bystander would be likely to interfere with two strapping young bullies who wore some great man's livery. "What did you do with the notebook?"

"We looked it over," said Bruno. "There was nothing in it but musical notes—pages and pages of them. It didn't mean anything to us. When we got home that night, we went to Marchese Lodovico and told him the Frenchman had dropped the notebook, and we'd found it."

Julian cocked an eyebrow. "Did he believe you?"

"I expect he knew what was what," said Tommaso. "After all, the Frenchman had been mighty unwilling to give up the notebook, and wasn't very likely to drop it in the street, understand? But we didn't tell him any more, and he didn't ask. He thanked us and said he'd take care of the notebook, so we gave it to him."

"What became of it after that?" asked Julian.

Tommaso shrugged. "We never saw it again, or the Frenchman, either—until today. Of course, we didn't spend much time in Milan after that. We went to the lake with Marchese Lodovico when he took up with the singer Orfeo, then after he died, we were always off travelling with Marchese Rinaldo."

"So this happened not long before Marchese Lodovico's death," Julian mused.

"It happened at the end of the autumn season at La Scala," said Bruno.

Which would make it a month before Carnival, thought Julian, when Orfeo came into his life. "Have you confronted Monsieur de la Marque about this?"

"We'd like to, Milord!" said Bruno. "We'd like to take him by the throat and ask him how he dares show his face here at the marchesa's villa, and her not knowing there was bad blood between him and her husband. But with the *sbirri* so near at hand, we didn't like to stir up trouble."

"You were very wise," said Julian. "Will you leave Monsieur de la Marque to me for the present?"

Bruno and Tommaso looked at each other. At last Tommaso nodded. "All right, Milord. We'll keep out of the Frenchman's way—for now."

"That won't be hard tonight," said Bruno. "Marchese Rinaldo's given us the night off—which he doesn't do very often!—and we're going to the village." He winked broadly. "We're both going to have a try at that Rosa, and may the best man win!"

Dipper smiled in a way that made Julian wonder if the best man had won already. But perhaps he was only thinking about how Rosa's mother would deal with the footmen's project.

After the footmen had clapped on their gold-braided tricorne hats, made their bows, and left, MacGregor said, "What was that all about? I couldn't follow it at all."

"I'm sorry, my dear fellow," said Julian, "I didn't want to put the footmen off by translating as they were talking. I'll tell you all about it now. But first—" Julian leaned further back in his chair, a smile playing around his lips. "Dipper, will you ask Monsieur de la Marque to have the goodness to join us?"

CHAPTER 28

De la Marque sauntered into Julian's and MacGregor's room as if he were making the rounds of the fashionable boxes at La Scala. "Good evening, *mon vieux*—my dear Doctor. How delightful of you to invite me for a comfortable coze, as you English say." He lifted his black brows and looked about. "I don't see any cards—not even a bottle of wine. If anyone comes in, we shall be taken for Methodists."

"I have every confidence you'll soon set them right on that score," said Julian. "Won't you sit down?"

De la Marque dropped into a chair opposite Julian and MacGregor. His eyes travelled to Dipper, who had once again taken up his post by the door. "Tell me," he enquired conversationally, "have you stationed your man there to keep me in, or to keep Grimani out?"

"To keep Grimani out, of course," said Julian. "I've never observed it was necessary to imprison you in order to make you talk."

"Touché." De la Marque leaned back in his chair and smiled. "But why should you wish to exclude our friend the commissario from this important interrogation?"

"Because I gave my word to the footmen that I would keep Grimani out of it if I could."

"How convenient!" De la Marque smiled more than ever.

"What do you mean by that?" demanded MacGregor.

De la Marque studied him keenly for a moment or two. "Merely that I've noticed some friction between Mr. Kestrel and the so-zealous commissario," he said mildly.

"Of course," said Julian, "if you insist on my sending for Grimani—"

"You are bluffing, *mon vieux*," laughed de la Marque. "But you do it so well that I'll submit with grace. You wish you to interrogate me. Ask away."

Julian met his gaze coolly. "As you'll have guessed, the footmen told us how they thrashed you, stole your notebook, and left you for dead in the street."

De la Marque no longer smiled. Julian saw the muscles tighten in his face and up and down his arms. He had sometimes wondered whether de la Marque was really related to the noble family with whom he claimed kinship; since the Revolution, Europe had teemed with counterfeit French aristocrats. Now his suspicions on that score were laid to rest. There was no mistaking the feelings that gripped de la Marque at this reminder of the footmen's assault: humiliation, affronted honour, cold patrician rage.

De la Marque said with careful deliberation, "I knew the footmen would talk, of course. It appears they gave you a fairly complete account. What do you wish to know from me?"

"Why didn't you report this robbery to the police?"

"Would you have done so?" De la Marque gave his characteristic Gallic shrug. "I had no witnesses, and I knew Marchese Malvezzi would protect his servants. I also knew he would keep my notebook as long as he wanted it. He'd been very avid to see it. I hoped he might return it of his own accord in the end."

"He couldn't very well do that," Julian pointed out, "since you went to Turin shortly afterward and stayed there for the next three months."

"So I did." De la Marque's black eyes were steely. "You could hardly expect me to hang about Milan, meekly waiting for him to have the grace to return my property."

"Did you ever confront him about the notebook?"

"That would only have enraged him. By holding my tongue, I might hope he would unobtrusively send it back when he was finished with it."

"So you swallowed the insult, and did nothing about it," said Julian.

"More readily than I will swallow one from you," said de la Marque softly, "if you mean to call me a coward, *mon vieux*."

MacGregor sat up sharply. Julian laid a reassuring hand on his arm, but kept his eyes on de la Marque. "That was not my intention," he said equably. "Have you ever told anyone about this robbery?"

"Was I likely to? As you are fond of pointing out, the story doesn't exactly rain credit on me."

"It might have been of interest to the police when the marchese's murder became public," Julian observed.

"The police would have attached far too much importance to it. A man doesn't kill a powerful nobleman over a few notes on singing."

"Not even if that nobleman's servants stole them, and beat him senseless in the process?"

De la Marque settled more deeply into his chair, looked thoughtfully at the ceiling, stroked his moustache. "It grieves me to say this, *mon vieux*, but you are singularly unamusing this evening."

"I am desolate." Julian widened his eyes in subtle imitation of de la Marque's usual mocking manner.

"It seems to me," said MacGregor, "a man might resort to violence if somebody stole the notes he'd been taking for months, or years, for a book on singing. The footmen said you used to go to the opera and write down the singers' fior—, fior—, that music they make up as they go along. You could never have re-created all that from memory. It was a deal of effort gone down the wind."

"On the contrary," de la Marque rejoined, "I owe the footmen a debt of gratitude. They helped ensure that my much-vaunted book would never be finished. Making notes and having them stolen is rather like Penelope weaving in the daytime and unweaving her work at night: at that rate, the project will entertain me for years."

"Rubbish!" said MacGregor. "Sooner or later you'll want to hold the book in your hands and say, 'Here's something I've accomplished.'"

"That sounds unutterably dreary," said de la Marque, "like a death. I enjoy activity, not accomplishment. *Process* enthralls me." He looked affably at Julian. "Speaking of process, what are you going to do now?"

"I take it you deny killing Lodovico Malvezzi?"

"I do."

"And you have no information as to who might have killed him?"

De la Marque glanced off meditatively, resting his chin on the knuckles of one hand. "I wouldn't say that I had *no* information. An idea has struck me lately, and this seems as good a time as any to mention it."

"Please do," Julian invited.

De la Marque abruptly looked Julian in the eyes and asked with a faint smile, "Have you ever heard of the Comte d'Aubret?"

"He was a French nobleman," said Julian slowly, "a liberal, reputedly somewhat eccentric. He died a few years ago, of a wasting illness."

"All very true," said de la Marque approvingly. "I knew him slightly. We were fellow émigrés in England. He was fifteen or twenty years older than I, and his eccentricity was more than reputed. When the émigrés returned to France after the Restoration, most of us were delighted to take up our old lives and privileges and make the most of them. Not so d'Aubret. He was a philosopher: thoughtful, sceptical, and—to the horror of France under the restored Bourbon monarchs—

irreligious. He admired the British Constitution—he even had one or two good things to say of Bonaparte. The King distrusted him, other nobles murmured against him, priests execrated him, his own peasants couldn't make him out. The police would no doubt have liked to catch him plotting against the government, but as far as I know, they never did. He didn't meddle in politics. He was very jaded. If I were to sum him up, I should say that no gentleman was ever more cynical in public matters, or more kind in private life."

"From all I know of him," said Julian, "you've described him very well."

De la Marque smiled broadly. "From you, that's a great compliment—you being such a shrewd judge of character."

"What has this Comte d'Aubret to do with Lodovico Malvezzi's murder?" MacGregor wanted to know.

"Well, you see, my dear Doctor," de la Marque explained, "the Comte d'Aubret had an English protégé: a young man who, I believe, would have been about Orfeo's age. D'Aubret sent this young man to Italy for polishing a year or two before the murder. And I seem to remember hearing that he could sing."

Julian regarded de la Marque intently. "What was this young man's name?"

"That's the very devil of it, Mr. Kestrel. I simply cannot recall. I never met him, you see." De la Marque smiled, catlike. "Of course, it may come back to me at any time."

"Of all the bamboozling tricks!" MacGregor exclaimed. "Do you think you can make a May-game of us with your French counts and English protégés? You say you remember how old this young man was and when he came to Italy, but you can't remember his name?"

"Sadly, *mon très cher médecin*, that is the case. You must understand, this young Englishman sparked considerable interest among d'Aubret's acquaintances. He wasn't very much seen—d'Aubret mostly kept him at his château—but there were all manner of rumours about him. Some people said he was d'Aubret's natural son, sired in England when d'Aubret was very young. Others were convinced d'Aubret used him as a spy and a go-between with the English. There was even a romantic story of how the young man was wandering destitute in the streets of Paris, and fainted into d'Aubret's arms outside Tortoni's. Whatever the explanation, d'Aubret took an extraordinary fancy to him. I'm not speaking of *l'amour à la Grecque*—I don't think d'Aubret's tastes ran that way. He may have been developing a system of education, like Rousseau. Or perhaps he was merely bored."

"I take it you don't believe in disinterested kindness," Julian observed.

"I don't believe in disinterested conduct of any sort. Whoever tells you he acts without regard for the consequences to himself is either a lunatic or a liar." De la Marque sat back and smiled. "But you haven't answered my question, *mon vieux*. What are you going to do?"

"There's only one thing I can do." Julian rose and turned to Dipper. "Will you please find Commissario Grimani and bring him here?"

"Yes, sir." Dipper went out.

De la Marque started to his feet. "What—what are you doing?"

"I'm reporting what you've told me to Commissario Grimani. I can't keep information of this importance from him."

"But—but—" De la Marque looked blank. "I thought you promised the footmen you would keep them out of it."

"I promised I would try. It isn't possible. The theft of your notebook and your story of the Comte d'Aubret's protégé have to be disclosed."

"You must be completely mad! Don't you know that Grimani—"

Julian lifted his brows. "Don't I know that Grimani—what?"

"Nothing!" De la Marque threw himself back into his chair. "Do as you like! Bring the whole benighted house down on our heads if it amuses you. But may the Devil and all his legions take me if I understand what you're about! I am lost in the labyrinth of your mind!"

MacGregor snorted. "Happens to me around Kestrel every day."

Julian gave Grimani an account of the footmen's theft of de la Marque's notebook and de la Marque's speculations about the Comte d'Aubret's protégé. Grimani naturally wanted to question the footmen, but Julian said they had gone to the village for the night. As he had promised them, he asked Grimani for leniency on their behalf as informers. He need not have bothered: the footmen were nothing to Grimani. He was far more interested in making a case against the victim of their crime.

"What precisely was in this notebook of yours?" he asked de la Marque.

De la Marque leaned back, threw one leg negligently over the arm of his chair, and sighed, a martyr to boredom. "All manner of musical jottings. Fioriture I heard at the opera. Musical exercises I'd read of or invented. Tonal and rhythmic sequences I'd heard singers mangle. I was trying to determine which combinations of notes are most challenging, and why."

"Did you include any advice on composition?" asked Julian. "Or perhaps any compositions of your own?"

"I have no pretensions to be the next Rossini," de la Marque said lightly.

"I only wondered," said Julian, "because Ernesto thought Marchese Lodovico was composing a piece of music before he died. And it occurred to me that he might have been using your notebook to do it."

De la Marque regarded him more keenly. "You interest me."

"Conte Carlo told me he'd never had any success at composition before," Julian went on. "If he had wanted to use your notebook to write—say, an opera, or merely a song—would he have found the materials there?"

De la Marque slowly withdrew his gaze. "I did try my hand at composing. I'd laid the foundation—anyone with a little knowledge of music might have constructed the edifice."

"Do you mean to accuse Marchese Lodovico of plagiarizing your music?" Grimani demanded.

"I don't mean to do anything so energetic as that," said de la Marque with a yawn. "Mr. Kestrel suggested it, and I was obliged to admit that it was possible."

"What finally became of this notebook?" said Grimani.

"I don't know, Signor Commissario. I can only tell you that I never got it back."

"It wasn't found among Marchese Lodovico's possessions," Grimani pointed out.

"I can't account for that," shrugged de la Marque. "Perhaps Orfeo has it."

"And perhaps," said Grimani, "you are Orfeo, and you wormed your way into Marchese Lodovico's good graces in order to retrieve your notebook and revenge yourself on him for his footmen's assault."

"Actually," mused Julian, "doesn't the theft of Monsieur de la Marque's notebook make it far less plausible that he's Orfeo? With such bad blood between him and Marchese Lodovico, it's hardly likely that the marchese would turn round and invite him to a musical idyll at the lake."

"Unless he couldn't resist his voice," put in MacGregor. "Everyone says that when the marchese heard a fine voice, he forgot everything else."

"This is all vastly flattering," said de la Marque. "Within the past quarter-hour, I've been hailed as a promising composer, a sublime tenor—though I grieve to remind you all that I am a baritone—and the most subtle and diabolical criminal imaginable. But as we've rather exhausted the subject of my achievements, licit and illicit, don't you think, Commissario, we might give a moment's attention to the Comte d'Aubret's protégé?"

"I haven't forgotten him," said Grimani. "This d'Aubret was a notorious liberal. Our government knew all about him, as the French authorities knew of potentially dangerous radicals here. If he really did have an English protégé who could sing, and who came to Italy not long before Orfeo appeared, the matter is worth looking into. Maestro Donati did say that Orfeo claimed to have learned French before he learned Italian. But your story is a little too convenient, monsieur. It may be nothing more than an invention to divert suspicion from yourself. I'll have enquiries made to discover this name you can't remember. But I won't absolve you of being Orfeo until I have firm proof that someone else is."

Grimani departed. De la Marque undraped his leg from over the arm of his chair and rose, saying with a bow, "Thank you, gentlemen, for a most diverting evening." He caught MacGregor's eye and added softly, "I'll leave you with Mr. Kestrel. You may wish to say goodbye to him—while you have the chance."

He went out. MacGregor sputtered, "What did he mean by that? He threatened you!"

"I don't know that it was an outright threat," said Julian. "But I imagine that if I were carried off by a rapid consumption, he wouldn't go into mourning."

He looked after de la Marque with a touch of regret. He did not trust the Frenchman an inch, yet he felt a twinge of liking for him. This was all the stranger, since de la Marque clearly had designs on the marchesa—a motive for murdering her husband that Grimani seemed to have overlooked.

There was a pattering sound from the balcony. The rain that had impended all evening was beginning. Dipper closed the French windows, and the mist gathered thickly against them, like an excluded creature looking in. Julian sent Dipper for extra blankets from the linen closet. One of the marchesa's rare touches of Milanese parsimony was her reluctance to light fires.

As Julian and MacGregor prepared for bed, they could hear the rest of the villa party going to their rooms up and down the corridor. Julian made out Carlo's genial *"Buona notte,"* St. Carr's complaint about the rain and Fletcher's long-suffering response, the marchesa's melodic voice alternating with Nina's childlike trill. Then there was silence.

Suddenly there came a loud drunken laugh. "Come on! Anybody would think you were on your way to be hanged!"

Julian opened his door a crack. Rinaldo was bundling Francesca into their room at the other end of the hall. By the light of an oil lamp in his hand, Julian saw her backing away from the threshold, her hands out beseechingly. Rinaldo pushed her inside and shut the door behind them both.

Julian closed his own door. His grip on the knob was tight—on his anger, less so. "If she weren't his wife, there would be a name for what he's going to do to her."

"But she *is* his wife," said MacGregor. "That makes all the difference in the world. *Whom God hath joined together*, Kestrel. You can't interfere between them."

At that moment, Julian felt scant respect for the sacrament of marriage. But he knew he could do nothing for Francesca. If he rescued her from Rinaldo, she would never get her children back. She would have broken with Valeriano to no purpose.

It was one thing to conclude that he could not help her—another to put her out of his mind. He sent Dipper to bed, but did not feel like going to bed himself. Clad in trousers, shirt, and dressing-gown, he stood by the French windows, watching the rain accumulate in puddles and run off the balcony.

MacGregor tried to distract him. "The more I think about it, the more I think there's a ring of truth to this story of de la Marque's, that Orfeo was the Comte d'Aubret's protégé. We know Orfeo was a rare hand at creeping into favour with people of consequence. He won over Lodovico Malvezzi—why shouldn't he have done the same with d'Aubret?" When Julian did not respond, he prompted, "What do you think?"

"I think that finding out whether d'Aubret had a protégé, and if so, who he was, is the kind of methodical task we can safely leave to Grimani. I'm more interested in the notebook."

MacGregor furrowed his brow. "Funny thing, its disappearing like that. Do you think Lodovico brought it with him when he came to the lake with Orfeo?"

"Whether he did or not, it ought to have been found among his papers after he died."

"Has anyone been through all the papers?"

"That's a good question," said Julian thoughtfully. "Conte Carlo told me he'd given Lodovico's private papers to Rinaldo after Lodovico died. We ought to ask Rinaldo tomorrow what became of them."

MacGregor yawned. "Well, I'm for Bedfordshire. After everything that's happened, we'll both be the better for a good, sound sleep."

"I thought I might sit up a while, if you don't mind. Downstairs, so as not to keep you awake."

"Why?" MacGregor demanded.

"I'm not sleepy. Perhaps I'll play the piano quietly until I am."

"Look here: I'm not to be fobbed off with Banbury stories. You're up to something. I should think tonight of all nights you wouldn't want to wander around the house in the dark, with de la Marque itching to do you a mischief—" MacGregor rounded on him. "That's it, isn't it? You think he may be dangerous, and you want to face him alone! Well, you may put that out of your mind! You're staying right here."

Julian could see there was no gainsaying him. "Very well." He pondered a moment. "I don't think de la Marque's threat was serious. But I suppose we should pay him the compliment of treating it as if it were."

He took out the case containing his pistols. They were already loaded, but he screwed new flints into the cocks and sprinkled fresh powder into the shallow pan beneath the hammer, ready to ignite at the striking of flint to steel. He left the case open beside the bed. Then he locked the door and propped a chair before it, the back tucked under the knob. He propped another chair against the balcony window in the same manner.

MacGregor watched him, fascinated. "Anybody would think you'd been fending off murder threats all your life."

"I don't think these precautions are really necessary. But on the chance de la Marque is in earnest, I shouldn't like my last thought on earth to be, 'Why the devil didn't I prime my pistols?'"

"I suppose I ought to be in a fright." MacGregor shook his head, marvelling. "But somehow all I can think of is that for the first time, I really feel I'm in the land of the Borgias."

Dipper was awakened by sunshine streaming through the window of his tiny attic room. The rain was over, the mist all but lifted, leaving only a few gossamer threads around the highest mountain peaks. The two menservants who shared his room ran to the window, greeting the sun as if they had not seen it for forty days and forty nights.

Dipper washed, shaved, dressed, and nipped down the service stairs to the basement. There he exchanged greetings with the kitchen servants and collected a tray with Mr. Kestrel's morning coffee and Dr MacGregor's tea. On his way back up the stairs, he had to dodge a group of the villa servants coming down. They were waving their hands excitedly, shouting curses at one another, and shaking their fists under each other's noses. Dipper would have thought a fight was going to break out, if he had not seen similar passions flare up among them, only to vanish as serenely as last night's rainstorm.

After they had passed, he inspected the tray to make sure he had not spilled anything. Just then he heard a slow, measured tread approaching up the stairs. Ernesto appeared with a pitcher of water and an armful of fresh towels. They continued up the stairs together.

"What was that kick-up about, Signor Ernesto?" Dipper asked.

"They're arguing over who forgot to bar the front door last night."

Dipper's brows came together. "But it *was* barred. Giacomo done it before he went to bed. I seen him."

"Well, it isn't now," said Ernesto. "I mean to find out who unbarred it, and if it was one of the servants, I'll see that he's punished. With things so uncertain, and my dear master's murder still unsolved, we can't have the villa open at night to anyone who wants to come in."

They parted at the top of the service stairs, Ernesto going toward Marchese Rinaldo's room at the other end of the hall. Dipper looked after him curiously for a moment, wondering how the reunited couple were getting on. Then he turned and went to Mr. Kestrel's door.

From the other end of the hall came a crash and a wild cry. Dipper plunked the tray on a table and ran down the hall to Marchese Rinaldo's room. The door was standing open. Ernesto was on his knees in a pool of spilled water, surrounded by towels and broken crockery. He was praying incoherently, crossing himself, and staring at the bed. Dipper stared, too.

At first all he saw was blood. Blood soaking the coverlet, sheet, and pillowcase. Blood spattered on the bed-curtains and wall. Blood coating the blade of the silver-handled razor lying at the foot of the bed. Rinaldo lay on his back, his nightgown open at the neck, the covers turned back below his breast. His eyes were closed, his throat hideously open. Francesca was nowhere to be seen.

Part Four

OCTOBER 1825

Vile assignations, and adulterous beds,
Elopements, broken vows and hearts and heads.

George Noel Gordon,
Lord Byron
Beppo

Grimani shot out of his room across the hall. Carlo, his face half shaved and half covered with soapsuds, was close behind. Fletcher ran out of his room next door to Rinaldo's dressed in shirt and trousers, his wet hair towelled into spikes. St. Carr followed, still in his nightclothes, his nightcap flopping over one ear. De la Marque approached at a more leisurely pace, clad in a dressing-gown of purple silk, his hair and moustache elaborately combed. Julian and MacGregor raced past him, both in dressing-gowns, MacGregor clutching his battered leather medical bag.

They were all brought up short on seeing Rinaldo. Carlo gasped, "Ah, Madonna!" and crossed himself. De la Marque blinked and seemed vaguely affronted, as if he thought such a sight had no business to assail him at this hour of the morning. Fletcher looked shocked but could gaze at the bed without flinching; Julian recalled that he was accustomed to dissecting animals.

MacGregor pushed past the others to Rinaldo. Grimani seemed about to stop him, then changed his mind and followed, watching him tensely as he felt and listened for signs of life.

"Dead," said MacGregor, in English. "Has been for some time."

Julian, who had quietly joined them by the bed, translated this. Grimani scanned the ranks of people in the doorway. "You," he said to Dipper. "Fetch me Zanetti."

Julian nodded to Dipper to obey. Dipper ran off.

Grimani's eyes raked the room. He went to the rosewood wardrobe, opened the doors, and twitched apart the clothes inside. No one. He strode to the balcony facing the lake. The French doors were closed but not secured. Grimani opened them wide, letting in a flood of sunshine that made the horror in the bed at once more real and more pathetic.

There was no one hiding there, nor on the balcony overlooking the south terrace. All at once Julian had a terrible thought—one Grimani must have shared. They went out onto first one balcony and then the other and looked over the marble railings. There was no broken body beneath. Francesca had simply disappeared.

"Has anyone seen Marchesa Francesca?" Grimani demanded of the group in the doorway.

Shakes of heads, bewildered gazes, stammered *No*s.

Servants were gathering in the hallway, crossing themselves and craning their necks for a glimpse of Rinaldo's corpse. Julian saw Guido's grizzled head among them, conspicuous by the heavy gold earrings. His eyes were narrowed, calculating; his lips moved in rote, indifferent prayers.

The marchesa appeared. Carlo said quickly, "Beatrice, stay back, don't look."

She came forward all the same, the others making way for her. She wore a loose white satin morning robe over a white nightdress. Her dusky hair, alive with combing, floated above her shoulders. She might have been an angel come for the dead man's soul. She looked steadily at Rinaldo, crossed herself gravely, and bent to raise Ernesto, who was still on his knees in the spilled shaving water, babbling broken prayers.

"Hugo," said St. Carr faintly, "I'm going to be sick."

Fletcher gave him his arm to lean on. "We'll be in our room."

Grimani turned to the marchesa. "I want you and the guests to dress and wait in the drawing room, and the servants to gather in the servants' hall. No one is to leave the house. Doctor, you will remain here. I want to know how long he's been dead and whether he could have done it himself." He turned to Julian. "Tell him."

Julian repeated it in English. MacGregor grunted, "I'll do my best."

"You stay as well, Signor Kestrel," Grimani added unwillingly. "I need you."

Julian knew better than to think Grimani wanted him for his detection skills. Someone had to interpret between Grimani and MacGregor, and Carlo, the victim's uncle, was too close to the crime. No matter: this might be Julian's only chance to observe the murder scene. He would make the most of it.

The crowd in the doorway dispersed, the marchesa giving her arm to Ernesto, who leaned on it like an old man. Grimani shut the door behind them—then he and Julian stared at the lock on the inside. The key was in it, and both lock and key were covered with blood.

"The knob is clean," Julian noticed.

Grimani looked at the hand he had used to close the door. Sure enough, the knob had left no blood on it. He crossed to the washstand, Julian following. The water in the basin was so red that the Chinese landscape at the bottom could scarcely be seen. The white linen towel was covered with red-brown stains.

Julian stepped back and took a survey of the room. It was rectangular, with the door at the end of one long wall. The bed jutted out from the centre of that wall, all but bisecting the room. On the right side of the bed, nearest the door, was a small night-table with an oil lamp on it. The opposite wall ran along the lake, with the balcony in the centre, the rosewood wardrobe and washstand to the left, and a round, marble-topped table to the right. The fireplace was in the short wall nearest the door. Opposite was the balcony over the south terrace.

Julian and Grimani approached the bed. Its blue damask curtains were closed at the foot and along the left side. On the right side, nearest the door, they were open but not tied back. MacGregor was busy about Rinaldo's body: looking into his eyes, scrutinizing his hair, hands, fingernails, fearlessly probing the raw, red gap in his neck. Julian and Grimani turned their attention to the razor lying at the foot of the bed. Its silver handle was elaborately moulded with vines and clusters of grapes. The blood on the blade had made a deep crimson stain on the blue coverlet beneath.

"Don't touch anything," Grimani warned.

"Of course not," said Julian civilly.

They moved on to the marble-topped table. A dressing-case of purple Morocco leather lay open there. It contained the accoutrements one would expect: ivory-handled toothbrushes, tortoiseshell combs, nail-scissors. Beside the case was an empty leather sheath of exactly the size to fit the bloodstained razor.

Crowded to one side of the table were two silver candelabra. The candles were tall and new, the wicks unburned. Julian crossed to the night-table and peered inside the lamp. "There's a great deal of oil left," he observed. "It must not have been burning long."

"We don't know if it was lit at all last night," said Grimani.

"I saw it lit," said Julian. "Marchese Rinaldo brought it to his room when he went to bed."

"What time was that?" Grimani asked quickly.

"A little after midnight, I should think—perhaps ten minutes. I saw him from the doorway of my room."

"Was Marchesa Francesca with him?"

"Yes."

"Did you hear them say anything?"

"Yes," owned Julian reluctantly. "Rinaldo was urging her to come inside—scolding her for hanging back." He supposed he had better make a clean breast of it, ominous though the implications were. "He was laughing loudly and seemed drunk. She looked very frightened. He pushed her into the room and shut the door behind them."

"Hmm," said Grimani.

There was a tap at the door. Grimani called brusquely, "Come in."

Zanetti joined them, hastily dressed and bearing his portable writing-desk.

"You've taken your time," snapped Grimani. "Don't explain—I don't have time to hear it. I want you to make sure no one leaves the villa. Lock all the outside doors, and collect the keys. Find out if any doors or windows have been forced—Yes? What is it?"

"The front door was found unbarred this morning, Signor Commissario, though the servants swear they barred it before they went to bed."

Grimani nodded briefly, as if this were what he would have expected. "Leave me your writing-desk. And bring me a servant whose whereabouts for the whole night are accounted for. I need someone to take messages to Solaggio."

"Yes, Signor Commissario." Zanetti hurried out.

MacGregor turned to Julian and Grimani, wiping his blood-stained fingers on his handkerchief. "All right. Here's as much as I can tell you without a complete examination. The body is cold. Rigour's set in, but it's only partial. The blood isn't coagulable—that is, it's ceased to clot. What all this says to me is that he was probably killed between four and seven hours ago."

Julian translated this as accurately as he could. He had never learned the Italian for *coagulable.* He glanced at the mantelpiece clock and found that it was nearly half past eight. "So he would have been killed between one and five in the morning."

MacGregor nodded. "The wound is deep," he went on. "Severed the carotid artery and both the external and internal jugular veins. He probably died almost instantly. The depth and shape of the wound are consistent with the razor's being the weapon."

"Is there any chance he did it himself?" asked Grimani.

"Very unlikely. A man in my village cut his own throat, and the wound was just what you'd expect to see in a suicide: deepest at the commencement, and slanted down from left to right. And there were little cuts around it, where he'd made false starts. This wound is straight across the throat, equally deep at both ends, and there are no tentative tries."

"How much strength would the murderer have needed?" Julian asked.

"Not much," said MacGregor. "Strong nerves and a firm hand would have been more important."

Their eyes met. Julian knew they were thinking the same thing. This whole discussion was hauntingly familiar, conjuring up memories of their first meeting, in another country house, over another corpse. MacGregor had been anything but favourably impressed with Julian then—had thought him a coxcomb at best, a murderer at worst. Julian smiled at the memory, and MacGregor looked at him askance. But of course he had chided him for levity then, too.

"Was he in that position when he was killed?" Grimani asked MacGregor.

"I'd say so, to judge by the flow of blood from the wound and the lividity—what there was of it, after such a loss of blood."

Julian surveyed Rinaldo's body. "He may well have been sleeping very deeply, after all the wine he'd drunk. Lying as he was, on his back with his throat exposed, he would have been an ideal target for anyone who wanted to do him a mischief."

He knew it was high time he took a close look at the body. His chest knotted up at the prospect. In all his experience of solving murders, he had never confronted a corpse so gruesome. He steeled himself, went to the bed, and gazed down at what had once been Rinaldo Malvezzi. To his surprise, he saw more than blood, torn flesh, and death. Within that ugly gash was the wreck of a miraculous mechanism: the network of veins and arteries that pumped life into eyes, ears, lips, and brain. He had been prepared for the tragedy, but not for the desecration, the waste.

He looked closer. Matted in Rinaldo's bloodsoaked chest hair was a small gold crucifix. It was strung on a gold chain some twenty-five inches long, the ends lying unfastened on Rinaldo's shoulders.

"Was it you who unfastened this chain?" Julian asked MacGregor.

"No. I didn't touch it."

Julian bent nearer. "The clasp seems very secure. I don't think it would have opened of its own accord while he was sleeping."

Grimani had been standing with arms folded, thinking things out. "It's clear what happened. Marchesa Francesca didn't want to come to bed with her husband. He locked the door to keep her in, and strung the key on the chain around his neck for safe-keeping. It was there when she slit his throat, which explains why it has so much blood on it."

"She used it to unlock the door," Julian went on, "thus getting blood on the lock—"

"Then she went downstairs and let herself out by the front door, leaving it unbarred," Grimani finished. "It's as simple a case as I've ever seen."

"Wait till Julian Kestrel gets hold of it," muttered MacGregor.

Julian forbore to translate this. With an apologetic look at MacGregor, he said, "Don't you think it strange that there's a great deal of blood on the key and the lock, but none on the knob? That would mean that Marchesa Francesca killed her husband, took the key, unlocked the door—and only then, before she left the room, decided to wash the blood from her hands."

"There's nothing strange about that," said Grimani. "She was in a passion when she committed the murder. But after she'd unlocked the door she came to herself enough to realize that she couldn't leave the room with blood on her hands. So she washed them."

"If she had the presence of mind to do that, why didn't she wash the key and lock as well? She must have realized that the bloodstained key and open chain would heavily incriminate her."

"She was a hysterical woman," said Grimani. "You can't expect her to have acted logically."

"Emotion has its own sort of logic, Signor Commissario. People don't calculate about one thing, while being wholly reckless about everything else."

"No Milanese judge would take any account of evidence like that," Grimani said coldly. "The explanation I've given fits all the objective facts."

There was a shade of regret in his voice. Julian thought he knew why. If Francesca had killed Rinaldo, she had almost certainly killed Lodovico as well. Which meant that Orfeo was innocent—of murder, at all events.

It seemed pointless to argue any further. Julian returned to his scrutiny of Rinaldo's body. Grimani sat down at the table with Zanetti's writing-desk before him, sharpened a quill, and rapidly wrote, folded, and addressed several notes. MacGregor paced back and forth, head down, hands clasped behind his back.

All at once Julian said, "Signor Commissario."

"What is it?" said Grimani, without looking up.

"I've found something."

Grimani joined him by the bed. Julian pointed to a white spot on the bloodsoaked sheet, a few inches to the right of Rinaldo's neck. Grimani squinted at it, touched it lightly with his finger. "Candle wax." He looked up at Julian. "What of that?"

"It's on top of the blood, Signor Commissario. That means someone stood over Marchese Rinaldo with a candle after he died." Julian went quickly to the candelabra on the table. "These are the only candles in the room—and none of them has been lit."

Grimani's eyes met Julian's—exasperated, but suddenly unsure.

Zanetti came in with the footmen, Bruno and Tommaso. They looked a little bedraggled, their flame-coloured frock-coats crumpled, their lace not overclean. They gaped at the corpse of their master, crossed themselves, and muttered the *de profundis.*

"These two servants spent the night in the village, Signor Commissario," Zanetti announced. "They left before Marchese

Rinaldo went to bed and were never out of each other's sight all night. They've only just returned. I thought one of them would do for a messenger."

Grimani ran his eyes over them. "You're Marchese Rinaldo's footmen, are you? The ones who stole a notebook from Monsieur de la Marque?"

The footmen exchanged alarmed glances. "Yes, Signor Commissario."

"I shall want to talk to you later," said Grimani ominously. He turned back to Zanetti. "What else have you learned?"

"No doors or windows have been forced," Zanetti reported, "and no one has seen Marchesa Francesca since last night. Marchesa Beatrice and her guests are assembled in the drawing room. She's ordered coffee to be served there." He sounded a little wistful, as if he would have liked a cup himself.

Julian asked the footmen, "Do you know how these new candles come to be here?"

"I brought them, Milord," said Tommaso.

"When was that?"

"Last night, before Bruno and I went to the village. Ernesto told me to take away the stumps that were here and replace them with new candles."

"They were just for show," put in Bruno.

"What do you mean?" asked Grimani.

"The marchese didn't like to have open flames about him, especially at night. He was afraid of them. He wouldn't admit it, but we all knew." Bruno's lip curled contemptuously.

"Did you leave any of the old candles behind when you brought the new ones?" Julian asked Tommaso.

"No, Milord."

"Were there any candles in the room besides these?"

"I didn't see any, Milord."

Grimani handed the notes he had written to Zanetti. "Seal these with the police seal, and give them to—Which one are you?" he asked Bruno.

"Bruno Monti, at your service, Signor Commissario."

"Can you read?"

"A little, Signor Commissario. My father—"

"Make sure he knows which note is which," Grimani told Zanetti. Turning back to Bruno, he asked, "Do you know where to find Comandante Von Krauss, the podestà Signor Ruga, the priest Don Cristoforo, and Dr. Curioni?"

"Yes, Signor Commissario."

"Then you will deliver these notes to them as swiftly as possible. You will not loiter along the way, and you will not speak to anyone—*anyone*, do you understand?—about this crime."

"Yes, Signor Commissario."

Julian thought this was asking too much of Bruno, chatterbox that he was. But he kept this to himself. Grimani had made it abundantly clear that he took no interest in Julian Kestrel's views of human character.

"Thank you for your assistance, signori," said Grimani to Julian and MacGregor. "Now please be good enough to dress and join the others in the drawing room."

"Isn't anybody going to look for Marchesa Francesca?" said MacGregor.

"I've requested that Comandante Von Krauss and Signor Ruga initiate a search for her," Grimani said. "If there are any results that are pertinent for you to know, you will be advised."

Julian and MacGregor had no choice but to withdraw. "How do you like that?" MacGregor fumed. "After all the help we gave him, he talks as if the murder were none of our business!"

"You know he's not overfond of amateurs," said Julian absently.

MacGregor cocked his head at him. "Do you think he's right? About Marchesa Francesca's killing her husband?"

"It's hard to imagine. But Rinaldo had insulted her, laid violent hands on her, torn her from her lover. Who can say what she might have been driven to, locked in with him and at his mercy?"

"Poor woman." MacGregor shook his head sombrely.

"We don't know that she's guilty," Julian reminded him. "But if she isn't—where is she?"

CHAPTER 30

Julian and MacGregor came down to the drawing room some twenty minutes later, having washed, dressed, and, in Julian's case, shaved. For once Julio envied MacGregor his thick, salt-and-pepper beard. He himself would have been glad to be relieved of the need to handle a razor this morning.

The company were scattered about the drawing room, tense yet aimless. Fletcher stared doggedly at the ornate Malvezzi family tree, as if he had set himself the task of memorizing it. St. Carr leaned against the nearby wall, restlessly kicking the skirting-board. Carlo stood with his elbow propped on the mantelpiece and his face sunk in his hand. Donati occupied a chair in a corner, Sebastiano standing sentinel beside him. De la Marque sat with Beatrice on the turquoise and white striped sofa, leaning close to her and talking with her softly.

Julian felt a stab of jealous frustration. While he had been poring over bloodstains and candle wax, de la Marque had been here comforting and cheering Beatrice—with some success, to judge by her faint smile and de la Marque's triumphant glow. What did de la Marque care how she felt? Her shock, her vulnerability, were merely to be played upon for his own obvious ends. —But what do you care, either, Julian asked himself in all honesty, when you grudge her consolation because it doesn't come from you?

When she saw Julian, she rose and came to him. She was dressed in her white dimity morning frock, with the black veil she usually wore to church draped lightly over her head and around her shoulders. She laid her fingertips eagerly on his arm. "Signor Kestrel, what news?"

"Grimani has sent Bruno with messages for Von Krauss, Ruga, Curioni, and Don Cristoforo."

"But what have you learned so far?" she pressed him.

Julian limited himself to obvious and elementary facts. For all the damning evidence against Francesca, her guilt was by no means proved. Until it was, God help him, he must regard the whole family, including this woman, as suspects. "Marchese Rinaldo's death was clearly murder. He was killed with the razor from his dressing-case—"

"Is that Signor Kestrel?" Donati half rose from his chair in the corner, holding out questing hands.

"Yes, Maestro." Julian went to him quickly. He saw with concern what this second murder had done to the old man. His sightless eyes were red with weeping, and he looked so gossamer-frail, a breeze might have blown him away.

"Signor Kestrel." Donati raised his hands as if in supplication. "How could this have happened? *Why* did it happen?"

"I don't know, Maestro. But I swear to you, upon my honour, that I will find out."

Ernesto came in. "Comandante Von Krauss and Signor Ruga are here, Your Ladyship. Commissario Grimani ordered me to show them straight up to him. They've left some soldiers waiting on the terrace."

"Offer the soldiers refreshment," said Beatrice. "And if they're going to be milling about for some time, ask them to take off their sabres. They do tend to knock into the urns and lampposts."

"Yes, Your Ladyship." Ernesto bowed and withdrew.

Julian returned to the marchesa. "There's something I should like to ask you."

"Of course there is," she said, with a wry smile. "I never doubted you would ask more questions than you would answer."

"Yesterday evening you told me you'd asked Marchese Rinaldo to stay the night because you were afraid of what Francesca might do if she were isolated with him at Castello Malvezzi. What did you mean?"

"What did I mean?" Her slim brows drew together. "Not that I expected her to attack or harm him. She's so gentle, I can hardly imagine it, even now. I believe I was more afraid she would lay hands on herself. But I really didn't think it out."

They were interrupted by the arrival of Don Cristoforo, who hastened upstairs to administer the Last Rites to Rinaldo. Julian knew that Rinaldo would not be officially pronounced dead until this was done, whereupon, by a compassionate fiction, he would be treated as having received the sacraments before he died.

The marchesa called for fresh pots of coffee, and the others subsided into restless inactivity again. Julian at last decided to go outside and have a look around, in spite of Grimani's orders to remain indoors.

On his way down the stairs to the terrace, he was met by half a dozen blond soldiers politely requesting him, in German-accented Italian, to go back inside. He submitted with grace, having no other choice. But as he was returning up the stairs, a noise from across the terrace caught his ears. He looked around. A sergeant and two soldiers were just stepping onto the terrace from the shore path. Walking between the soldiers, shoulders slumped, head drooping, was Francesca.

One of the soldiers waiting on the terrace raced up the steps past Julian—to alert Grimani, no doubt. Julian remained looking over the stairway balustrade. Francesca's guards brought her to the foot of the stairs. Her hair was half undone, her pale-yellow gown creased and dirty, with grass-stains around the hem. Her white petticoat showed through a long rent in the skirt. Though the morning was chilly, she had no shawl, and her cheeks were red and pinched, her hands crossed over her breast and chafing her upper arms.

When she saw Julian, her taut face relaxed ever so slightly. She must have been relieved to see any man not in uniform. He started down to her, but two soldiers crossed their bayonets at the bottom of the stairs, blocking his way. "We can't permit you to speak to the prisoner, signor," said one.

"The—prisoner?" faltered Francesca.

"At least allow me to give her my coat," said Julian.

"We can't permit that, either," said the soldier, regretful but firm. "We don't know what may be in the pockets."

Julian reined in his exasperation. "Then perhaps you'll be good enough to search me."

"That won't be necessary," said Grimani's voice.

Julian looked around to the top of the stairs. Grimani stood there, a look of cold satisfaction on his face. He was flanked by Von Krauss, handsome and immaculate in his white coat with gold epaulets, and Ruga, his plump face pasty and anxious.

Grimani looked a question at Von Krauss, who inclined his head, allowing Grimani to take the lead. "Sergeant," said Grimani, "your report."

The sergeant stepped forward smartly, saluted, and said, "We found Marchesa Francesca in the villa chapel, Signor Commissario, at the southwesternmost corner of the garden. She was on her knees before the statue of the Madonna. When we came in, she got to her feet quickly and seemed frightened."

"Did she say anything?" asked Grimani.

"Yes, Signor Commissario." The sergeant's stalwart soldier's mask slipped a little. He looked suddenly like a goodhearted peasant from some Alpine village, confronted by the unthinkable. "She said she'd been asking the Madonna for forgiveness and guidance. Then she said, 'Perhaps I shouldn't have done it, but I wanted so desperately to get away.'"

All eyes turned to Francesca, appalled.

She shrank from the stares and would have turned away, but the soldiers restrained her and held her facing Grimani, Von Krauss, and Ruga, who looked down on her from the top of the stairs like judges from the bench. She asked in a small voice, "Does—does Rinaldo really mean to charge me with a crime—just for running away from him?"

"That is absurd, Marchesa Francesca," paid Grimani. "You can't suppose your husband survived such an attack?"

"Attack?" Her colour faded. In a voice as high as a little girl's, she asked, "What—what do you mean?"

"I mean that your husband lies murdered in his bed, Marchesa Francesca. As you well know."

Francesca collapsed.

Francesca was revived and brought inside to recuperate a little before being questioned. Grimani, Von Krauss, and Ruga remained on the terrace for a brief council of war, which Julian was permitted to overhear. Ruga was to go back to the village to calm the agitation there, while Von Krauss would return to his barracks, where he had other pressing business. Soldiers and gendarmes would be seconded to Grimani, who would supervise the investigation of Rinaldo's murder from the villa. If he determined there were adequate grounds to make an arrest, Ruga would provide him with a warrant.

Julian also learned that Dr. Curioni had been summoned to an outlying hamlet and might not return for some time. This was to Julian's advantage, because Grimani wanted a doctor present when he interrogated Francesca, both to judge whether her statements were consistent with the medical evidence, and to tend her in the event of another collapse. He had no choice but to rely on MacGregor, and as Zanetti was busy questioning servants, he was compelled to ask Julian to be his interpreter once more.

Before they went inside to join Francesca, Julian asked if he might pose a few questions to the sergeant. Grimani grudgingly called the sergeant over. Julian asked, "When you found Marchesa Francesca in the chapel and brought her here, did she give any sign that she knew her husband was dead?"

"No, signor. After she said what I reported just now, I told her she should make her confession to the police, not to me. From then on, she only said one thing more."

"What was that?"

The sergeant thought a moment, then repeated carefully, "'Holy Mother, forgive me, I know it's a sin, but I wish I had died in climbing down from the balcony.'"

"Climbing down from the balcony!" exclaimed Grimani. "Are you sure you heard her aright?"

"Yes, Signor Commissario. 'Climbing down from the balcony.' That's what she said."

Grimani looked up to the balcony of Rinaldo's room, three stories above and bare of any trees or trellising. "That's ridiculous. She must think us utter fools."

"She may not mean this balcony," said Julian slowly. "The room also has a balcony over the south terrace."

"No one could climb down from that one, either," said Grimani, "least of all a woman. She's either lying or mad."

"Did she resist coming with you?" Julian asked the sergeant.

"No, signor. She came very meekly."

"Did she?" said Julian thoughtfully.

"This is a waste of time," said Grimani. "Come, Signor Kestrel. I'll get to the bottom of this."

Francesca did claim to have climbed down from the balcony to the south terrace. Grimani, unbelieving, took her outside to show him how she had done it. Julian and MacGregor accompanied them, Julian giving Francesca his arm. She was pale and walked a little stiffly. Julian supposed she must still be in shock.

They went around to the south terrace and stood beneath the balcony of Rinaldo's room, three stories above. There were no creeping plants or trellising to aid in climbing down, and the fruit trees were separated from the house by a gravel walk.

"She might have managed it with a rope," said MacGregor doubtfully, "or some sheets knotted together."

Julian translated this for Francesca. She shook her head timidly. "I didn't have a rope, and there weren't any extra sheets."

"Then how did you do it?" Grimani challenged her.

Francesca swallowed hard. Julian said gently, "Perhaps it would be easier if you began at the beginning. How did the idea of climbing down from the balcony first come to you?"

She looked away. Twin spots of colour kindled in her cheeks. "It was late. It was dark. The house was quiet. Rinaldo was asleep. His arm was over me, across my chest. I wanted to get up, but I was so afraid to wake him—" She drew a long, shaky breath. "You wouldn't understand."

"Be patient with us," said Julian. "We're trying our best."

Her eyes softened. "I knew that you were a kind man, Signor Kestrel."

"Go on, Marchesa Francesca," said Grimani impatiently.

She turned her face away again. "I was lying in bed. I felt I was drowning, dying. I thought of Pietro, how lonely he must be, and how I would never see him again. 'Never' is so long, you can't grasp it all at once, but I knew that days and weeks and months would go by, and I wouldn't know if he was well or ill, I wouldn't hear his voice or hold him in my arms. I felt sure he wouldn't eat. He could die of despair. And then I thought of Rinaldo—of what my life would be with him. I couldn't bear it. I had to get away. I prayed to the Madonna to help me. And suddenly—" She lifted wide, wondering eyes. "Rinaldo turned over on his back and took away his arm. It was like a sign that the Madonna had heard my prayer."

"The Devil heard your prayer, not the Madonna," said Grimani. "Do you suppose the Madonna would help a wife to leave her husband?"

"N-no, I know she wouldn't," she said confusedly. "But all the same, it felt that way to me. I got out of bed very carefully, so as not to wake him, and tiptoed to the nearest window—that one." She pointed up to the balcony. "I opened the French doors—so slowly, because I didn't want to make a sound! Rinaldo was sleeping deeply after all he'd drunk, but I couldn't be sure he wouldn't wake, and—and want me there with him again." Her voice died away.

"Would you like to sit down, Marchesa Francesca?" Julian asked.

"No, Signor Kestrel. You are very good. Thank you." She resumed, "I went out onto the balcony. I wasn't thinking then of climbing down. I only wanted a breath of air. I didn't know what to do—how to get away. You see, Rinaldo had locked the door of our room and hung the key around his neck, with his crucifix, and I didn't dare try to undo the chain while he was sleeping.

"It was raining, but I went to the edge of the balustrade and looked down. The mist was all lit with moonlight, and I could see the side of the house very clearly. I looked over to the other balcony." She indicated the balcony to the left of hers, nearest the back of the villa. "It—it would be yours, I think, Signor Commissario."

"Yes," said Grimani. "What of that?"

"Well, you see, it overhangs that wall." She nodded toward the brick wall that backed the south terrace. "I thought that, if I could get to your balcony, I could let myself down from the balustrade to the walkway at the top of the wall. And then—I could get away." Her eyes travelled down the narrow flight of stone stairs from the walkway to the south terrace.

"And how did you mean to get to my balcony?" asked Grimani with a sneer of disbelief.

"There's a little ledge, Signor Commissario, between your window and mine." She pointed hesitantly.

There was, indeed, a grey-painted ledge along the white wall, just beneath the windows of the upper floor. Julian pictured the ledge as seen from the window of Francesca's room, formerly his. "That ledge can't be more than three inches wide. Do you mean to say that you walked some thirty feet along it on a rainy night, with nothing to cling to for support?"

"There wasn't any other way," she said simply.

"This is preposterous," said Grimani. "No woman could have done it. Even a man would be mad to try."

"But I'm good at climbing, Signor Commissario. I used to climb trees and fences with my brothers when I was a child."

"So you told me," Julian recalled.

She went on with her story. "I dressed as quietly as I could. But first I blew out the oil lamp that Rinaldo had left burning beside the bed, so that if he woke he wouldn't see me dressing."

Julian pricked up his ears. "Did you have any light in the room?"

"Just a little moonlight from the window. But I knew where to find my clothes."

"Did you light a candle at any time?"

"No. Rinaldo didn't like them in his room at night. He would have been angry if he'd awakened and seen one.

"I went out onto the balcony and climbed over the balustrade onto the ledge. I inched along it, with my hands and cheek pressed flat against the wall. It seemed to take hours. When I got to the hall window between the two balconies, I tried to open it, but it was bolted. So I had to go on.

"Finally I reached Commissario Grimani's balcony and climbed into it. I just sat down with my back against the railing and stayed there for a while. My heart was beating so hard, and all the fear I'd kept at bay while I was on the ledge seemed to rush at me, so that I couldn't stop trembling. But finally I made myself get up and climb over the balustrade. I let myself down slowly, feeling with my feet for the top of the wall. At last I found it and let go of the balustrade. And I was free.

"I came down from the wall and went around to the front terrace, thinking I would take a boat from the pier and row to Como. I wanted to follow Pietro back to Venice. But when I got to the pier, I was suddenly confused. I didn't have any money. I didn't know how I would hire horses. But what was more, I didn't know if I ought to go at all. I *had* been happy at the prospect of seeing my children—it was all that sustained me after Pietro left me. He might even refuse to take me back, knowing how my heart was divided. I asked myself, could I endure life with Rinaldo for the sake of Niccolò and Bianca? Or—I could hardly bear the thought of it—would I end by hating them for what they'd done to me?

"I walked about the garden in the rain. Finally I went to the chapel and asked the Madonna what to do. But she turned her face away from me, and I had no answers—only the same questions running through my head. I couldn't bear to go—I couldn't bear to stay. Finally I was so tired, I fell asleep in front of the Madonna's statue. When I woke, I prayed again. And then the soldiers found me."

"Did anyone see you climb down from the balcony?" asked Grimani.

"I don't think so. I suppose anyone who saw me would have tried to stop me."

"Did anyone see you in the garden or the chapel?"

"Not until the soldiers came."

"So you have no witnesses," said Grimani. "You have no evidence whatsoever, except that your dress is torn and soiled, which you might have done deliberately in order to back your story." Grimani's eyes narrowed. "Were you wearing a nightgown when you went to bed?"

Her cheeks crimsoned. "Yes."

"It wasn't found in your room. What became of it?"

"I—I don't have it anymore."

"What do you mean, you don't have it? Where is it?"

She said, so faintly that the others had to strain to hear, "I threw it in the lake."

"Ah!" Grimani's eyes lit up. "Because it was stained with blood!"

"Yes," she whispered, turning her face away.

"So there you have it, gentlemen," said Grimani. "Marchesa, evidently you omitted from your romantic story that you killed your husband before you made your escape."

"I didn't!" she said piteously. "He was sleeping. I could hear him snoring when I left."

"Then how did your nightgown come to be stained with blood?"

Her eyes squeezed shut, and tears spilled out. "I don't want to tell you. Please, I'll tell a woman. I'll tell Beatrice."

Julian felt sick. He said with the greatest delicacy, "Let me help you, Marchesa Francesca. Was the blood on your nightgown your own?"

She nodded, eyes closed. "He—Rinaldo—he was rough—and I wasn't used to—I didn't know I was bleeding until I went to put out the lamp. And then I looked down and saw the blood on my nightgown, and I—I didn't want to leave it, for everyone to see—" She broke into sobs.

It was all too clear to Julian now why she had been walking so stiffly and gingerly. He was angry with himself for not coming to her rescue last night—angry with MacGregor for preaching about the sanctity of marriage. "Marchesa Francesca, it was for your husband to be ashamed, not you."

"I'd left him," she said helplessly. "I'd humiliated him for years. I suppose he had the right. But all the same, I didn't want anyone to find my nightgown after I'd gone. I took it with me, and when I reached the pier I tied it around a stone and threw it in the lake." She looked timidly at Grimani. "Please, Signor Commissario, may I wash and change my clothes?"

"Very well. But you'll have to give me everything you're wearing now as evidence."

They returned to the house. Beatrice met them in the Hall of Marbles and told them that Dr. Curioni had arrived and was in Rinaldo's room preparing a death certificate. When she learned that Francesca wished to wash and change her clothes, she offered her own room. Grimani arranged for two soldiers to stand guard outside and be handed every article of clothing she was wearing. They were to remain there until she emerged, whereupon they were not to let her out of their sight.

"When may I see my children?" she asked Grimani.

"That's impossible. They're in Milan, and you must remain here until I determine how to proceed."

"But their father's been murdered! They'll hear of it and be frightened!"

"You ought to have thought of that sooner, Marchesa Francesca," he said coldly.

"I don't understand," she faltered.

"Suffice to say, it's very probable that you will shortly be arrested for your husband's murder. I leave you to judge whether it would be fitting for you to see your children with such a charge hanging over your head."

"Oh, no." She put her hands to her face. When she lowered them, her eyes were glassy. "Will they let me see my children before I die?"

"I have no idea," said Grimani. He turned to the soldiers. "Take her away."

"I'll go with you," Beatrice told Francesca.

"If you remain with her while she changes her clothes," warned Grimani, "it may be necessary to search you when you come out."

"If any of your soldiers touches me," said Beatrice calmly, "I shall expect my brother-in-law to kill him. I think he'll oblige me. He hasn't much love for the Austrian army."

She linked her arm in Francesca's and went upstairs, the two soldiers following with disconcerted faces. Grimani looked after them sourly, then turned to Julian and MacGregor. "Thank you for your assistance. Now that Dr. Curioni has arrived, I needn't trouble you to take any further part in this investigation."

Julian was resolved to speak his mind before he was given his *congé*. "Do you seriously mean to arrest Marchesa Francesca?"

"If I did," said Grimani, "it would be no business of yours. However, since you've been good enough to assist me, I'll admit I haven't made an official decision yet. I want to question the household and hear from the soldiers who are making enquiries in the neighbourhood, to see if anyone can substantiate this fairy-tale she told us."

"It could be true," said Julian. "There's nothing impossible in it, and it's consistent with all the evidence."

"Barely consistent," said Grimani. "The best that can be said for it is that we can neither prove nor disprove it. No one is likely to have been watching that side of the villa at that hour. And if Marchesa Francesca left any smears or footprints on the balconies or walls, the rain would have washed them away. But her story leaves all manner of circumstances unexplained. If she escaped as she says she did, why was Marchese Rinaldo's chain unfastened, the bloodstained key in the lock, and the front door unbarred?"

"Oh, there's no doubt," said Julian softly, "if Marchesa Francesca is innocent, then someone has deliberately set out to pin the murder on her."

"That's pure fancy," scoffed Grimani.

"You will allow, Signor Commissario, that there was no reason for anyone but Francesca, who was locked in with Marchese Rinaldo, to take his key after he was dead and use it to unlock the door. That he was killed with his own razor would be all of a piece with the scheme to implicate her. So would the unbarred front door, meant to suggest that she left the villa that way."

"Why should we pursue such a tortuous theory, when we can make sense of all the evidence by concluding that she's guilty?"

"But we can't," Julian objected. "Take the nightgown, for instance. You seem to think she disposed of it because she was wearing it when she killed Rinaldo, and it was stained with his blood. But if she were so concerned to cover her tracks, why the devil did she leave Rinaldo's chain unfastened, and the bloodstained key in the lock?"

"I'm aware that such inconsistencies intrigue you. For my part, I accept that a woman who has just atrociously killed her husband is unlikely to behave very rationally. Last night she was mad; today she is sane, and has made up a clever story to account for her disposal of her nightgown, and at the same time gain sympathy for herself and throw blame on her victim."

"A medical examination would tell us whether she was roughly handled last night," said MacGregor.

"She may have one if she likes," said Grimani, "but it's immaterial. If that's all the evidence she can muster, she'll certainly be convicted."

Julian asked musingly, "Don't you wonder that she didn't try to escape from the neighbourhood, assuming she'd killed her husband? She had hours to get away. She might have taken one of the boats or lost herself in the mountains."

"We would have found her," said Grimani imperturbably. "She probably knew that."

"When the soldiers found her in the chapel, she came with them willingly, though if she'd resisted I can't think they would have dragged her from the altar."

"She'd made up her mind by then to pretend she didn't know her husband was dead," said Grimani. "So naturally she had to return with the soldiers as if nothing were amiss."

Julian played his trump card. "What about that drop of candle wax on top of the blood on Rinaldo's sheet? The only candles in the room had never been lit."

Grimani's brows came together. "She could have had a candle hidden in the room and used it to commit the murder, then afterward thrown it into the lake along with her nightgown."

"Why should she have needed a candle, when the oil lamp would give her perfectly adequate light?"

"The lamp might have gone out," said MacGregor.

"Then she would have had no means of lighting a candle," said Julian, "except by striking a light with the tinder box, which takes a long time and makes an infernal amount of noise. More to the point, Tommaso said he'd removed all the old candles. That means Francesca would have had to smuggle a candle into the room before she went to bed. And why should she have done so?"

Grimani glared at him and took an impatient turn about the room. "One drop of wax is nothing, compared with all the evidence against her."

"How can it be nothing," Julian countered, "when it can't be explained?"

Grimani resumed his pacing. He had integrity of a sort, Julian thought. That drop of wax was an objective fact he could not blink away. It might not prevent him from convicting Francesca, but all the same, he wanted it accounted for.

"What are you suggesting?" he said at last. "That someone came into the room and killed Marchese Rinaldo after Marchesa Francesca had left by the balcony? By her own account, the door was locked, and the key was around Marchese Rinaldo's neck. Neither the lock nor the door was tampered with. So how would this person have gotten in?"

"I suppose that if Francesca escaped by the balcony, the ledge, and the south terrace wall, someone could enter by the same means. But I suspect there was an easier way. With your permission, Signor Commissario, I should like to try an experiment—one that won't disturb any of the evidence."

"Very well." Grimani sounded sceptical, but also a little intrigued.

Julian led them upstairs to Rinaldo's room. Curioni was there, making out the death certificate. When they had all exchanged greetings, Julian and Grimani went out of the room, and at Julian's behest, MacGregor locked the door from the inside.

"Now, Signor Commissario," said Julian, "I should like a key to one of the nearby rooms. Your own will do."

Grimani eyed him dubiously but fetched his key. Julian tried it in Rinaldo's lock. The door opened.

Grimani stared. Then his eyes flashed angrily. "Exactly what do you claim to have proved?"

"Not that you committed the murder, Signor Commissario," said Julian with a faint smile. "Though it does appear, theoretically, that you might have done so. Your key opens this lock, and I shouldn't be surprised if some of the other guests' keys do as well. It's not uncommon in houses like this for bedroom keys to match. It facilitates discreet visits—"

"I understand, Signor Kestrel." Grimani took stock. "So you think Marchesa Francesca escaped as she says she did, and afterward someone entered the room, killed Marchese Rinaldo, and tried to pin the murder on her. It's far-fetched. To begin with, how did this intruder know he would find the marchese alone?"

"Because he saw Marchesa Francesca escape. He might have looked out of this window"—Julian went to the window at the end of the hallway, between Rinaldo's and Grimani's rooms—"or one of the south-facing windows downstairs. He might even have gone for a stroll in the garden, though that's not very likely, on account of the rain."

Julian was mindful that the person most likely to have witnessed Francesca's escape was Grimani, whose window overlooked the south terrace, and whose balcony she had actually entered. But he tactfully kept this to himself.

Curioni and MacGregor came out of Rinaldo's room. Curioni confirmed MacGregor's conclusions about the time and cause of Rinaldo's death. It was agreed that, with the permission of Conte Carlo, Rinaldo's nearest adult male relative, the body would be cleaned, dressed, and taken to Solaggio for display in the church.

"I'll leave those arrangements to you," Grimani told Curioni. He cast Julian a look of icy acknowledgement. "I'm going to ask the marchesa how many other keys open this door."

When Grimani, Julian, and MacGregor came downstairs, they found a contingent of Ruga's gendarmes waiting in the Hall of Marbles to report to Grimani. Their discoveries were mostly negative. No one in Solaggio had seen Francesca last night or observed any suspicious strangers in the neighbourhood. But there was one surprising fact: Valeriano, thought to be well on his way to Venice, had spent the night at the Nightingale and was still in Solaggio.

"Have you made enquiries at the inn to find out if anyone saw Marchesa Francesca last night?" asked Grimani. "She may have known Signor Valeriano was there and gone to him after the murder."

The gendarme who was acting as spokesman shook his head. "Signora Frascani says she takes care to secure all the doors and windows at night, Signor Commissario, and nobody goes in or out without her knowing."

Julian could well believe this, although it was anyone's guess whether the landlady's precautions were to keep thieves out or to keep her daughter Rosa in. "You say Marchesa Francesca never went in. Did Signor Valeriano go out?"

"Yes, signor," said the gendarme. "He was out from before midnight until two or three in the morning."

"He met her somewhere and helped her concoct that story of climbing down from the balcony," said Grimani. "That explains any inconsistency between her recklessness last night and her artfulness this morning."

"It didn't look like art to me," said MacGregor.

"If you had any expertise in police matters, Signor Dottor," said Grimani, "you would know that suspects fighting for their lives develop extraordinary acting abilities where they had none before. I know what you will say, Signor Kestrel: that drop of wax on Marchese Rinaldo's sheet has yet to be explained. I've been thinking about that. All the evidence suggests that Marchesa Francesca killed her husband, unlocked the door of their room, went downstairs, and left the house by the front door. Someone in a bedroom along the hall might have looked out, seen her leaving, and taken advantage of her absence to go in and speak to Marchese Rinaldo. This person found him dead, and while looking at his body, dropped wax from a candle he had brought into the room."

Julian nodded resignedly. Grimani was very far from being a fool: he was bound to think of this sooner or later.

"Why didn't this person raise the alarm?" MacGregor wanted to know.

"He might have been afraid of being accused of the murder," said Julian. "Or perhaps he feared to incriminate Francesca. Then again, he might have seen an opportunity to do something hole-and-corner—to search the room, perhaps even take something away with him."

"I'll have all the rooms on the corridor searched," said Grimani. "You," he ordered the gendarmes, "bring Signor Valeriano here at once."

The gendarmes departed. Grimani, Julian, and MacGregor went into the drawing room, where the guests were still unhappily congregated. Don Cristoforo was with them, discussing funeral arrangements with Carlo. Grimani asked where the marchesa was, and on learning she was still upstairs with Francesca, rang for a servant to ask her to join them. He also sent for Zanetti to interpret and take notes.

Zanetti hastened in with his portable writing-desk. He had finished questioning the servants, and reported that they all slept two or three to a room and had thus been able to give one another alibis. It was always possible, of course, that one of them had slipped away without awakening his companions, but Zanetti had uncovered no cause for suspicion against any of them. Moreover, all their rooms were equipped with chamberpots—as, for that matter, were their masters'—which eliminated the most obvious reason for roaming the halls at night.

"Do even upper servants like Ernesto and Guido share rooms?" asked Julian.

Carlo looked around at him rather sharply.

"Ernesto and Guido are doubled with one another, signor," said Zanetti. "They gave each other alibis."

Julian had no faith in Guido's word, but he did trust Ernesto's. Which meant he must scratch Guido from the list of suspects.

The marchesa came in. Carlo went to her at once, asking, "How is Francesca?"

"A bit more tranquil. I've persuaded her to try to sleep a little."

Grimani walked brusquely up to her. "How many other rooms in the villa have keys that fit Marchese Rinaldo's lock?"

"Three," she replied. "The two across from Rinaldo's—your own and Carlo's—and the one next door, which is shared by Signor St. Carr and Signor Fletcher."

Grimani turned to Carlo. "Did you know those four rooms had locks in common?"

"I arranged it, Signor Commissario," said Carlo calmly. "The villa used to be mine, remember. Some of my guests found it—convenient."

"What about the rooms at the other end of the corridor?" said Grimani. "Do they have keys in common?"

"No," said the marchesa. "Monsieur de la Marque's, my own, and the one across from mine, occupied by Signor Kestrel and Dr. MacGregor, all have keys that open only their own locks."

"Are there spare keys to Marchese Rinaldo's room?" Grimani pursued.

"I have several," she said coolly.

"Where are they kept?"

"In a box in my room."

"Is any of them missing?"

"I have no idea."

"I'll look into that directly I finish this interrogation. Now I wish to know from all of you where you were between the hours of one and five o'clock this morning."

Beatrice, Carlo, Fletcher, St. Carr, and de la Marque all claimed to have been asleep in their rooms. So did Donati and Sebastiano, who in any case slept on the floor below and did not have a key that fit Rinaldo's lock. Donati declared, moreover, that he slept very lightly and would have heard if Sebastiano had left their room during the night.

"And you, Signor Kestrel?" Grimani proceeded.

"Dr. MacGregor and I were in our room as well."

"And neither of us could have left without waking the other," MacGregor added, "because Kestrel had put a chair against the door, with the back tucked under the knob."

"Why did you do that?" Grimani asked Julian.

Julian wished MacGregor had not brought this up. Their precautions last night seemed absurd, now that it was so clear the danger had not been to them. But MacGregor responded eagerly, "Because Monsieur de la Marque threatened Kestrel before he left our room last night!"

The Frenchman's black brows rose as high as they would go. "Threatened him? How, my dear Doctor, did I do that?"

"You know very well," retorted MacGregor. "You said I might want to say goodbye to him while I had the chance."

"Oh, yes," murmured De la Marque. "I did say that. I suppose I was a little out of temper. I crave your pardon, Mr. Kestrel."

"You may have it, Monsieur de la Marque."

They bowed ceremoniously to one another.

"None of you has a satisfactory alibi," said Grimani.

"We haven't heard *your* alibi yet, Commissario," said Beatrice.

"I am not obliged to set up an alibi, Marchesa."

"I don't see why not," objected Carlo. "Your being a police official doesn't place you above the law. Your room is across from my nephew's, and your key matches his. We have a right to know where you were between one and five this morning."

"As usual, Signor Conte, you confuse liberal bombast with law. This is my investigation, and I am accountable for my conduct of it only to the Director-General of Police."

"It isn't your conduct of the investigation I'm challenging," Carlo flashed back. "I'm suggesting that you're a suspect like the rest of us and ought to have to answer the same questions."

"I beg to differ, Signor Conte. I am not a suspect 'like the rest of you.' I didn't know my key opened Marchese Rinaldo's door. What is more, I had no motive to kill either him or Marchese Lodovico. You, on the other hand, knew about the matching keys. Furthermore, in the past five years, two of the three people who stood between you and the Malvezzi title and lands have been brutally murdered, leaving only the child Niccolò."

"How dare you?" Carlo shook with rage. "How *dare* you! This is beyond all bearing! Do you realize who I am? Do you know that my ancestors stood high in rank and honour in the days of the Visconti, when yours were peasants labouring in their vineyards and begging at their doors?"

Julian regarded Carlo more closely. For all his liberalism, he was exactly like his brother under the skin: a proud, imperious patrician.

"I mean no disrespect to your rank," said Grimani imperturbably. "But I have a duty to the Viceroy of Lombardy-Venetia to investigate and solve these murders. And in his name, I wish to know where the key to your room was between one and five o'clock last night."

"I care nothing for you or your Viceroy," said Carlo. "But in the name of truth, I will say that I believe my key was in the lock on the inner side of my door. That's where I usually leave it. But I'm not certain. I wasn't expecting anyone to make off with it."

"Signor Fletcher and Signor St. Carr." Grimani turned to the two Englishmen. "Where was your key?"

St. Carr opened his mouth to speak, but Fletcher cut him off. "I locked the door and put the key in my dressing-gown pocket. It was still there this morning."

"Why did you put it there?" asked Grimani.

"It seemed as good a place for it as any."

"Are you in the habit of leaving your bedroom key in your dressing-gown pocket?"

"Not particularly," said Fletcher.

"Why did you lock the door at all? Had someone threatened your life, too?"

"I rarely threaten more than one person's life in an evening," remarked de la Marque.

"Look here, Mr. Commissario—" began St. Carr.

"Take a damper, Beverley," said Fletcher.

"But, Hugo, he's implying that you're trying it on with him. And I can back you. Everything Mr. Fletcher said is true, Commissario. I found the door locked when I got up this morning and asked Hugo where the key was, and he fished it out of his dressing-gown pocket."

"You didn't know he'd locked the two of you in?" said Grimani quickly.

"No, he must have done it—" St. Carr broke off.

"After you were asleep?" prompted Grimani.

St. Carr was silent.

Grimani turned his ice-water eyes on Fletcher. "Why did you lock the door without telling him? Were you afraid he would leave the room during the night?"

"It was just a precaution. I only thought of it after he'd gone to sleep."

"So you knew where the key was, and he didn't. Did *you* leave the room during the night?"

Fletcher glanced toward de la Marque who regarding him with amused, expectant eyes. "Yes," he owned reluctantly. "I went downstairs for a short time."

"When was that?" asked Grimani.

"I didn't look at a clock. It was well after everyone had gone to bed."

"It was about a quarter to three," said de la Marque.

"How do you know that?" said Grimani.

"Because I heard Mr. Fletcher coming up the stairs, which are next to my room, and came out to see who was wandering about at that hour."

"What were you doing awake?" Grimani asked.

"I wasn't awake," said de la Marque. "I was sleeping the blissful sleep of the just. Mr. Fletcher's footsteps woke me."

"What did you do?"

"We exchanged a few words. I believe I asked him if the maidservants are as compliant as they are pretty. He didn't seem to find that amusing. He begged my pardon for waking me, and I went back to bed. *Voilà tout.*"

Grimani turned back to Fletcher. "Why did you go downstairs?"

"I heard a shutter banging and went to close it."

St. Carr drew in his breath sharply.

"Where was this shutter?" asked Grimani.

"Just below our room," said Fletcher, "in the music room."

"Was it a south-facing shutter?"

"I—I really can't recall."

"Can't you?" Grimani's eyes bored into him. "If it was a south-facing shutter, you might have seen Marchesa Francesca climbing down from the balcony and known you would find Marchese Rinaldo alone."

"Why should I care if he was alone? I hardly knew him. I hadn't a blessed thing to say to him."

"Did you take a candle with you when you left your room?"

"Yes."

"So you had a key that opened Marchese Rinaldo's door—"

"I didn't know I had," interrupted Fletcher.

"—and you could have dripped wax on his sheet. When Monsieur de la Marque saw you, were you returning from fastening the shutter—or from unbarring the front door, to make it appear that Marchesa Francesca committed the murder?

"You've got it all wrong," broke in St. Carr in a shaking voice. "I'm the one who went downstairs to fasten the shutter. If Hugo got up, it must have been only to look for me."

"Don't be silly," said Fletcher.

"It's true! Stop being so deuced heroic! My parents asked you to look after me, not to make a confounded martyr of yourself! Mr. Commissario, I couldn't sleep, and that shutter was plaguing my life out, so I said I was going to go downstairs and fasten it, and Hugo half woke up and grunted something. I lit a candle at the lamp that's kept burning in the hall, then I went downstairs, fastened the shutter, and came straight back."

"Was Mr. Fletcher there when you returned?" asked Grimani.

"I don't know. I didn't look to see. I just put out the candle and went to sleep."

"What have you to say to that, Signor Fletcher?" said Grimani.

Fletcher bit his lip. "All right. I admit it—I came fully awake after he was gone and didn't like the idea of his knocking about the house alone at that hour, so I went looking for him. I suppose we missed each other somehow, because I came back to our room to see if he'd returned, and he was there asleep." Fletcher shook his head in some exasperation. "I locked the door so he couldn't stray off again, and hid the key in my dressing-gown pocket. Neither of us can have been gone more than a few minutes."

"How do you know how long he was gone?" Grimani challenged him. "Can you say for certain how much time passed between his leaving and your waking up and going after him?"

"I think it was only a minute."

"But you don't know?"

"No," ground out Fletcher.

Grimani's cold glance took in Fletcher, St. Carr, and de la Marque. "So none of you has a complete alibi, and you all left your rooms last night."

"I beg leave to point out," said de la Marque, "I merely came to my door to speak to Mr. Fletcher. And as I don't have a key that fits Marchese Rinaldo's lock, how are you suggesting I might have got into his room?"

"If Marchesa Francesca killed him and went out by the door, you would have found it unlocked."

De la Marque opened his eyes at Grimani. "But in that case, my dear Commissario, what am I supposed to have done? Gone in, found him horribly slaughtered, and decided it would really be a shame to wake everyone from a sound sleep?"

"I haven't yet determined what you might have done. But you did have reason to want to speak to him. You said last night that you never got your notebook back after Marchese Lodovico's death. Marchese Rinaldo might have had it or known where it was."

"What notebook?" the marchesa asked quickly.

"A musical notebook that Monsieur de la Marque kept, and that Marchese Lodovico borrowed without his permission."

De la Marque let out a scornful breath at this innocuous version of events, but said nothing.

"Do you deny it?" Grimani persisted. "That you went to Marchese Rinaldo's room to ask him about your notebook?"

"Deny it? Only the greatest self-restraint prevents me from laughing it out of countenance."

Grimani gave him a withering look. "That reminds me: does any of you know of any connexion between Orfeo and the Comte d'Aubret? Monsieur de la Marque claims the comte had an English protégé who could sing, and who was in Italy at the time of Marchese Lodovico's murder."

They all shook their heads. The marchesa regarded de la Marque in intrigued speculation.

"I'm finished with you all for the moment," said Grimani. "I require you not to leave the villa, and not to return to your rooms until I give you leave. I intend to conduct a search of your rooms and your belongings."

"That's a wholly unnecessary intrusion," said Carlo.

"That is for me to determine, Signor Conte." Grimani turned to Beatrice. "Marchesa, I must ask you to come with me to your room and tell me whether any of the spare keys is missing."

The marchesa inclined her head and went out, Grimani and Zanetti following.

"Blood of Diana!" Carlo exploded. "The insolence of that man! Does he suppose we've littered our rooms with bloodstained garments?"

"Actually," mused Julian, "I should be very surprised if he found any bloodstains at all."

"What do you mean?" asked Fletcher.

"If I were going to commit this murder, I know how I should do it. I should go to Marchese Rinaldo's room in my nightgown and dressing-robe. I should lock the door from the inside to prevent anyone from coming in and taking me unawares. Then I should strip to the skin. After I'd slit the marchese's throat, I should go to the washstand and clean off the blood from wherever it had splashed on my body. After that, it would be safe to put on my nightgown and robe and slip out of the room. Assuming I were blackhearted enough to attempt to pin my crime on Marchesa Francesca, I should have done that before I washed: taken the bloodstained key from around Marchese Rinaldo's neck and unlocked the door."

"A magnificent re-creation!" exclaimed de la Marque. "May I say, *mon vieux*, if you didn't commit this crime, you ought to have done so?"

"You're very kind."

Carlo was pale. "You make it all seem so terribly real."

"My son," said Don Cristoforo, laying his hand on Carlo's arm, "we ought to attend to the body."

"Yes, of course." Carlo gave himself a little shake and gestured for Don Cristoforo to precede him. The priest departed with a benediction and a rustle of black cassock. Carlo followed.

Fletcher came up to Julian and MacGregor. "What's going to become of Lucia Landi? Everyone seems to have forgotten all about her."

"I haven't forgotten about her, Mr. Fletcher," said Julian. "But if Grimani has, it's just as well."

"He'll remember her again soon enough," warned Fletcher.

"But by then she may not matter anymore. Grimani is all but convinced that Francesca killed Rinaldo. If so, she almost certainly killed Lodovico as well. If she's arrested, Lucia can reveal Orfeo's identity without fear that he'll be charged with murder."

"It didn't look to me as if Grimani had made up his mind to arrest Marchesa Francesca," said Fletcher. "He certainly pitched into Beverley and me when he found we'd been out of our room last night."

"He was merely being thorough. And he would have liked to build a case against you or de la Marque, because he believes that one of you is Orfeo, whom he's loath to let slip through his fingers. But the evidence against Francesca is overwhelming."

"I see. Thank you, Mr. Kestrel." Fletcher thrust his hands in his pockets and went off, somewhat reassured.

"He seems mightily interested in that young lady," said MacGregor.

"Lucia?" Julian smiled. "She does seem to have made impression on him."

"But did she make it in the past few days, or four and a half years ago?"

"More than ever, my dear fellow, I don't think it's of any importance."

"Well, what *do* you think is important? Who do you believe killed Rinaldo and his father?"

Julian considered. "I'm still disposed to absolve Francesca, though Grimani may be right that I elevate character above fact.

The idea of her as the murderer simply doesn't ring true to me." He paused, then went on steadily, "If any woman killed Rinaldo, it's more likely to be Marchesa Beatrice. He'd insulted her, thrown her childlessness in her face, threatened to wrest the villa away from her. It was at her urging that he passed the night here instead of going on to the castle. She told me that she was afraid Francesca might do something desperate if she were isolated with him, but that may have been part of her plan to implicate Francesca in the murder."

MacGregor stared. "You can accuse her of murder—this woman you seem to have such a regard for?"

"I do have a regard for her. That's why I work very hard to suspect her. Otherwise I shouldn't be able to do it at all."

MacGregor shook his head gravely. "Still, when all's said and done, there's no evidence against her. And Carlo had at least as good a motive as she did. As Grimani pointed out, Lodovico and Rinaldo stood between Carlo and the Malvezzi title and wealth. Of course, there's still Rinaldo's son to consider."

"Niccolò is a child, and Carlo will be his natural guardian. And children die all the time, of a myriad of causes. Carlo would find him by far the easiest of his victims to dispose of."

"You're not suggesting he would murder a little boy?"

"If he would shoot his own brother and cut his own nephew's throat, I hardly think we'd need credit him with any scruples about child-murder. But in fact, I don't believe he committed either of those crimes—at all events, not for material gain. The thing makes no sense. At the time Lodovico was killed, Carlo was head over ears in debt. He might have been driven to murder his brother if he'd had something immediate to gain by it. What I can't accept is that he embarked on a hazardous murder plot that wouldn't bring him profit until years later—if it ever did at all. He couldn't count on having an opportunity to kill Rinaldo. Any opportunity he did have might not come for years, and in the interval Francesca might have returned to Rinaldo or died—either way, Rinaldo might have had more sons. The Malvezzi are an impatient race, and though Carlo seems the most temperate and judicious of the lot, I don't think he would risk so much for such a remote, uncertain end."

MacGregor threw up his hands. "*Somebody* must have committed these murders!"

Yes, thought Julian, and the sooner we find out who it was, the better for us all. This murder, in a house full of people and almost under Grimani's nose, was extraordinarily reckless. Our murderer is growing bolder—or more desperate. And the Devil only knows what he, or she, may do next.

Rinaldo's body was taken to Solaggio in a black-draped boat, with Don Cristoforo and Dr. Curioni at either end. The villa party, which had gathered on the terrace to watch it depart, trooped sombrely back indoors, like prisoners returning from a bout of air and exercise. It was then that Valeriano arrived.

He entered the Hall of Marbles flanked by four gendarmes, just as Francesca was coming downstairs with her two soldiers. She gasped, "Pietro!" and would have run into his arms, but at a sign from Grimani, the soldiers barred her way. She looked over their crossed bayonets with anguished eagerness. "Oh, my love, what are you doing here? I thought you'd gone away! And why are you under guard?"

Valeriano's eyes flickered expressionlessly over her and her escort, then took in the villa party, standing about like a Greek chorus, and came to rest on Grimani. "You sent for me, Signor Commissario?"

"Why are you still in Solaggio?" Grimani fired off. "I thought you meant to return to Venice."

"I had unfinished business here, Signor Commissario."

"What was that?"

"Marchese Rinaldo was still alive, Signor Commissario."

There was a shocked silence.

"What are you saying?" Grimani asked sharply. "Are you implying you had something to do with his murder?"

"I'm saying that I killed him, Signor Commissario. I thought you knew that. Didn't you send these men to arrest me?"

"It isn't true!" cried Francesca. "He's only saying it for my sake, to protect me!"

Valeriano turned his remote, dead eyes on her. "This has nothing to do with you."

"What do you mean?" she faltered. "Why do you look like that?"

"I'm sorry," he said quietly. "There's a great deal I ought to have told you."

She lifted trembling hands to her brow. "This isn't happening. Everyone, everything has gone mad—"

"Your confession is convenient, Signor Valeriano," Grimani cut in, "but you do have a motive to lie. I don't want a culprit I can't convict."

"You don't believe me?" Valeriano started to reach into an inside pocket of his coat. The gendarmes on either side moved closer. Valeriano smiled faintly. "It's not a weapon. I'll take it out very slowly."

Suiting the action to the word, he drew out an object and held it up for everyone to see. It was an elbow-length glove of cream-coloured kid, ornamented with green silk myrtle leaves and a ruby heart pierced by a diamond shaft.

"Where did you get that?" Grimani exclaimed.

"It belongs to me. It's the mate of the one I left for Marchese Lodovico on the night before he was killed."

"You're saying that you killed him?"

"Yes, Signor Commissario."

"No, Pietro!" Francesca's fingers clenched around the crossed bayonets that kept them apart. "Don't do this—"

"Francesca," he said, "let go of those bayonets."

She did. A few drops of blood fell from her hands to the marble floor. MacGregor strode to her side, his eyes daring the soldiers to keep him back. He took her hands, examining the cuts and stemming the bleeding with his handkerchief.

Francesca paid him no heed. "I won't let you do this! I won't let you sacrifice yourself for me!"

"I've told you," he said wearily, "this has nothing to do with you. I resolved to kill Lodovico Malvezzi long before you and I ever met."

"Why?" said Grimani. "What was Lodovico Malvezzi to you?"

"He was my greatest enemy," Valeriano said quietly. "He was also my father."

CHAPTER 32

"Your father!" Carlo broke from the little group of onlookers and confronted Valeriano in astonishment. "It can't be!"

The others stared at the two of them juxtaposed. Julian, for one, felt he was seeing them with new eyes. He had never thought to look for a resemblance, but it was there—in Valeriano's good looks, but above all in his height. To be sure, castrati were apt to be tall. But in his elegant figure, his easy grace, the proud set of his head, he was the mirror image of Carlo—who in turn was so like his dead brother.

Grimani asked Carlo and Beatrice, "Did Marchese Lodovico ever give the smallest hint that this man was his son?"

"No, never," said Carlo.

Beatrice slowly, silently shook her head.

"He didn't know," said Valeriano calmly.

Francesca stammered, "But—but that would mean that I ran away with—with my husband's—"

"Brother," supplied Valeriano. "Half-brother. Yes."

She trembled so violently that MacGregor put an arm around her shoulders to support her. "This woman needs to lie down," he told Grimani, "and have the cuts in her hands dressed."

"We'll go into the drawing room," said Grimani. "You can attend to her there. I want her present when I question Signor Valeriano, to see what she makes of his story."

In a few minutes they were all settled in the drawing room. Francesca lay on a sofa, her eyes dull with shock. MacGregor made her sip a little wine, but it brought no colour back to her face. When he drew up his chair before her and took one of her hands to bind the cuts with sticking plaster, she submitted like a doll.

Valeriano stood with his back to the fireplace. The four gendarmes still flanked him, two on either side. Grimani stood before him, surveying him with cold, assessing eyes. Zanetti perched on an ottoman, his portable desk on his lap. Beatrice sat in an armchair with her hands in her lap, quiet and contained, as if she were waiting for the curtain to rise at La Scala. Carlo, Julian, de la Marque, Fletcher, and St. Carr were scattered about the room. Even Donati was there, in his preferred seat in the corner, Sebastiano by his side.

Valeriano regarded them all, unruffled. After so many years on the stage, he was not a man to be daunted by an audience. "You will be wondering who my mother was. She was Giulietta Petroni—a name that may mean something to you, Maestro, if to no one else here."

Carlo drew in his breath sharply.

Donati knit his brows. "She was a singer, no? A beautiful girl—a Venetian. I don't believe I ever heard her, but I understood she had an exquisite voice, only a little too delicate to last. She sang at the San Carlo in Naples, but not for more than a season or two. And then—" Donati shook his head. "I don't know what became of her."

Julian looked at Carlo. "Signor Conte, you seemed shocked just now, when Signor Valeriano mentioned his mother's name."

"And well I might be," said Carlo fervently. "I recognized her name, too. I knew she was a singer in Naples years ago. And I remembered that Lodovico was sent there when he was eighteen, to finish his education. So this mad story could be true—Valeriano could indeed be my nephew."

"I am your nephew," said Valeriano.

"Can you prove that?" said Grimani.

"I have abundant proof—letters, trinkets, and such things. If my story doesn't convince you, you may send to Venice for them.

"My mother was Venetian, as Maestro Donati says, but she studied music in Naples, where most of the best singers were trained in those days. She made her debut there, and according to her maid—my dear Elena, who brought me up—all the city fell in love with her. They had every cause. She was young and ardent, her voice was sweet, and even when I knew her—ravaged, wretched as she was—she was agonizingly beautiful."

Beatrice closed her eyes for a moment. The others hardly breathed as they waited for more.

"Lodovico Malvezzi fell in love with her," Valeriano went on. "He couldn't have married her, of course. For a man of his ancient name to unite himself with a gondolier's daughter would mean ostracism—indelible disgrace. If he had only seduced her, I might have forgiven him and so might she. But what he did was far worse. He bribed an educated rascal to masquerade as a priest and marry them in secret. In her simplicity, my mother succumbed to the trap. She believed she was his wife; and in that belief, she let him make her his whore.

"She gave up the stage and went to live in a little house outside the city, where he visited her in secret. He had told her he didn't dare reveal their marriage until he was of age. He tired of her soon enough—brought the pretended priest to her and revealed the trick. He gave her money, as if that could atone for her broken career, her lost virtue, her shattered heart. My mother had always given herself unreservedly to whatever passion ruled her. In the spring of her life, it was music. In the summer, it was

Lodovico Malvezzi. In the autumn and winter, she wanted only to die.

"She fled to Venice, but she didn't try to see her family. For the rest of her life—and she was destined to drag out another eight years—she lived as a recluse. Her greatest fear was that Lodovico would discover she was with child. She couldn't bear him to have that final triumph over her—worse, she was terrified he would take the baby away. She travelled deep into the country to give birth to me and left me there with her faithful Elena. She herself returned to Venice and only came to visit us now and then, with the greatest secrecy. She always believed Lodovico was having her spied on. Once or twice she failed to come to us as planned, because she thought there were followers on her heels.

"Elena pretended that I was her grandson, and so I was given her name, Brandolin. I knew that Giulietta was my mother, but Elena said she was too ill to live with us. She also told me my father had died before I was born, and that was why my mother was always so sad.

"My mother's only pleasure was in teaching me to sing. Her own voice was ruined by grief and illness, but she carefully nurtured mine. I quickly came to love music, but even if I hadn't, I would have learned or done anything to please her. So I made great progress from a very early age."

Valeriano drew a long breath. "When I was eight, my mother's health broke down completely, and Elena was summoned to her bedside. My mother had come to two decisions about me. One was that when I was old enough I should be told who my father was—but only if I promised never to reveal to him that I was his son. The other—" Valeriano paused, then went on quietly, "My mother had little money to leave me, and knew I would have to make my way in the world. My obvious vocation was music. My voice at eight was beautiful and sweet; when it changed it might be ruined. So she resolved it should not change.

"Elena had never been able to deny her anything. She promised all that was asked of her, and my mother died in her arms. A week later, Elena had me cut." Valeriano smiled sadly. "Three years after that, the French invaded Italy, and banned castrati from the operatic stage. The ban was later lifted, but castrati were on the wane in any case. My mother had been out of the world a long time, and probably didn't realize that. She meant the best for me. I don't blame her for the decision she made." The momentary quaver in his voice showed how great the temptation to blame her must have been. "I blame Lodovico Malvezzi. For her death, alone and almost friendless, and for my life, unnatural thing that it is—the guilt is his."

Valeriano paused. There was no sound in the room but the ticking of the clock and the distant murmur of the lake. Francesca had sat up on the sofa and was gazing at Valeriano in an agony of compassion. Beatrice's face remained inscrutable. Carlo shuddered and passed a hand across his eyes.

"With the little money my mother had saved, Elena sent me to a music school in Venice. I lived there for some years and worked devotedly at my music. When I was twelve, I paid a visit to Elena in the country. There I was set upon by boys who mocked me for being a eunuch and the chance-born son of a Venetian whore. The first insult was nothing to me, but the second I could not bear. I wept with rage and tried to fight them. They beat me savagely before Elena could rescue me. I urged her to tell me the truth about my mother. I remembered her infrequent visits and the mystery surrounding her. I was only a child, but I lived among adults and saw life through their eyes. I wasn't suffering because I thought the boys were wrong, but because I feared they were right.

"Elena told me the truth at last—the story as I've just told it to you. The one fact she held back was my father's name. I begged her to reveal it. I was all on fire for some wild act of revenge. It maddened me to think that my mother had borne me out of wedlock, just as the boys had taunted, but only because the villain, my father, had inveigled her into believing she was an honourable woman. Elena held true to the promise she had made my mother. She wouldn't tell me unless I pledged myself never to breathe a word to my father of who I was. I took the oath she demanded. I had to know the truth. And I learned that my father was Lodovico Malvezzi—that, but for his vile trick, my mother would have been a lady of rank, and I the heir to a marquisate. Strange, isn't it, Francesca? It would have been I, not Rinaldo, who would have married you. Your children would have been mine. Instead, I am a bastard and the murderer of my father, and you are my brother's wife—"

"Oh, please!" She flung up her hands. "I cannot bear it!"

He withdrew his gaze from her and went on levelly, "I kept my oath to Elena. I never told Lodovico of our kinship. I let the scandal that my mother was a prostitute stick, sooner than reveal anything that might allow Lodovico to guess the truth. But I never promised not to take revenge on him for my mother's wrongs, and my own."

"You waited a very long time to do so," Julian observed.

"Revenge was my paramount ambition, Signor Kestrel, but not my only one. A great sacrifice had been exacted of me to make me a singer; I didn't wish that sacrifice to have been in vain. So I chose to make my name in music before I committed a crime for which I might have to pay with my life. And then—" Valeriano looked away for a moment, then went on in the same steady, inexorable voice, "I discovered that bloodshed wasn't the only form of revenge open to me. In the case of a proud family like the Malvezzi, it wasn't even the best."

Francesca looked up slowly. "Oh, no," she whispered.

"I tore that family apart," Valeriano said with quiet pride. "I humiliated not only my father but my brother, who occupied the place that should have been mine."

"And I, Pietro?" Francesca broke in. "What was I to you?"

He looked at her, not without compassion. "You were useful."

"Useful!" Her hands clenched convulsively around the sofa cushions. She was shaking. "Do you mean that I left my husband, gave up my children for six long years—so that I could be *useful* to you?"

"I'm sorry," he said.

Her voice came from low in her throat, like the growl of an animal. "Rinaldo was right. You are a monster. Ah, Madonna!—when I think of your kindness, your tenderness all those years! All acting? All pretense? Of course, why not? You were on the stage for years! And yet, it must not have been easy for you to keep me happy—to prevent me from going back to my children and my home! For a creature like you—without a heart, without a human feeling in your breast—truly, Signor Valeriano, it was the performance of your life!"

She burst into wild, helpless laughter. MacGregor took her by the shoulders and gave her a quick, firm shake. Beatrice held a smelling-bottle to her nose and lightly chafed her hands. Gradually she grew quieter. Valeriano stood very still through it all, saying nothing.

Grimani's hard voice rose above the confusion. "This is a police investigation, not an opera stage. Signor Valeriano, I don't want to hear any more of your grievances against the Malvezzi family. Your motives for killing Marchese Lodovico are clear enough. What I require of you now is a plain account of the murder."

"You shall have it," said Valeriano. "For a year or two after Marchesa Francesca came to live with me, I was content. I had triumphed over Lodovico. I had given Rinaldo a taste of the shame and impotence I had always felt. But Lodovico lashed back at me by impugning my name and destroying my career. Without music to live for, I began to feel restless. My victory over him wasn't complete. When Francesca proposed to return to Lombardy and appeal to Rinaldo to see her children, I agreed, but my purpose was different from hers. The better to accomplish it, I borrowed a villa across the Lake of Como from Marchese Lodovico's. I knew—all the musical world knew—that Marchese Lodovico had gone to the lake with a mysterious English tenor he was grooming for the stage.

"Once at the lake, I heard that Lodovico was staying at Castello Malvezzi, while Orfeo and Maestro Donati were at the villa. I had to lure him out of the castle; he was all but invulnerable there. To lie in wait for him on the road between castle and villa was too uncertain. I determined to lure him to some isolated spot after dark. I had my mother's gloves—the gloves he had given her—to use as bait. I felt sure he would remember them. And I was almost equally sure he would tell no one of the rendezvous. He had always kept his infamous liaison with my mother a secret. Perhaps even he felt a twinge of shame where she was concerned.

"I chose the belvedere as the place of rendezvous. I was familiar with the villa and its gardens. Lodovico once brought me there to sing at a *fête champêtre.* As Signor Kestrel was quick to observe"—Valeriano bowed in Julian's direction—"I went riding on the night before the murder and again on the night it occurred. The first time, I left the package containing the note and glove at the castle. The second time, I went to the belvedere."

Valeriano's voice dropped. He gazed into the distance as if he could see it all unfolding again before him. "I arrived at about midnight and tethered my horse outside the villa gate. It was unlocked, and I went in. I walked along the shore path to the belvedere. There were one or two boats on the lake, but no lights on the shore to reveal my presence to them. I had brought a lantern with me, but I shuttered it and felt my way in the dark. When I reached the belvedere"—he paused, drew breath, and went on—"my father was waiting. I gave him no chance to ask questions or tempt me to break my oath and throw our kinship in his face. Perhaps he guessed in his last moments who I was and why he had to die. But I kept the letter of my promise.

"He lay stretched out at my feet with his head toward the balcony on the lake and his arms flung out. I'd shot him at such close range that the bullet had left a great, powder-blackened hole in his breast."

Julian asked, "What did you use for a wad?"

Valeriano came out of his trance with a start. "I can't remember. What does it matter?"

"The wad was found in the wound, Signor Valeriano."

Valeriano looked shaken. "I can't tell you what it was. When you load a gun, you use any rag or scrap of paper that comes to hand."

"It was a piece of paper ruled with musical staffs," said Grimani shortly. "There's nothing remarkable in that. You're a singer—you must have had plenty of that sort of paper ready-to-hand."

"Yes," said Valeriano. "Of course I did."

"Go on with your story," said Grimani.

"I had one thing left to do," Valeriano continued. "I went through Lodovico's pockets on the chance he had brought my note and my mother's glove to the rendezvous. I thought it unlikely anyone would ever connect them with me, but I would have liked to retrieve them if I could. I found his watch and his pocketbook and a loaded pistol, but I didn't find the note and glove, and I couldn't risk searching inside the villa. So I went home. Marchesa Francesca was worried about me and had rashly gone out searching in the dark. Otherwise, nothing untoward occurred, and I've kept my secret to this day."

Carlo crossed himself, his eyes blank with shock. Beatrice looked at Valeriano with loathing. Francesca rocked back and forth, moaning softly. De la Marque stood strangely at his ease, his shoulders propped against the wall, his gaze interested, detached. In a corner of the room, Fletcher, who had been straining to follow Valeriano's Venetian-accented Milanese, was explaining in whispers to a bewildered St. Carr what it was all about. Julian looked away from Valeriano long enough to take in all their reactions, then fastened his eyes once more on the self-confessed parricide.

"All right," said Grimani. "Now tell us about Marchese Rinaldo."

Valeriano inclined his head. "For a long time, it was enough for me to humiliate Rinaldo. I wouldn't have killed him but for the final indignities he inflicted on me before you all."

"In fact," put in Julian, "at one time you risked your own life rather than harm him."

"Ah." Valeriano was silent for a moment. "You're speaking of the duel."

"Yes. The duel in which you braved his fire twice, and fired into the air yourself."

"There was no heroism in that, Signor Kestrel. Rinaldo was terrified—shaking like a leaf. He was almost certain to miss me. And I knew that any wound I could give him with a pistol would be trivial compared with the shame of being defeated by a eunuch who didn't even return his shot.

"So the score was settled between us: I had his wife and had trampled on his honour; he had my rightful name and patrimony. It was he who upset the balance. He took Marchesa Francesca back, and in the process insulted me in a manner no gentleman could have borne, and even a castrato was bound to avenge."

"You chose to relinquish Marchesa Francesca," Julian reminded him.

"Yes," said Valeriano, "when I saw she would have left me for her children in the end. I thought: If we must part, let it be by *my* act. Rinaldo shall never say it was he who dealt the final blow."

"Were you merely playacting when you tore yourself away from her—when you called her your one and only love?"

Valeriano lifted his eyes with a faint air of exasperation. "I'm a singer, Signor Kestrel. The lover parted from his beloved is a staple of the repertoire—almost the first thing one learns."

Julian recalled the first time Valeriano had sung for the villa party. *I go, I go, but you, my love, make peace with me...*

"After I parted from Marchesa Francesca," Valeriano went on, "I hung about the neighbourhood, hoping for a chance to strike at Rinaldo. I came to the villa last night with that in mind."

"How did you get through the gate?" Julian asked.

"I didn't use the gate. I walked along the shingle beneath the embankment and climbed up into the garden. I stood beneath Rinaldo's window, wondering if there were any way I could get inside. Suddenly, incredibly, I saw someone come out and climb over the balcony railing, then edge along the ledge to the other balcony and climb down to the south terrace wall. By that time, I could make out her shape well enough to see, first, that it was a woman, then that it was Francesca.

"I hid among the trees until she had come down from the wall and gone away. All the while I was thinking: if she could come down by that means, I could go up. I ascended to the walkway at the top of the wall and pulled myself up to the balcony—that would be yours, Signor Commissario. I sidled along the ledge as I had seen Francesca do and climbed into Rinaldo's balcony."

"What time was this?" asked Julian.

"I didn't look at my watch. It was between midnight and dawn—that's the best I can say. When I reached the balcony, I looked through the French doors and saw Rinaldo lying face up in bed, asleep."

"So there was a light in the room," said Julian interested.

"There was no light in the room. I had brought a small dark lantern with me."

"You climbed up the side of the villa with a lantern?"

"I hung it on one of my braces. May I continue?"

Julian bowed.

"I took off my boots," said Valeriano, "in order to move about the room silently and without leaving muddy footprints. I left them on the balcony and came in through the French doors. I started to approach Rinaldo with the lantern in my hand, but it made a clanking sound, and I was afraid it might wake him. So I opened it and took out the candle and continued toward the bed with that."

Julian and Grimani exchanged glances. Then a grim smile settled on Grimani's lips. The drop of wax on Rinaldo's sheet was explained at last.

"Rinaldo's dressing-case was on the table," Valeriano went on. "I found his razor, and used it to slit his throat."

Julian asked curiously, "How were you proposing to kill him if there hadn't been a razor ready-to-hand?"

"I had a knife with me."

"Then why go out of your way to use his razor?" Grimani challenged him.

"There's nothing strange in that, Signor Commissario. I have waited all my life for an opportunity to use a razor."

Even Grimani seemed a little nonplussed. "Go on," he said at last.

"There's little more to tell. After Rinaldo was dead, I saw the key on the chain around his neck. I understood it all at a glance: he'd locked himself and Francesca into the room, which was why Francesca had had to leave by the balcony. I used the key to let myself out and escape through the house instead of hazarding the balcony again. I preferred being caught alert and conscious in the villa to being found in the garden with broken limbs."

"But didn't you realize Marchesa Francesca would be likely to be blamed for your crime?" asked Julian.

"It never occurred to me. But if I wronged her, I've made it up to her now by absolving her."

"You could never make up for what you've done to me!" Francesca came shakily to her feet. "I climbed down from the balcony last night because Rinaldo had used me worse than a slave, or a woman of the streets. He had mocked and degraded and raped me. I tell you, I would rather have last night back, and a hundred such nights, than this horror of knowing I was nothing to you! What are you, that you could do this to me? What *are* you?"

He said in a low voice, "I am what God and Lodovico Malvezzi made of me."

Grimani turned to Zanetti. "Prepare a written statement for him to sign. Then take it to Solaggio and have Ruga draw up a warrant for his arrest."

"Yes, Signor Commissario. What's to be done with him in the meantime?"

"Lock him in one of the rooms," said Grimani, "and have the gendarmes stand guard at the door."

"You could use the billiard room," Carlo suggested bleakly. "It's at the back of the house, out of everyone's way."

"All right." Grimani turned to the gendarmes flanking Valeriano. "See that he remains there, and that no one holds any communication with him. And remove anything he might use as a weapon against himself." Grimani smiled with cold satisfaction. "I won't have the gallows cheated of its prey."

CHAPTER 33

After the gendarmes had taken Valeriano away, Francesca abandoned herself to wild, keening grief. MacGregor bathed her temples in vinegar and water and ordered a soothing infusion of herbs for her to drink. Beatrice sent a servant to fetch Don Cristoforo to pray with her. Julian, rather to his own surprise, sat down beside her and gathered her into his arms. She clung to him and soaked his shoulder with weeping. He thought that, in her misery, she probably had very little idea who he was.

When sheer exhaustion had calmed her a little, MacGregor helped her to her room. Beatrice promised to follow and sit with her till she fell asleep. When they had gone, she turned to Grimani, her eyes bright and bitter. "I congratulate you, Signor Commissario. You've found your murderer—and without even having to lift a finger."

"It's a satisfactory solution," Grimani said shortly. "Signor Valeriano's story that Marchese Lodovico was his father will have to be verified. But the rest of his confession verifies itself. He knows details about Marchese Lodovico's murder that were never made public—the position of his body after he was killed, the search of his pockets, and the loaded gun in one of them."

Grimani had every reason to be pleased with himself, Julian thought. He had solved Rinaldo's murder on the very day it was discovered. What was more, his superiors would find the culprit highly acceptable. It would have offended the aristocratic principles of Austrian Milan to arrest a member of the Malvezzi family. Valeriano, a Venetian singer's bastard, gave rise to no such squeamishness. Yet Julian perceived that Grimani was not quite satisfied. How could he be? The investigation was over, and Orfeo was still unidentified and free.

"What do you make of his confession, Signor Kestrel? Beatrice asked.

"If all he said is true, I can easily believe he hated Marchese Lodovico enough to kill him. It's Marchese Lodovico's role I find incongruous." Julian turned to Carlo. "Would you say it was like your brother to inveigle a woman into a mock marriage?"

"No," said Carlo slowly, "I wouldn't. He didn't accomplish things by stealth—certainly not by deception. He considered it his privilege as Marchese Malvezzi to speak his mind and direct the opinions of others. He was honest, not out of religious or moral principle, but because he felt he owed it to himself to be."

"He was very secretive about Orfeo's identity," de la Marque pointed out.

"That was different," said Beatrice. "He liked knowing things other people didn't. It was a form of power, and he liked power of all sorts. But a secret isn't the same thing as a lie."

"Still," said Carlo, "I can't say for certain what he might or might not have done at the time he was studying in Naples. I didn't see him for two or three years."

"Who did see him?" Julian asked.

"If I were you," said Carlo, "I should talk to Ernesto."

Julian found Ernesto in Rinaldo's room, tidying his possessions and supervising a crew of servants who were changing the bedclothes and mopping up the blood. At first he was reluctant to be drawn away. "Heaven knows what they'll be at if I don't keep an eye on them, Signor Kestrel. Half of them think they see Marchese Rinaldo's ghost popping out of every corner, and the other half keep trying to count the bloodstains so that they can bet on that number in the lottery."

"I'm sorry to distract you, but I need information that only you can give me."

"But I thought the murders were solved, signor."

Julian smiled. "I am very hard to please."

Ernesto stared. But all he said was, "I will go with you, signor."

They went to Julian's room at the other end of the hall. Ernesto sank into a chair with an involuntary sigh of relief. Julian realized that this second murder of a Marchese Malvezzi had taken a greater toll on him than he cared to acknowledge. His eyes were haggard, and his grey skin seemed to hang on him like a husk.

Julian began, "You've heard the gist of Valerian's confession—in particular, his story that Marchese Lodovico was his father?"

"Yes, signor."

"Conte Carlo says you were with Marchese Lodovico in Naples."

"Yes," said Ernesto. "I was given to him as his servant just before he was sent there. My father was servant to the old marchese, his father. That was—Holy Virgin, it must have been forty years ago. Marchese Lodovico and I were of an age, seventeen or eighteen."

"Did you ever hear anything of a mock marriage between Marchese Lodovico and Giulietta Petroni?"

"No, signor. And I find it hard to believe."

"But not impossible?"

"No." Ernesto shook his head gravely. "Not impossible, signor. My master was a little mad in those days."

"What do you mean?"

"It was his first taste of freedom, signor. He'd never flown so far from the family nest before. All his life, the old marchese had watched him like a hawk and ruled him in everything. He was the only person my master was ever afraid of. Afraid—that's not the word for it. Terrified is what he was.

"Now all at once he was on his own, in a city that turned out the finest singers in the world. He'd always loved music, but in Naples he was well-nigh drunk on it. He was forever losing his heart to one voice or another—and if it was a woman's voice, you could be sure he'd find his way to her bed one way or another."

"Marchesa Malvezzi told me he never took a singer as his mistress."

"He didn't," said Ernesto slowly, "after Naples."

"Can you recall anything about his relationship with Giulietta Petroni? Did he ever mention her name? Did you see them together?"

Ernesto squinted back into the past. "I seem to remember he fell in love with a *prima donna* who left the stage suddenly. I thought he'd set her up privately somewhere. He was out a good deal and spent money like water. But that's to be expected of a young nobleman let loose in the world for the first time."

"None of this proves he deceived her into thinking she was his wife," Julian mused. "Could he have carried out such a long, elaborate ruse without your knowing anything about it?"

"Oh, yes," Ernesto said sadly. "He would have taken care to keep it from me. He didn't trust me in those days. He thought, since my father was the old marchese's servant, that I'd been sent with him to spy on him. He wronged me there: I was his man, not his father's. But it took him a few years to realize that."

"Would his father have been so very angry at his seducing a singer?"

"Not at his seducing her, no, signor, nor even at his getting her with child. But to pretend to marry her—that was a low, sneaking thing, and the old marchese would have taken it ill."

Julian considered. "Do you suppose Lodovico knew or guessed that Valeriano was his son?"

"I'm sure he never had any idea there was a child, signor. He would have wanted him. He always regretted not having more sons. No matter what sort of scrape he'd got into with the mother, he wouldn't have rested till he got his hands on the boy."

"Valeriano said his mother feared something of the sort," Julian recalled. "She believed Marchese Lodovico had set spies on her."

"I don't know anything about that, signor."

"Could Marchese Lodovico have found out about his relationship with Valeriano after Valeriano had grown up and become a singer? That would explain why he made such an effort to cultivate him."

Ernesto shook his head. "He would have been more direct, signor."

"Perhaps he was reluctant to acknowledge the relationship because his son was a castrato."

"If he was," said Ernesto quietly, "he was deceived. Signor Valeriano is more of a man, and more truly my master's son, than his dead brother ever was. His crimes were terrible, but the wrongs done to him and his mother were terrible, too. He revenged himself like a man, and my master would have respected him for that. And, you know, it does seem fitting, signor—"

"What seems fitting?"

"That it took one of my master's own blood to destroy him."

On parting from Ernesto, Julian decided he could do with a breath of air. He went out through the front door to the top of the stairs. There he paused, looking down on the terrace from the stairway balustrade.

The marchesa sat in a wicker chair by the lily pond, leaning down to dip her fingers in the water. Her black veil had slid from her head and fallen about her shoulders. The afternoon sun slanting across the terrace made her white gown a little transparent, showing him the graceful arm inside her long, full sleeve and the delicate ankles beneath her skirt. He was struck by her beauty as if he had never seen it before. Murder had no right to exist in the same world with her. Nothing that troubled her had any right to exist.

He came swiftly down the stairs and joined her by the lily pond. She looked up to see who it was. "Giuliano."

"Am I disturbing you?"

"No." She dipped her fingers in the water again, sending goldfish darting in all directions.

He drew up a chair beside hers. "May I help?"

"Help with what?"

"With whatever is troubling you."

"I'm not troubled, Giuliano. I was only thinking."

He watched her disturbing the goldfish. Why could he not love a woman like Francesca? he mused. A woman who sought comfort confidingly, like a child—who wanted only the simple things: to love and be loved, protect and be protected.

"What were you thinking?" he asked.

"I was thinking about Orfeo. Do you suppose he'll reveal his identity, now that he's no longer in danger of being arrested for Lodovico's murder?"

"He may have other reasons for keeping it dark."

"I suppose it doesn't matter, anyway. Now that we know he didn't kill Lodovico, he's become unimportant. He always was unimportant—a mere distraction. You sensed it long ago, and I ought to have believed you."

"Why are you so bitter?" he asked.

She did not answer. After a moment she said, "What will you do now?"

"In the next half hour, or generally?"

"After you leave the villa."

"I shall offer to show MacGregor anything else in Italy he cares to see. But he's had his fill of Continental travel. All he'll want now is a courier to take him back to England."

"And you? Where will you go?"

He considered. "I've never been to Peru. I actually know very little about it, but I rather like the name."

She leaned down to the pool again, her fingers rippling the water. "You are pleased to laugh at me."

"Such a question deserves such an answer. You must know that I shall go wherever you are."

She sat up slowly, still keeping her eyes averted. "I can't think you would like living in Milan."

"Risotto, the opera six nights a week, and you? I should struggle along."

She looked around at him then, with a smile that all but knocked him off his seat. He took her hand. "I speak English, French, and Italian, and there are no words to tell you how I love you."

He lifted her hand to his lips. She stroked his cheek lightly. He thought of that night in the belvedere—imagined her breathless and yielding in his arms. It was all he could do not to draw her to him. But they were under the eyes of the boatmen on the lake, and of who knew what servants looking out of the windows overhead. He let go of her hand reluctantly.

"What are you going to do in the next half-hour?" she asked, smiling.

"I should like to conduct an experiment—one that our scientific friend Mr. Fletcher would approve of."

"What sort of experiment?"

"I want to try climbing up from the south terrace wall to Marchese Rinaldo's balcony."

"Why?" she asked in astonishment.

He shrugged. "I think it would illumine the crime for me."

"But you could break your neck! It's a miracle Valeriano didn't—" She broke off, her eyes widening. "You want to see if he really could have done it."

Julian smiled noncommittally. "I think someone ought to find out, don't you?"

Julian's experiment inevitably became a public spectacle. All the servants turned out to watch, shout encouragement and warnings, pray, shriek, and generally distract him from keeping his footing. Several ran about beneath him with an old boat-awning, but Julian would not have wagered on its effectiveness in breaking his fall. Dipper and MacGregor likewise watched from below, MacGregor with his medical bag in his hand and grim disapproval written all over his face. Beatrice waited on Rinaldo's balcony, like the prize at the end of Julian's climb.

He took off his coat and left it with de la Marque, who was amusing himself by playing valet to the mountaineer. Then he ascended the stairs to the walkway at the top of the south terrace wall. From here, by standing on tiptoe he could just catch hold of the base of Grimani's balcony. He hoisted himself up into it. Then the difficult part began.

He put a foot cautiously over the balustrade onto the ornamental ledge between Grimani's window and Rinaldo's. The ledge was barely half the width of his foot. He fought off the urge to look down at the gravel walk and the excited bystanders three stories below. He put his other foot over the balustrade and set out.

From the ground, the ledge did not look very long, but it seemed to go on interminably. He had to sidle like a crab, his body pressed to the wall, his arms spread out on either side for balance. He marvelled that Francesca and Valeriano should have done this at night, in the rain. His hands groped instinctively over the wall, feeling for some purchase. There was a cornice moulding overhead—a deep groove with a tantalizingly protruding edge—but it was some six or eight inches out of his reach.

His right foot slipped. An anguished cry rose up from below. He threw all his weight to his left foot, flattened his body as hard as he could against the wall, and righted himself. The onlookers groaned with relief. Beads of sweat broke out on his brow, and his heart beat hard and fast. He took half a dozen deep, measured breaths and edged forward again.

Rinaldo's balcony was before him at last. Three feet away—two feet—near enough now to get his leg over the balustrade. Beatrice caught his hand and helped him in. "Giuliano!" she breathed.

He saw that she had in full measure an Italian woman's hero-worship of physical courage. Seeing her eyes shining on him with a naîveté as rare in her as it was adorable, Julian could only wish he had thought to climb up the side of a building before.

MacGregor was not going to let him off so easily. "Well?" he called from below, his voice snappish with pent-up worry. "What do you think you've accomplished by these antics?"

Something of the greatest importance, if Julian did not miss his guess. But he was not prepared to shout it from the balcony. They would all know soon enough.

For the next three-quarters of an hour, Julian was very busy. He had something to inspect and someone to interrogate. He had no sooner finished these tasks than the dinner bell rang. It was late for dinner, by the villa's standards—nearly half-past five. The marchesa had decreed that, after all the strains of the day, no one should bother to dress.

The villa party began assembling in the drawing room—all except Francesca, who was not expected down to dinner. Grimani stood looking out of one of the front windows, his back very straight and his hands clasped behind him. Julian suspected he was watching for Zanetti to return from Solaggio with the warrant for Valeriano's arrest. Fletcher and St. Carr hung about by another window, talking with forced unconcern about cricket. Carlo leaned his arm on the mantelpiece, brooding. MacGregor paced back and forth before the fireplace. Beatrice and de la

Marque talked in low voices in a corner. From the music room, Donati could be heard playing a Scarlatti sonata.

Julian went over to the ornate Malvezzi family tree, with its golden apples bearing the names of past and present family members. He sought out Lodovico: born 1765, married in 1790 to Isotta Marini. One child, Rinaldo, born 1795. Married again in 1817, to Beatrice de Goncourt, no issue—

"Signor Commissario!" Zanetti hastened in and presented Grimani with an official-looking paper. Grimani glanced over it and said, "All right. Bring in Valeriano."

Zanetti skittered out. He returned a minute later with Valeriano and the four gendarmes who had been guarding him. Valeriano looked pale and listless. When Grimani told him he was under arrest and would be confined in the village gaol, preparatory to his removal to the Santa Margherita prison in Milan, he hardly seemed to be listening.

Julian stepped forward suddenly. "Signor Commissario, I should like to ask a favour on behalf of the prisoner."

"I don't need you to ask any favours on my behalf, Signor Kestrel," said Valeriano, with strained courtesy.

Julian paid him no heed. "I should like to ask that before he's committed to gaol, he be allowed to sing for us once more."

"That's ridiculous," said Grimani.

"It's not ridiculous." Donati appeared in the doorway to the music room, leaning on Sebastiano's arm. "It would be a great kindness to a singer—perhaps the greatest kindness you could bestow."

"I want no such kindness," said Valeriano. "I don't wish to sing."

"Consider," said Julian, "this may be your last opportunity, not only to sing for an audience, but to sing at all." He turned to Grimani. "I don't suppose singing is allowed in the Santa Margherita?"

"Of course not," said Grimani. "The prisoners would be singing all the time, and using their songs to send messages to each other."

Valeriano looked taken aback. He had prepared himself for disgrace, imprisonment, and death, Julian thought, but not for having the great gift and consolation of his life torn away. At last he said in a low voice, "If you please, Signor Commissario, I should like to sing one last time."

Grimani rolled his eyes in exasperation. "Very well. One song."

Julian gave Donati his arm into the music room. "Maestro," he whispered as he seated him at the piano, "play *Che farò*."

Donati did not ask questions. He played the introduction to the famous castrato air: Orpheus's lament over the corpse of his beloved Euridice. The company filed soberly into the music room, Valeriano still flanked by his guards. He began:

"What shall I do without Euridice?
Where shall I go without my love?"

The melody unfurled, exquisitely tender and anguished, entreating earth and Heaven to answer the unanswerable.

The door leading to the Hall of Marbles opened. Francesca stood there, staring across at Valeriano as he sang. She wore an ill-fitting black dress that Julian recognized as one of Beatrice's. Her face was white and gaunt. Her eyes expressed her feelings more eloquently than speech. *How dare you say those words? How dare you sing of love?*

"Euridice! Oh, God! Speak to me!
I am still your faithful lover...

Still Francesca stared. Valeriano's voice began to falter.

"What shall I do without Euridice?
Where shall I go—"

He covered his face with his hands and wept.

Julian went to him and laid a hand on his shoulder. "The

masquerade is over, Signor Valeriano. You know you didn't kill Marchese Lodovico or Marchese Rinaldo."

"I did kill them. This is just a moment of weakness—it means nothing—"

"I don't say I suspect it," said Julian Patiently. "I *know* it. And I shall tell you how.

"There were several things about your confession that I doubted, but my first piece of concrete evidence came when I climbed up to Marchese Rinaldo's balcony, as you said you had done. There's a cornice moulding above the ledge between the two balconies. I tried to grasp it, but it was six or eight inches out of my reach. Marchesa Francesca couldn't have reached it, either. But you have the advantage of us in height, Signor Valeriano. You could have grasped that moulding—and you would have. Anyone venturing along that narrow ledge would have taken advantage of whatever support came to hand.

"Afterward I went upstairs to the garrets and leaned out of the windows to look at that cornice moulding. There's a deep groove along it that last night's rain didn't penetrate. It has quite an elaborate collection of leaves and spiders' webs—and they haven't been disturbed at all. You were never on that ledge, Signor Valeriano. Your confession was an ingenious tissue of lies.

"Or rather, I shouldn't say of lies, but of truth and lies ingeniously mixed. I believe Lodovico really was your father, and you lured him to the belvedere rendezvous using the glove he had given your mother. But you didn't intend to kill him. You meant to use his treatment of your mother to blackmail him into letting Marchesa Francesca see her children. Your note told him to meet you in the belvedere 'after eleven,' but as you told us earlier today, you didn't arrive until midnight. And by the time you arrived, he was already dead.

"That's how you knew so much about the condition of his body. You even knew about the loaded gun he had with him: you found it while you were searching his pockets for your note and your mother's glove. But I disconcerted you when I asked you about the wad that had been used to load the gun that shot him. That was something you couldn't have known."

"But—but Rinaldo's murder?" broke in Carlo. "How could he have learned so much about that so quickly? He wasn't even in the house when it was discovered."

"No," said Julian, "but he was in Solaggio. Commissario Grimani sent Bruno to Solaggio this morning to deliver messages to Comandante Von Krauss and others. He warned Bruno not to speak to anyone along the way, but I'd had a little experience of Bruno, and I didn't think he was capable of obeying that order. He had just seen Marchese Rinaldo's body and had a good look around his room. He wouldn't be able to resist giving the villagers a first-hand account of the murder. I cornered him a little while ago and prevailed on him to admit it. He gathered a group about him in the piazza and told them every detail he could remember: the bloodstained razor lying on the bed, the unfastened chain around Marchese Rinaldo's neck, and the rest of it. And he remembers distinctly that Signor Valeriano was there."

Grimani's eyes sparked angrily.

"Of course Bruno didn't know about Marchesa Francesca's climbing down from her balcony," Julian went on. "But that story must have spread very quickly: the soldiers who found her in the chapel knew it, and they weren't instructed to keep it to themselves."

"How did Signor Valeriano know about the drop of candle wax on the sheet?" Grimani objected. "That wasn't something Bruno or the soldiers would have seen."

"I wondered about that, too," said Julian. "Then I remembered that you and I discussed it in the presence of the gendarmes you sent to fetch Valeriano from the Nightingale. I'll wager they talked about it as they were bringing him here. At all events, from one source or another, he gained all the information he needed to confess convincingly to Marchese Rinaldo's murder. He had a great deal to memorize in a very short time. But he was accustomed to learning major opera roles in a matter of days. This can't have been very different."

Jaen turned to Valeriano. "To be sure, you had compelling reasons to want Marchese Rinaldo dead. But when you had an opportunity to kill him in the duel, you risked letting him kill you instead. Your explanation for that was clever but implausible. You fired into the air for the simple reason that you weren't willing to kill your brother.

"I don't know why you felt the need to convince Marchesa Francesca you had never loved her, but I should guess you wanted to mask the fact that it was for her sake you were doing all this. You knew she was in danger of being arrested for both murders, and the only way you could think of to save her was to condemn yourself. Perhaps you also hoped, by repulsing her, to discourage her from making any effort to prove your innocence, and so put herself at risk again. She said your pretence of love for her was the performance of your life. But in reality you gave the performance of your life earlier today, when you persuaded her you felt nothing for her, at the very moment when you were giving up your life in her service."

"Is that true?" Francesca asked Valeriano breathlessly.

"I'm sorry," he whispered "I tried to save you. I couldn't carry it through—"

He got no further. Francesca launched herself at him, beating him with her fists, kicking him, tearing at his clothes. "How could you? How could you tear my heart out, and think it was for my good?"

"I was trying to protect you!" he pleaded. "I was out of my mind with fear for you! And I thought that, once you were free of me, you could marry again and have more children—"

"Oh!" She flung him from her in disgust. "How can you be so stupid and selfish?"

"Selfish?" he echoed in astonishment.

"Yes!" She looked around at the others. "I expect you think he's brave. He isn't brave! He throws away his life because he thinks it of so little value! Dare to live, Pietro! Dare to believe that you deserve to live! That and nothing else will make you truly a man!"

"You despise me," he said bleakly.

Her face crumpled. "No, I love you. Else why would I care so much?"

They fell, exhausted, into each other's arms.

Grimani asked abruptly, "Why were you still in Solaggio this morning, Signor Valeriano, when you said yesterday that you meant to return to Venice?"

Valeriano turned toward him, flushed and happy, his arm still about Francesca's shoulders. "That was my intention. But it was hard enough to give Francesca up—to leave her so completely was beyond me. Besides, I was worried about her. I hardly knew what I feared, but when I thought of Rinaldo's cruelty and her despair, I couldn't desert her. So I put up at the Nightingale, thinking I would wait a few days to be sure she was safe—then I would go."

"You recant your confession of murder, then?" said Grimani.

"I have no choice." Valeriano lowered his eyes. "Everything Signor Kestrel said was true."

"I ought to have believed in you," said Francesca remorsefully. "I ought to have known you would never kill anyone."

Valeriano took her gently but firmly by the shoulders and looked into her eyes. "You must understand, my dear love—my confession was convincing precisely because there was so much truth in it. I drew on my most ignoble and savage feelings. I did hate my father. I did want to kill him, when I first learned what he had done to my mother. But Elena reminded me that it would be a mortal sin. I was trained as a singer—bred up on the classical myths. I thought of Orestes, and Oedipus. If I shed a parent's blood, I would be polluted, damned. That couldn't have been what my mother wanted. She wanted me to sing. So I tried to avoid Lodovico. But he wouldn't have it so. He hunted me down, courted me unmercifully. And so I met you, Francesca.

"I didn't want to love you. I never dreamed I would love anyone. When I realized what you meant to me, I was panic-stricken. I tried to dissuade you from coming to me. I couldn't bear to seem, even to myself, to be using you as an instrument of revenge. I feared that if you ever found out I was your husband's brother, you would be filled with horror at me—worse still, at yourself. But in the end—" He lifted his hands helplessly. "I wanted you too much."

Grimani broke in on their reunion again. "Were you telling the truth when you said you arrived at the belvedere at about midnight on the night of Lodovico's murder?"

"Yes. And as Signor Kestrel guessed, I found him dead." Valeriano turned back to Francesca. "The strange thing is, I was sorry. Against my will, against all reason, there must have been something in me that acknowledged him as my flesh and blood."

"Was his body cold?" asked Grimani.

"Yes."

"So he'd probably been dead at least half an hour. That would mean he was killed between half-past ten and half-past eleven."

Julian thought this of secondary importance. Far more significant was Valeriano's revelation that the murderer and the person who lured Lodovico to the belvedere were not one and the same. How, then, had the murderer known that he would find Lodovico there? Lodovico had had a lantern with him—perhaps the murderer had seen the light from somewhere on the lake and come to investigate. But surely it was too much of a coincidence that someone with both a motive to kill Lodovico and a weapon had been in the vicinity of the villa that night. Julian would lay any odds the murderer had known Lodovico would be all but alone there. Yet how had the murderer found this out?

Lodovico had come to the villa that morning and announced he would spend the night there and would not bring any servants. That meant that Donati, Orfeo, Tonio, Lucia, and Matteo had known of his plans. Could one of them have passed this information on to the murderer? Lucia and Matteo might have talked idly to some stranger—or, even more likely, some trusted and respected acquaintance. And Tonio—Tonio had been sacked that day. Might he not have wagged his tongue indiscreetly before he fell into the drunken stupor in which he had passed the night? That might account for why he had run away the next morning: because he feared he would be blamed for Lodovico's murder—

No, that cock would not fight. It had not been made public that Lodovico's death was murder. In fact, at the time Tonio fled from the Nightingale at eight in the morning, it had not even been discovered that Lodovico was dead. Julian was not sure what to make of all this, but he began to have a very bad feeling about what had become of Tonio.

"What's going to happen now?" Carlo asked Grimani.

"The murder isn't solved," said Grimani, "so the investigation will continue. In the meantime, you will all remain here."

"I was hoping I might go to Milan to see my children," Francesca faltered.

"Out of the question," said Grimani. "You are once again the chief suspect in your husband's murder."

Valeriano passed a hand across his eyes.

"There's nothing to link her to Lodovico's murder," Carlo pointed out.

"She was at the lake when it happened," said Grimani. "But in fact I don't think she killed Marchese Lodovico herself. That murder required a degree of calculation and boldness beyond a woman's capacity. She must have acted through an accomplice."

"Not Pietro!" Francesca said quickly.

"No," said Grimani. "Orfeo."

Julian sighed. He might have known Grimani would bring the investigation round to Orfeo again. The idea of Orfeo as Francesca's paid assassin ran counter to the theory that he was a Carbonaro agent. Yet Grimani probably would not put it past him to be both.

Francesca had no thought to spare for Orfeo or for her own danger. "Couldn't I send for my children to come here?"

"That's of no consequence to me," said Grimani.

"May I, Beatrice?" she asked eagerly.

"Yes, of course," said Beatrice. "I'll send Ernesto for them if you like."

"Marchesa Francesca," Julian intervened, "I must advise you not to do this. Wait until things are more settled."

"You don't understand, Signor Kestrel," said Francesca. "It isn't just a matter of my wanting to see them. They'll have heard of their father's murder. They'll be lonely and frightened. If I can't go to them, they must come to me."

"Forgive my bluntness, Marchesa Francesca," said Julian gently. "The last two men to hold the title Marchese Malvezzi have been murdered. Your son holds it now. Do you really want to bring him into this house?"

She stared. "But—but he's only a little boy!"

"And very likely he's not in danger. But if there's the smallest chance—"

"Yes, yes," she said. "He must remain where he is." She looked around at the others. "Would one of you go to my children, to bring them my love and make sure they're all right?"

"I would go," said Valeriano, "but I'm loath to leave you."

"Oh, no." She clung to him. "I can't be parted from you now. But perhaps Carlo or Beatrice—"

"They're implicated in the murders," said Grimani. "I can't allow them to leave."

"I take it you don't seriously consider *me* as a suspect, Signor Commissario?" Julian asked.

"You?" Grimani's eyes narrowed. "You want to go to Milan?"

"Just for the day," said Julian. "I could leave early tomorrow morning and return by nightfall—if Marchesa Francesca will favour me with her commission."

Francesca hesitated. "The children don't know you—"

"I give you my word, I shall be as kind to them as I know how."

Her face softened. She went to him and laid her hand lightly on his breast. "You believed in Pietro when no one else did—when even I had lost faith in him. You restored us to one another. I would trust you with my children. I would trust you with my life."

"I'm honoured, Marchesa Francesca. I shan't give you cause to regret those words." He turned to Grimani. "Have I your leave to go to Milan, Signor Commissario?"

"By all means." Grimani's lip curled contemptuously. Julian had no difficulty reading his thoughts: *If you want to dash off to Milan and play nursemaid to a pair of children, you may do so with my blessing. I never wanted you here, anyway.* He did not grudge Grimani his triumph. It was better than his knowing the real reason Julian wanted to go to Milan.

CHAPTER 34

Dinner at the villa was short and silent. The household was worn out with shock and suspense. The knowledge hung heavily over them that the murder remained unsolved, and the murderer might be among them even now. If anyone could have forgotten, the soldiers standing guard in the hallways and patrolling the grounds would have been a constant reminder.

Francesca and Valeriano stayed close together and seemed to find a measure of peace in each other's sight, in spite of the threat to Francesca. Carlo looked at Valeriano bemusedly from time to time, as if he could hardly credit that he had lost one nephew and gained another in the space of four-and-twenty hours. Only de la Marque seemed in spirits. As the evening wore on, he looked more and more like the cat that had swallowed the cream. Julian determined to find out what he was up to.

The company drifted off to bed early. Grimani had stationed soldiers outside their rooms, but the marchesa took exception to that. "If you're concerned about our escaping, you need simply post guards at the outside doors and under the windows. Unless you were proposing your men should listen at our keyholes?"

Grimani grudgingly dispatched the soldiers downstairs, and the company retired to their rooms. But Julian did not undress. "Aren't you going to bed?" MacGregor asked.

"Not yet. I want to talk to Dipper about my trip to Milan tomorrow. There are a few things I should like him to attend to in my absence."

"You're not taking him with you?"

"I'm only going for the day, and I think I can fend for myself for that amount of time."

"Why don't you just ring for him? You never go to bed without him fussing about you, anyway."

"The servants' quarters are more private. We can speak English there without fear of being understood by anyone around us. I'll be back presently, but you needn't sit up. Good night, my dear fellow."

He went out into the broad, still hallway, lit only by a lamp at either end. He felt a twinge of conscience at having all but lied to MacGregor: he did want to talk to Dipper, but that might have to wait till tomorrow morning. There was something more important he had to do tonight.

Next to his and MacGregor's room was a door leading to the servants' stairs. He slipped silently through it, then opened it a crack to look out. From here he had a view of the main staircase across the hall and the two rooms on either side of it: Beatrice's and de la Marque's. Now there was nothing to do but keep an eye on de la Marque's door, and wait.

The minutes ticked by. The church bells chimed eleven, then the half hour after. Weariness stole on Julian. Perhaps he had only imagined that de la Marque was engaged in some devilry. But he could not desert his post yet—not before midnight, the time-honoured hour of trysts and conspiracies. He leaned into a corner of the little staircase hall, making himself as comfortable as he could without taking his eye from the crack in the door.

The church bells counted up to twelve. Nothing happened. Julian straightened and started to open the door. Then all at once there was a sound across the hall.

The door to de la Marque's room opened a little way. De la Marque put out his head, looked swiftly up and down the hall, and came out, closing the door soundlessly behind him. He tiptoed toward the main staircase. Julian held his breath. De la Marque passed the staircase and moved on to Beatrice's door.

He tapped softly, three times. The door opened at once. For an instant, the lamp at the end of the hall revealed Beatrice's face. Then she stepped aside to let de la Marque in, and the door closed behind them.

Julian felt as if he had been kicked very hard in the stomach. How often? he wondered—how many nights had they been together, while he himself slept so near? Of course she had promised him nothing. She had never said she returned his love. But still, she had given him hope; she had looked at him, touched him in such a way—Why? To induce him to solve the murders? Or to distract and mislead him from solving them?

And what the devil was he to do now? His chief desires were to pick a quarrel with de la Marque and to crawl into a hole—neither very practical. To leave them together was unbearable. Yet how could he interrupt them? What could be more pointless and ridiculous than to storm in and say, *Aha!*

All at once the investigator awoke in him. Suppose this was not an amorous assignation—or not that alone? He had once speculated that Beatrice and de la Marque were lovers or political allies at the time of the Piedmontese revolt. He had even suspected them of acting in concert to kill Lodovico. What they were talking of now might be of vital importance to the investigation. Could he bring himself to listen?

As a gentleman, he was repelled by the thought. As a lover, he shrank from it as from a lash. As an investigator, he had no choice. He crossed the hall, thankful for the carpet that muffled his steps, and put his ear to Beatrice's door.

She and de la Marque were speaking in French, so softly that, but for the silence in the house, Julian would not have heard them. "But my dear Gaston," Beatrice was saying, "I'm only complying with your wishes. A man doesn't constantly hint at a thing unless he wants to be asked about it."

"Ah, but wanting to be asked isn't the same thing as wanting to answer."

"Then you do know?"

"I am desolate, my angel, but I don't."

"Then you've deceived me."

"I beg to disagree. I never told you I knew who Orfeo was."

"You implied as much. And you know I asked you here so that we might talk of it."

"We *are* talking of it."

"But not to the purpose." Her voice changed—became warmly enticing. "Come, my dear, you have no reason to keep Orfeo's secret. Unless Grimani is right to suspect you of being Orfeo yourself?"

"If I were, forgive me, my love, but I would hardly admit it."

"You aren't afraid of me, surely?"

"What man isn't afraid of a beautiful woman?"

"I mean, you aren't afraid to confide in me? You can't think I would run to Grimani with the information?"

"What would you do with it?"

"Keep it. Lock it away. Enjoy the pleasure of knowing something Grimani doesn't."

"And what pleasure would *I* enjoy?"

There was a silence. Then Beatrice said, "Whatever you wished."

"You want to know so badly?" he asked, interested.

"You hardly flatter yourself."

"Considering that you've never honoured me with such favour before, I can't quite deceive myself into thinking I've succeeded by my charm alone."

"You haven't succeeded at all yet," she reminded him.

"Won't you give me something on account? A kiss, perhaps, to show you're in earnest?"

"You can see that I'm earnest. If I weren't, you wouldn't be here. And I swear to you upon my honour that I'll repay you in the coin you wish. Who is Orfeo?"

"Alas, I don't know."

"Then good night, Monsieur de la Marque."

"My dearest—"

"Good night. If you're having difficulty finding the door, I shall ring for a footman to point it out to you."

"Wouldn't you find that a trifle embarrassing?"

"I promise you, monsieur—I shall ensure that you find it more so."

"I believe you!" De la Marque laughed softly. "Very well, my dear Marchesa, I leave you—with the greatest regret! Good night."

The door opened. De la Marque and Julian confronted one another.

Beatrice appeared behind de la Marque, her face softly illumined by the shaded lamp in her hand. Julian held his ground, obstructing de la Marque's way, so that he and Beatrice had no choice but to step back and let him into the room.

As soon as they were inside, Beatrice moved away, leaving the lamp by the door. She was still dressed in the white cotton morning frock she had worn all day. She stood at the foot of the bed, half turned away, one hand upraised and clasping one of the posts.

Julian and de la Marque stood by the door, braving the light. De la Marque glanced toward Beatrice. "It seems, Marchesa, you were right to be concerned about people listening at keyholes. But you were mistaken in supposing such tricks were confined to the police."

"I beg your pardon for listening," said Julian. "But I should say that, of the three of us, I have the least to be ashamed of."

"You insult me," de la Marque observed.

"You may have satisfaction whenever you wish."

"No, *mon vieux*." De la Marque broke into a laugh. "I don't want to kill you—not yet, at all events." He studied Julian's face.

"I'm afraid the feeling isn't mutual. What a pity! You really ought to be grateful to me."

"Ought I?"

"But of course! First, because you heard from my own lips that I've never enjoyed this lady's favours. And second, because I didn't tell her Orfeo's identity." De la Marque smiled. "You wouldn't want me sharing information with her that I've never imparted to you?"

"You said you didn't know who Orfeo was." The marchesa's voice was muffled, her face still turned from the light.

"And of course I don't," de la Marque said smoothly. "But if I did—forgive me, my dear Marchesa, but I would not have betrayed him."

"Thank you, monsieur," she said, very low. "It needed only that."

"Now I'll grant you both a further boon," said de la Marque. "I'll withdraw and allow you to settle your differences with a kick or a kiss." He bowed and went to the door. "What a pity the stairs intervene between my room and this one! I can assure you, I should have had my ear to the wall!"

He went out. The silence he left behind was so deep, Julian almost seemed to hear his own heart beating. He glanced around him, thinking with unnatural detachment how like Beatrice this room was. Her favourite white was everywhere: in the graceful bed hangings, the marble table-tops, the ceiling mouldings of scrolls and rosettes. The walls and chairs were covered in sky-blue silk. Over the mantelpiece was a tall, gilt-edged mirror. That was fitting, Julian thought. What work of art could compare with Beatrice's own image?

He said, "You brought me here to investigate your husband's murder. It's now tolerably clear that that is all you ever wanted of me. As part of my investigation, I must ask you why you offered to sell yourself to de la Marque in exchange for his revealing Orfeo's identity."

"To sell myself!" She was pale. "How dare you?"

"May I not dare to name what you dared to do?"

She looked away again. "Very well. Yes. What you say is true."

"I've been too forbearing with you. The reason, you know all too well. Now I will have an answer. Why were you willing to go to such lengths to identify Orfeo?"

"I offered Gaston the bait I thought he would be most likely to take."

"That is not the question I asked. Why were you so determined to find Orfeo that you would give yourself to a man you don't love—a man who would see you as nothing but a fleeting conquest?"

She lifted her slim brows. "Isn't that a rather personal question for an investigator?"

He went to her suddenly and looked into her face. She could not meet his eyes. He said in a low, urgent voice, "I think you owe me an explanation. After all that has passed, or nearly passed, between us, I'm entitled to know why you would lower yourself and torment me, in order to go questing after a singer of whom you know so little?"

She lifted her chin and looked at him unflinchingly. "I want to find Orfeo so that I can destroy him."

"Destroy him?"

"Yes."

"Because—" He was stunned. "Because you believe he killed your husband?"

"He did kill him. It makes no difference whether he actually fired the shot. It was on his account that Lodovico was at the lake. If he hadn't been isolated in the country, the murderer couldn't have sought him out secretly and killed him."

"But surely you must realize—"

"What? That I'm behaving like a silly, irrational woman? That I'm not being fair?" She shook her head. "You don't understand. You can't know anything of what I feel."

"Then make me understand."

"If you must." She drew a long breath. "There's one thing you must know at the start. I have only ever loved one man in my life, and that was Lodovico Malvezzi. It isn't the fashion to love one's husband—in fact, it's considered rather bad taste. But I had loved him long before I married him—long before I even married Philippe. When I was a little girl, he was a god to me—the handsomest, strongest, most manly man I knew. Of course as I grew older I saw his faults. He was vainglorious, selfish, ruthless toward anyone who crossed him. But by then my love was so deeply rooted, I couldn't tear it out.

"I accepted my marriage to Philippe. Lodovico was married already, and only saw me as a child in any case. But I never forgot him. Even after I went to live in Paris, I studied to be all that would please him. I even tried to learn to sing, but I had to give it up. I had no gift for it at all.

"I told you how I returned to Milan after Philippe was killed, and Lodovico fell in love with me at last, and married me after Isotta died. I was happier than I'd ever been in my life. But I didn't trumpet my feelings to the skies. I hugged them close to me—hid them even from Lodovico. Some hearts open like flowers, and some must be cracked like nuts. Mine was never one of the flowers, Giuliano.

"I wasn't lying when I told you I didn't mind Lodovico's having mistresses. I knew they meant nothing to him. He would always come back to me in the end. But there were two griefs eating away at me—growing more bitter year by year.

"Lodovico badly wanted more children. Rinaldo was a mistake, an abortion, a pathetic thing foisted on him in place of a son. He talked gleefully of the children he and I would have—how healthy and handsome and brave they would be. I was gleeful, too. I had never conceived with Philippe, but I thought that was only because he'd been away on campaign so often. But I found that I couldn't give Lodovico a child, either. Every month I hoped and prayed, and every month I was disappointed. I spent whole nights on my knees before the Madonna. She never relented. She knew me for what I was: a proud, worldly woman, who read Voltaire and laughed at the Pope, then put on religion like this year's fashions, just to wheedle a baby out of God!

"If I'd borne Lodovico a child, I would have been special to him—set apart from all other women. As it was, I was little more than a favoured mistress—the chief concubine of his seraglio. All his deep devotion, all the madness of his love, he poured out on his singers." Her voice caught on a sob. "At night he would get out of my bed and go to the window, just to listen to some sweet-voiced gipsy passing in the street.

"But he never loved any singer as he loved Orfeo. Do you know the real reason he hid him away at the Lake of Como? It wasn't only to make a mystery about him. It was because he was a virgin. In all Milan—in all Italy—only Lodovico had heard him sing. He wanted him all to himself, before the world had its turn. Do you know what *droit de seigneur* is?"

Julian's throat was so dry that for a moment he could not find his voice. "Yes."

"The first night," she nodded. "That's what Lodovico wanted. And perhaps he would have wanted it, even knowing it would cost him his life. Can you wonder—" She caught her breath, her great eyes burning into Julian's. "Can you wonder I hated Orfeo? I wanted to take him by the throat—to squeeze and squeeze until he had no voice left! I believe I could have done it, if only I could have got near him. But Lodovico wouldn't share him, even with me.

"I went to Turin to escape all the talk in Milan of Lodovico and his tenor. I'd heard there was political trouble brewing in Piedmont, but I felt too reckless to care. I even had the sort of stupid idea children do, that if anything happened to me, Lodovico would be sorry.

"The weeks wore on. Lodovico wrote me blithe letters about Orfeo's progress. I lay awake at night with my head on fire, thinking of Lodovico happy and fulfilled without me—hating him, hating Orfeo. Then the revolt broke out in Turin, and in my wretchedness, I made use of it. Can you guess how?"

"You deliberately went missing on the road between Turin and Novara, so that Lodovico would leave Orfeo and come looking for you."

She inclined her head. "It was quite easy, actually. I travelled in a simple hired chaise, with only a few servants out of livery. I didn't give my name at the inns where we changed horses and forbade my servants to address me by my title. But I didn't tell the courier I sent on ahead that I was travelling incognito, so that he and the others searching for me wasted a great deal of time asking after Marchesa Malvezzi, and of course hearing nothing. The countryside was in confusion, anyway. The King of Piedmont had abdicated, and the people were caught between the rebels in Turin and the loyalist troops in Novara. In all the upheaval, I could count on passing unnoticed.

"Of course my plans went hideously awry, as such idiotic plans deserve to. Rinaldo was too terrified of his father to send him word I'd disappeared. He traced me to Belgirate and fetched me home to Milan like a piece of stray baggage. I arrived only to find that Lodovico was dead. All I cared for in the world died with him. I didn't know yet that he'd been murdered, but I blamed Orfeo for his death. And whatever the solution to the murders, I always will."

Julian felt as if a cold hand had gripped his heart. He knew she had no idea what she had revealed. And he could not tell her because she would stop him going to Milan tomorrow and dragging the truth about the murders into the light. He had lost all stomach for the task, but it must be finished.

He asked, "Why were you so convinced that de la Marque could lead you to Orfeo?"

"First, because I think that he's more likely than either Signor Fletcher or Signor St. Carr to be Orfeo himself. The night you and I met at La Scala, you told me his English was so good, he could pass for a native. Soon after, Maestro Donati mentioned that Orfeo's accent sounded more French than English. Gaston was the right age and knew a great deal about singing, for all that he affected to regard it as a science rather than an art. On top of everything else, he was terribly interested in you and your investigation. He came to my box at La Scala the night before we left Milan, and asked me all manner of questions about you. That he could be Orfeo—here, at our mercy—seemed too much to hope. But all the same I invited him to come here with us, to find out.

"From the beginning, he taunted us with hints that he knew more of Orfeo than he was saying. I felt absolutely certain that either he was Orfeo himself, or he knew who Orfeo was. But I could never penetrate his secret. I watched him, flirted with him—flirted with you in order to make him jealous. Nothing was of any avail."

Julian looked away. She paused, then came to him and hesitantly laid her hand on his arm. "Giuliano, that wasn't all there was between us. That night in the belvedere—Gaston wasn't with us. I was thinking only of you and me."

"And Orfeo. Even then, you pleaded with me to find him."

"So that I could be free of him! So that I could give you a heart that wasn't twisted up with hatred! I wanted to love you. I—I could love you—it terrifies me to say so." She added in a low voice, "But I suppose that after tonight you could never love me."

"I do love you. That is my misfortune. Please finish your story. What prompted you to try such desperate measures to make de la Marque speak?"

"After Valeriano confessed to the murders, I felt desolate, knowing that Orfeo would never be caught, because it was no longer worth the authorities' while to pursue him. I had no love for Valeriano—he was one of Lodovico's singers, too, and now it turns out he's Lodovico's son by another woman. But I wanted Orfeo to be the murderer, or at least to be exposed, and it seemed he never would be. Then you told me you wanted to try climbing up to the balcony, and I realized that you, at least, doubted Valeriano's guilt. I have great respect for your intellects, Giuliano. I felt sure you would be proved right in the end. But in the meantime, perhaps Gaston could be cajoled into betraying Orfeo, in the belief that it was safe now, because the murders were solved.

"I sought out Gaston. You can imagine the conversation. I said the investigation had left me unsatisfied—that it seemed only half finished as long as Orfeo remained unknown. He said he was desolate that I should lack for anything I desired. And so on. The end of it was, we agreed he should come to my room tonight to speak of it further. Then you demolished Valeriano's confession, and so put Orfeo in danger once more. But I'd gone too far to draw back. I received Gaston, and offered him what I knew he wanted in exchange for what I believed he had. I failed. And now you know all my story. I told you once that we should only play hide-and-seek with one another. You can see now that it's true."

"Yes, Marchesa."

"Marchesa," she repeated. "Not even Beatrice now."

"I've disturbed you long enough," he said. "You must wish to go to bed, and I'm leaving for Milan early in the morning. Good night."

He went to the door. She followed. As he grasped the knob, she covered his hand with hers and looked up into his face. "Stay with me."

His heart jerked in his breast. One night, he thought—what can it matter? One night—then let it all come crashing down around our ears! His heart hammered wildly; his face and hands were hot—

"I can't," he said bleakly.

She slowly took her hand from his. Her wide eyes searched his face. "It must be that you suspect me of the murders. You think that, in my madness over Orfeo, I came here secretly from Belgirate and killed Lodovico."

He did not answer.

"I see." She walked a little away. "Then good night, Signor Kestrel. Don't you think it rather funny that such a famous beauty should be rejected by two gentlemen in one night?"

"De la Marque wasn't willing to pay your price."

"And you?"

"I doubt very much, Marchesa," he said quietly, "that you would be willing to pay mine."

He went out, crossed the hall, and entered his own room. MacGregor had gone to sleep, leaving a lamp burning on a table by the door. When Julian came in, he started up. "Everything all right?"

"Yes," said Julian briefly and untruthfully.

MacGregor nodded and fell asleep again.

Julian did not bother to ring for Dipper, but undressed, washed, cleaned his teeth, and blew out the lamp. He got into bed beside MacGregor, and lay for a long time gazing up into the darkness, waiting for a dawn that could only bring him sorrow and regret.

CHAPTER 35

Julian awoke the next morning resolved to proceed in a businesslike manner with his trip to Milan and its aftermath. He tried to think of himself as an actor in a play—the lines already written, the ending already resolved, and his own task merely to perform his part as well as he could, and to see that no one made any untoward entrances or exits. He dressed and breakfasted early, intending to leave by eight o'clock. Just before he departed, he and Dipper went up to Dipper's room on the attic floor for the confidential talk that Julian had been planning last night.

The other servants had long since left their rooms to go about their work, but all the same Dipper had a look up and down the hall and in the rooms on either side before he and Julian closeted themselves in his room. It was simply but comfortably furnished, with a boxlike oak wardrobe, a small iron washstand, two cane chairs, and a bed large enough for half-a-dozen people, although only Dipper and two other menservants slept there. A murky painting of Madonna and Child hung on the wall; the wood floor beneath was worn away by servants' knees.

Julian said, "You know that this trip to Milan may be decisive. If Palmieri confirms my theory, we shall be in a fair way of solving these murders. I want you to keep a close watch while I'm away. I don't think our fox will break covert, but if it does, I should like to know which way it ran. But don't on any account go in pursuit: this fox is deadly enough without being cornered."

"Yes, sir."

Julian frowned and took a turn about the room. "The risk is that I may not be able to see Palmieri in time. We know he was in Milan a few days ago, because Rinaldo said he'd consulted him about his effort to wrest the villa from the marchesa. Actually, it's a mercy he made that threat—otherwise we shouldn't have known who the family lawyer was. But I can't be certain of finding him today. And I can't stay the night, because the three days' respite Grimani gave Lucia will be over this evening, and devil only knows what he'll do to her." Julian stopped walking abruptly and looked at Dipper. "If for any reason I don't return in time, you must protect her."

Dipper stared back, wide-eyed. "What do you want me to do, sir?"

"Whatever you must." Julian took up his hat, gloves, and walking-stick, and they left the room in silence.

The door to the wardrobe slowly opened. Nina put out her head, looked around to see if the coast was clear, and darted out. She paused before the Madonna, crossed herself, and whispered a quick prayer. Then she was gone.

Julian left the villa without seeing Beatrice. He heard she had a headache and was passing the morning in her room. He told himself he was fortunate to have avoided a meeting. But all the same he felt an ache of regret.

One of the servants rowed him from the villa pier as far as Como. There he hired a post-chaise to take him to Milan.

His progress was slower than he had hoped. The roads were clogged with waggons bearing tubs of grapes to the winepress. Each waggon was drawn by six or eight grey oxen, their horns tipped with steel, their girths bedecked with flowers. The grapes were secured with such a mass of iron rings and chains that the oxen could only move at a funeral pace. Julian's postillions cursed ferociously and passed them when they could.

It was one o'clock by the time the post-chaise reached Milan. Julian proceeded to Casa Malvezzi. Much as he wanted to see Palmieri, he felt a duty to Francesca to call on her children first. He had letters from her and from Carlo, the children's presumptive guardian, authorizing their tutor, Abbé Morosi, to admit him. Morosi proved to be an earnest young cleric in spectacles. He told Julian he had already broken the news of Rinaldo's death to Niccolò and Bianca. "Of course they are very distressed," he said gravely. "They adored their father."

Julian found this hard to imagine. But perhaps Rinaldo had looked different through his children's eyes. "May I see them?"

Morosi conducted him to the nursery and presented him to the nine-year-old marchese and his sister. Bianca was a slight child with eyes too big for her face and soft brown hair like her mother's. Niccolò had nothing of either parent about him. He was tall for his age, with black hair, hazel-gold eyes, and a slightly beaked nose—the youthful image of Lodovico.

Both children seemed in good health, though pale and in need of sleep. Bianca was unabashedly frightened and distressed, but Niccolò held up his head and tried to speak like a man. "Have the police found out yet who killed Papa, Signor Kestrel?"

"No, Signor Marchese. But I think they may be very close." Julian took a seat, so that his eyes were on a level with theirs. "I have a message for you from your mother."

"From Mamma?" Bianca clasped her hands. "Is she better?"

Julian was not sure how to answer this.

Morosi interceded hastily, "It's been a great grief to the children that their mother is too ill to live with them."

"She lives with the nuns," said Bianca shyly. "She's been with them for years. But Papa always said she would come home when she was well enough."

"Will she be coming home?" Niccolò asked.

"She's much better," said Julian. "She hopes to come home very soon. In the meantime, she asked me to give you her love, and to tell you that she never ceases to think of you and counts the moments till she sees you again."

"Please give her our love, too," said Niccolò quietly. Bianca could only nod, her eyes swimming in tears.

Julian took his leave of them and walked out with Morosi. "Marchesa Francesca was under the impression that they knew why she had gone away."

"Oh, no!" Morosi looked shocked. "Marchese Rinaldo took the greatest care to keep it from them. I'm afraid the boy has begun to guess the truth—he's old enough now to understand servants' gossip. But Marchese Rinaldo always tried to shield them from having to be ashamed of their mother."

Julian was glad he could relieve Francesca of one of her burdens. For his own part, he was not sure if he thought more of Rinaldo for sparing his children, or less of him for lying so viciously to his wife.

As he was leaving, he casually asked Morosi for Palmieri's address. He hoped Morosi would assume he was seeing the lawyer on some business of the Malvezzis. Sure enough, Morosi not only directed him to Palmieri's chambers but sent for a sediola to take him there.

The chambers were in a little street off Piazza Fontana, convenient to the Palace of Justice. The street was so narrow, the iron-railed balconies nearly met in the middle. Julian rang at the door of a tall house with crumbling mouldings and green shuttered windows. A wizened clerk poked out his head. His gaze ran over Julian's clothes and lingered approvingly on his boots, which showed by their lack of mud that he had come in a carriage.

"What is your business, signor?"

Julian presented his card. "I wish to see Signor Palmieri at once."

"Have you an appointment, signor?"

"No. But I have letters from their Excellencies Marchesa Francesca and Conte Carlo Malvezzi." Julian drew the letters just far enough out of his pocket to show the Malvezzi seal.

Fortunately, the clerk did not ask to read them. He bowed obsequiously and ushered Julian into a small back parlour that looked as if it had been furnished with odds and ends from other houses. Julian supposed Palmieri received few visits from clients in his chambers. Families like the Malvezzis would expect their lawyer to come to them.

The clerk left Julian for a few minutes, then returned and bade Julian follow him upstairs. He waved Julian into a narrow but lofty front room, its walls and ceiling painted with unconvincing *trompe-l'oeil* reliefs. The shutters were nearly closed, leaving the roam in a murky half-light. A thin, dark, elderly man rose from behind a desk. "Signor Kestrel? I am Camillo Palmieri. Please sit down."

They shook hands, then Julian took a chair opposite. Palmieri dismissed his clerk and sat down, tucking a gold-rimmed eyeglass into one eye. "Now then. I understand you have letters for me from my unfortunate clients."

He held out his hand. Julian smiled. "Actually, Signor Palmieri, I came here merely to ask you a question."

"Ah." Palmieri smiled faintly and clasped his hands before him on the desk. "I am sure you understand that I cannot discuss my clients' affairs with a stranger."

"I do understand," said Julian. "My question is simply this. I know that Lodovico Malvezzi married Isotta Marini in 1790. Did he ever go through a second marriage with her?"

Palmieri's eyeglass dropped on the desk with a clink.

"I can even tell you the year," Julian added helpfully, "1793. The marriage was conducted with the greatest secrecy, but Marchese Lodovico was obliged to confide in his family lawyer about it, in case it should ever have to be proved."

"But—but how—?"

"How do I know?" Julian rose, smiling. "I am sure you understand that I cannot discuss my friends' affairs with a stranger. Thank you for seeing me, Signor Palmieri. Good afternoon."

On leaving Palmieri's chambers, Julian began to reflect that he had not eaten for eight hours. He wanted to return to the lake at once, but he knew he could not afford to let his strength lapse. He betook himself to a little blue-awninged café in the bustling Corsia dei Servi. Over millet bread and strong coffee, he realized his next move was not so simple as he had supposed.

If he laid his evidence before Grimani, would Grimani act on it? Or would his mistrust and dislike of Julian hold him back from accepting a solution to the murders at Julian's hands? It would be disastrous if the murderer were warned of the impending danger, yet left at liberty. Then, too, there was always the chance that Julian might meet with some misadventure on the road. He must not be the only person who had all the information needed to make his case.

He needed an ally in Milan, and there was only one person he could turn to. He took a last swallow of coffee and set off quickly for Conte Raversi's palace.

Raversi received him as if he had been hovering in anxious expectancy ever since Julian came to see him a fortnight ago. "Signor Kestrel, words cannot express my shock and concern when I heard that my poor friend's son had died in the same brutal manner as his father. What in the name of the Virgin Mary could the Carbonari have had against Rinaldo? Or was it enough for them that he was Lodovico's son?"

"Signor Conte, I believe I know why both murders were committed, and by whom."

He unfolded his solution. Raversi listened in increasing astonishment. When the story was concluded, he crossed himself and pressed a gaunt white hand to his heart. "That there should be such wickedness! It's beyond belief!"

"But you do believe it, Signor Conte?"

"After what you've told me, Signor Kestrel, I have no choice. But why have you come to me with this story? Why not go to the police?"

"I don't know any senior police official in Milan. And I thought you would be particularly eager to bring this murderer to justice."

"What do you mean?" Raversi searched his face.

"Merely that Marchese Lodovico was your friend, Signor Conte."

Raversi walked back and forth broodingly for a moment "What do you wish me to do?"

"I should be very grateful if you would present my case to the Director-General of Police. Knowing how high you stand in the government's esteem, I'm sure you could do it more effectively than I."

"I see. Very well, I will go with you to the police."

"If you wouldn't mind, Signor Conte, I should like to return to the villa at once. I'm afraid Grimani may harass Lucia in my absence." Julian thought a moment. "I should be very grateful if you would do me one last service."

"What is that?"

"Will you write a letter for me to take to Grimani, requesting that he take our suspect into custody pending official instructions from Milan? Without the backing of a man of your rank and importance, I can't answer for his cooperation. And it's vital that we act quickly, if we're to take our quarry unawares."

"As you wish, Signor Kestrel."

Raversi sat down at his battered writing-table and composed a letter briefly stating Julian's case against the suspect and bidding Grimani make an arrest. He gave it to Julian to read, then folded it up very small, addressed it to Grimani, and sealed it with his family device, a mermaid blowing a horn.

"Shall I order you a post-chaise to the lake?" Raversi asked.

"You're very kind. Thank you."

The two men shook hands. When Raversi would have withdrawn his, Julian held it a moment longer. "I want you to know that I'm very grateful to you."

Raversi searched Julian's face again. But Julian only smiled, bowed, and waited for Raversi to ring for the post-chaise.

To Julian's exasperation, the roads to the lake were still choked with waggons of grapes. He did not reach Como till nearly eight in the evening. At least he had no difficulty finding a boat to take him to the villa: the harbour was full of idle craft. He beckoned to one of the boatmen, who nosed his boat up alongside the pier so that Julian could board.

Julian got in. "Why are there so many of you in the harbour?"

"There's been a terrible storm, signor! One moment the afternoon sun was smiling on us—the next, the winds swept down, lightning filled the sky, thunder roared like a thousand cannons, and the lake churned with waves fit to crack our boats like nuts. It's over now, thank Santa Pelagia, but those of us who were caught in it weren't in any hurry to venture out again!"

As he talked, the boatman took his place standing in the bow and pushed away from the pier with his long oar. The boat glided into the open lake, the lantern in the prow cutting a gold swathe through the water. The night air was mild, the sky clear and flecked with stars. It was hard to believe a violent storm could have raged so recently. But the weather on the lake was famous for its treachery.

There were few boats out even now. But just as Julian made out the lights of the villa in the distance, a boat slid out of the shadows along the bank and headed toward them. The lantern in the prow showed a large, muscular figure plying the oar.

The boat cut smoothly in front of Julian's, stopping it in its course. The man in the prow leaned down, peering through the gloom. The lantern light caught the glint of gold rings in his ears. "Signor Kestrel?"

"Good evening, Guido," said Julian.

"Good evening, signor." Guido sounded anxious. "Have you seen my master?"

"No. I've only just arrived from Milan."

"He went out rowing before the storm, and he hasn't come back." Guido turned to the boatman. "Have you seen him?"

"No," said the boatman. "I pray he's not drowned. Poor gentleman, he handled a boat better than any Excellency I ever saw."

Guido shook his head somberly. "If you see him, will you tell him I'm out looking for him, and the people at the villa are getting worried?"

"I will," the boatman promised.

"I almost forgot, Signor Kestrel." Guido reached into his pocket. "I have a letter for you. You may want to read it at once. I was told it was important."

He handed Julian a folded paper. The boatman unhooked the lantern from the prow and placed it on the seat in front of Julian, so that he could see. Julian unfolded the paper. A lock of brown hair fell out.

Julian's heart jerked. He held the letter to the light. It was in English, in Carlo's firm, flowing hand:

> *I am sorry to resort to these measures, but you* would *interfere. When I learned you intended to see Palmieri in Milan, I could take no further chances.*
>
> *I have your servant, and the girl Nina as well. You will see from the lock of your servant's hair that I speak the truth. We are awaiting you at the caves. Even now Guido will be making a signal to let me know that you are reading this letter.*

Julian looked up. Guido had unhooked his boat lantern and was waving it up and down and from side to side in an immense sign of the cross. If Carlo were watching from the foot of the crag, outside the caves, he could not fail to see that light sweeping the darkness.

> *When you finish reading it, you will give it back to Guido. Then you will get into his boat and let him bring you to me. If you are not at the caves with him fifteen minutes after I see his signal, then you may come at your leisure, and bury whatever is left of your servant and the girl.*

Julian drew a long breath, controlling his anger—controlling, too, the wave of panic rising in his chest. What had he done to Dipper—Dipper, who had begged him to stay out of this investigation? Of course, Carlo might be bluffing—might not have Dipper at all—but Julian could not gamble with Dipper's life. He had no illusion about what lay before him. His going to the caves would not bring about Dipper's and Nina's release. Carlo could not afford to let any of them live. Yet Julian must do as he demanded, and quickly. Fifteen minutes was barely enough time to reach the caves.

Julian's boatman had been watching Guido's manoeuvres with the lantern curiously. "What are you doing?"

"It's a custom in Naples," said Guido. "We do it for luck, after a storm." He leaned toward Julian. "I'm going in the direction of the villa, signor. I'd be happy to take you the rest of the way."

"Thank you." Julian rose and handed him back the letter.

"Now, for the love of the Madonna, that's not fair!" cried the boatman. "I've brought this gentleman nearly all the way, and you want to rob me of my fare—"

"You'll be paid," said Julian. "Here." He reached into his trouser pocket. His hand touched Raversi's letter.

He tucked the letter into his palm, along with as many coins as he could grasp. Under cover of darkness, he put both coins and letter into the boatman's hand. The boatman stared. "Signor—"

"Isn't it enough?" asked Julian quellingly.

"Y-yes, signor. But—"

"Then good night." Julian stepped into Guido's boat, and Guido rowed quickly away.

The boatman gazed after them blankly. Julian prayed that he could read, or if he could not, that he would have the sense to take the letter to the villa. It would not tell the villa party where Julian was, but at least it would reveal Carlo's guilt and suggest there was something sinister about Julian's disappearance. Search parties might be sent out. But could they arrive in time?

Julian had little hope of that. He must watch, think, make the most of his opportunities. There would be no second chances now.

Once Guido had pulled well away from the boatman, he shipped his oar and stepped to the middle of the boat where Julian sat. Plumping down in the seat opposite, he drew out a pistol and pointed it at Julian's heart. With his free hand, he felt in Julian's pockets. Finding Julian's pistol, he tossed it over the side of the boat.

"Was that really necessary?" said Julian. "You've broken up a pair."

"You won't have any use for them now." He threw Julian's bullets and powder flask after it, then thrust the oar into Julian's hand. "Here. You row. And remember, I'm watching you all the time, and if you make any sudden move, I'll shoot you dead."

Julian rose and began to ply the oar with quick, deliberate strokes. Guido burned Carlo's letter in the boat lantern. Then he drew out a second pistol—he was taking no chances his first shot might miss—and kept both barrels trained on Julian as he rowed.

"I must say," Julian observed, "your master has managed all this with his usual discretion. The boatman saw you with me, but Conte Carlo has contrived not to be seen at all."

"That's no matter. I'll let on that the note I brought was from your servant, and you asked to be set down on the shore to look for him, and that's the last I saw of you."

"That won't be very convincing, once the police realize you were the last person to see me alive."

"That won't mean much, because no one will ever see you dead. It's hard to prove a murder without a body, signor—very hard."

"You mean to throw me in the lake? That can be dragged."

"Not the lake. We have something else in mind. You're going to disappear, signor. Just like Tonio."

CHAPTER 36

When Julian's and Guido's boat drew near the promontory, Guido took the lantern from the prow and closed the shutter, rendering them all but invisible to any night fishermen who might be abroad. Then he ordered Julian to row around to the side of the promontory away from the villa. Straining to see by the faint moonlight, Julian guided the boat around the crag and concealed it in a rocky inlet. They got out, Guido still covering Julian with both pistols.

Guido hung the lantern on his wrist by an iron ring at the top. Then he opened the shutter enough to let out a sliver of yellow light. He and Julian began climbing over the rocks toward the cave mouth. Julian remembered Carlo's telling him how pirates used to hide their boats behind the crag and creep over these rocks to steal wine from the caves. *The lake was a lawless place in those days,* Carlo had said. From Julian's perspective, it had not much changed.

Their progress was agonizingly slow. How many of the precious fifteen minutes were they consuming, getting over these great, ungainly rocks—wedging their feet in hollows, slipping on lake wash, tearing their trousers and skin on knife-like protrusions? Each time Guido stumbled, he cursed fiercely in Neapolitan, and Julian knew that here was an opportunity for him to jump into the lake and escape—and, of course, leave Dipper and Nina to die. He clambered on, using feet and hands to propel him forward, like a monkey.

At last they reached level ground. It was only a few more steps to the cave mouth. Carlo was waiting just inside, looking out through the curtain of blood-red creeper, a double-barrelled pistol in each hand. "Come in, come in," he said affably, under his breath.

Julian passed into the great round cave known as the Salon, Guido behind him. "I'm delighted to see you, Mr. Kestrel," Carlo continued. "Also a little relieved, I must confess. I couldn't be certain my stratagem would fetch you. It was hard to believe that even an Englishman would give up his life for his servant."

"I'm sure there's no danger of your making such a gesture," said Julian, for Guido's benefit. "Where is my servant?"

"I shall take you to him." Carlo made a motion with his guns, indicating that Julian was to go before him to the trapdoor at the center of the cave.

The trapdoor lay open, a lantern beside it. Guido went down the ladder first, then Julian. Carlo waited above, holding his lantern over the trapdoor and pointing a gun at Julian, so that Julian was lit and covered from both above and below. The silence closed over him as he descended, leaving only the sounds of this dark, enclosed world. Guido's harsh, heavy breathing filled his ears; his own footsteps steadily marked his descent, like the drums leading up to an execution.

He reached the bottom and felt the familiar haunting sensation of being under water. The lantern light was suffused with the blues and greens of the mosaics on the walls and vaulted ceiling. Exotic fish stared from all sides; plants seemed to reach out living tentacles for prey. I am going to die in an under-sea fantasy, Julian thought. His investigator's mind, like a disembodied thing, tried to make sense of this prospect. *Why* am I going to die here? What can they possibly do with my body? They'll only have to drag it up again—

There were strained murmurs behind him. He turned. Dipper and Nina stood close together, their backs to the wall. Julian perceived that their four wrists were bound together behind them and tied to an iron bracket. Their mouths were stopped with linen rags. Dipper's eyes above the gag were full of anguished remorse at the sight of his master. Julian's throat closed. Not a whit of reproach, although this horror is all my fault—

He beat down his guilt. It was a luxury he could not afford. He turned back toward the ladder, where Carlo was just descending. On reaching the bottom, he set his lantern on the floor and levelled both his guns at Julian. Guido covered Dipper and Nina.

"You have four guns between you," said Julian. "Surely you can untie them now, or at least take off their gags."

"You may do that yourself presently," said Carlo. "You'll have time for that before you die."

He's enjoying this, Julian thought. All the better, if it makes him prolong it. I must keep him talking. Every moment of delay is precious. "Why is Nina here?"

"She was the bait we used to catch your servant," said Carlo.

"She was in league with you?"

"No, no," laughed Carlo. "She was the victim of her own jealousy. Guido told her he'd been to Solaggio and heard Rosa bragging that Dipper was coming to see her tonight. Poor little Nina was in despair. Guido counselled her, 'You must ask Dipper to walk with you this evening—away from the village, toward the caves.' Nina did exactly as she was told. She and Dipper went walking here after the storm, and Guido and I were waiting."

"We're wasting time," muttered Guido.

"Bah!" said Carlo. "There's no hurry. No one will intrude on us here. These grottos are reputed to be haunted, and the servants never like to come here after dark. Besides, we're all accounted for, more or less. People think I was caught in the storm, and you're out searching for me. These two are lovers"—he glanced toward Dipper and Nina—"so their disappearing together won't excite remark. And Mr. Kestrel will simply appear to have been delayed."

"The gardens are swarming with soldiers," Guido reminded him.

"Yes, my chicken-hearted friend, but they're Germans, which means they do everything according to a precise, methodical pattern. I've observed their rounds, and they never come anywhere near the caves. Why should they? They have no reason to think anything sinister will happen here."

"That's no reason to take chances," Guido insisted. "We ought to kill them and be done with it."

Nina whimpered through her gag. Dipper looked at her sympathetically. Julian said to Guido, "Not a very fitting sentiment from one of your calling."

Guido's eyes narrowed, and his thumb tapped tensely on the barrel of his pistol.

"We knew you'd guessed that," Carlo remarked. "You must have suspected it very early, else why would you have tried to find out if Guido knew Latin?"

Julian shrugged. "I happened on the knowledge that he could read and write, which I thought surprising in a Neapolitan of his class. Not only would he have had little opportunity to learn—he would have seen little need. But there's one large body of men in Naples for whom literacy is essential. Once I discovered that Guido understood Latin, I was certain he had been one of their number. Or rather, he still is—I believe a Catholic priest remains ordained to the end of his life, and however debased he becomes, the sacraments he administers are binding."

Carlo's face hardened. "That is correct. I suppose it has occurred to you by now that you're too clever for your own good?"

"At the moment, I can find it in my heart to wish I were a little more obtuse."

Carlo smiled suddenly, giving Julian a glimpse of his everyday self—the courteous patrician, the charming courtier, the warm-hearted liberal. The man was so *likeable.* No wonder he had come so far.

The next moment his smile faded, and the murderer looked out of his eyes again. "I've watched you gathering all the strands together bit by bit. You expressed doubt that my brother would have contracted a mock marriage. You studied our family tree. You warned Francesca not to bring Niccolò here. But I consoled myself by thinking that you couldn't have any proof. Then I found out you intended to see Palmieri."

"How did you know that?" Julian asked.

"Once again, I have little Nina to thank. Soon after we came to the lake, I began to think I had better find some way to keep abreast of what you suspected, and what you were going to do. Guido reported to me that your servant was both loyal and clever, which meant we couldn't bribe or trick him into betraying your plans. So we set Nina to spy on him. It was quite easy. Guido befriended her—a priest knows how to make women talk—and in no time at all she was pouring out to him that she feared Dipper was deceiving her with Rosa. Guido told her she must find proof—watch his every move, listen to his conversations, steal his letters. She did—and of course brought every tidbit she discovered to Guido to be talked over.

"This morning she was in Dipper's room looking for love-tokens from Rosa, when she heard you and Dipper coming and hid in the wardrobe. She heard your whole conversation. Of course she didn't understand very much of it, since it was in English, but she heard you mention Palmieri's name twice. She told Guido as much. I suppose Palmieri gave you the information you wanted?"

Julian saw no point in pretending otherwise. "Yes. I know that Marchese Lodovico secretly married his wife Isotta a second time in 1793. And I know why."

"The strange thing is," mused Carlo, "that it never occurred to me he'd resorted to such a simple expedient. When Guido sought me out and told me how he'd married my brother to Giulietta Petroni all those years ago, all that mattered to me was that Giulietta was alive when Lodovico married Rinaldo's mother. That made Lodovico a bigamist, Rinaldo a bastard, and me Lodovico's direct heir." His tips twisted. "I never thought to ask if Giulietta was still living when Rinaldo was born."

Julian forbore to explain how he had made the deductions he had. He wanted to entice Carlo to talk, not to trumpet his own acuteness. "You'd known nothing of Lodovico's marriage to Giulietta until Guido told you of it?"

"No, nothing. But Guido's story made sense of a good deal I hadn't understood before. My poor brother!" Carlo laughed with bitter satisfaction. "He must have been off his head when he realized what an act of folly he'd committed in marrying a singer. He couldn't get an annulment without making the marriage public, and he would sooner have cut his own throat—if you'll pardon the allusion—than braved our father's anger. In the end he rid himself of Giulietta by convincing her, with Guido's help, that Guido was no priest, and the marriage was no marriage. But when he returned to Milan from Naples, our father began pressuring him to take a wife. He was the eldest; it was his duty to produce an heir. He resisted for a long time—I couldn't fathom why. But in the end he was more frightened of our father than he was of committing bigamy. But why should I tell you all this? You've obviously guessed."

He straightened, suddenly businesslike. Guido stood to attention. Julian felt his sands running out. He said quickly, "I haven't guessed everything. I don't understand, for instance, why Guido waited more than thirty years to tell you about Giulietta."

"Lodovico paid him off and insisted he leave Italy," said Carlo. "He went to Spain, where he led a distinctly unclerical life and eventually was put in prison. When he got out, he was penniless. He came to me and offered to sell me his information about Lodovico's marriage to Giulietta. I persuaded him to let me have it on account, with the promise that he would be well paid—when I became Marchese Malvezzi."

"Which you proceeded to arrange," said Julian. "Which of you actually killed Lodovico?"

"I did," said Carlo. "And now, Mr. Kestrel—"

"I must say, you accomplished it brilliantly," said Julian. "You didn't leave the slightest trace that could identify you. You even thought to use a piece of paper ruled with musical staffs as a wad. I suppose you hoped to implicate Orfeo?"

"The thought occurred to me," Carlo acknowledged. "Of course I didn't know he would be so obliging as to disappear, and so bring suspicion on himself—or that Conte Raversi would be such an ass as to keep the murder a secret, and thus make a hash of the initial investigation."

Carlo smiled reminiscently. "Fortune favoured me from the beginning. I travelled from Parma to Milan with Guido, then sent Guido to the lake to reconnoitre. A few days later he brought the word that my brother planned to spend the night nearly alone at the villa. I was at the lake by nightfall, and rowed out in a boat Guido had stolen for me. I intended to go to the villa, but I saw the light in the belvedere and decided to investigate, hoping I would find Lodovico there. As, of course, I did."

"You climbed up the embankment into the garden, I suppose."

"Yes." Carlo cocked his head at Julian appraisingly. "I notice you haven't asked how Guido found out that Lodovico would be all but alone at the villa that night?"

"No," said Julian, with interest. "How did he know?"

Carlo smiled unpleasantly. "Don't pretend you haven't guessed. Guido got it out of Tonio, whom he met in the village after Tonio had got the sack. This, of course, made Tonio's continued existence inconvenient. So in the morning, Guido sought out Tonio and told him Lodovico had been killed. He warned Tonio that he would be suspected of the crime—after all, Lodovico had brought about his dismissal only yesterday. The boy was in such a panic, he didn't stop to reflect that he had an alibi. Guido persuaded him to hide here in the grottos until nightfall. He was never seen again—just as you and your servant and his sweetheart will never be seen again."

Julian cast about for another question. "How did you know I would come back from Milan alone tonight? I might have had a troop of police at my back."

"I didn't know," said Carlo. "But desperate straits call for desperate measures. I had two choices: flight or attack. Flight would have been too costly. And if I attacked and lost, I would at least have the satisfaction of bringing you down with me."

He came closer, stepping out of the light of the lantern at his feet, so that Julian only saw him in outline and heard the scowl in his voice. "I've had one disappointment after another. The fall of Napoleon left my life in ruins. Lodovico had everything, and I had nothing. In Parma I was a mere courtier—a lapdog to the Archduchess—I, who had been one of the chief ministers of the Kingdom of Italy! For six years I struggled to rebuild my fortunes and support my children, but I only slid deeper and deeper into debt. And then Guido came, and offered me Lodovico's rank and wealth and all he possessed, if only I could eliminate that one life standing in my way.

"My plan was that, as Lodovico's executor, I would miraculously 'discover' his marriage to Giulietta. But when I met with Palmieri to discuss Lodovico's estate, he told me how he had helped Lodovico arrange a secret second marriage to Isotta." Carlo laughed harshly. "Lodovico had said he feared there was an irregularity in the first marriage! Palmieri, being the soul of discretion, never asked what the irregularity was. But he thought I should know, as executor, that whatever it was, it had been corrected before Rinaldo was born.

"I was staggered. I had killed my brother for nothing. Rinaldo and Niccolò both stood between me and the title. I couldn't kill all three of them and hope to escape detection. Who would have had a motive but me?"

"My life became more wretched than ever. I had to play the affectionate uncle to Rinaldo, who had everything I wanted. And I had to keep this one with me." He jerked his head at Guido. "He knew what I'd done. If he got safely away, he might betray me. I had to endure his demands for money and the insulting tone he thought he could take with me, once I'd stooped to become his fellow criminal. For years it went on! And then—"

Carlo breathed hard. "My chance came again. I had the perfect opportunity to kill Rinaldo and throw the blame on Francesca. With both of them gone, I would have charge of Niccolò and could deal with him at my leisure. But I must have been born under an unlucky star—fated to win battle after battle, only to have the prize snatched away. Valeriano revealed he was the son of Lodovico and Giulietta, and that gave you the information you needed to piece together what I'd done, and why. Do you know what it means to steel yourself to commit two murders, and have both of them rendered futile? I had no one to punish the first time it happened. But, by the Madonna, you will suffer for it now!"

"There's something you don't know," said Julian. "Before I left Milan I entrusted my evidence against you to Conte Raversi, and he promised to lay it before the Director-General of Police. So you'll gain nothing by killing us, except to increase the number of murders for which you'll be held accountable."

Carlo's whole body stiffened. "I'm not sure I believe you. But if you really have denounced me, I have little to lose. What worse punishment could befall me for six murders than for three? And Guido and I may still be able to escape before the local police have cause to suspect us."

"Not if we keep hanging an arse here," Guido rasped. "Let's have done with this, Master!"

"Very well," said Carlo. "We'll bring this comedy to a close."

Julian dared not reveal how he had slipped Raversi's letter to the boatman. If Carlo thought he was in imminent danger of arrest, he might shoot them all out of hand. "Let them go," Julian urged, glancing toward Dipper and Nina. "I'm the only one who's seen Palmieri. They don't understand what we've been saying, and the authorities wouldn't take their word over yours in any case."

"Very heroic," Carlo sneered. "But I don't doubt for a moment that your servant is in your confidence. And surely little Nina wouldn't want to live without her lover."

Nina sobbed and twisted in her bonds. Julian knew he must do something—but there was nothing left to do. A numbing exhaustion crept over him. His lungs were parched for a breath of fresh air. He felt the dry, dead cold of this place in all his bones. Every scrape and bruise he had got climbing over the rocks ached. There was no hope left, only a faint curiosity about how he was going to die—

He must not give up. He would soon have all eternity to rest in. *Concentrate.* There is always something more to do. Kick over one of the lanterns? No, the other would still provide light enough to shoot Dipper and Nina. Start a scuffle? Not while they were such helpless targets.

"We'll go up now," Carlo was saying. "Mr. Kestrel, you may come with us. This will interest you."

"He'll try to get away," Guido warned.

"You don't understand the English," said Carlo. "Mr. Kestrel will never abandon the ship while his crew remains in danger. And, really, it seems only right, after promising him a tour of the caves, to show him the sights I omitted when we were here last. Go ahead of us, Guido: I'll cover him from the rear!"

Cursing under his breath, Guido ascended the ladder. Carlo slung the ring of his lantern over his right wrist, leaving both hands free to cover Julian with his guns.

Julian ascended the ladder, Carlo following. The air above ground, even inside the cave, was deliciously fresh. Julian took several deep breaths and felt his head clear, his senses sharpen.

He gazed around the Salon. Its walls looked white and bleak in the lantern light, every fissure and pockmark thrown into relief. Nothing could be hidden there. In all the Salon, there was not a spot that could mask a mystery. Except—

Yes, Carlo and Guido were bringing him to the little marble pool, with its rectangular basin hollowed out of the ground and its back, some three feet high and four feet wide, set into the cave wall. At the centre of the back, the small grotesque face stared out, its mouth in an astonished *O*, the nozzle protruding from it. While Carlo covered Julian, Guido set down his lantern, put his guns in his pockets, and took hold of the nozzle with both hands. He wrenched it sharply to the left and twisted it.

With a long, low moan, the marble back of the pool swung slowly outward. Guido took up his lantern again, revealing a recess, hardly big enough for a man to stand upright or lie at full length. There appeared to be nothing in it but a large horizontal drum, with a chain wound several times around it and a winch at the side. The other end of the chain seemed to disappear through an opening in the ground.

Carlo's eyes shone. "You remember my telling you about Achille Delborgo, Mr. Kestrel—the man who built the grottos two centuries ago? I showed you his little trick of hanging a mirror at the end of a passage in the grottos, to frighten guests. But that was only a trifle. Now you are about to see his *pièce de résistance*."

Guido crawled into the recess, lantern in hand, and crouched before the winch. Julian was preposterously reminded of a surly dog looking out of its kennel. "Now, Master?" he grunted.

"Now," said Carlo.

Guido grasped the winch with both hands and leaned into it with all his strength. It yielded. Panting with the effort, he forced it round and round. The chain clanked fiercely as more and more of it coiled around the drum. From below in the grottos came a rumbling, like some underworld god disturbed.

"That's enough," said Carlo.

Guido stopped. In the sudden silence, his heavy breathing resounded through the cave. He still gripped the winch—half lay on it, using his weight to help hold it in place. Julian realized that if he let it go, the drum would spin out of control, the chain unwind, and—what would happen?

"Come, Mr. Kestrel," said Carlo. "You must be curious to see what the mechanism is for." He shot a look at Guido. "Whatever you do, don't let go of that winch until I give the signal."

Guido nodded, wasting no strength on speech. Carlo drove Julian before him to the ladder and made him descend. Julian heard Carlo following and thought of seizing him by the foot.

But Carlo stayed just out of reach, while keeping Julian within range of his guns.

When they got to the bottom, Carlo went to Nina and held one gun to her temple, while with his other hand he drew a knife and cut the rope that tied her wrists and Dipper's to the bracket. Their four wrists remained bound together behind, their gags in place. "Now," said Carlo, "go ahead of me, all of you—that way."

He herded the three of them toward the blocked passage with the mirror at the end. Dipper and Nina shuffled and stumbled, trying to walk with their wrists linked behind. The four of them entered the passage, and the light from Carlo's lantern danced in the mirror—but the mirror was in the wrong place. It was leaning against the side of the passage, and the narrow wall at the end, where it had hung, was not there at all. Carlo held his lantern aloft, and Julian saw that the wall had risen up along grooves on either side, so that what was once a wall was now an open doorway.

"So that's what the chain is for," he said.

"Yes," said Carlo. "I call this wall the portcullis, because it can be raised like the gate of a castle. You can see that it all but disappears into the space between the ceiling of the passage and the floor of the cave above. Unfortunately, there's no way to keep it lifted except to hold onto the winch handle. And as I don't want to tax Guido's strength too long, you will oblige me by passing through."

Julian, Dipper, and Nina walked under the portcullis into utter darkness. Carlo stepped in after them, and his lantern burned away a little of the gloom. Nina screamed and dropped to her knees, dragging Dipper down with her. Julian gazed around him, somehow not at all surprised to find that Carlo had thrust them into Hell.

It was actually another grotto room about the size of the one they had left. But, instead of whimsical marine motifs, the walls were covered with scenes of the punishment of sinners. Naked bodies plummeted into fires, struggled on hooks, had their sides torn open by demons and their living entrails dragged out. Angels looked down from above and wrung their hands. Lightning gleams shot out from gilding and fragments of mirror, giving a terrible life to the scene.

"Welcome to the Day of Judgement," said Carlo, "the finest of Achille's tricks. He would have the mirror removed and the portcullis raised, so that the guests would walk innocently in here, thinking it was merely another grotto. And while they were suffering agreeable terrors at the sight that met their eyes, Achille would drop the portcullis and trap them inside. All meant to be harmless fun, no doubt, but I suspect that it led to someone's death, even if only by mischance. That would explain the dark legends that cling to the grottos. It would also account for why the existence of the portcullis was hushed up. I learned of it from some obscure papers that came to me when I purchased the villa. I experimented with the mechanism and found that it still worked. But I kept it to myself—even after I sold the villa to Lodovico."

Julian was only half listening. His eyes were on a dark shape on the floor just inside the entrance. Carlo held his lantern toward it, revealing a human form lying face down. Buff trousers and a brown jacket pooled about its skeletal frame. One hand, coated with shrivelled, blackened skin, was stretched out toward the portcullis. Julian's heart twisted. *Tonio.*

He said, "You might at least have killed him before you left him here."

"He didn't suffer long," Carlo shrugged. "Once the portcullis is closed, there's no means for air to enter. I suppose that's why he's so little decayed, even after four and a half years. Now then: you will all be good enough to step back."

Carlo advanced on them, both guns levelled, compelling them to back away from the entrance. Julian thought of making a desperate rush at him. But that would be suicide. Carlo's pistols were double-barrelled: he could miss once and still have bullets enough for all three of them before he would have to reload.

Having driven them well away from the entrance, Carlo began backing toward it. In a matter of moments, he would step out of the Day of Judgement and give the signal, and Guido would drop the portcullis—

"I'll leave you the light, so that you can take proper leave of each other." Carlo set the lantern down in the centre of the room. "Goodbye, and God have mercy on your souls."

The signal, thought Julian feverishly. What is the signal? It must be a sound—one high and penetrating enough to carry all the way from the grottos up to the caves. There was only one sound he could think of. He put his fingers to his lips and emitted a piercing whistle.

There was a clatter of chains overhead. The portcullis dropped with a thundering crash. Carlo spun around, trying to get out before it fell. In that moment, Julian rushed at him from behind and shoved him against it.

The shock sent one gun spinning from Carlo's hand to the floor. Miraculously, it did not go off. Julian grasped the other gun by the barrel, squeezing Carlo's wrist with his free hand, till he wrenched the gun away. Carlo twisted free. The remaining gun lay almost at his feet. He lunged at it.

Dipper darted forward, jerking Nina after him, and kicked the gun across the room. Carlo and Julian both dove for it. Julian reached it first. He seized it, rolled over onto his back, and sat up, pointing both guns at Carlo's heart. Carlo froze, then sank slowly back on his haunches.

Julian came to his feet. "Stand up," he said softly.

Carlo rose.

"Take out your knife," Julian went on in the same quiet, deliberate voice, "and lay it on the floor, then back away from it."

Teeth clenched, Carlo obeyed. Julian put one gun in his trouser pocket long enough to pick up the knife and cut Dipper's and Nina's bonds. They flexed their wrists, wincing, and took off their gags, taking in great gulps of air. Nina hid her face in Dipper's shoulder, and he put his arm around her waist.

Julian gave Dipper one of the guns. "Now—"

"Master!"

The voice seemed to come from everywhere and nowhere, filling the room. Dipper and Nina stared around in bewilderment. Julian looked at Carlo. He was gazing up at a point in the vaulted ceiling a few feet above the portcullis. Julian took the lantern and held it up as high as he could.

The ceiling was covered with scenes from Revelation. The Four Horsemen of the Apocalypse seemed to be galloping straight down into the room. The Sons of God and the Daughters of Men twined their naked limbs in savage embraces. Leviathan loomed up above the portcullis, its immense jaws open. Carlo was gazing directly into its mouth.

"Master!" the voice repeated.

"Guido!" Carlo shouted. "Lift the portcullis!"

It must be some sort of pipe, thought Julian, leading down from the recess where the winch mechanism was to Leviathan's mouth.

"Master, what are you doing in there?

"There's been a mishap. Let me out!"

"Why did you give the signal while you were still inside the Day of Judgement?"

"I didn't. Signor Kestrel did."

"I don't like this. Kill them, Master."

Carlo stared helplessly at his former captives pointing his own guns at him. "Guido, damn you, lift the portcullis!"

"Something's gone wrong," said Guido.

"Be calm," warned Julian in a low voice. "Tell him everything is all right."

"Guido." Carlo's voice sank to a growl in his effort to keep it level. "There's nothing amiss. The Englishmen are dead."

"No." Guido's disembodied voice dropped, as if he were speaking half to himself. "I didn't hear any shots. Even without my ear to the pipe, I would have heard that."

"Guido, in the name of God—" Carlo began.

A low, singsong chant began to issue from Leviathan's mouth. They all strained to make out the words.

"My God," whispered Carlo. "The prayer for the dead."

Nina shrieked.

"Guido, you bastard!" Carlo shook his fist up at the ceiling. "You'll pay for this! My sons will track you down! I swear to you, one way or another I'll get out of here and kill you myself!"

It all made inexorable sense, Julian thought. Guido must be finding it altogether too perilous to be tied to Carlo, who had grown so reckless lately, and who would surely bring Guido down with him if he were caught. If Carlo were left here, everyone would assume he had perished in the storm. Even if they suspected foul play, they would not be able to bring it home to Guido. As Guido had said: *It's hard to prove a murder without a body.*

Guido's voice ceased. There was a faint creaking, followed by a distant thump. Then silence.

"He's pushed the back of the fountain into place," said Carlo. "We're completely sealed off—buried alive."

"No!" Nina fell to her knees. "Blessed Madonna, have mercy on us!"

"If you know any way out of here," Julian observed to Carlo, "this would be an excellent time to mention it."

"There is no way out," said Carlo hollowly.

Julian went over to the portcullis and shone the lantern on it. Its dark, shining surface was almost like metal. He tapped on it, and it gave out a dull thud. "Is it wood?"

"Seasoned wood," said Carlo, "six inches thick. A dozen men couldn't break it down."

"Most Holy Madonna," Nina was praying frantically, "if you'll let us out of here, I promise to wear blue for a year—no, no, for the rest of my life—and to go to confession every day and give all my money to the Church—"

Julian walked around the Day of Judgement, lantern in hand. It was oval, about fifteen feet long and ten feet wide. The floor was paved with marble, the walls and ceiling encrusted all over with ghastly mosaics and paintings. He ran his fingers over the walls and tapped on them, but could not find a chink or a hollow sound anywhere.

Nina's prayers had given way to uncontrollable sobbing. Dipper coaxed her up from her knees. "Don't take on. Why, Mr. Kestrel and me, we been in worse scrapes than this, and we always done the trick in the end."

Julian could not think of a scrape that had been quite this dire, but he kept that to himself, as he did the fact that there was barely an inch of candle left in the lantern. He did not want to think what this place would be like when the light was gone.

He told Dipper and Nina how he had given Raversi's letter to the boatman. "If he delivers it to the villa, they'll guess that Carlo is behind our disappearance and send out search parties."

"They won't know where to find us." Carlo seemed to take a perverse satisfaction in the hopelessness of their plight. "Nobody living knows about the portcullis and this room except Guido and ourselves."

"You said you experimented with the portcullis after you purchased the villa," said Julian. "You must have had someone to help you, if only to hold it open while you came in here. And I'll lay any odds you found a use for the device before you sold the villa to Lodovico. Didn't you tell me you were suspected of hiding arms from the Austrians during the final days of the Kingdom of Italy?"

Carlo smiled thinly. "You have a good memory, Mt Kestrel. I did confide the secret to one person: my old gardener, Matteo Landi. But, as you know, he's dead."

"He may have told someone before he died."

"He swore a holy oath never to breathe a word of it, and he was a superstitious man. But never mind. Suppose someone can be found who knows the secret of the portcullis. And suppose the boatman actually delivers Raversi's letter, instead of throwing it in the lake, as is far more likely. That won't be of any consequence to us. Because by the time they come to let us out, we'll have long since run out of air."

"It's a quarter to ten!" Fletcher paced distractedly about the terrace. "Grimani's had Lucia penned up in the billiard room for more than two hours! What is he doing to her?"

"If you ask me," said St. Carr, "Orfeo's not a gentleman, whoever he is. It just isn't the thing, letting a female get into hot water on your account, while you play least in sight and do nothing."

"And if my aunt had been a man, she'd have been my uncle!" Fletcher retorted. "We know that, Beverley! The question is, what are we going to do about it?"

De la Marque shrugged. "What can we do? Mr. Kestrel is resident performer of miracles, and he isn't here."

The three of them glanced toward the balustrade, where MacGregor was walking tensely up and down, watching for Kestrel's boat. The rest of the villa party was scattered about the terrace, paying no heed to the conversation.

Fletcher turned to the marchesa, saying in his awkward Milanese, "Can't Your Ladyship do something to help Lucia? At least make Grimani give her a respite. No one should be questioned for hours without any rest."

The marchesa did not seem to hear. From her seat by the lily pond, she was watching the lake as intently as MacGregor. But after a moment she looked around, saying, "I don't think Commissario Grimani would be willing to hear any more from me about Lucia. It was all I could do to persuade him to bring her here and question her again, instead of committing her to gaol out of hand."

"I know that," said Fletcher, "and I'm grateful. But—"

The villa doors swung open. Grimani stepped out and came swiftly down the stairs, alternately appearing and disappearing as he passed beneath the stairway lamps. Zanetti followed at a prudent distance. Grimani crossed the terrace to join the others, his shoulders set, his eyes narrowed and glinting. "Zanetti!" he rapped out.

Zanetti approached him, quaking. "Signor Commissario?"

"Gather a party of soldiers, and take Lucia to the village gaol. She is to have a crucifix and a blanket—nothing more. And no one is to visit her, not even Don Cristoforo."

"You would deny her religious consolation?" said Donati in dismay.

"This isn't your affair, Maestro!" Grimani snapped. "I advise you to keep to your province, and leave me to mine!"

"Look here, Signor Commissario—" Fletcher began.

"A boat!" MacGregor shouted.

"A boat!" The marchesa ran to join him at the balustrade.

There was indeed a boat approaching the villa pier. The marchesa and MacGregor strained to see who the passenger was. But there was no passenger—only the boatman plying his oar in the prow. The marchesa turned away from the balustrade.

"I know," said MacGregor in halting Milanese. "I hoped it was Kestrel, too."

"He must have been lost in the storm," she said in a low, unsteady voice. "He was determined to return this evening. He would be here if he could."

The boat nosed up to the pier, and the boatman hopped

out. Bruno, who was on duty on the terrace, went down to meet him. "What's your business?" he asked haughtily.

The boatman was a spry, elderly man, with wrinkled brown skin and fingers permanently curled from years of holding an oar. "I should like to see the Englishman."

"Which one?" Bruno puffed out his chest. "We've got a whole parcel, you know."

"The one that's always dressed so smart," said the boatman.

"That'll be Milord Kestrel. And you can't see him—even supposing he *would* see the likes of you—because he hasn't come back from Milan."

"But he has," said the boatman. "I brought him from Como myself, after the storm."

"You're daft, old one."

"I'll show you how daft I am! He gave me this." The boatman pulled a letter from his jacket pocket and thrust it at Bruno. "But I can't read, and I don't know what he wants me to do with it, so I thought I'd best bring it back to him."

Bruno gaped at the seal on the letter. He screwed up his eyes, painstakingly sounding out the words of the address. "*Comm-mis-sario Al-fon-so Gri*— It's for the Commissario! You'd better come with me at once!" He ran up the stairs. "Signor Commissario!"

Everyone came forward to see what the excitement was about. Bruno bowed to Grimani and held out the letter. "The boatman brought this. It's from Conte Raversi. I recognized his seal straightaway, because him and my master—"

"Hold your tongue." Grimani tore the letter open and read it under one of the lamps. When he finished, he lifted startled eyes.

"What is it?" the marchesa urged.

"Signor Kestrel has presented evidence to Conte Raversi that Conte Carlo committed these murders, with the connivance of his servant Guido."

"Carlo?" she breathed. "That's impossible!"

"He couldn't have!" chimed in Francesca. "Why would he kill his own brother and nephew?"

"The letter doesn't go into that." Grimani turned to the boatman, who was hovering behind Bruno. "Where did you get this?"

"S-Signor Kestrel gave it to me, Signor Commissario. I was bringing him here from Como, but Conte Carlo's servant, the Neapolitan, came along and said he would take him the rest of the way. So Signor Kestrel got into his boat."

"Oh, no—" The marchesa put out her hands as if to ward off a blow. "He can't have done so! Why should he, knowing what he knew?"

"I don't know, Your Ladyship. But he did, and they went off—to come here, so I thought. But first Signor Kestrel gave me three times my fare, and also that letter."

"How long ago was this?" Grimani asked.

"I don't know, Signor Commissario. Perhaps an hour. I wasn't sure what to do, you see—I didn't want to make trouble—"

"You know, Dipper's missing, too," said MacGregor. "I haven't seen him in hours."

"So is Nina," said the marchesa.

"Which way did Guido take Signor Kestrel?" Grimani asked the boatman.

"He—he said he'd take him back to the villa—so—"

"So you didn't take any notice." Grimani shook his head. "He'll be dead by now."

The marchesa's colour fled. "You don't know that."

"What are you going to do about this?" MacGregor demanded of Grimani.

The commissario turned to Zanetti. "Gather together all the soldiers stationed in and around the villa. Divide them into parties and have them search the shore north of the villa and the countryside further inland. And send someone out to question any boatmen still on the lake. I'll have Signor Ruga and Comandante Von Krauss arrange a search to the south, in and around the village."

"Yes, Signor Commissario. What about the two soldiers guarding Lucia?"

"They're to remain at their posts outside the billiard room. I don't want anyone taking advantage of this crisis to let her out."

Zanetti bobbed his head and ran off.

"I'm going to write to Ruga and Von Krauss," said Grimani. "I'll be in the library."

He went indoors. The Hall of Marbles was in a flurry, with soldiers streaming in, the news of Carlo's guilt and the Englishman's disappearance spreading like fire among them. Grimani left them to Zanetti. Taking a candle, he went into the library and wrote his notes.

As he was sealing them, Zanetti came in. Grimani handed him the notes. "Have these delivered at once."

"Yes, Signor Commissario. But Signor Commissario, I came to tell you, Lucia is asking for you. She's been banging on the billiard room door and telling her guards she must see you at once."

"Is she ready to talk?"

Zanetti hesitated. "She's ready to talk about something, Signor Commissario. But I don't know what."

Grimani went to the billiard room, which was in a back corner of the villa. The two soldiers standing guard outside the door stood to attention. Grimani unlocked the door and went in.

Lucia ran up to him. "Signor Commissario, thank the Blessed Virgin you've come! I have something to tell you!"

Grimani set his candle on a table, locked the door behind him, and put the key in his coat pocket. "Well?"

"I heard all the noise in the house. I wanted to know what it was about, so I listened to the two soldiers talking outside the door. They said Guido took Signor Kestrel away in a boat, and he and Conte Carlo are going to kill him because he found out they killed the marchese and his son. Signor Commissario, I think I know where they've gone!"

"How would you know that?"

"There's a secret place Conte Carlo knows about. He hid some guns there when the Austrians came back, after the French were beaten. My father helped him. He hadn't any choice—Conte Carlo was his master then. I followed them there one night. I didn't know then what they were doing, but I was worried about Papa—he seemed so afraid."

"Where is this hiding place?"

"I didn't see it for myself. It's underground, in the grottos, and I couldn't go to look at it, or Papa and Conte Carlo would have seen me. But I saw Conte Carlo go down the ladder with some guns, and when he came back, he didn't have them anymore."

"He probably put them in the grottos," said Grimani.

"No, Signor Commissario, because I went down there the next day, and they weren't there. There's some secret place that you can only get to by turning a great handle that's hidden behind the fountain in the Salon."

"This is nonsense," said Grimani.

"It's true! I saw my father do it! He twisted the nozzle of the fountain, like this, and the back of the fountain came away from the cave wall. There was a recess with a great crank inside, and my father turned it and held it in place while Conte Carlo carried the guns down the ladder."

"If there really is such a device, and it was used to hide arms from the Austrians, you ought to have reported it long ago."

"What does that matter now?" she cried impatiently. "The important thing is to prevent another murder. If Conte Carlo and Guido were going to take Signor Kestrel somewhere to kill him, that's where they would have gone! You must go after them and stop them!"

Grimani regarded her with a steady, measuring gaze. At last he said, "I have only your word for it that this hiding place exists. And you've shown yourself to be a thoroughly untrustworthy witness. I can't give any credence to your story."

She stared. "You don't believe me? Why would I lie?"

"Why should I trust you?" he countered.

"But I'm telling the truth! I swear by God and the Madonna and all the saints! What can I do to make you believe me?"

"Give me Orfeo."

She drew in her breath sharply. "But—but you know now he didn't kill Marchese Lodovico or Marchese Rinaldo."

"I want him," said Grimani.

"But why?"

"He's defied the law. He's lurked here, making his presence known but refusing to identify himself. He's mocked my authority, which comes from the Viceroy. I'm not convinced he isn't the murderer. I have no proof of Conte Carlo's guilt except a letter from Conte Raversi, based wholly on Signor Kestrel's evidence. And Signor Kestrel isn't here to give that evidence himself."

"But I'm telling you how to find him," she urged, "if you would only listen!"

"I have listened. And I repeat, I do not believe you."

He turned to go. Lucia ran after him, caught him by the coat-tail. "Let me see the marchesa!"

Grimani turned back to her. "You will see no one. And no one will know what has passed between us. If Signor Kestrel dies in those caves, you will be responsible. I know you don't like him, but are you willing to be his executioner? And not only his—there are two other people missing: his servant and the marchesa's maid."

Lucia wrung her hands. "Blessed Madonna, help me, tell me what to do—"

"The minutes are ticking away, Lucia. They may all be dying. Would Orfeo want that? And if he would, is he worth all this devotion? If you believe he hasn't done anything wrong, then you've nothing to fear for him—"

"You'll find something to use against him! You hate him so much, you might even—" She broke off.

"I might even what?"

She shook her head, saying nothing.

"It's pointless to go on with this," said Grimani. "Good night, Lucia."

"No!" She caught his arm and looked beseechingly into his face. "You would let three people die?"

"It's you who are letting them die. I'm only doing my duty as a policeman."

She let go of his arm and stepped back, breathing hard. He waited. At last she said, "Are those three men here—the ones you brought to me at Signor Ruga's?"

"Yes," said Grimani quickly. "Is Orfeo one of them?"

"Yes." She hung her head. "If you take me to them, I'll point him out to you."

"I'm not to made a game of! Just tell me which one is Orfeo."

"How can I? I don't even know their names." She lifted her chin. "Besides, if I must betray Orfeo, I want to look him in the eyes and tell him why. Even Judas didn't betray our Lord behind his back."

"That's blasphemy! What's more, it's an obvious ruse to warn the man and give him a chance to escape."

"It isn't! I promise I'll go straight to him and give him up to you."

"Will you swear to that by God, the Madonna, and your hope of Heaven?"

"I swear," she whispered.

At about the time that the boatman brought Raversi's letter to the villa, Julian was holding his lantern close to the portcullis to examine it. It was so thick and hard, Carlo's small, sharp knife would not make a dent in it. There was no protrusion on its surface to catch hold of, and nothing with which to lever it up. It was wood, which meant it would burn—but slowly, and in the meantime they would smother in the smoke.

"We could let fly our pops at it, sir." Dipper brandished his pistol hopefully.

Julian shook his head. "That won't answer. A bullet would only lodge in it—or worse, glance off it and hit one of us." He added musingly, "But you've given me an idea. Signor Conte, do you have a powder flask?"

Carlo's hand went involuntarily to his trouser pocket. "Why?"

"Be so good as to lay it on the floor and step away from it."

"What are you going to do?" Carlo persisted.

"If Dipper and Nina agree, I'm going to have a try at blowing up this door."

"You're mad!" Carlo exclaimed. "It's too thick! You'll only kill us with the explosion—or the passage will collapse and seal us up!"

"As we're already quite thoroughly sealed up, I can't see that that makes any odds. And I'm not looking to blow a hole through the portcullis—only to shatter enough timbers to allow us to kick it in." He turned to Dipper and Nina. "What do you say? I think we've a chance of escaping by this means, but Conte Carlo may be right—it may merely seal our doom."

"I'm for having a go, sir," said Dipper.

"Yes, please!" Nina begged. "Anything to get out of here!"

"Very well," said Julian. "Your flask, Signor Conte."

Carlo did not move.

"You must realize," said Julian, "I care very little whether you give it to me, or I kill you and take it."

Carlo pulled the flask from his pocket and threw it down. Nina jumped back in fear.

"It's harmless as long as it isn't lit," Julian assured her.

He came forward and picked it up. It was of copper, pear-shaped, and embossed on either side with the Malvezzi serpent and sword. He shook it, and found it tolerably full. He opened the valve that let powder into the pourer at the tip. Then he stood on a spot about ten paces in front of the portcullis and walked toward it, pouring out a thin trail of powder as he went.

"What is he doing?" Nina asked.

"He's making a fuse," said Carlo.

Julian set down the flask at the foot of the portcullis, the open nozzle touching the end of the end of the trail of powder. "When I light the other end," he explained to Nina, "the flame will travel along the powder till it reaches the flask."

"But won't the powder explode when you light it?" asked Nina.

"Loose powder doesn't explode," said Julian, "it merely burns. Powder explodes when it's tightly packed—which means the powder in the flask should give us a considerable blast."

He went over to where he had left the ropes that had bound Dipper's and Nina's wrists. "Here," he said, giving them to Dipper. "Tie Conte Carlo's hands behind him."

"Is that necessary?" asked Carlo haughtily.

Julian smiled wryly. "Oh, I think no amount of caution could be wasted on you, Signor Conte."

Dipper bound Carlo's hands. Julian glanced around the vaulted room, brows knit. "We had better stand as far to the side as we can. The explosion will blow straight back."

Dipper, Nina, and Carlo retreated to one side of the Day of Judgement and pressed themselves against the wall. Julian took the candle from the lantern and lit the fuse. Then he joined the others by the wall, and they all watched, mesmerized, as the tiny, sparkling, hissing light crept slowly toward the flask.

The night grew so chilly that MacGregor persuaded the marchesa to withdraw from the terrace to the drawing room. There she resumed the same anguished pacing she had been engaged in on the terrace ever since the news of Kestrel's danger had arrived. MacGregor joined his pacing to hers. Francesca and Valeriano sat on the sofa, looking on in silent sympathy. Donati occupied his favourite chair in the corner, Sebastiano standing beside him. St. Carr and Fletcher sat in one of the window embrasures, while de la Marque lounged against the wall close by.

The two soldiers who had been guarding Lucia brought her in. Grimani and Zanetti followed. "Well?" said Grimani to Lucia.

She looked across at de la Marque, St. Carr, and Fletcher. De la Marque straightened, and St. Carr and Fletcher came to their feet. She drew a long breath and went toward them slowly. She passed de la Marque, passed St. Carr, and stood before Fletcher, looking pleadingly into his face. "Forgive me. If I don't denounce you, three people may die. You are Orfeo."

He stared, opened his mouth to speak, then paused, searching her face. His own relaxed into a smile. "I forgive you."

Her eyes closed. She let out a shuddering sigh of relief.

"She's mad!" declared St. Carr. "Hugo is no more Orfeo than I am! Tell them, Hugo!"

"I'm sorry, Beverley." Fletcher's eyes were still on Lucia. "I couldn't tell you before."

St. Carr gaped at him, speechless.

"But this is marvellous!" cried de la Marque. "Of all possible outcomes to the search for Orfeo, this is without a doubt the most delicious! You must sing something for us directly!"

Fletcher looked at him in exasperation. "This is hardly the time for that!"

Grimani was smiling in grim triumph. "Signor Fletcher, I arrest you in the name of the Viceroy of Lombardy-Venetia." He turned to the soldiers. "Take him."

The soldiers came forward and gripped Fletcher by either arm. "You don't have to do that!" Lucia chided. "He wasn't trying to run away!"

"Don't worry, Lucia," said Fletcher.

Her face softened. "Call me Barbarina, as you used to."

"Barbarina, then," he said, smiling.

She turned fiercely to Grimani. "I've given you Orfeo. Now you must save those people before it's too late!"

"It's probably too late already," said Grimani. "But what I can do, I will."

A voice from the doorway said, "I wouldn't dream of putting you to so much trouble, Signor Commissario."

Everyone spun around. Kestrel stood there with Dipper, Nina, and Carlo. Their clothes were torn and dirty, their faces and hands powder-blackened, the stench of sulphur thick about them.

"Thank God!" broke from MacGregor.

Lucia's eyes lit up—then filled with remorse and dismay as they fell on Fletcher.

The marchesa gave a cry, ran past them all, and flung herself into Kestrel's arms.

Julian clasped her close, even as he whispered, laughing, "You'll reek of sulphur!"

"I don't care!" Her voice was muffled in his shoulder. "If you knew what I've been through when I feared I might lose you—lose all chance of mending things between us—" She gave a little gasping sob and drew away from him. "I can't tell you now, but I will—later, when we're alone."

MacGregor, who had been hovering behind her, pressed forward and wrung Julian's hand. "You've given us all a fright I won't soon forget! I did warn you, when you wanted to get mixed up in this investigation—"

"Yes, my dear fellow," said Julian affectionately, "you were entirely right and prudent, and I was entirely foolhardy and rash."

"Well, I wouldn't go so far as to say that," said MacGregor gruffly. "You did solve the murders, and came out of it with a whole skin—though only just!"

Grimani confronted Julian, unsmiling. "Are you prepared to make a statement against Conte Carlo?"

"Very much so," said Julian.

He gave a brief account of how Carlo and Guido had meant to bury them alive in the Day of Judgement, how Carlo had been trapped with them, and how they had blown open the portcullis with the powder flask. The others listened in amazement. There was great curiosity about the Day of Judgement, and the marchesa, suddenly light-hearted, promised they would all go and look at it tomorrow.

"I shouldn't advise that," said Julian. "The passage leading into it is full of debris and may collapse in the wake of the explosion."

"I'll send for workmen to find out if it's safe," she said. "I simply must see it—the scene of your triumph, Giuliano!"

"And someone ought to remove poor Tonio's body and give it a proper burial," said Donati.

Francesca was gazing in troubled bewilderment at Carlo, who stood a little apart, his bound hands behind him, a patrician sneer on his face. "Why did he do it?" she appealed to Julian. "How could he kill his own brother and nephew?"

"We all want to know that," said Beatrice. "But we mustn't tax Signor Kestrel with questions until he's had a chance to rest and change his clothes and take some refreshment. And Nina and Dipper must be ministered to as well. Ring the bell, will you, Sebastiano? I want candles, hot baths, coffee—a great deal of coffee! I'm sure none of us will want to go to bed till Signor Kestrel has told his story!"

Grimani said to Zanetti, "Have a party of soldiers take Conte Carlo to the barracks in Solaggio. I expect Comandante Von Krauss can find some place of confinement for him more appropriate to his rank than the village gaol. And have the search parties who were going to look for Signor Kestrel hunt for Guido instead."

He turned to Fletcher. "It seems you have a respite from interrogation, signor. It won't be long, I promise you." He said to the soldiers, "Lock him in the billiard room, and keep him there under guard. And, Zanetti, keep a close watch on Signor St. Carr. He may know more than he lets on about Signor Fletcher's activities."

"He doesn't know anything," Fletcher said quickly.

"No, you saw to that, didn't you!" St. Carr lashed out. "I expect it was easy for you. Bird-witted Beverley, who can be told any old story and won't know any better than to believe it!" His lip trembled. "I trusted you! I trusted you, and you lied to me!"

"I'm sorry," Fletcher said helplessly.

"Take him away," ordered Grimani, bored.

"Let me go with him," begged Lucia.

"Out of the question," said Grimani.

The soldiers moved to take Fletcher away. Lucia called out to him, "I'm so sorry!"

"There's nothing to be sorry about," he reassured her. "I'll be all right."

"I knew you would understand! I *felt* it." She pressed her hands to her heart. "I'll stand by you, whatever happens. I'll never desert you, as long as you're in any danger."

Fletcher smiled. "Then I've nothing more in the world to wish for."

The soldiers marched him out.

MacGregor took Julian's arm. "Come. Let's get you upstairs and into a hot bath. You must be chilled to the bone."

Julian let himself be led away. As soon as he and MacGregor were out of earshot, he asked, "What has Fletcher done to get himself arrested?"

"He's confessed to being Orfeo."

Julian stopped in his tracks. "What?"

"Caught you by surprise, has it?" MacGregor chuckled. "Well, after all, you can't know everything."

"I'm absolutely floored. What in the name of all that's marvellous possessed him to do that?"

"Lucia gave him away. I'm not sure why, but it seemed to have something to do with rescuing you."

"Good God. What an infernal tangle."

"Can you do anything to help him?" MacGregor asked.

"Yes. I have one card left in my hand. And I can see I shall have to play it."

CHAPTER 38

Dipper joined Julian in his room a quarter of an hour later, as clean and neat as if he had never set foot outside the villa that night. He began laying out Julian's evening clothes, blissfully unheeding of Julian's suggestion that he take the rest of the night off. "Have you at least taken some refreshment?" Julian asked. "I don't want you dropping from fatigue and cluttering up the carpet."

"I had some wine and a biscuit, sir."

"Very fortifying, if you happened to be a mouse."

"Sir." Dipper put down his clothes brush and looked at Julian in pained remonstrance. "I can't have you looking anything less than togged out to the nines. Puts me in a bad light, don't it, sir, on account of everybody knows it's me as rigs you out."

"Yes, I quite see. I shouldn't like to hazard your reputation."

He compromised by making Dipper share the cold meats, cheeses, and other delicacies that shortly arrived on a tray. After they had eaten, Julian finished dressing and regarded himself in the mirror. It seemed extraordinary that he should look just as he did on any other night—his white cravat tied with exquisite simplicity, his black coat and trousers moulded to his body without a crease, his white cashmere waistcoat shimmering with a trace of white satin embroidery, his black shoes mirror-bright. White kid gloves hid the scratches on his hands. He glanced toward the clothes he had been wearing before, now piled in a corner like a snake's sloughed skin. He hoped the boots could be saved. He would not find another pair like them before he returned to England.

He was procrastinating, he knew. He must go downstairs. He owed a great many explanations, and the time had come to pay the debt.

He had no sooner emerged from his room than Beatrice looked out of her room across the way. "I've been listening for you," she whispered. "Come in for a moment!"

He complied. She closed the door behind them, leaned back against it, and looked at him with rueful, laughing eyes. "I had to speak to you alone. I've been hovering in wait for you like a peasant girl for her sweetheart."

"It suits you," he said, smiling.

"I'm behaving horribly, I know. I have every reason to be angry with you. Last night you spurned me—you even seemed to suspect me of the murders. Pride ought to keep me from approaching you first; resentment ought to harden my heart against you. But when you fell into danger I forgot my anger, and now that you've returned I've lost my pride. I'm not afraid to make the first advance. Forgive me, Giuliano, for everything."

She held out her hand. He took it, bent over it, and kissed it. When he straightened, she was looking at him with dazzled eyes. "Come to me tonight, Giuliano," she breathed. "Tell your doctor friend something, anything, but come to me."

He drew her into his arms. She abandoned herself to him. He felt that she kissed him with her very soul on her lips.

When at last they moved a little, apart, he, asked, "What of Orfeo? Have you forgotten your anger against him, too?"

Her face set. "We know now who he is. I can leave him in Grimani's hands. I believe Grimani has no more love for him than I have." Her features softened once more. "So you see, I'm free of him. We need never think of him again."

He clasped her once more to his heart and kissed her, letting the moment engulf him—blot out all that had passed and all that was to come.

At length she drew away. "We must go downstairs. Everyone is waiting for us."

"Beatrice—"

"I know, love. I wish them all at the devil, too. But we can't disappoint them." She laughed softly. "And it would never do, would it, if they came looking for us here?"

The drawing room at midnight was as bright as day. Beatrice must have sent for every candle in the house. They stood on tables, in candle-stands, along the mantelpiece, and in the windows. It was like being in a votive chapel on the feast-day of a patron saint.

Carlo had been taken to the barracks in Solaggio, and Fletcher was still confined in the billiard room. The rest of the villa party were all there: Beatrice, Francesca, Valeriano, de la Marque, St. Carr, MacGregor, Grimani, Donati, and Sebastiano. Ernesto, Dipper, and Nina had been invited to join their masters on this festive night, though they kept respectfully in the background, Ernesto standing, Dipper and Nina sitting on the carpet hand-in-hand. Lucia was there, too, seated on an ottoman at the centre of the room, where Grimani could keep her under his eye. Zanetti sat with his portable desk on his lap, taking notes.

Julian stood before the mantelpiece and embarked on the story of how he had uncovered Carlo's guilt. "It was partly a process of elimination. Signor Valeriano's confession was false. Marchesa Francesca's very real agony on hearing it convinced me that she believed it—and thus couldn't possibly be the murderer herself. Still, I sensed that Signor Valeriano's kinship with the Malvezzis lay at the heart of these murders—if only I could fathom how.

"The more I thought about it, the more implausible it seemed that Marchese Lodovico would have made a mock marriage in the first place. Assuming he had done it, why had he kept it such a secret, and why had he ever after eschewed love affairs with singers? Forgive me, Signor Valeriano, but a nobleman's friends are unlikely to think less of him for playing a trick of that sort on a woman of Giulietta Petroni's birth. And so I began to wonder if by any chance the marriage could have been real."

Valeriano stared.

"I asked myself who alive would have first-hand knowledge of the marriage. Giulietta, her maid Elena, and Lodovico were all dead. That left only the priest. I pictured a Neapolitan of at least sixty, sufficiently educated to be, or pass for, a priest. He also had to be unscrupulous enough to perform a mock marriage—or disavow a real one."

"And you thought of Guido," said Beatrice.

"Yes, Guido, who, I had discovered, knew Latin, and who had appeared in Carlo's life very suddenly not long before Lodovico's murder. I speculated that he had told Carlo about Lodovico's marriage to Giulietta. But the information would have meant nothing to Carlo unless the marriage was real. I learned from the family tree"—he went over to it—"that Lodovico had married Rinaldo's mother, Isotta, in 1790. Giulietta hadn't died until 1793. I knew because Valeriano mentioned that his mother died three years before the French invaded Italy.

"I asked myself whether Lodovico would have been rash enough to marry Isotta, when he already had a legal wife. I remembered Ernesto's telling me that the only person Lodovico ever feared was the old marchese, his father. Since Lodovico was the eldest son, his father might well have compelled him to marry. And Lodovico might have committed bigamy sooner than tell his father the truth.

"If Guido revealed to Carlo that Lodovico's marriage to Isotta was invalid, that would give Carlo every reason to kill his brother. After the murder, he could pretend to discover that Rinaldo was illegitimate, and he himself was Lodovico's direct heir."

"Just what I would expect of a liberal," said Grimani. "They have no religion and no respect for authority. How can they know right from wrong?"

"With respect, Signor Commissario," said Julian, "I think Carlo's much-vaunted liberal ideals are a consequence of his ruthlessness, not a cause. He threw in his lot with the French because he saw it as the best means of advancement. After the French were driven out, he had nothing to gain by forswearing liberalism. He was so heavily compromised in the Austrians' eyes that they would never have restored him to government office. He might as well at least keep the character of a man of principle. But it galled him unspeakably that his brother was at the pinnacle of wealth and power, while his own star had set, and he had nothing in the world but debts and memories. He once spoke to me of the Wheel of Fortune. When Guido came to him with the story of Lodovico's first marriage, it must have seemed to him that Fate was letting him give the Wheel a turn, bringing himself to the top again, and his brother to the bottom.

"But there was one gaping flaw in this theory I'd devised: four and a half years went by, and Carlo never revealed that Lodovico's marriage to Isotta was invalid. He might have discovered too late that he couldn't prove it, but I couldn't credit that. He wouldn't have taken the risk of killing his brother unless he was confident of the gain. So it must be that after Lodovico's death he learned something that dished his scheme.

"I went back to the family tree. It told me that Rinaldo had been born in 1795, two years after Giulietta died. I remembered Valeriano's saying that his mother believed Lodovico had set spies on her. That might not have been all her fancy: Lodovico might have been hoping to hear of her death so that he could make his union with Isotta legal by the simple expedient of marrying her again.

"He would have wanted to keep that second marriage a secret, but still, he would surely have left some evidence of it, in case Rinaldo's legitimacy was ever called in question. The best repository would be the family lawyer, Palmieri. What was more, if Palmieri knew of the second marriage to Isotta, it could have been he who revealed it to Carlo. Carlo was Lodovico's executor: what more natural than that Palmieri should have discussed intimate family business with him after Lodovico's death?

"Carlo would have had no choice but to swallow his losses and keep the secret of Lodovico's marriage to Giulietta. He only renewed his project of inheriting the family estate when chance presented him with a golden opportunity to kill Rinaldo. That explains the long gap between the two crimes, which I had initially thought made Carlo an unlikely suspect, at least if the motive were pecuniary.

"We may not ever know precisely how Rinaldo's murder came about. But this is what I should guess: Carlo was wakeful that night and came out of his room. He happened to look out of a south-facing window—probably the one at the end of the hallway—and saw Francesca climbing down from the balcony. He guessed that Rinaldo must have locked her in with him. Moreover, Rinaldo must be deeply asleep, else Francesca wouldn't have been able to escape. So he cold-bloodedly killed Rinaldo and did all he could to pin the crime on Francesca, knowing that if she were found guilty, her son, Niccolò—the only person who stood between him and the title—would fall neatly into his hands."

"Thank God you warned me not to bring my children here!" Francesca exclaimed.

"I could hardly credit that Carlo would be so rash as to strike at Niccolò so soon after Rinaldo's murder," said Julian. "But how could I take that chance? As it turned out, your sending me to see the children gave me the perfect opportunity to speak with Palmieri. Unfortunately, Carlo learned of my intent." Julian saw no need to reveal how this had come about, for which Nina looked at him gratefully. "Give Carlo his due: he excels at devising schemes on short notice. By the time I returned with the information I'd sought, he had laid a trap that nearly finished me."

MacGregor knit his brows. "But wasn't he afraid Palmieri would reveal you'd come asking questions about Lodovico's marriage to Rinaldo's mother? If he did that, someone else might make the same deductions you did."

"You don't know Signor Palmieri," said Beatrice. "He would have volunteered nothing to the authorities. His career is built on keeping clients' secrets."

Valeriano could no longer contain himself. "If all this is true, then Lodovico Malvezzi was more of a villain than even I ever dreamed!" He jumped up and walked back and forth, his hands lifted as if to throttle the empty air. "That he should have seduced my mother by pretending to marry her was bad enough. But that he made her his lawful wife, then deceived her into thinking she was his whore, and her child was a bastard—by God, if he were alive now, I really could kill him!"

"Pietro!" Francesca was at his side, taking him lovingly by the arm. "My dear, don't think of the past. It's too late to change it now. Think of the future we shall have together—you and me, and my children, too—your niece and nephew!" She turned to Grimani. "Signor Commissario, may we go to them now?"

"You'll have to remain here until the investigation is officially closed," said Grimani.

"We could send for the children," said Valeriano. "Marchesa Beatrice, would you be kind enough to help us?"

"But surely you don't need my help," said Beatrice, smiling.

Valeriano looked puzzled. After a moment he said tentatively to Ernesto, "Could you arrange for a servant to take a message to the children's tutor?"

Ernesto bowed. "You have only to ask, Excellency."

"There, you see," said Valeriano to Francesca, "it—" He froze, then turned slowly back to Ernesto. "What did you call me?"

"If I've understood Signor Kestrel aright, you're my master's eldest true-born son. That makes you Marchese Malvezzi."

"But—but that's impossible! I can't be a marchese! You know what I am!"

"It doesn't prevent you inheriting a title," said Beatrice.

"But I can't even produce an heir—"

"You don't have to!" Francesca clasped his arm. "If Rinaldo was legitimate, then Niccolò can inherit. My son will be your heir. Oh, Pietro, it will be almost as if—"

They looked into each other's eyes, hardly believing in this new turn of the Wheel of Fortune. The others murmured congratulations, then tactfully dispersed into small groups about the room—all except St. Carr, who was half asleep in his chair.

Just then a soldier arrived and reported to Grimani that Guido had been found at a tavern a mile or two up the coast. He had been taken to the Solaggio barracks. Grimani said he would interrogate both him and Carlo tomorrow morning.

"What will happen to them—Carlo and Guido?" MacGregor asked Julian.

"Guido would most likely be hanged if he weren't hand-in-glove with Carlo. It would be awkward to hang one and not the other, and the authorities are loath to execute men of Carlo's birth. Still, Carlo killed his own brother and nephew, both marchesi. He may have to pay the supreme penalty. I believe that, being nobly born, he has an ancient right to insist on being beheaded rather than hanged."

Another messenger arrived. This time it was one of Ruga's gendarmes, with a warrant for Fletcher's committal to the village gaol. Grimani ordered Zanetti to have Fletcher brought in.

"What are your grounds for holding him?" Julian asked.

"He may have been in league with Carlo," said Grimani. "At the very least, I mean to find out once and for all why he fled from the villa on the night of the murder, and why he announced his presence to us on the evening of the festival, while keeping his identity a secret. It all smacks of Carbonarism."

The two soldiers who had been guarding Fletcher brought him in. Grimani went up to him. "Signor Fletcher—"

St. Carr started fully awake. "Look here, Commissario, you can't do this."

"Can't?" Grimani's head snapped round at him. "I advise you to keep out of this, Signor St. Carr."

"I can't keep out of it. I won't. You're all wrong if you think Hugo had anything to do with those murders. He may have masqueraded under a silly Greek name and gone about singing under people's windows at night. He's odd enough for anything. But he wouldn't commit a murder—certainly not a shabby, craven murder of an unarmed man. He's a man of honour."

"He's a liar and a trickster," said Grimani. "He deceived us all, you among the rest."

"If he did," said St. Carr, working it out slowly and painfully, "he must have had a good reason. He must have been serving some end that was more important than telling the truth."

"He'll have ample time to reflect on that," said Grimani. "He won't get out of prison till he's unburdened himself of all his secrets."

"I don't believe he has any secrets," said St. Carr. "And if he has, I expect they're no business of yours."

"Beverley—" began Fletcher, alarmed.

"Oh, don't be an ass, Hugo!" exclaimed St. Carr. "This is no time to be trying to keep me out of trouble. Who the deuce is going to keep *you* out? Signor Commissario, my father knows the British consul in Milan and the British ambassador in Vienna, and I'll see to it that they make it hot for you if you harm a hair of Mr. Fletcher's head!"

"Have a care, Signor St. Carr," said Grimani. "I can easily make you out an accomplice."

"Sir," said St. Carr, trembling with indignation, "I shouldn't advise you to try!"

"Signor Commissario." Donati's gentle voice silenced both combatants. "I have a favour to beg of you. Before you take my pupil away to gaol, I should like to hear him sing."

"Don't be ridiculous," said Grimani.

"This may be my only chance," Donati pleaded. "I trained that voice. It would mean a great deal to me to hear it one last time."

Fletcher was shaking his head violently. "No. No. I couldn't."

"You will if I order it!" said Grimani.

"But I can't—I'm not—"

"We know you've had no chance to practise," Donati soothed. "We'll understand if you're not in voice."

"I'll allow it," said Grimani. "But I warn you not to play any tricks, Signor Fletcher. I know how prisoners send messages by their choice of songs, and by inventing their own lyrics."

"I'll choose the song, by your leave," said Donati. "Or better still, let Signor Kestrel choose it. He deserves the honour, after all he's done."

"Thank you, Maestro." Julian thought a moment. *"My peace depends on hers."*

"Mozart!" beamed Donati. "Orfeo's favourite!"

"I'm not well," stammered Fletcher, who did look a little green. "I should only make a hash of it. Perhaps tomorrow—"

"Don't worry." Lucia slipped her hand in his. "Everything will be all right."

"Take me into the music room, Sebastiano," said Donati. "I want to accompany him, just as I used to."

Sebastiano led Donati into the music room and seated him at the piano. The others gathered around them, Lucia still holding Fletcher's hand. Donati played the opening chords. Orfeo drew a long breath and let fly:

"My peace depends on hers,
Whatever pleases her gives life to me—"

"Bravo!" Donati broke off playing and clapped his hands. "That is my pupil! That is his voice!"

No one else spoke. They were all staring, dumbfounded, at the singer—not Fletcher, but Julian Kestrel.

"You!" burst out MacGregor, "*You* are Orfeo!"

"I am Orfeo." Julian's heart was pounding. He could not look at the marchesa—not yet.

"But, good God, man!" MacGregor sputtered. "Do you mean to say that you came all the way to Italy to carry on a hunt for *yourself*?"

"Not for myself. For the marchese's murderer—and I was the only one who knew for certain they weren't one and the same. So you see, I was in a unique position to solve the murder—if I could only avoid being convicted of it first."

"Just a moment!" MacGregor's brows drew together. "On the night of the festival, I saw you on the library balcony while Orfeo was singing on the south terrace. How did you contrive to be in two places at once?"

"In the time-honoured tradition of comic opera, I exchanged clothes with my servant. Dipper went out on the balcony wearing my coat and hat, with pattens on his feet to give him a little more height. He had the light behind him, so that you only saw him in silhouette. He can imitate the way I walk and stand well enough to be mistaken for me at that distance. Afterward, while everyone else rushed to the south terrace to look for Orfeo, Dipper ran north up the shore path and jumped into the lake. He left a white rag tied to the branch of a tree so that I would know he'd got away safely."

Julian turned to Lucia. She smiled at him, the recognition she had hidden for so long shining in her face. He went to her and took her hand. "My dear Barbarina, how can I thank you for what you did for me? If it hadn't been for your courage, your loyalty, and your faith, I should be in prison, the murders unsolved, my own life in danger, and Carlo free to wreak whatever villainy he liked. For all that's been accomplished here, the credit is yours."

"I'm sorry I had to be so harsh with you," she said. "I didn't want you to give yourself away. The longer I could stop you, the more time you would have to find the real murderer."

Grimani was white with rage. "Signor Kestrel, I arrest you in the name of the Emperor of Austria and the Viceroy of Lombardy-Venetia," He turned sharply to the soldiers. "Handcuff him and take him to gaol!"

"We don't have a warrant," stammered Zanetti.

"I'll answer for that!" Grimani snarled.

"On what charge am I arrested?" Julian asked.

"You've obstructed a police investigation."

"Really?" De la Marque raised his brows in amusement. "I should have thought that Mr. Kestrel's solving the murders would have been of some slight assistance to the police."

"Mind you," MacGregor told Grimani sympathetically, "I can understand your wanting to blow up Kestrel. I'd like to myself. He's led us all a dance I've never seen the like of. But he's not a criminal. What's more, he has powerful friends—the new Marchese Malvezzi, for one."

Valeriano stepped into his unaccustomed role like the seasoned performer he was. "Of course I should feel compelled to take it up with the Viceroy."

"And I'll tell the British consul," piped up St. Carr, "and the ambassador—"

"I've already heard the list of your official acquaintances!" Grimani spat back. "And the devil with them all!" He waved a hand at Julian. "Take him to gaol!"

"Signor Commissario," murmured Julian, "won't it be a little awkward explaining to the Director-General of Police that you took your chief suspect as your ally in this investigation?"

"You were never my ally! I tolerated you, nothing more!"

"It may not appear to the Director-General in quite that light. You might rather let on that you knew all the time I was Orfeo, but, having perceived I was innocent, you kept me here as a first-hand witness to Marchese Lodovico's last days."

Grimani breathed hard through his nostrils. Julian waited. All the while, he was acutely aware of the marchesa standing in a corner of the room, just beyond his view. He steeled himself and started to turn toward her. But Grimani's voice pulled him back.

"Before I decide anything, I want some questions answered. Why did you run away on the night of Marchese Lodovico's murder?"

"I knew nothing about the murder. I didn't even hear he was dead until some days after I left the villa. He and I had fallen out several times lately, and I believed our natures were too hopelessly at odds for us to get on any better in the future."

"Did you continue your training?"

"No."

"Why not, if your voice showed such promise?"

"I should have been hard-pressed to find another teacher the equal of Maestro Donati." Julian added more quietly, "I'd never whole-heartedly embraced the idea of a stage career in any case. I'd been swept away by the marchese's enthusiasm, Maestro Donati's genius, and my own love for music."

"If you had such a regard for Maestro Donati," sneered Grimani, "why didn't you take proper leave of him, instead of disappearing in the night?"

"You're right," said Julian gravely. "It was an appalling failure of courtesy. I ask your forgiveness, Maestro."

"And I give it, my son." There was just the faintest tinge of amusement in Donati's voice. Julian felt a rush of affection. My dear Maestro, he thought, you always knew when I was keeping something dark!

"All the same," said Donati wistfully, "I'm sorry to see my training go to waste."

"That could never be, Maestro. You taught me not only to sing, but to *listen*—to understand music as I never had before. You taught me what it was to be an artist. I shall always remember and be grateful for that."

"I'm glad to see how much technique you still remember. You're out of practice, but your voice is in better form than I should have expected."

"I must own," said Julian, "I've been practising."

"I thought as much," said Donati, smiling. "But where?"

"The grottos. I used to go them sometimes when I was out walking, before Rinaldo's murder confined us all here."

MacGregor exclaimed, "That's why you did that experiment to see if noise in the grottos carried outside the caves! But were you already planning that prank of serenading us in the garden?"

"No. That only came to me after Commissario Grimani declared the investigation was making no progress here, and Conte Carlo proposed enlisting the Bow Street Runners to search for

Orfeo in England. Carlo's motives are obvious now. But his proposal was reasonable in itself—unless you knew, as I did, that Orfeo wasn't guilty. I didn't want our party to break up, and I certainly didn't want any effort wasted on hunting for Orfeo in England. So I thought it best to let you all know that Orfeo was here."

"But why were you writing a letter to that Bow Street Runner to ask for his help in finding Orfeo?" MacGregor asked.

"I needed an excuse to withdraw to the library while the rest of you were on the terrace. I also thought I owed it to Vance to warn him, in the event there really was a search for Orfeo in England, that he would be hunting for a mare's nest. I would have found some veiled way of conveying that in my letter."

"But my son," said Donati, "if you didn't plan your serenade in advance, why were you practising your singing in the grottos?"

"Maestro," said Julian simply, "how could I come back to this place and not wish to sing?"

Donati smiled.

"What I want to know," said Grimani, "is how you, Maestro, could possibly have spent the past ten days under the same root with Signor Kestrel and not recognized him as Orfeo."

"There's nothing astonishing in that," said Julian quickly. "Maestro Donati knew me as a penniless music student—he wouldn't have expected me to be resurrected as a dandy. And when I first met him as Julian Kestrel, I had catarrh, so he couldn't have recognized my voice."

"That was convenient," Grimani bit off.

Julian smiled ruefully. "A little snuff in my handkerchief was of the greatest assistance. For that, too, Maestro, I ask your pardon. I had no means of confiding in you about what I was doing, and if I were discovered to be Orfeo, I wanted you to be able to say truthfully that you didn't know. Of course I was disconcerted to learn that you would be coming here with us. I couldn't feign catarrh indefinitely. I could only avoid you as much as possible and hope for the best."

But of course Donati had found him out soon enough. Julian had guessed as much when Donati made a point of telling him how he had instructed Sebastiano never to leave him alone. Donati had trusted Julian sufficiently not to betray his secret, yet he had recognized that his trust might be misplaced and had wanted Julian to know he was on his guard. In response, Julian had advised Sebastiano to keep a loaded pistol at hand, thus arming Sebastiano against himself. Donati, it seemed, had understood this for the pledge of good faith it was.

Grimani broke in on Julian's reflections. "Where did you go when you left the villa on the night of the murder?"

"I roamed about the mountains for perhaps a week, then entered Switzerland at Lugano."

"And why this sudden desire to go mountaineering?"

Julian smiled. "I thought it would be good for my health."

"Your whole proceedings reek of secrecy and intrigue." Grimani stalked back and forth for a few moments, then rounded on Julian again. "This story Monsieur de la Marque told about the Comte d'Aubret's protégé. Was that you?"

Julian was silent for a moment. "The Comte d'Aubret was my benefactor, yes."

"He was a notorious liberal," said Grimani.

"He had far too much taste to become notorious for anything."

"Be that as it may, he was a liberal. He sent you into Italy to spy for him—perhaps to assist the Carbonari."

"The Comte d'Aubret was not an incendiary. He had an open, enquiring mind, which gave him the reputation of a liberal among the Ultras of the Faubourg St. Germain. But whatever his politics, he didn't involve me in them. In fact, he strongly advised me to keep out of Italian political disputes."

Grimani rounded on de la Marque. "Did you know Signor Kestrel was the Comte d'Aubret's protégé, whose name you claimed not to remember?"

"I hadn't the least idea." De la Marque laughed. "I wonder how Mr. Kestrel kept his countenance while I told him all about the comte and his protégé! You must have found that extraordinarily amusing, *mon vieux*. Or perhaps not: I daresay you had a bad moment or two, wondering if I would suddenly remember the protégé's name and expose you. And of course you were obliged to pass on my information to Commissario Grimani, even at the risk he might ferret out the protégé's identity. If it were discovered you'd kept such an important clue to yourself, people might have wondered why."

Grimani cogitated, his eyes screwed into slits. At last he said to Julian, "I don't for a moment believe you've told me the whole story. But after such a lapse of time, it would be pointless to try to build a case against you. So here's what I've decided. You will leave Lombardy tomorrow morning. The official reason will be that you may have made enemies in the course of this investigation, and I can't answer to your government for your safety. I'll give you an escort of gendarmes to accompany you to the Swiss border and see that you cross it."

Julian bowed. "You're very kind, Signor Commissario."

"One thing more, Signor Kestrel." Grimani's ice-water eyes held Julian's gaze. "In the future, I must advise you, *for your health:* stay out of Austrian Italy." He turned on his heel and went out.

The others began to retire. Valeriano and Francesca thanked Julian warmly for all he had done to transform their prospects. They had no sooner gone than MacGregor approached with Fletcher, Lucia, and St. Carr.

Julian said to Fletcher, "I owe you a debt of gratitude for taking on Orfeo's identity as you did. But I don't precisely understand why you did it."

"Lucia asked me," said Fletcher.

"I told Commissario Grimani about the hiding place in the grottos," Lucia explained. "But he said he wouldn't believe me unless I told him who Orfeo was. I was afraid to tell him it was you. He hated Orfeo so much I thought he might not rescue you—he might even do you a mischief and blame it on Conte Carlo. So I decided to pretend that one of those three men was Orfeo. I knew that, once you were safe, you would set things right. And if the worst happened, and you were dead, I could always tell Commissario Grimani the truth."

"Why did you choose me?" asked Fletcher shyly,

Lucia smiled. "Just something I saw in your face." She turned to Julian. "Good night, Signor Orfeo. You don't mind if I still call you that, do you?"

"No, Barbarina. But where will you stay tonight?"

"I'll go back to Signora Ruga's," she said. "She's been very kind to me. I'm sure she'll let me stay the night, even if I'm not a prisoner anymore."

"May I walk you there?" asked Fletcher. He reddened a little and added hastily to Julian, "Unless you'd rather?"

"I should like to very much," said Julian. "But *I* haven't earned the right, as you have."

"I'll go with you, Signor Fletcher," said Lucia.

"I'll come, too," offered St. Carr.

Julian regarded him critically. "You seem rather tired. You might prefer to catch a few hours' sleep. Looking peaked isn't at all the thing, you know."

"Isn't it?" said St. Carr. "I *am* rather fagged out. Do you think you could manage without me, Hugo?"

"I expect so," said Fletcher, grinning. He shot Julian a grateful look. "Good night, Beverley, Mr. Kestrel."

"Will I see you again before you go?" Lucia asked Julian.

"I shall insist on it," he promised.

"Goodnight, then," she said, "and God bless you."

"God bless you, Lucia," said Orfeo.

Fletcher and Lucia went out. St. Carr said his good nights and followed. At long last, Julian turned to the marchesa. She stood like a statue in her corner, her face immobile, giving nothing away.

MacGregor looked from one of them to the other. "Er—I'll go up and wait for you, shall I?"

"Thank you, my dear fellow," said Julian.

MacGregor shuffled out.

Julian and Beatrice were left alone. She came out of her corner and stood before him. They looked at each other in silence. Then she lifted a hand and struck him across the face. "Get out of my house."

He had known this was coming. For the past twenty-four hours, he had steeled his heart to accept it. Why, then, was it so hard to bear?

"I'm sorry," he said. "I had no idea until last night how you felt about Orfeo. I thought that, once the murder was solved, I could tell you the truth, and you would understand my deception and forgive it."

"I understand it." Her voice broke. Tears sprang to her eyes. "But why, why, having deceived me, did you have to tell me the truth? We could have been happy, if only I had never known!"

"I couldn't leave Fletcher at Grimani's mercy."

"How noble you are!" she flung at him. "How honourable—in everything but love!"

"Would you have wanted me to go on deceiving you—to let you give yourself to a man you hated?"

"Yes! Because we would have had some joy together, even if it was founded on a lie, and now we have nothing!" She caught her breath on a sob. "You may stay here the rest of the night. But you won't see me again. Now go."

He went. At the door, he turned to look at her one last time. She was moving silently about the room, blowing out the candles. He went out.

Gaston de la Marque was waiting, as Julian had known he would be. "Where can we go?" de la Marque asked softly.

Julian thought briefly. "The lake."

CHAPTER 39

Julian and de la Marque shipped their oars and let their boat drift on the black, star-scattered mirror of the lake. Although it was two or three in the morning, and there were no other boats in sight, they kept their voices low and spoke in English for added safety.

De la Marque regarded Julian appreciatively. "I think you must be completely mad, *mon vieux*. I've thought so from the beginning. Do you realize it's only by the merest chance that you aren't cooling your heels in the Santa Margherita prison?"

"If I were, at least I would have the consolation of your company."

"I know." De la Marque flashed his brilliant teeth in a smile. "What do you think has kept me so remarkably well behaved?"

"I haven't noticed you putting yourself under any great strain in that regard."

"Oh, come, I could have been much worse. I came very close to throttling you when you told Grimani about my notebook."

Julian smiled. "MacGregor thought you were meaning to make away with me."

"Now that is most unjust. I wouldn't have dreamed of it, except as a last resort."

"That's very good of you."

"*Mon vieux*, whether you believe it or not, I came here as much to guard you as to guard against you. I admire you enormously. I've been fascinated by you from the first. If one of us were a woman, I would be in love with you. I can't say more for you than that, can I?"

"It's certainly one of the more singular tributes I've received."

"You don't believe I'm in earnest." De la Marque leaned back on one elbow, surveying Julian quizzically. "I wonder if you can have any idea what the loss of that notebook meant to me? Have you ever been inadvertently responsible for a disaster? I used to lie awake at night second-guessing my every move—cursing myself for a too-clever idiot." He sat up suddenly and leaned toward Julian, elbows propped on his knees. "The curse of revolutionary activity is that one must write things down: names, places, sources of money and arms. But if those writings fall into the hands of the police, scores of people may fall—a whole movement may collapse. It happened to Maroncelli, and Andryane. The written word is damning."

"And you thought written music might be less so."

De la Marque sighed. "It seemed such a good idea at the time. Who would make better spies than singers? They move about constantly from city to city, they meet everyone: the nobility, army officers, labourers. And when they perform each night, they can add any variations they like to their songs. *Voilà: a* spy who can pick up information, then pass it on in public, before hundreds of people."

"While you quietly take it down in your notebook and translate it at your leisure."

"It was an excellent cipher. I designed it myself. Nothing so banal as a mere substitution of musical notes for letters of the alphabet—the resulting sequence of notes would be impossible to sing. No: combinations of notes had certain meanings, depending on their intervals, time values, and so on. It sounds complex, but it was quite easy to use once you understood it. I suppose Aeneas didn't tell you how it worked?"

"All he told me was that it was built around the *tritone*: the interval of three whole tones, known as *diabolus in musica* because it's awkward to sing."

"Yes. It was a pun on the society's name, of course. We called ourselves Angeli, but the police nicknamed us Diavoli. So 'the devil in music' seemed an appropriate key to the cipher."

"Marchese Lodovico had guessed that *tritoni* lay at the heart of it," said Julian. "He took to scribbling them everywhere. Marchesa Malvezzi and I found two he'd written on some old sheets of music, and I saw him jot down others when he came to the villa for my lessons. Ernesto noticed it, too, and jumped to the conclusion that he was composing a piece of music."

De la Marque nodded. "I'm not surprised he guessed the notebook was in cipher. If nothing else, the recurrent *tritoni* were an oddity that a connoisseur of music would have noticed. But why didn't he turn it over to the police out of hand?"

"I should guess, because he hadn't broken the cipher," said Julian, "and he couldn't bring himself to relinquish the notebook until he had. At all events, when I saw him jot down those *tritoni*, I knew for certain that he'd brought the notebook to the lake—and what was more alarming, he'd begun to penetrate its secret. That's why I took the risk of going to the castle on the night before the murder. I hoped to get inside to search for the notebook, but Marchese Lodovico caught me out."

"Now, this is exactly the sort of thing I've been pining to know. I heard very little about your mission after I left Milan. My colleagues insisted I go: they were afraid Lodovico would guess the notebook was in cipher, and I would be arrested and induced to talk. I suppose I would have felt the same way in their place. So I went to Turin to assist in the revolt there. Sadly, it was too disorganised and too late—hopeless from the beginning."

"It must have been," said Julian politely, "if even you couldn't save it."

"Now you are jesting with me. But, really, if I could have induced my colleagues to be a little more ruthless, we might have accomplished something. The Piedmontese are too sentimentally attached to their royal house—they *would* put their trust in Carlo Alberto, though anyone could see he hadn't the stomach to lead a revolution. But that's neither here nor there. My flight from Lombardy robbed me of the honour of making your acquaintance, which was rather unfair, when it was I who proposed you as our agent to retrieve the notebook. Did you know that?"

"No. I had never heard of you before we met at La Scala."

"But I had heard of you. As you later discovered, your patron the Comte d'Aubret was a friend to the Angeli. When he proposed sending his English protégé to Italy, we—the Angeli—thought we could use you to carry information from one city to another. D'Aubret disabused us of that notion. He didn't want you drawn into our activities. He was very protective of you."

"That was good of him."

"Hardly a passionate statement about the man for whom you risked your life."

"The fact that I risked my life for him ought to be statement enough."

"To be sure," said de la Marque, smiling. "Pardon me, *mon vieux*—I forgot you were English. But to return to the theft of my notebook: you must realize it couldn't have come at a worse time. The government in Milan was moving aggressively against political dissenters. The first arrests had come a month or two before, and we knew there would be others. We Angeli had contrived to keep our movement very secret, but if my notebook were deciphered, it would be all up with us.

"We canvassed possibilities. We knew it would be useless for me to confront Marchese Lodovico directly: he would either deny the theft or carry it off with a high hand. The police would side with him—not that we cared to have anything to do with the police in any case. To break into Casa Malvezzi would be worse than useless—the Marchese had hordes of strapping footmen at his beck and call.

"It was at this juncture that I chanced to hear you had come to Milan for Carnival. I had a friend at the Santa Margherita, who kept me apprised of the latest foreign arrivals. I saw at once that you would make a perfect agent. You were English and had no connection with Italian politics, so you were the last person Lodovico would suspect of being a Carbonaro. You were a gentleman and had an entrée to exclusive circles. And by all accounts, you were a music lover. I didn't know then that you could sing like an angel, but I was more than willing to believe you were sent from Heaven. The question was, had you the ingenuity to ingratiate yourself with Lodovico, and the boldness to find my notebook and steal it back?

"I persuaded Aeneas to sound you about it. He was reluctant at first. He said: Why should you, a young English traveller, wish to throw in your lot with us? I reminded him that my notebook heavily incriminated the Comte d'Aubret in our activities, and if it were deciphered, the Viceroy would think it his duty to inform the French authorities. D'Aubret had many enemies in France. His intellects were too sharp and too ungoverned. All those whose vanities he'd wounded, whose pretensions he'd torn down, would seize on the chance to have him imprisoned or exiled as a revolutionary. He was your benefactor. It was even rumoured he was your father. If affection for him didn't move you to help us, surely self-interest would."

Julian did not reply. He thoughts were far away, in Milan on the night of December the twenty-sixth, 1821—the first night of Carnival. The streets were thronged with laughing, singing, jostling people. Enticements were everywhere: the smell of freshly baked *panettone*, the sound of popping corks, the flash of black eyes above a fan or through the slits of a mask. Then all at once there came the hand on his shoulder, the black-cloaked man at his side, the whisper in his ear: *"Signor Kestrel, I must talk to you."*

He remembered the hushed conversation on the little canal bridge near Porta Romana—the sable water shot with reflections of candlelight from nearby windows, the confused fragments of songs borne on the air. And of course there was Aeneas's voice, ludicrously businesslike behind his beaked black Carnival mask. The whole thing seemed a scene from an opera. But the danger to d'Aubret had been all too real.

A turmoil of feelings had rushed on him. Fear for d'Aubret—remorse at having left him at the mercy of his enemies—strangest of all, exhilaration at being able to repay a little of the debt of gratitude that weighed on his heart.

"I heard an account of your meeting with Aeneas long afterward," de la Marque was saying. "I gather he was more than a little astonished to discover he had caught a nightingale."

Julian shrugged. "He told me that music was the best avenue by which to approach Marchese Lodovico. So I asked him if the marchese interested himself in aspiring singers. Aeneas said he did."

"But you must understand, Signor Kestrel," Aeneas had gone on, *"in Italy every other man you meet thinks he can sing, and most of them are right. The marchese would be interested only in a voice that was extraordinary."* Julian had observed mildly that he had been told his voice had great potential, though he had chosen not to pursue a career on the stage. *"Very well, let's hear it,"* Aeneas had said. So Julian had applied for a Carbonaro mission by singing a serenade to a masked man, two ducks, and half a dozen appreciative pairs of lovers leaning out of windows along the canal.

"Now you must tell me everything," said de la Marque. "How you induced Marchese Lodovico to carry you off to the lake, and how you found my notebook at last."

"I didn't induce him. He thought of the idea himself. I was a bit nonplussed. When I sang under his window, I hoped merely to awaken his interest. I had no notion he would take me up in that fashion."

"But you must have had some idea of keeping your identity a secret—else why approach him so stealthily?"

"I wasn't trying to be stealthy. I sang under his window for the romance of the thing—because I'd heard he was impulsive and imaginative, and I thought a serenade would appeal to him more than a letter of introduction. I also knew that men of his rank set no store by anyone who seems to court their favour. Which is why, when he first proposed to launch me on the operatic stage, I was very hard to convince."

"But this is delightful!" De la Marque leaned back, his head resting on the seat at the end of the boat. "Go on!"

"I told him I was very poor, but my father was a gentleman and wouldn't have wished me to go on the stage. I said I was thinking of giving music lessons. Marchese Lodovico was beside himself. 'Give music lessons! With a voice like yours? Surely if you must earn your bread by your talent in music, it would be far better to win fame and fortune on the stage than to toil in some conservatory.' I said, at least I needn't drag my name through the theatres or see it on playbills. That may have been what gave him the idea of weaving a mystery around my identity. At all events, I allowed him to talk me round."

"Machiavellian, *mon vieux*!"

It was, rather, Julian thought. But it was not the whole story. He remembered Lodovico pacing up and down his room at Casa Malvezzi. A single lamp burned amid the crimson curtains and wall hangings, so that the whole room swam in a red glow. *"You really think I could be successful?" "I know it! Put yourself in my hands, Signor Kestrel. I will make you the greatest tenor in Italy!"* Julian half believed him. He had a dazzling vision of himself on the stage at La Scala, the Théâtre Italien in Paris, the King's Theatre in London—no, not London. That was not how he had meant to go home. Yet his heart hammered, his head spun, and he asked himself which of them was really the one being seduced.

"From then on," he continued, "Marchese Lodovico took charge of everything. He brought me to sing for Maestro Donati and persuaded him to accompany us to the lake. In the meantime, he enjoined absolute secrecy on me about our project. His concealment of our connexion was inconvenient, since I couldn't get near him to look for the notebook. But I had great hopes of our sojourn at the lake. Since the notebook contained vocal exercises and ornamentation, there was at least a chance the marchese would bring it with him to use in my training. Failing that, he might let fall some clue to what he had done with it. After we came to the lake, I lost no opportunity to discuss exercises and ornamentation with him. But it wasn't until we'd been there some six weeks that his scribblings of *tritoni* revealed he was trying to break the cipher."

"You were remarkably patient."

"I had no choice."

The truth was, he had hardly noticed the days flying by. Absorbed in his training, challenged by Donati's demands, aglow with achievement when he met them, he often had to remind himself of why he had come here. As he listened to Donati's anecdotes of singers and their triumphs, he was fired with ambition and a kind of reverence for his own talent, as if it were not a possession to be flaunted, but a gift he must strive to deserve. He felt guilty at all the effort Donati was investing in him. He even felt some compunction toward Lodovico, who was doing so much for him. But of course Lodovico had known how to chill gratitude, as frost does flowers.

"How did you find my notebook at last?" asked de la Marque. "*Where* did you find it?"

"On the morning after Marchese Lodovico caught me at the castle, he came to the villa and announced he would be spending the night there. I determined to have another try at getting into the castle while he was at the villa. That night he sent Maestro Donati and me to bed early. After I'd helped Maestro Donati prepare for bed, I went downstairs again, hoping to slip out without Marchese Lodovico's seeing me. I was just in time to see him going out by the front door. I nipped into the library and looked out of the window to see where he was going. He was striding off down the shore path—to the belvedere, as we know now, to keep the rendezvous with Valeriano.

"I turned away from the window, and the light from my candle fell on the writing-table there. I saw the very notebook I was looking for lying open, with a pile of papers beside it. Aeneas had described it to me—its size and thickness and the colour of the binding. I looked through it quickly and found the pages contained music, with *tritoni* scattered throughout. The loose papers were covered with *tritoni*, letters of the alphabet, and stray words. They showed the whole history of Marchese Lodovico's efforts to break the cipher.

"There was no time to think, no room for hesitation. I thrust the papers into the notebook and took it up to my room. I couldn't destroy it, because I'd promised Aeneas I would return it to him if I could. We'd met a second time, before I left Milan, and he had given me the names of a pair of brothers in the neighbourhood to whom I could safely entrust the notebook. I retrieved my pistols and whatever else was essential to take away with me, and bolted.

"I found the brothers Aeneas had told me of and left the notebook with them. They gave me a horse, money, and other provisions. They warned me to travel north into the mountains and cross the border at a point well above Chiasso, which was swarming with customs officers. I spent a week in the wilds of the Val Cavargna, sleeping in barns or under trees and dodging the customs men, till I felt quite like one of the local smugglers. Finally I descended to Lake Lugano and bribed a boatman to take me clandestinely into Switzerland."

"How did you learn of Marchese Lodovico's death?"

"I read about it in the newspapers when I reached Lugano. I was considerably surprised. The papers said he'd died of heart failure, but I'd never seen the least sign of ill health in him. Of course, looking at the thing cold-bloodedly, his death was a stroke of luck for me. He was the only one who'd known my real name, and now I might well be able to keep dark that I was Orfeo. That seemed prudent, since the newspapers also reported that the Milanese police were looking for Orfeo—I assumed because my disappearing so suddenly had made them suspect me of being a Carbonaro, or some less exotic variety of criminal."

De la Marque nodded. "My colleagues sent word to me in Turin of your success and the lengths to which you'd gone to achieve it. Because of course," he added nonchalantly, "we assumed you'd killed Lodovico to get the notebook back. I was immensely relieved, and only sorry I would probably never have an opportunity to tell you of my admiration and gratitude. Later I heard how you'd taken London society by storm and become the most celebrated dandy since Brummell. I could only think what a shame it was to waste such talents on leading a pack of aristocrats about by the nose. With your audacity and cleverness, what a revolutionary you would have made!"

"You're very kind."

"What did you make of me," de la Marque asked curiously, "when I turned up in the midst of your investigation? Did you know from the beginning it was I who'd compiled the notebook?"

"No. The idea did occur to me when I heard of what you call your parlour tricks—your perfect pitch and your ability to write down a melody after a single hearing. But you must understand, Aeneas had told me nothing of who compiled the notebook or how it came into Lodovico's hands. I was forced to look about among all Lodovico's acquaintances for a Carbonaro who might have passed the notebook on to him. Of course, when you came to the lake with us and persistently dropped hints that you knew more of Orfeo than you were saying, I strongly suspected you. But I had no proof until the footmen told me how they'd stolen your notebook and given it to their master."

"Did you think I had killed Marchese Lodovico?"

"I entertained the possibility. I could see you were smarting from his footmen's treatment of you. And you might have feared he'd learned so much about the cipher and the contents of the notebook that it would be dangerous to let him live, even if I were to get the notebook back for you. But once Rinaldo was killed, my suspicion of you receded. I couldn't conceive of any reason you would have to want him dead."

"If it's any consolation, *mon vieux*, I can't have baffled you half as much as you baffled me—even though I had the advantage of knowing from the beginning that you were Orfeo.

We—the Angeli—were mystified when you turned up in Milan after the truth came out about Lodovico's murder. Why in the name of the devil and all his minions would you be courting discovery like that?

"We couldn't afford not to know, in case you were proposing to turn informer against us. I took it upon myself to keep an eye on you, which is why I watched you and La Beatrice through that little device you detected at the opera. A few nights later I called at her box and asked her all about you, and to my surprise, she invited me to join your party at the villa. Of course I realized the theft of my notebook might come out. But I had to keep abreast of what you were up to. Besides, you'd put me on my mettle. If you were willing to take such daring risks, surely I could do no less.

"Of course, once I came to know you, I understood why you had come here: you were a mad, quixotic Englishman, and you couldn't let the police make a hash of the investigation, when you could set things right. What took me utterly by surprise was that I—*I*, and not you—was suspected of being Orfeo! That really was a sublime farce. Molière couldn't have written anything better.

"It seemed a trifle less amusing when those troublesome footmen turned up. That, *mon vieux*, was when I concluded you were not merely eccentric but a raving lunatic. Whatever possessed you to tell Grimani about my notebook and the Comte d'Aubret's protégé? The footmen wanted no trouble with the police. They would have held their tongues if you had."

"You left me no choice," said Julian. "You conveyed to me very clearly, through your account of the Comte d'Aubret's protégé, that you knew I was Orfeo and could reveal it to Grimani at any time. You made a direct threat: Say nothing about the notebook, or I shall miraculously remember the protégé's name. But that was a double-edged sword: if I were exposed as Orfeo, I would have nothing to lose by telling Grimani all I knew of the Angeli. So I turned your threat against you. I passed on all the information to Grimani, including your story about the comte's protégé."

"I must admit, you took the wind out of my sails. But surely for you, it was a Pyrrhic victory. If the murders hadn't been solved, Grimani would have sent to Paris for information about d'Aubret, and would have ferreted out that the young English wag with the marvelous voice was a certain Julian Kestrel. And where would you have been then?"

"Exactly where I would have been in any event, if Lodovico's murder hadn't been solved when it was. Because Grimani had given Lucia only three days' respite before he meant to sink his fangs into her. And that I could not allow."

"Do you mean to say you would have given yourself up? Even though you would almost certainly be hanged or sent to the Spielberg?"

Julian smiled wryly, thinking of his sombre outing with MacGregor to Villa Pliniana. "I must admit, I was a bit blue-devilled."

"So I should think!" De la Marque shook his head indulgently. "Mad, utterly mad, just as I said."

"Is there no one you would consider dying for?"

"Only liberty, *mon vieux*."

They both fell silent. Julian lay back in the boat, feeling its gentle rise and fall and listening to the soft wash of the water against its sides. The stars blurred before him. He closed his eyes and let his conscious mind slip free—

De la Marque called it back. "There's one thing more I should like to know. Why did you take Conte Raversi as your ally after you'd solved the murders?"

"I had to confide in someone. Raversi was Lodovico's friend, he had influence with the authorities, and it would probably be a relief to him to find that the killer was someone other than Orfeo, since it was his own secrecy about the murder that had helped Orfeo escape. Or at all events—" Julian smiled. "That's one explanation."

"What do you mean?"

"Here's one I like better. Conte Raversi is one of you, isn't he? He came to the lake while Lodovico and I were there, in part to keep an eye on my mission, and in part to gauge the strength of the local military in the event of a rebellion—which he did very cleverly by organising a meeting of the local landowners with Comandante Von Krauss. After he learned of Lodovico's murder, he helped me in the only way he could: by hamstringing the investigation so that I was able to get away."

"I am shocked," said de la Marque delightedly, "utterly shocked that you could accuse such a pillar of orthodoxy of being a Carbonaro!"

"If I had any doubt of it," Julian added, "you settled the matter when you told me that, after you heard how I'd retrieved your notebook, you assumed I'd killed Lodovico. Who told you he'd been murdered, if not Raversi?"

"*Mon vieux*, you are magnificent! Is there any chance you would consider coming over to our cause?"

"I should have thought your cause was a bit moribund at the moment."

"In Italy, yes. The people are too much at odds with one another for concerted action. The pot simmers, but the lid stays securely in place. The revolution will come first in France. We have experience. We know what to do."

"And what comes after? Another Terror? Another Bonaparte?"

"I don't concern myself with that. Europe is encrusted with institutions that need to be torn down. Let someone else worry about what to erect in their place. If a revolutionary thinks too much about consequences, he becomes incapable of action. As your poet put it, conscience makes cowards of us all."

"Doesn't that strike you as a trifle irresponsible?"

"That's your English sense of order. Order belongs to art. Real life should be all disorder and struggle."

"I see," said Julian. "It's a philosophy. I'm glad you explained that. Otherwise I should have been in danger of thinking you took up Carbonarism out of sheer devilry."

De la Marque's eyes danced. "But, *mon vieux*, don't you think a man ought to like his work?"

"It is an advantage," Julian allowed. "I shall fall asleep presently."

"Do so. I'll row us back."

"You're very good." Julian closed his eyes, then opened them again. "I owe you three thousand francs."

"Three thousand francs?—oh, but of course. I wagered three thousand francs that if you found Orfeo, you would be sorry. I forgive the debt. What's more, if it would please you, I'll abandon my pursuit of a certain lady. Though it does seem a shame—when you've gone, I shall be exactly what she needs."

No, thought Julian. But I think you may be exactly what she wants. "Just don't leave her more alone than you found her. That's all I ask."

The lights outside the villa had all burnt out by the time Julian and de la Marque returned. They had to make their way across the terrace by moonlight and memory. Halfway to the stairs, they heard footsteps pacing ahead. De la Marque stopped, and Julian sensed him go taut with alertness. A revolutionary must suspect every shadow.

"Bonna sera," called Julian experimentally. *"O mei, bon giorno."*

"Good morning." Fletcher's lanky figure took shape out of the gloom.

"Can't you get in?" asked Julian.

"I haven't tried. I didn't want to go to bed yet. You mustn't mind about me—I don't want to keep you up."

"I shall take you at your word," said de la Marque. "I'm quite done-up. Good night, Mr. Fletcher. *Mon vieux*, you are absolutely forbidden to leave tomorrow without saying goodbye."

He sauntered inside. Julian asked, "How is Lucia?"

"Fine." Fletcher heaved a long sigh. "You know, you mean the world to her. You couldn't find it in your heart to love her a little?"

"Oh, very easily. But I think she deserves to be loved more than a little, don't you?"

Fletcher thrust his hands in his pockets and walked about. "She promised to stand by me as long as I was in any danger. But I'm not in danger now."

"You've humbugged a powerful police official. You'll be in danger as long as you remain in Austrian Italy. If I were you, I should remain a long time."

"But—I don't want to use her promise to trap her."

Julian laid a hand on his shoulder. "My dear fellow, take some advice from one who knows. Don't try to be fair to her. You're in love, and you're in Italy. Show her no mercy."

❀ ❀ ❀

There was a lone lamp burning in the Hall of Marbles. Julian lit a candle at it and started toward the stairs. As he passed Cupid and Psyche, his light cast a warm glow on them, giving their marble limbs the softness of flesh and their faces the illusion of living tenderness. It hurt Julian's eyes to look at the thing. He went upstairs.

MacGregor was lying crosswise on their bed, asleep in his clothes. Hearing Julian come in, he struggled up, dashing the slumber from his eyes. "All right. I want some answers from you. Start with the Comte d'Aubret. Was he your father?"

"My father was Richard Kestrel, son of a Yorkshire country squire."

"What about those other rumours de la Marque talked about? Were you some sort of spy between d'Aubret and the English?"

"He didn't have spies. He merely had opinions, which unfortunately weren't popular in court circles."

"Well, what was it, then?"

"You're forgetting *l'amour à la Grecque.*"

MacGregor reddened. "Well, I know it wasn't *that*!"

"It wasn't, as it happens."

"Well then—" MacGregor broke off uncertainly. "There's one other story de la Marque told—something about your wandering destitute in the streets and fainting into d'Aubret's arms."

Julian withdrew his gaze but spoke quite matter-of-factly. "I didn't faint into his arms. I dropped on the pavement outside Tortoni's, and he came out to investigate."

MacGregor stared. "How old were you?"

"Sixteen."

"What were you doing there? Why did you faint? Were you ill?"

"I—" It sounded absurd, even somehow shameful. "I was hungry."

"But how—why—" MacGregor stammered.

"I had no money and nothing left to pawn. I knew no one in Paris. My father had taught me French when I was young, but I was hopelessly lost trying to understand the Parisians. My manners were too good for me to beg with any plausibility, and my clothes were too wretched for anyone to entrust me with honest work. There's an assumption in the *beau monde* that, with so much food about, and so many resources for earning a few pence, no one healthy and enterprising can possibly starve. But actually, it's quite easy."

"But what were you doing in Paris all alone at that age?"

"I'd been living with my uncle in London, and I didn't like it. So I ran away."

"All the way to Paris?"

Julian smiled wryly. "That *was* rather mad. It was just after Waterloo, and I'd heard there was a rage in Paris for all things English. I had an idea I might find work, make my fortune—God knows what I thought. I wanted to be somewhere new—completely different from the world I'd known."

"But whatever prompted you to leave your uncle's house for a city where you had no place to go—where you'd be a foreigner with no friends?"

Julian did not answer at once. "My uncle wouldn't let me play the piano anymore."

"There must have been more to it than that!"

"That was enough. Under the circumstances."

MacGregor looked at him almost fearfully. "What circumstances?"

Another pause. "I thought you wanted to hear about the Comte d'Aubret."

"You mean, you don't want to tell me about your uncle."

"Not particularly. He wasn't an evil man, only narrow and unimaginative, worshipping money because it was a good he could hold in his hand—one that had no mind of its own and nothing so elusive and immeasurable as beauty. My mother had run away from him before me, so you see, it was something of a family tradition."

"All I see is that you don't want to talk about it, and I can't do anything to loosen your tongue. So go back to your meeting with the Comte d'Aubret. What happened after you dropped on the pavement?"

"When I came to myself, I was alone in a fiacre—a Parisian hackney coach—and a servant was offering me cheese and ices and other odds and ends through the window. D'Aubret had put me there so that I could eat without being stared at by the fashionable set at Tortoni's."

"That's a singular thing to have thought of," said MacGregor.

"He was like that. He put himself very readily into other people's shoes."

"If you were a common urchin, you wouldn't have cared who saw you eating."

"But the comte suspected I wasn't. In fact, he'd made a bet with his friends about it. When he found me on the pavement, he'd noticed that my linen was dirty, but my nails were clean. One of his maxims was: if you want to know a man's breeding, look at his hands."

"Sounds as if he had a knack for the sort of divining *you* do."

"He did, now you come to mention it. At all events, he talked to me for a bit, and finding I was English and could write a good hand, he took me into his household to help with his English correspondence. He'd lived in England for some years after the Terror, and had a great many friends there. But as he hadn't enough correspondence to keep me occupied, I was given all sorts of odd jobs. For a while I helped look after his clothes."

"His clothes?" MacGregor's jaw dropped. "You mean you were a—a *valet*?"

"Not exactly," said Julian, amused. "His real valet, Justin, wouldn't have permitted that. But sometimes I was allowed to help Justin with small tasks, especially ironing, which he disliked."

"Ironing," repeated MacGregor dazedly. "How did you even know how?"

Julian's lips curved wryly. Apparently MacGregor thought he had spent his boyhood conning Latin verbs. "I have unexpected talents. At all events, I was often underfoot when the comte dressed in the morning or undressed at night, and he talked with me about one thing or another in order to keep up his English. Soon he was telling me what he thought about all manner of subjects—politics, the theatre, love affairs. Insensibly, my position began to change. The comte would say, 'Your accent needs polishing, *Julien*, you must study elocution.' Or, 'You must learn to ride, *Julien*, in case I wish you to accompany me out.' When he found out I could play the piano, nothing would do but that I should continue my musical studies.

"His friends couldn't fathom what he was about, but I think I understand it. The comte was five-and-thirty but had never married. He would have been expected to take a colourless, convent-educated wife, and their children would have been swallowed up in the atrophied world of the Faubourg St. Germain, where his mother and sisters were desperately trying to re-create the *ancien régime*. D'Aubret was liberal, cynical—a traitor to his class, a Christian only in his conduct. His family disapproved of him violently, and if he'd had a child, they would have been determined to save it from him. But no one cared how he educated or befriended a mere English stray he'd found on the street."

"That all sounds like fustian to me. Did it ever occur to you that he was lonely, and he liked you?"

Julian thought a little, then smiled. "Thank you, my dear fellow. I think that may be what I was trying to say."

"Now, when did you take up singing?"

"That was a matter of chance. I was telling the comte the tune of some instrumental piece, by putting wordless syllables to the notes. He looked at me strangely. Then he said offhandedly that perhaps I ought to take a few singing lessons. The next thing I knew, he'd found me a singing master. I thought nothing about it. I'd always loved music, but I thought of myself at best as a gifted amateur on the piano. I'd never considered singing at all.

"The singing master gave me perhaps a dozen lessons. He declared that my voice was wholly untaught, I didn't know the first principles of breathing or phrasing, I could hardly tell one register from another. I was simply—a natural singer. The comte told me I was at a crossroads. I could either go on as I was or cultivate this gift and make a career on the stage.

"I didn't want to become a singer. It wasn't the life I'd envisioned for myself. But I felt I had no choice. Because it dawned on me all at once how dependent I'd become on the comte. My duties in his household had become very light, and the expenses of my education very heavy. I couldn't live indefinitely on his charity. I owed it to him to stand on my own feet, now that a way had opened before me.

"I told him I wished to be trained as a singer, and that if he would be good enough to assist me, I would repay him as soon as I was able to earn a living. He wasn't deceived. The language of duty and obligation was foreign to our discourse. He told me he had been selfish. He'd kept me tied to him by a golden thread of patronage and money, and there was only one way to set me free. He settled a sum of money on me—enough to dress, keep a horse, and live in the manner of a gentleman. He told me it was a *fait accompli*, and nothing I could say or do would change it. 'Now,' he said, 'our relations will be amicable and without strain. I shall do nothing more for you, so you needn't worry about appearing to curry favour. And you will greatly displease me by feeling a sense of obligation. A gentleman must learn how to receive a favour gracefully, which for a man of spirit is much more difficult than conferring one.'"

"He sounds a good man," said MacGregor, "even if he was irreligious. I'd like to have known him."

"You do, in a way. Much of the best of me that isn't my father is Armand d'Aubret."

"So you went to Italy," MacGregor pursued, "and Marchese Lodovico took it into his head to make a singer of you after all."

"Yes. But that part of the story you know."

"I know it now that everybody else does," MacGregor grumbled. "You didn't see fit to confide in me before."

"I was afraid you would try to stop me coming to Milan."

"Why didn't you tell me the truth after I followed you here?"

"You'd put yourself in far more danger than you knew by attaching yourself to me in this investigation. The one thing I could do to protect you was to keep you in ignorance."

"You thought I wasn't to be trusted," MacGregor accused him.

"I thought you the most honest and forthright man I knew, and I didn't want to set you at war with your own nature."

"Fiddlesticks! You've the prettiest way I ever heard of telling a man he can't keep a secret."

Julian was all too aware that he had not told MacGregor the whole truth even now. But what would it profit MacGregor to know about his mission for the Angeli? He and MacGregor were not out of Italy yet. Far better for MacGregor to have nothing to hide from the police.

"I suppose Dipper knew everything from the beginning," said MacGregor.

"Yes. I believe I rose enormously in his estimation when he found there was a country where I was wanted by the police. But when he realized I meant to walk straight into their clutches, he was scandalized. It went against every tenet of his creed."

"What will your London set make of your escapade as Orfeo?"

"The details will probably never be understood even in Milan. By the time they reach London, they'll bear only the most glancing resemblance to the truth. The whole affair will appear to be a lark, perhaps prompted by a wager."

"People may want to hear you sing," MacGregor warned.

Julian shrugged. "I shall say I gave it up when I discovered that tenors wear flannel neckcloths and make unspeakable grimaces whenever they hit any note above a high *B*."

"Quips like that may fool your London friends. But I know you were speaking from the heart when you told Maestro Donati what his training meant to you. With a gift like yours, how could you give up singing?"

"I wasn't brought up to it. My mother was on the stage, but she died when I was born. My father raised me to be a gentleman, even if in the most reduced of circumstances."

MacGregor nodded. "You've told me how his family cut him off for marrying your mother. You mean he wouldn't have approved of your becoming a singer?"

"I think he might have been pleased, actually," Julian reflected. "He always said my mother had a lovely voice."

"Well then, what was to stop you pursuing a career on the stage?"

"It isn't a gentleman's calling."

"Do you mean to say you let a God-given talent go to waste, because it wouldn't pass muster in the London drawing rooms?"

Julian said nothing for a time. He went to the open window and stood looking out on the trees tipped with moonlight and the glimmer of lake away to the east. "When I was nine or ten years old, my father and I went to deliver some manuscript pages to a bookseller in Paternoster Row. My father had become a hackney writer after my mother died. He worked at fair-copying, translation, indexes—whatever the booksellers would give him. It was January—a cold, blustery day. My father was dressed in a shabby old greatcoat and patched shoes, with a moth-eaten green shawl tied around his shoulders. His nose was blue, and so were his fingers where they poked through the holes in his gloves. God knows what sort of miserable object I presented.

"We were walking along the pavement, when suddenly we saw a gentleman looking in the window of a bookshop ahead. He was a stout, prosperous-looking fellow, with a greatcoat all over capes, a black felt hat, and shiny black Hessian boots. 'But that's Wrentham!' my father exclaimed. 'I knew him at university!' He started toward the gentleman with his hand outstretched. Mr. Wrentham looked around. I saw surprise in his face, then recognition, then embarrassment and distaste. And just before my father reached him, he crossed the street and cut him dead.

"Not long ago, this same man's son applied for admission to White's, which, as you may know, is the most exclusive gentleman's club in London. The outcome was uncertain. I used my influence."

"You kept him out?"

"My dear fellow, that would have been spite. No: he owes it to me that he got in. That was revenge."

MacGregor stared. After a moment he faltered, "But you can't mean to spend the rest of your life avenging slights to your father."

"Why not? It passes the time. And I do solve the odd murder."

MacGregor shook his head gravely. At length he asked, "What's going to happen here, now the investigation is over?"

"Our party will break up quickly, I expect. Grimani will want to get to Milan as soon as possible, to collect all the credit he can for the investigation, and to promote his own version of events. The marchesa will plunge back into Milanese society, and de la Marque will dance attendance on her as long as he has nothing more pressing to do. Valeriano will take his place as head of the Malvezzi family, with Francesca at his side. I shall warn him to keep a close watch on Niccolò: Carlo has three sons, and it seems too much to hope for that they should be nothing like him. Fletcher will go wherever Lucia does, and won't have cause to regret it. If St. Carr is wise, he'll continue his travels alone and learn to get himself out of scrapes. You'll go back to England, I imagine."

"All the better for having come here, thanks to you. But what will you do?"

"I don't know. Perhaps I shall go somewhere I haven't been—Spain, for instance."

"That wouldn't be my prescription." MacGregor came over to the window where Julian stood, and held his gaze with his own calm, direct brown eyes. "You're a little heartsick now, just as I was when you persuaded me to come on the Continent with you. Now I'm telling you that the best thing for you is to come back with me to England."

From somewhere in the distant hills, a boy's voice rang out in a peasant's song. A shepherd, Julian supposed. It must be nearer dawn than he had thought. The voice was sweet and sure. But where could one go in this country and not find music?

"There's something I ought to explain," he said quietly. "I've told you why I chose not to become a singer. But since I came back to this villa, there hasn't been a day when I haven't felt regrets. I thought I made the right choice, returning to England. I'm not sure anymore."

"*I'm* sure," said MacGregor.

Julian looked at him in surprise.

"It isn't that I think you've done right to devote your life to fighting your father's battles. I can't believe he would have wanted that. But I can see now that you wouldn't have been happy singing on the stage. Maestro Donati said you didn't have the temperament, and he was right. Do you remember when you told me that singing in public would be like appearing naked before a crowd of strangers? That would never have done for you. You're the most *dressed* man I've ever known. You like being in the public eye, so long as the public sees only what you want it to see. As a singer, you would have poured your whole soul into every performance, before all the world. You have many kinds of courage, Julian, but not that kind. And you were wise enough to know it."

The boy was still singing. Julian listened a moment longer, then drew the window closed. He laid a hand briefly, affectionately, on MacGregor's shoulder. "All right, my dear fellow. Let's go home."

AUTHOR'S NOTE

The characters in this novel are fictitious. Historical figures are mentioned in passing, including the political prisoners Pellico and Andryane and the singers Velluti, Pasta, and Catalani. Giovanni Battista Rubini, who performs at La Scala in chapters 9 and 10, was a renowned tenor of the period, but I've taken a liberty with history by having him sing in Milan in 1825 (he was actually in Paris that year).

All the Milan locales, apart from the private houses, are authentic. Some streets now have different names, and the dreaded Santa Margherita police headquarters is no more. La Scala has substantially the same structure as in Julian Kestrel's day, but a reverent silence is now observed during performances.

Solaggio is patterned on several Lake Como villages, notably Bellagio. Villa Malvezzi is loosely modelled on the real Villa Melzi d'Eril, which also has a Moorish belvedere. Canova's voluptuous life-sized sculpture of Cupid and Psyche, which I've transported to Villa Malvezzi, can be seen at Villa Carlotta, near Cadenabbia. Villa Garuo, mentioned in chapter 14 as the former home of the estranged wife of Britain's George IV, is now the luxury hotel Villa d'Este. Villa Pliniana, with its ancient intermittent spring, is unfortunately not open to the public.

All the music in the book is genuine, apart from Donati's compositions. If any reader would like a list of the songs by their Italian names, with their composers and (where appropriate) the operas they come from, by all means write to me.

I am grateful for the help and encouragement of the following people: Julie Carey, Cynthia Clarke, Molly Cochran, Shelagh Ellman-Pearl, Glenn Morrow, Robert O'Connell, Louis Rodrigues, Inger Ross-Kristensen, Al Silverman, Ilene Robinson Sunshine, Christina Ward, and Gene Wicker. I would also like to express my appreciation to Dana Young for listening so patiently to the travails of Julian Kestrel and his creator. Finally, I would like to thank my father, Edward Ross, who introduced me to opera at a vulnerable age, and whose wealth of knowledge and enthusiasm about the subject has been of the greatest assistance to me in writing this book.

PUBLISHER'S NOTE

The following is a list of the songs that appear in the novel, in chronological order:

"Ecco, ridente in cielo," from *Il Barbiere di Seviglia*,
by Gioachino Rossini (Chapter 1)
"Caro mio ben,"
by either Giuseppe or Tommaso Giordani (Chapter 2)
"Ner cor piu non mi sento," from *L'Amor Contrastato*,
by Giovanni Paisiello (Chapter 4)
"Son tutta duolo,"
unknown author (Chapter 5)
"In quegli anni," from *Le Nozze di Figaro*,
by Wolfgang Amadeus Mozart (Chapter 5)
"Languir per una bella," from *L'Italiana in Algeri*,
by Gioachino Rossini (Chapter 9)
"Cruda sorte," from *L'Italiana in Algeri*,
by Gioachino Rossini (Chapter 10)
"Nel vedervi a un altro in braccio," from *Amor Rende Sagace*,
by Domenico Cimarosa (Chapter 11)
"Che invenzione prelibata," from *Il Barbiere di Seviglia*,
by Gioachino Rossini (Chapter 14)
"Parto, parto ma tu ben mio," from *La Clemenza di Tito*,
by Wolfgang Amadeus Mozart (Chapter 20)
"Che farò [senza Euridice]", from *Orfeo*,
by Christoph Willibald Gluck (Chapter 33)
"Dalla sua pace," from *Don Giovanni*,
by Wolfgang Amadeus Mozart (Chapter 38)

For more information about the music in this novel, please visit our website:

www.felonyandmayhem.com/book/the-devil-in-music-by-kate-ross